"You must accept that I am now your betrothed and we will be wed in two days."

"Even over my refusal? You cannot force me." He cupped her face with warm palms, and she felt the force of his light touch clear down to her toes.

"I can," he said softly. "Believe me, I prefer not to use force, but you continue to resist what you cannot prevent. Our fates are sealed. Yield, Gwendolyn."

"Never." She expected anger but received an unnerving smile.

"Never is a long time." His kiss was whisper soft against her lips, and only the power of magic could turn it all-encompassing, banishing her resistance and common sense so thoroughly. Every part of her became aware of how closely they stood, how little fabric covered either of them. Too easily she could grab his tunic and pull him closer yet, feel the heat of him against her. Too easily she could melt into a puddle at his feet. She couldn't yield, couldn't let him win.

PRAISE FOR SHARI ANTON
AND HER NOVELS

"Shari Anton is a master who weaves magic onto every page."

—*Rendezvous*

"Anton is a superbly talented writer of medieval historical fiction."

—TheRomanceReadersConnection.com

Please turn the page for more reviews...

AT HER SERVICE

ONCE A BRIDE

"Anton weaves a spellbinding romance, rich in historical backdrop, fiery characters, and sexual tension."
—*Romantic Times BOOKclub Magazine*

"Bravo . . . Ms. Anton has painted a marvelous and witty novel of love."
—*MyShelf.com*

"A keeper! This is a delightfully charming novel, extremely well written, with characters who blossom throughout each page."
—*TheRomanceReadersConnection.com*

THE IDEAL HUSBAND

"Anton weaves history into her highly romantic tale with aplomb, crafting a beautiful love story brimming with period atmosphere."
—*Romantic Times BOOKclub Magazine*

"A historical romance for readers to savor."
—*Southern Pines Pilot* (NC)

"A lovely, lovely tale . . . The well-proportioned mix of narrative and dialogue; passion and romance; challenge and triumph sets a brisk pace . . . I'm eagerly looking forward to her next book."
—*RomRevToday.com*

ALSO BY SHARI ANTON

At Her Service

Once a Bride

The Ideal Husband

Midnight Magic

SHARI ANTON

Christine,
Enjoy! Thanks!

Shari Anton

WARNER
FOREVER

NEW YORK   BOSTON

Book design by and text composition by L&G McRee
Cover design by Diane Luger
Cover illustration by Alan Ayer
Typography by David Gatti

Warner Books

Time Warner Book Group
1271 Avenue of the Americas
New York, NY 10020
Visit our Web site at www.twbookmark.com.

Printed in the United States of America

First Paperback Printing: December 2005

10 9 8 7 6 5 4 3 2 1

To the wonderful ladies who populate
the Medieval Enthusiasts loop.
Goddesses, every one.

ACKNOWLEDGMENTS

Today theories abound on the very existence of King Arthur and Merlin. Geoffrey of Monmouth had no doubts. His *Historia regum Britanniae*, finished c. 1136, contains both *The History of the Kings of Britain* and *The Prophecies of Merlin*. For its day, the book was a best-seller and subject to both praise and criticism for its content. As a basis for my research, I chose to use GEOFFREY OF MONMOUTH: THE HISTORY OF THE KINGS OF BRITAIN, translated and with an introduction by Lewis Thorpe.

I also would like to thank DeborahAnne MacGillivray, who provided the Welsh phrase I needed to finish this book.

Chapter One

England, 1145

WHEN THE ROYAL TEMPER RAGED, prudent men held their peace.

Alberic of Chester considered himself a prudent man. With his helm securely tucked under one arm, he stood quietly near his fellow soldiers, holding a sword still too bloody to sheathe.

Chilly rain mingled with sweat to soak his hair and trickle down his neck to seep under the layers of chain mail, padded gambeson, and linen shirt. His chain mail weighed down on shoulders beginning to stiffen from exertion, his body too weary and spirit too heartsick to feel victorious.

A skirmish shouldn't have been fought in this field, where sprouting oats were now ruined. So many men shouldn't have died today. A frightful waste.

Alberic yearned to return to the austere comforts of the royal army's camp, where everyone from the lowliest pikeman to exalted King Stephen had idled away weeks while laying siege to Wallingford Castle. There awaited him a canvas tent where he could get out of the rain and, if the supply wagons had arrived, drink enough ale to drown out the wails and moans of the wounded and dying.

Except he dared not move until given the order.

So Alberic watched tall, robust King Stephen pace the road alongside the freshest battlefield in the ten-year dispute over the rightful possession of England's crown. Unconcerned for either the rain wetting his woolen cloak or the mud splattering his leather boots, the king focused his fury on two men: Ranulf de Gernons, the earl of Chester, the living, stoic target of his wrath; and Sir Hugh de Leon, a baron who lay facedown in blood-soaked grass, beyond hearing and earthly cares.

"An unfortunate death, Chester."

The king's deceptively placid statement reeked of ire and accusation.

With nearly as regal a mien as the monarch's, Chester retorted, "His death could not be avoided, Sire. Sir Hugh refused to surrender when given the chance."

The king gestured toward a young, fair-haired man sprawled not far from the baron. Alberic tensed, aware of whose blood dried on his sword, and prepared to acknowledge his part in the senseless carnage if need be. But the king continued to address the earl.

"The son, also?"

"Young William followed his father's foolhardy example. Had they allowed, I would have captured both and held them for ransom."

"So instead you allowed both to die!"

Chester tossed a hand in the air, his usually unshakable composure fraying. "Their goal was to attack the camp and take you as their prisoner. What would you have us do, Sire? Not defend our own lives? Stand aside? Perhaps allow them to escape and return to Maud's service?"

"We would *prefer* our land-rich subjects be captured and brought before us! Sir Hugh might have been turned to our service if given sufficient enticement."

The twitch of Chester's jaw made Alberic wonder how long the recent, brittle alliance between the earl and the king would last. Chester's reputation for acting only in his best interest was well earned and widely known. And given the king's mistrust of Chester, a breach could come at any time, for any reason, the alliance split asunder by either man.

"As I said, Sir Hugh gave us no choice," Chester stated, firmly indicating he would argue no more.

Wisely, King Stephen didn't push the earl further. Instead, he glanced at the field littered with dead, at the wounded men-at-arms being tended, and finally at the poor souls who'd been taken prisoner: those of Sir Hugh's small force who'd survived.

Too small of a force to have a prayer of prevailing against the earl's. Alberic still didn't understand why Sir Hugh, who had been vastly outnumbered, hadn't surrendered. Or why William had fought on with such vicious zeal knowing his father had fallen and their mission was doomed.

All pondering over the de Leon men's actions halted when King Stephen's gaze settled on him. Alberic endured the full force of the dark-eyed, measuring stare for several uncomfortable moments before the king asked of Chester, "Your whelp?"

Alberic almost smiled at the earl's obvious chagrin.

For several years now, Chester had dismissed the familial similarities between himself and Alberic as slight and utterly no proof of paternity. To have the king notice the resemblance so quickly and accurately must be irritating. Alberic also knew better than to hope for the answer he'd waited nigh on half a lifetime to hear—full acknowledgment from Chester. Even so, his heartbeat quickened.

"So his mother claimed," Chester finally answered.

"Have you provided for him as yet?"

"He has a place in my household."

A place grudgingly given and not the one Alberic had hoped for as a lad of twelve. After his mother's death, having no means to support himself, he'd shown up at Chester's castle and confronted the earl. While Chester hadn't acknowledged Alberic as his son, neither had the earl tossed him out the gate. Disappointed, but needful of shelter and sustenance, he'd responded to Chester's scant generosity by working hard to earn the earl's respect, if not his affection.

Most days Alberic believed he'd made strides in winning Chester's acceptance. On others he suffered pangs of sorrow for that skinny lad, raw with grief, needing to belong *somewhere* and fearful he never would.

"Is he knighted?" the king wanted to know.

Alberic's heartbeat kicked up another notch. That coveted honor hadn't occurred yet, though he'd long since passed beyond the age when most squires acquired their knighthood. Chester, however, was decidedly reluctant to bestow the honor.

"Not as yet."

Then Alberic wondered why the king took so pointed and unwarranted an interest in the baseborn son of the earl of Chester. Especially now, when more important matters begged attention.

Discomfited, Alberic watched King Stephen squat beside Sir Hugh and slide a large gold ring from the baron's limp hand, pausing to study it before clenching it in his fist.

"The seal of the dragon," the king said softly. "We remember the first time we saw this unusual ring many years ago, on an occasion when Sir Hugh attended our uncle's court. He said he wore the ring in honor of his wife, a Welsh princess, whose family claims lineage from that of Pendragon."

Pendragon? The fabled King Arthur?

All around him Alberic heard both awed murmurs and snickers of disbelief. The muttering stopped when the king rose from beside Sir Hugh.

"Disbelieve, do you?" Stephen called out. When no one answered, his attention again returned to where Alberic didn't want it. On him.

"What of you? Do you believe?"

Alberic considered his answer carefully, well aware he was being judged.

"I know naught of the descendants of King Arthur, Sire, so cannot give you an informed opinion on the matter."

The king came toward him, his steps purposeful, his intention impenetrable, stopping a mere arm's length away. "What is your name, young man?"

"Alberic of Chester, Sire."

"On your sword dries the blood of William de Leon?"

Asked mildly, but with an undertone of cold steel.

Apparently the messenger whom Chester had sent to camp to inform the king of the skirmish had described how the baron and his son had met their end.

"Aye, Sire."

"Do you now consider yourself the better man?"

Alberic glanced over at William de Leon—young, fair-haired, and damned good with a sword.

"William fought with both zeal and skill. He had already vanquished several others before he and I crossed swords. I consider myself blessed to have come away the victor."

"His equal, then?"

Only by citing legitimacy of birth could anyone make a case for William de Leon's superiority, and Alberic chose to ignore that unfortunate circumstance of birth whenever possible.

"As you say, Sire."

The corner of the king's mouth twitched with humor, and approval softened his eyes.

"As we say, is it? Then we believe you may be ripe for what we have in mind." The king drew his sword, a fighting weapon instead of the fancy blade one might expect a royal personage to wield. "Kneel before your king, Alberic of Chester."

Doubting Stephen had lost his wits and intended to behead a man who'd committed no crime, Alberic could think of only one other reason for the king's drawn sword and the accompanying order.

Knighthood.

Alberic hesitated, overjoyed at the prospect of receiving the coveted rank, but wary of why King

Stephen had singled him out. Kings didn't confer knighthood as an act of kindness, nor had Alberic done anything on the battlefield this day to warrant a field knighting. Therefore, the king had an unfathomable motive of his own—not good.

And Chester frowned in stark disapproval. Alberic knew their fragile relationship might suffer if he accepted the king's offer. Dare he risk what the earl might consider betrayal?

But hadn't Chester taught him by example that only dolts refused to seize an opportunity to gain honor, or land and wealth, and then hold tight to the favor and grants given?

And hellfire, Alberic wanted this. He'd craved the honor and rank of knighthood from Chester, and been loyal and patient only to be denied. What he hadn't received from his father, he'd be a fool to refuse from King Stephen.

Misgivings brushed aside, ignoring the unrelenting drizzle, Alberic knelt in the mud and soon felt the weight of the king's sword on his right shoulder.

"We dub thee knight, Alberic of Chester, with all the rights and responsibilities that come with the honor. We charge thee to uphold the laws of our beloved England, to serve as protector for widows and orphans, to hold fast to the teachings of the Holy Church and praise Almighty God for His blessings. Do you so swear?"

His mouth dry as dust, he answered, "I do so swear."

The sword lifted from his shoulder and he tensed, steadying for the *colée*. The king's open-handed buffet to the side of Alberic's head nearly knocked him over, eliciting a cheer from the soldiers and thus serving its purpose—to fix in the witnesses' memories the events of this day, of the oath given to the king when Alberic of Chester became *Sir* Alberic.

Through the ringing in his ears he heard the king continue. "And now, Sir Alberic, we propose to grant you a living to support your new rank. Upon swearing your homage and fealty to our royal person, we shall bestow upon you Sir Hugh de Leon's castle at Camelen, along with all his other holdings."

Stunned, Alberic stared at the ring the king held out, eager to grasp it but wary of accepting.

"What of Sir Hugh's widow?"

"His Welsh princess died many years ago. William was his only son. Three daughters remain. We charge you to take one as your wife, send another to our court, and give the last to the Church."

Alberic's curiosity nearly burst with questions about Camelen, which he knew lay somewhere south of Shrewsbury, and the extent of the estates and the income he could expect. Verily, for wont of a simple oath the king meant to make him a rich and powerful man.

He gave fleeting thought to the daughters. Surely one of the females would be tolerable enough to wed and bed, and thus produce an heir, firmly establishing his claim to Camelen.

Only a witless fool would hesitate longer or argue further.

Alberic put down his sword and helm, slipped on the baron's ring, then raised his clasped hands for the king to enfold. When next he stood, only two men within sight outranked him: the earl of Chester and the king of England.

Ye gods, how quickly men's fortunes rose and fell given the vagaries of war.

The king slid his sword into an intricately tooled leather scabbard belted at his waist. "Take de Leon and his son home. Bury them with the honor due them, then hold Camelen in our name."

"As you say, Sire."

King Stephen smiled wryly. "'As you say.' Do you hear how easily and sincerely he says the words, Chester? You could learn much from your own get."

The king spun and headed toward his horse, and the unease Alberic felt earlier returned. Why in the name of all the saints had the king granted knighthood and the wealth and power of a barony to the earl of Chester's bastard?

Something was definitely amiss here.

He stared down at the uncommon gold ring King Stephen called the seal of the dragon. A sparkling garnet graced the face of faceted black onyx, the mounting held securely by gold prongs fashioned as dragon's claws.

Oddly enough, though sizable, the ring didn't sit as heavily on his hand as Alberic thought it should. Odder still, it fitted as though a goldsmith had made it especially for his finger—loose enough to twirl but snug enough to stay on.

"A handsome gift," Chester commented, still frowning in disapproval. Though the earl stared at the ring, clearly he meant the entire royal gift.

Alberic bent over and wiped the blood from his sword on the long grass, his stomach tightening as it always did when he spoke to Chester.

"A handsome gift, indeed. My mind would be easier

about accepting it all if I knew what game the king plays."

The earl shrugged a broad shoulder. "Simple enough. He believes he has now purchased your loyalty, and thereby firmly fixed mine."

Then the king believed wrongly, the grandiose gift given for naught. Alberic glanced at the bodies of the baron and his son. The two had fought and died together for the same cause, loyal to each other to the very end. With either father or son, the king might have struck a bargain and gained the cooperation of the other. The same steadfastness could not be assumed regarding Ranulf de Gernons and his bastard.

"Then the king does not know you very well."

"Nay, he does not. I wish you good fortune in claiming your prize."

The earl walked off, shouting orders to his men to fetch carts to carry the wounded, to begin burying the dead, to march the prisoners back to camp.

Prisoners Alberic would soon have to take charge of.

He took a deeper than normal breath, the problems associated with his new position beginning to surface. The faces of the men he'd recently fought against twisted with varying degrees of defeat, anger, resentment, and despair.

He needed only one of Sir Hugh's soldiers to lead him to Camelen. Would it be the pikeman who sat cross-legged in the mud, his head bowed into his hands, or the elderly knight who might understand that a man submitted to shifts of circumstances and accepted the changes wrought by war? Surely, if one man of Camelen swore allegiance to the new lord, others might, too, if only for the chance to return home.

Not that he could wholly trust the word of a one of them.

Accepting the king's gifts had been as easy as taking an oath; gaining possession of them wouldn't be so simple. Not only did he have to get to Camelen, but somehow get through the gate without someone on the battlements taking umbrage and shooting an arrow through his heart.

Alberic again inspected the ring, the garnet winking at him from atop the onyx, the dragon's claws seeming to dig deep into his gut. He'd come by the ring and Camelen fairly and honestly, but he knew others would feel he'd stolen them.

Too bad. Camelen was now his, and he would make his claim. How to go about it merely required a bit of careful thought and planning, something he was very good at.

Atop Camelen's battlements, Gwendolyn de Leon adjusted the ill-fitting helm in a vain attempt to keep the nose guard from interfering with her sight.

She understood Sir Sedwick's insistence that she wear the helm—and the shirt of chain mail her brother had worn as a young squire—whenever she ventured onto the battlements. During times of war one took precautions against threats. Except she saw no immediate danger to either Camelen or her person, merely two knights atop palfreys riding over the field separating the castle from the woodland beyond. One of the two, Sir Garrett, she had no trouble identifying.

For a few moments she focused on the woodland, hoping either her father or her brother would emerge, too. Neither did.

"I do not like the looks of this, my lady," Sedwick grumbled from beside her.

Her attention forced back to the field, Gwendolyn conceded that Sir Garrett shouldn't be here, but rather with her father and brother defending Wallingford.

"Perhaps Father sent Garrett home with a message."

In answer to her conjecture, Sedwick snorted through the battle-marred nose on his round face. "See you any sense of urgency? And why send two knights, one of whom we do not know, when a runner would have done? Nay, my lady. The very air stinks of trouble."

"Then send someone out to learn their purpose before they come closer."

"Without knowing who Garrett brings to our gate? His lordship would have my head on a pike were I to be so foolish. We will wait for Garrett to explain."

Gwendolyn bit her bottom lip to hold her peace. She might be in charge of the household in her father's absence, but Sedwick, her father's steward, currently held sway over the defenses. The knight's dour, suspicious nature made him perfect for the position, though she thought his current stance against lowering the drawbridge overly distrusting.

Sir Garrett certainly meant Camelen no harm. As for the knight who rode by his side, how much damage could one man do against thick stone walls and an armed garrison? He surely posed no menace.

The knight was tall, certainly, and young, she judged from the lack of bend to his back and his solid yet fluid seat in the saddle. His broad shoulders carried the weight of gleaming chain mail with ease. The belt of his scabbard circled a trim waist over narrow hips. Black leather riding gloves covered his hands.

He wore a helm, of course, concealing his hair, the nose guard obscuring his facial features. Except his jaw, which was both square and bold.

As the men traversed the field, Gwendolyn's curiosity kept pace with her rising impatience until, finally, the men had no choice but to halt at the outer edge of the moat. She caught herself wondering further about the coloring of his hair and eyes when Sedwick's shout halted her silly musings.

"You return to Camelen in strange manner, Sir Garrett."

Garrett removed his helm and ran a hand through his steel-gray hair. Sweet mercy, the man looked weary unto dropping from his saddle!

"Not the manner of my choosing, Sedwick." The weariness in Garrett's voice matched his appearance, and for the first time since she'd been called to the battlements, Gwendolyn felt a twinge of apprehension. "We bear news best not shouted over the wall, so I would be most grateful if you would lower the drawbridge."

Sedwick made no move to signal an affirming command to the guards posted near the giant winches that controlled the bridge's thick chains.

"Who do you bring with you?"

"Christ's blood, Sedwick, I will explain all after—"

Abruptly silenced by the young knight's hand to his forearm, Garrett's visage turned grimmer than before.

"I am Sir Alberic of Chester," the knight answered, his voice deep and clear, easily carrying up to the battlements without strain. "By my oath, I mean Camelen and its people no harm."

"And I shall vouchsafe his oath," Garrett stated.

Sedwick's eyebrow arched sharply. "My lady, if this Sir Alberic is of Chester, then he is a king's man and so our enemy. Yet Garrett bids us allow him entry! I like this not."

All true and worrisome. Her father firmly believed in the right of King Henry's daughter, Maud, to the English crown. He considered King Stephen the usurper and traitor for having swiftly claimed his uncle's crown at Henry's death. Ranulf de Gernons, the earl of Chester, had recently thrown the weight of his earldom behind King Stephen, infuriating her father, who'd vowed to present Chester's head to Maud on a gold platter.

Nay, Sir Hugh de Leon wouldn't be pleased if a man of Chester were allowed inside Camelen. And yet, Sir Alberic came in the company of Sir Garrett, a man her father trusted completely. And the young knight was willing to enter a hostile, fully garrisoned castle, so he must have a very good reason. The news the two wished to impart must be important and, she feared, grave indeed.

"Truly, Sedwick, what harm can come of Sir Alberic's entry? Garrett vouches for him, and I doubt any knight is slow-witted enough to challenge an entire garrison. I say we allow him inside."

Sedwick hesitated a moment more before tossing up a hand, signaling the guards to lower the drawbridge. The winches groaned and chains clanged as the heavy door of wide planks began its decent.

Gwendolyn swiftly headed for the gate tower stairway, removing the helm that had pressed hard against her thick braid and giving her head instant relief. She handed the detested headpiece to the page who'd held her veil and circlet, deciding to leave on the chain mail. Time enough to take it off after she heard Garrett's news.

The bridge thudded to the earth, sending her scurrying down the stairway, Sedwick and several guards close behind. By the time she reached the bailey, Garrett and his companion had crossed the bridge.

She halted at the base of the gate tower, her curiosity centered on the young knight who'd removed his helm, which struck her as arrogantly confident he wasn't in any danger.

And sweet mercy, Alberic possessed a riveting countenance.

He looked about him, taking in his surroundings with eyes as green as summer grass. Wheat-blond hair skimmed the wide shoulders she'd noted earlier, and framed a swarthy-skinned visage that had undoubtedly quickened the beat of many a careless maiden's heart.

Gwendolyn wasn't careless, having learned from her parents the importance of holding her heart on tight rein. So she appreciated Alberic's handsomeness as if admiring a finely sculpted statue, choosing to ignore the faster beat of her pulse.

She could tell nothing of his thoughts during his perusal of the castle and contents of the bailey. Then he turned to look at her, and his eyes narrowed in disapproval at the sight of her chain mail.

Understandable, she supposed, and of no importance. What he thought of her strange garb mattered not.

Garrett, who'd looked weary from a distance, looked nigh on haggard up close, but not for all the gold in the kingdom would she embarrass the proud knight by fussing over him.

The knights dismounted, Garrett with the difficulty of age, Alberic with the grace of a skilled horseman.

Garrett attempted a smile. "Thought that was you on the battlements, Lady Gwendolyn. A welcoming sight to these unworthy, weary eyes."

Now wasn't the time for smiles and gallantry.

"You bring news, Garrett. What has happened?"

Garrett took a long, steadying breath. "The worst news, I fear. My lady, I am given the sad duty of informing you that your father and brother have . . . fallen."

Nay! Sweet Jesu, nay!

For several long moments Gwendolyn could only stare at Garrett, unable to breathe, struggling to deny what she couldn't possibly have heard. Then Sedwick cursed, mocking her feeble attempt at disbelief. Grief hit hard. Tears welled up and spilled down her cheeks. To keep herself upright, she grabbed hold of Garrett's forearm.

"Fallen? Both?" she asked, almost choking on the words.

"In battle, near Wallingford."

Briefly her thoughts flew to her sisters. The elder, Emma, and the youngest, Nicole. *Orphans, all of us.*

But not poor, and not without resources. Father had been most specific on her course of action should the worst happen.

Gwendolyn palmed away her tears, forcefully setting

aside her grief. Later she would mourn, but now she must see to her duty to her loved ones, and then to the legacy.

With her father gone, she alone could ensure the safety and continuation of the legacy.

"Where are they?" she asked of Garrett, relieved to hear her voice sounded stronger.

"On a cart in the woodland." Then he sighed and put his free hand over Gwendolyn's. "We brought Hugh and William home for burial. However, we cannot bring them into the castle until we are assured all at Camelen are prepared to accept their new lord."

Shock left her speechless. Gwendolyn soon reasoned out who that *new lord* must be.

Sir Alberic of Chester.

She glared at the knight she'd witlessly allowed entrance. "You have no right to Camelen. My father's will clearly states that if William does not survive him on his death, Father's estates should be divided between his three daughters. Emma is entitled to the castle as her dowry, and Nicole and I to our proper portion of manors and fees. I suggest you seek your fortune elsewhere!"

"In time of peace, or had Sir Hugh supported the rightful king, then his will might have been honored," Alberic said in his deep, rumbling voice that now held a surprising and unwanted note of sympathy. "Unfortunately, your father rebelled against the king from whom he held the charters for his estates, which gives King Stephen the right to seize and dispense the lands as he chooses."

Garrett's hand pressed down on hers where she still clutched his arm. "Sir Alberic is right, my lady. I witnessed the gifting. We have no recourse."

She snatched her hand away, distraught Sir Garrett could so blithely abandon his loyalty to her father in favor of an upstart knight.

"What if we do not accept this new lord, Garrett? What stops us from tossing him out the gate and raising the drawbridge?"

Garrett, damn his hide, looked to Alberic, who answered.

"The king kindly allowed a company of royal soldiers to accompany me. They are in the woodland, guarding the men of Camelen who survived the skirmish and the cart bearing your father and brother. If I do not give their captain the signal to bring all into the castle, he will take everyone back to Wallingford for King Stephen to dispense with at his whim."

Gwendolyn's heart sank. "You dare hold the bodies of the lords of Camelen hostage? My father deserves a lord's burial in the church! My brother beside him! 'Tis unconscionable for you to deny them—"

"I do not deny them, my lady. Too many men of Camelen have already been lost—"

"How many?"

His countenance softened. "We bring sixty-three survivors with us, many with wounds. That I know of, five chose not to return and went on their way. Three were wounded too severely to chance the trip. I expect they will be buried at Wallingford with the others."

Gwendolyn quickly calculated, her heartache deepening. She looked to Garrett for confirmation. "Thirty-two men lost?"

He nodded. "One knight, several squires, including your father's and mine. The rest foot soldiers."

Sweet Jesu! So many. So very many.

Alberic continued. "So you see why I wish a peaceful transfer of lordship, my lady. Once done, you are free to bury Sir Hugh and William with all the honor and ceremony they deserve." Then he turned to Garrett. "Tell the captain of the guard to disarm the garrison. Until I am assured of the men's loyalty to me, only royal troops will carry weapons. Any man not willing to swear loyalty must leave by nightfall on the morrow."

Garrett bowed. "So it shall be, my lord."

My lord. God's blood, Garrett had truly gone over to the enemy! All those lives lost fighting an enemy of which Alberic had to be one, all for naught. How could he?

Gwendolyn opened her mouth to protest; Sedwick's hand landed gently on her shoulder.

"My lady, your father always knew he might one day suffer retribution for his part in the rebellion. It appears the day has come, and 'tis we who must pay the price. If what Garrett and Sir Alberic say is true, then we have no choice but to bow to our fate."

Gwendolyn closed her eyes and willed tears of anger and despair not to fall. If both Sedwick and Garrett, two of her father's most trusted retainers and advisers, conceded the battle to Alberic, then he'd won the day.

She glared at the knight who usurped her father's estates, and damned his cruelty in holding those she held dear as hostages against her cooperation.

Someday, when Maud won her crown, justice would be served. The usurper displaced. Camelen and its lands returned to the rightful heirs: she and her sisters.

For the nonce, she had no choice but to acknowledge

Alberic of Chester's lordship of Camelen, but swore she would never, ever recognize him as *her* lord. Thanks to the same father who'd lost Camelen to another man, she had resources of her own with which to flee and a safe haven awaiting her.

Soon after she retrieved the ring from her father's hand, she must leave Camelen. While leaving her home and sisters behind would hurt deeply, go she would. The legacy, and the fate of all England, might depend upon her success.

Chapter Two

"A MEN," GWENDOLYN SAID IN RELIEF, closing the bed-chamber door behind the departing priest. "I thought he would never leave us alone."

Emma pushed back the green velvet coverlet, revealing her buxom nakedness, and eased her legs over the side of the bed. "He certainly gave me no comfort."

Father Paul had stumbled over his words, the prayers he murmured with the intention of easing their grief having little effect at all. But then, perhaps the grief was simply too new and heavy for easing.

Gwendolyn helped her sister rise, grasping Emma's forearm to lend support. "One cannot judge Father Paul too harshly, Em. He did what he thought right, though I admit a prayer or two less would have done. Nicole, fetch Emma's chemise and surcoat."

Ten-year-old Nicole nimbly jumped down from the chair she'd slid under the window slit, where she watched for signs that their father and brother were being brought into the bailey. Her wide brown eyes were reddened and puffy from weeping, a condition she shared with her older sisters.

Nicole handed over the chemise, then announced, "I say we get a sword and run him through."

Emma gasped and sank down onto the bed. Shocked as well, Gwendolyn could only stare at the girl. Certes, Nicole tended to act first and consider the repercussions afterward, but the suggestion was beyond belief!

"Do you truly believe the priest deserves death for faulty prayers?"

Nicole placed her hands on her hips, ire twisting her pert, bow-shaped mouth. "Not Father Paul, this new *lord*. He is surely mean and . . . and evil. We cannot allow him . . ."

Fresh tears threatened to fall when Nicole's bottom lip began to tremble. Gwendolyn wrapped the angry, fear-filled child in an embrace and strove for a soothing tone.

Not easy, given her own distress.

"Hush, now. Murder is not a solution."

Nicole sniffed. "Why ever not? The king's men killed Papa and William, did they not? And is this Alberic not a king's man?"

The king's men most certainly had killed their loved ones, and many more, and Sir Alberic undoubtedly was the enemy. Gwendolyn's anger and grief threatened to overpower the need to chastise Nicole.

Gwendolyn released Nicole slightly in order to sit down on the bed next to Emma, who'd managed to put on her chemise. She shouldn't be out of bed. One could still see the glaze of pain in Emma's eyes, sense what it cost her to rise. Just leaning forward to take her surcoat from where it draped over Nicole's shoulder caused her to pale.

Nay, Emma shouldn't have to suffer so, and Nicole

shouldn't be driven to violence. And Gwendolyn wished she didn't have to be the strongest among them, again.

Damn war. Father and William shouldn't both be dead. But they were, leaving the de Leon daughters to grapple with the aftermath as best they could. Leaving Gwendolyn to hold heart and hearth together for the time left to her.

Gwendolyn swallowed her distress, grasped hold of Nicole's hands, and prayed for the strength to find the right words.

"Father and William were . . . killed by the king's men, 'tis true. But they fell in battle, with honor. There is no honor in murder, Nicole. Besides, we know not how they died, or at whose hand. But mark my words, 'tis probable they gave a good accounting of themselves. Never doubt that more than one king's man suffered the same fate as Father and William."

Knowing her father, he'd probably been in the thick of the fray, William close at his heels, their pride allowing nothing less. And look where pride led them: to their deaths.

"Would that this war would end," Emma said softly. "No more deaths, honorable or no. No families left to grieve."

"Stephen should surrender the crown to Maud," Nicole declared, mimicking an opinion heard often from their father, a sentiment his daughters shared.

"Aye, but that is not likely to happen soon." Gwendolyn pulled Nicole in for a brief but heartfelt hug. "Nor can we do aught about it just now."

But you might be able to now, a little voice whispered. Gwendolyn roughly shoved the nagging thought aside.

No sense contemplating invoking the legacy to put an end to the war. At least not for the nonce. All of the conditions hadn't yet been met and wouldn't be until she reached her betrothed.

Nicole nodded her acceptance of her powerless state, then asked, "Will Sir Alberic allow us to stay? What will become of us?"

Gwendolyn wished she had an answer to allay what she realized might be Nicole's worst fear, that the new lord might banish her from her beloved home.

"I know not for certain, but that is for Emma and I to worry over, not you. We will see you taken care of no matter what happens. Can you trust in us?"

Again Nicole nodded, though she looked no less concerned.

Indeed, what choice did the girl have but to trust her older sisters? Their mother had died ten years ago, shortly after Nicole's birth, leaving the babe in the hands of a disinterested father, a loving but hapless brother, and two sisters who were more than eager to try their hand at mothering. Gwendolyn hoped they hadn't done a bad job of it and ruined the imp beyond repair.

Sweet Jesu, may we all find the strength to bear whatever is to come.

She squeezed Nicole's hands. "Go back to the window and watch while I braid Em's hair."

Nicole assumed her post at the window slit without comment, an oddity for her, a measure of her upset.

Emma used Gwendolyn's shoulder as support when she rose, and Gwendolyn worried over Emma's ability to withstand the next few hours without collapsing.

"Perhaps you should return to bed. Nicole and I can—"

"And have it whispered about that Sir Hugh de Leon's eldest daughter gave her father and brother less tribute than their due? *Never.* Help me with my surcoat."

If Emma was determined to see this through, then she would. Such was the power of her will. Would that her aching head succumb to that will. Unfortunately, the sick headaches ran their own course, sometimes lasting for several days. Rest and herbal potions made them bearable, but nothing they'd tried over the years could give complete relief.

Surcoat in place, Emma shuffled over to the stool. Gwendolyn fetched the ivory comb and eased it though the tangles, knowing every tug must hurt.

Emma rubbed at her brow. "The new lord, this Sir Alberic. *Is* he evil?"

Gwendolyn bit back a hasty, hateful comment about evil lurking in the hearts of all men; an answer Emma's question might have evoked from Father Paul. Now was not the time to let loose her temper, not with Nicole in the chamber.

"I think not." And not unfeeling, she had to admit. Alberic had expressed genuine sympathy for her loss, which she hadn't wanted to hear from the man who'd benefited greatly from her grievous misfortune.

"Young? Old?"

"Perhaps a bit older than you."

"Ancient, then."

Gwen smiled at the attempted jest by a woman a mere two years older than herself. "Aye, beyond prime for certain."

"Bad tempered?"

"Not today." But from the solid set of his jaw, she didn't doubt Sir Alberic could be driven to bad temper. Truly, he'd shown stoic patience throughout her outbursts. Her own father wouldn't have allowed the loud, sharp barbs she'd tossed Alberic's way, and her father had allowed all of his daughters to speak their minds—to a point.

"What else must I know?" Emma asked.

Gwendolyn glanced at Nicole and lowered her voice. "Thirty-two others died at Wallingford."

Emma crossed herself. "Lord have mercy."

"The battle must have been horrific. I cannot help but wonder what part Sir Alberic played that the king saw fit to grant him Camelen."

Emma waved a dissenting hand. "Likely none at all. Kings do not grant baronies for performance in battle. We must assume Alberic is a highly placed noble and likely a king's favorite long before Wallingford. Camelen is quite a prize for one so young."

All quite true. "When he rode through the gate he looked around him, inspecting the place. I could not tell if he liked what he saw of Camelen or not."

Gwendolyn put down the comb, separated Emma's thick mass of silken, reddish-brown hair, and began braiding, all the while pondering her other impressions of Sir Alberic of Chester. His expression hadn't revealed his thoughts, at least not until he'd spotted her wearing chain mail. To that he'd reacted with definite dislike.

"I can tell you Sir Alberic does not approve of women wearing chain mail."

Emma glanced at the trunk into which Gwendolyn had placed the mail shirt, where it would remain until needed again by either sister. "Most men would object, I suppose, but it affords us protection."

It did, even if Gwendolyn disliked wearing the heavy chain mail. She handed her sister the end of the waist-length braid. "Hold this," she ordered, then took the two steps toward the table to fetch a strip of leather.

When she turned back to Emma, she noted her sister's puzzled expression.

"What?" she asked gently.

"Father held Camelen and his other manors by royal charter," Emma said slowly, obviously sorting thoughts as she spoke. "With Father and William . . . gone, we become royal wards. A frightening thought."

Frightening, indeed. But where Emma and Nicole faced an uncertain future, Gwendolyn had no choice in her course.

Not for the first time since their mother's death did Gwendolyn wish she could confide in Emma. But only now did she resent being her mother's choice as guardian of the legacy, which she alone knew about and must guard with her life if need be.

A pendant for the woman. A ring for the man. A scroll bearing instructions on how to recall King Arthur from Avalon during England's darkest hour.

The pendant and scroll rested safely and secretly behind a loose brick in the bedchamber's hearth. Once she retrieved her father's ring, she must take all the artifacts to a place of safety in Wales, to her betrothed.

Gwendolyn had always understood and accepted that her duty to the legacy must come before all else. She just hadn't realized that doing so might mean abandoning her sisters. Her heart broke for the loss, but she truly had no choice. She would have to leave Nicole to Emma's care and pray the two came to no harm.

Despite Nicole's fears of banishment from Camelen, Gwendolyn doubted Sir Alberic intended to blithely toss the daughters of Hugh de Leon out the gate. Control over the fates of high-born, unwed females was simply too valuable a right to squander away.

Emma again rubbed at her brow. "Damn ache. I need my wits about me and cannot think through the pain."

Gwen fetched a cup from the small bedside table. "I know this has cooled, but if you drink the rest you might feel some relief."

Emma's nose scrunched with disgust. "Foul brew."

"Merely willow bark in broth."

Emma drank, her distaste for the herb-infused broth visibly rising with each sip. "There. Satisfied? Believe me, Gwen, no potion will ever cure what ails me! The headaches are my penance to bear. Now leave off!"

Stunned by Emma's sharpness, Gwendolyn could think of no words to comfort her sister. The pain a penance? Surely not. Emma wasn't thinking clearly. Pain mixed with grief must be muddling Emma's thoughts beyond sense.

Into the silence, Nicole's voice rang clear and somber. "They come."

∽

Father Paul led the procession into Camelen's crowded great hall, his steps in rhythm to a harp's soulful song.

Alberic took his place, positioned directly behind the

litter bearers and in front of the six guards chosen to stand first watch during the overnight vigil.

Sir Hugh and William were garbed in the armor in which they'd fallen, with their swords in their scabbards and their helmets placed between their feet. Their battered shields rested on their chests.

Alberic's first impression of Camelen's great hall was that someone had been overly enamored of weaponry. While he tried to concentrate on the small ceremony beginning the funeral rituals, he couldn't help glance up and outward at the weapons hanging on the walls, on the six pillars supporting the roof's arches, and from the roof's support beams high above.

Groupings of swords, daggers, axes, lances, shields, crossbows, and claymores, most of them gleaming, all vied for his attention. Most spectacular were the swords, arranged in a stunning circle up high on the far wall.

Such a collection must have taken years to assemble, and the resulting effect of far-reaching and formidable power threatened to overwhelm the viewer. Likely each piece had its own tale to tell of victory or defeat, honor or shame, glory or disgrace. Someday he would have to ask Garrett, who walked stoic and somber at Alberic's side, if he knew the tales attached to some of the weapons.

'Twould also be fascinating to learn why the lord of a wooden keep, surrounded by a thick, stone wall and a deep moat, located a mere few leagues south of Shrewsbury, had thrown his lot in with the rebellion when most of the shire supported the king. And if Hugh owned all these weapons, why hadn't he armed a larger force of men to take with him to Wallingford?

Nagging questions that wouldn't be answered today.

Gently, the litter bearers lowered the deceased lords of Camelen onto two trestle tables placed side by side in front of the dais. Beside the tables stood three females. He recognized the one in the center as Gwendolyn, who'd removed her chain mail. A startling sight, that, but the armor hadn't detracted from her doe-eyed beauty one whit.

The other two must be her sisters, one a mere child.

From these three females he must choose a wife, but he had no time for more than a brief glance at them before the bearers bowed, then slipped away from the tables now become funeral biers.

The vigil guards took their positions. All done efficiently and quietly, with respect.

Along with Garrett, Alberic bowed his head and silently wished both father and son a speedy and safe journey to the hereafter.

Beg pardon, William. I did not mean . . .

Alberic squelched the guilt-induced apology. The two of them had met on the field of battle and crossed swords. In defending his own life he'd taken William's. 'Twas not the first time he'd killed a man, and he could think of no other reason why he should be sorry other than this was the first time he'd observed funeral rites for his victim. And William's death might continue to haunt his footsteps if the people of Camelen didn't consider their new lord blameless in the old lord's demise.

Unfortunately, there wasn't any way to keep his part in William's death a secret. The soldiers would talk among themselves. A servant would overhear. The tale would spread through the entire castle as fast as fire through dry brush.

Alberic wanted to avoid a revolt while establishing his lordship, but doubted the conversion would be completely peaceful, which was why he hadn't removed his sword. And why he'd ordered all of Camelen's soldiers disarmed until such time he no longer worried over being murdered in his bed. And why one of the king's soldiers walked at his back.

Necessary precautions he hoped wouldn't be necessary for too long.

So far, all had gone well and probably would continue to do so until after the burials, giving Alberic time to observe, assess, and take whatever preventive measures he deemed appropriate.

Again following Garrett's lead, Alberic approached the priest and Hugh's daughters, knowing all and sundry expected him to utter condolences.

Useless gestures. He well remembered that no words uttered by the villagers at his mother's burial had made him feel less wretched, frightened, or alone.

During the long, somber ride from Wallingford, Garrett had provided bits of information, among them the daughters' names and order of birth.

Indeed, the sisters crowded together for support. Emma and Nicole leaned inward, toward Gwendolyn. To prop her up or for succor? Whichever, they appeared as a cluster of feminine jewels in the masculine bedecked hall.

Exquisitely cut jewels. Their father had either indulged them outrageously or garbed them finely to proclaim his wealth.

To his surprise, Alberic saw nothing of the father in any of the daughters. All possessed fair skin and the wide, doe-like eyes he'd noticed of Gwendolyn earlier. He couldn't help thinking their mother must have been quite a beauty.

A Welsh princess. Or so the king had said. Alberic still didn't know whether or not to believe the family's claim of heredity from King Arthur. However, he had no trouble believing the sisters came from Welsh heritage, and their bearing, especially Gwendolyn's, was worthy of a princess.

All three wore chemises of the whitest linen, covered by silk surcoats of dove gray. Chains of gold links girdled their waists. Veils of a shimmery cloth he couldn't name covered their heads, held in place by circlets of spun gold set with large, exquisite jewels, coming damn near close to crowns.

Topaz studded Emma's circlet, putting Alberic in mind of the rising sun. The eldest—making her the expected choice for his wife—possessed a lovely face, graced by a full mouth. She was also amply endowed and wide-hipped. Desirable attributes in a wife for a man who needed heirs.

Young Nicole, with her emerald circlet slightly askew, snuggled up to Gwendolyn for comfort. She bore all the signs of becoming a great beauty, but was much too young to take on the immediate duties of a wife.

Glittering amethyst, the stones a pure, deep violet, adorned Gwendolyn's circlet. Willow slender and graceful, she impressed him as sturdy yet flexible, able to endure life's blows and then come right again. Perhaps he'd judged her too harshly in the bailey, put off by the sight of a woman draped in chain mail. In fully feminine garb, Gwendolyn was an enchanting vision.

Definitely suitable enough to wed and bed. According to Garrett, Hugh left her in charge of the household in his absence, so no one would need to become accustomed to a new mistress. And of all the females, she was the easiest to envision in his bed.

And of all the sisters, she paid him the least heed, staring hard at her father and brother.

Garrett bowed. "My ladies, I cannot fully express my sorrow at this luckless turn of fortune. All I can do is assure you that Sir Hugh and William fought bravely and died honorably. May God have everlasting mercy on their souls."

When Emma tried to smile at Garrett, Alberic sensed the pain that glazed her pale face was due to a physical hurt more than the depth of her grief. Was she ill?

"Sir Garrett," she said, her voice strong despite the pain. "We thank you for bringing our father and brother back to us."

"I wish the circumstances different, my lady. Escorting Lord Hugh to his final rest will be my privileged last service to a man I have served half of my lifetime. A good man, he was. A fair lord who will be missed by many."

Then Garrett raised a hand, palm upward indicating the sisters. "Lord Alberic, may I present to you the ladies of the house of de Leon. Emma, Gwendolyn, and Nicole."

Only then did Gwendolyn's head turn, her red-rimmed eyes fixing him with a stare, as if wondering who he was and trying to remember if she'd seen him before. He dismissed the dent to his male pride as inconsequential. The woman obviously grieved deeply and must be allowed a lapse or two.

"I also offer my condolences, ladies. Loss of family is most difficult and distressing to bear. May Sir Hugh and William find peace in the hereafter."

"Amen," the priest intoned. "Shall we begin, my lord?"

It took Alberic a moment to realize whose permission the priest sought. He didn't have to look around to know that everyone in the hall awaited his answer, the silence complete.

A heady sense of power flooded through him, knowing that in this hall his word was now law. Within an instant he could have everyone on their knees, groveling at his feet, as he'd seen the earl do when mightily displeased.

Alberic nodded his permission at the priest, then stepped off to the side to allow Emma, Gwendolyn, and Nicole full view of their father and brother.

The priest began the prayers. Alberic strove to listen attentively to the entreaties to God, Christ, and various saints to grant favor to Hugh and William. But God's bones, how much help did Hugh and William need getting through heaven's gate? A lot, apparently, given the priest's many and earnest pleas for intercession for mercy on their souls.

When Alberic no longer recognized the saints' names from whom the priest begged indulgences, his attention began to wander, discovering he wasn't the only one who no longer heeded the priest's prayers.

Gwendolyn seemed restless, but not overtly. A slight

shift of stance. A brief glance his way. A perusal of the crowd.

Then Emma leaned harder into Gwendolyn. Both women remained standing, but whatever ailed Emma affected her ability to keep upright on her own.

He thought it fitting his first order in the hall should be one of compassion for the females. Perhaps they would remember it when he informed them of the rest of the king's orders and not judge the bearer of the news too harshly.

Alberic waited for the natural pause between the crowd's "Amen" and the priest's intake of breath for the next invocation. He pointedly cleared his throat and, as he'd hoped, drew the priest's attention.

He pitched his voice low so only a few would hear. "I believe a bit of mercy for the living is in order, Father."

The priest pursed his lips in chagrin. "A last prayer?"

"Only if you must."

Gwendolyn looked at him fully then, her expression and small nod expressing her gratitude, though he also had the feeling she did so reluctantly.

The final prayer was mercifully short, followed by an invitation to any who wished to keep vigil to remain in the hall, and a reminder of the burial rites to be observed on the morrow, a mere hour after dawn.

Most of those gathered came forward for a long look at Hugh and William and to express their condolences to the ladies.

Emma seemed to rally, determined to do her duty. But whenever someone went on too long or became over-wrought, Gwendolyn hurried them along.

Then his stomach growled, reminding him of how

long ago he and the rest of his escort had eaten. Garrett overheard.

"Events have interfered with showing you proper hospitality, my lord. I will have someone take you to your chamber and order food brought up."

As lord, his place was in the hall, but he didn't think anyone would think too badly of him if he took a few minutes to wash and get out of his chain mail. He had passed his helmet off to Odell, the king's soldier who acted as his guard and squire, but hadn't yet taken off his riding gloves.

Before he could answer Garrett, the sisters clasped hands, and together approached the twin biers. They went first to William, who was closest to them. He couldn't see the sisters' faces, but could feel their grief.

Then they circled around to view their father, their grief nigh unbearable. Tears streamed down their cheeks. Nicole could barely look at her sire, hiding her face in Gwendolyn's skirts. Emma closed her eyes, her mouth moving in silent prayer.

Only Gwendolyn reached out to touch Hugh, her hand slipping beneath the shield to grasp his folded hands. She went very still, staring down at the shield covering her father's chest.

When she looked up she sought out Garrett, and Alberic could almost hear the question her expression asked of her father's trusted knight.

Father's ring. Where is it?

Not very gallant of him to hurt an already hurting woman, but maybe it was best this way. The daughters of Hugh de Leon must realize their lives had changed completely, that they were no longer the reigning princesses of Camelen.

He slipped off the riding gloves he probably should have taken off earlier, if only to allow all to see the ring, the visible proof of his lordship. As the garnet in the center of the onyx flashed bright in the torchlight, he turned to Garrett.

"I am ready for that room and food now."

"Immediately, my lord. This way."

They headed for the stairs. Gwendolyn bolted into his path, her ire high.

"That ring belongs to my father. You may not wear it."

"Lady Gwendolyn, I am sorry for your loss, but you must accept that whatever once belonged to Hugh de Leon now belongs to me. His holdings, his people, even his ring."

He thought he'd been gentle, but she recoiled as if he'd delivered a punishing blow. Like the willow he'd compared her to earlier, she didn't stay down long.

"There are some things the king had no right to give away. The ring is one of them. I should like to have it back."

"Step aside, my lady. Go back to your mourning. Now is not the time to air your complaint."

She looked about to object, then took a deep, steadying breath before delivering what sounded suspiciously like an order.

"Then we will speak of this later, *my lord*."

Chapter Three

A SERVANT HAULED the last full canvas sack out of the lord's bedchamber. Gwendolyn stood in the doorway, her hand on the latch, trying not to wallow in grief.

She'd thought burying her father and brother the most wrenching experience she'd ever endured. Now a full day afterward, she felt as though she'd barely survived ordeal by fire.

The lord's bedchamber didn't look very different from when she'd begun removing her father's belongings.

The huge, four-poster bed claimed its normal space, the golden velvet draperies tied back against the posts. Though her mother had died ten years ago, Gwendolyn could envision Lady Lydia lying there during her last days. Only months ago her father had perched on the edge of the thick feather mattress, complaining about how his new boots pinched his toes.

Mere weeks ago she spent nigh on an hour in this chamber with him, listening intently while he explained why he and William must go to Brian fitz Count's aid at Wallingford, a vital stronghold for the Empress Maud, and what he expected of her in his absence.

He had promised to return home before Beltane. And he did, but not in the manner he planned.

So now the ornate trunk along the far wall no longer held her father's tunics and breeches. His shoes and boots no longer stood beneath the wooden pegs where he'd hung his cloaks. A pewter flagon of wine and a gold goblet graced the heavy, round oak table where her father had tended to toss odd items until one could barely see the surface.

Alberic's gloves and helmet lay on the table. His cloak occupied a peg. She noticed no other of his possessions, and had thought it strange until remembering he'd come to Camelen straight off the battlefield. Surely he'd already sent someone to collect his personal belongings from Chester. Too soon he would make the chamber his own.

Fighting back tears, Gwendolyn closed the door behind her and strode down the passageway to yet another bedchamber. There, too, several sacks awaited her.

Stepping into William's chamber was akin to drowning. She struggled for breath while waves of grief battered at her resolve not to cry again. Her heart ached, her throat hurt, her eyes burned. Tempted to retreat, Gwendolyn swallowed the lump threatening to choke her as she crossed the room to yet another trunk that must be emptied.

She knelt down and opened the lid, only to lose sight of the contents through another wash of tears.

The swish of silk slippers on the rush mat alerted Gwendolyn to Nicole's entry. A deep breath helped steady her, bolstering her resolve to hide the worst of her distress. As she turned she hoped her smile didn't look too feigned.

"What is it, dear?"

Nicole bent over to pick up a sack from the stack, then brought it toward Gwendolyn. "Shall I help?"

She rose, feeling her face soften into a genuine smile at Nicole's offer. But if the task was agonizing for her, 'twould be sheer misery for Nicole.

"Nay. Truly, 'twill take me little time." She took the sack. "Done with your lesson?"

"Father Paul ended it early. Neither of us could concentrate on adding numbers." She waved at the trunk. "What will you do with it all?"

"Give some away to needy soldiers or peasants. Keep some." She shrugged a shoulder, not yet sure what to dispose of and what to keep.

Nicole glanced at the table that held several items dear to William. "Their weapons, too?"

Gwendolyn placed a hand on her sister's shoulder. "The swords and daggers should hang in the hall. The others? We shall see." She gave Nicole a brief hug. "Perhaps you should go sit with Emma for a while. I believe her headache begins to wane."

"All right," she agreed with lack of enthusiasm. Having never been sick a day in her short life, Nicole didn't deal with others' ailments with much compassion.

Gwen walked her little sister toward the door, wanting her out of the chamber so she could get the unpleasant chore over with.

"Will his lordship allow us to hang the weapons?" Nicole asked.

Gwendolyn hadn't thought to ask Alberic's permission. Would he give permission? Likely.

"I should think so. Weapons from Camelen's past lords hang among those Father collected. 'Tis tradition."

"Is it also tradition for the new lord to plunder the stores of the old?"

Gwendolyn stopped walking. "What do you mean?"

"Alberic inspected the storage rooms this morn. He pulled several ells of fabric from a crate and gave orders for the seamstresses to make him some tunics."

She tamped down a swell of ire. "Did he?"

"Aye. And Cook says he opened a sack of Father's favorite almonds and devoured a handful as if he had never tasted the like before."

Gwendolyn imagined Alberic going through the store-room, grabbing at this, handling that. Looting whatever suited his fancy. Laughing at her misfortune and his gain.

Except the vision didn't come clearly, nor ring true. As much as she hated to admit it, he had the right to the fabric, and she could hardly begrudge him a handful of almonds. He didn't need to loot or plunder what now belonged to him.

"What belonged to Father now belongs to Sir Alberic, both the fabric and the almonds. And the lands and the falcons and the hunting dogs. All of it, Nicole. We have no say in the matter."

"He does not own us, does he?"

"Nay, we are royal wards, not Sir Alberic's. Out with you now. Go pester Emma."

"She is likely asleep," the girl grumbled, but obeyed.

As Nicole disappeared into their bedchamber, the devil himself appeared at the top of the stairway. Alberic slowed as he came near, bobbed his head as he stopped.

"Lady Gwendolyn." He looked past her into William's

chamber, frowning. "A beastly task you set for yourself, and so soon."

"Someone must do it."

"Set a servant to the task."

Emma had suggested the same, and Gwendolyn had bristled then, as now. "Nay, 'tis a daughter and sister's duty."

His frown disappeared, and an odd, almost haunted look stole over him before his composure returned. "I was all of twelve when my mother died, and seeing her belongings disposed of was nigh as difficult as burying her. I commend you on your sense of duty, and your courage."

That damn lump in her throat threatened to swell again, this time moved by his admission. 'Twasn't hard to envision him as a young boy grieving for his mother. Except she found it hard to believe a noble male would take a hand in disposing of his mother's belongings. Still, she'd seen his genuine pain.

And truly, she didn't deserve his compliment on her courage. She'd taken on the task this morn in part because Sedwick—whom Alberic had asked to remain as his steward and on his council as the knight had done for her father—had told her of Alberic's plans to inspect the castle and lands this morn, so she'd known his chamber would be free of his presence. That suddenly seemed cowardly.

And given Nicole's upset over Alberic's right to loot the storage rooms, he'd apparently made a thorough tour of the castle.

"Have you been out to the villages yet?"

He shook his head, his blond hair skimming his shoulders. "We are about to leave, so I came up to fetch my cloak and gloves."

This struck her as odd. "Why not send up your squire?"

He stared at her, confused, then smiled. "You mean Odell? He is not my squire, merely one of the royal troops."

How was it a noble of high rank had no squire? Unless, like her father's and Garrett's, his squire had fallen at Wallingford, too. She bit her bottom lip to keep from offering condolences to a man she truly shouldn't feel the least bit sorry for.

He ran a hand through his thick mane, his green eyes narrowing. "Another task I must see to. I should imagine one or two of the younger guards would qualify to act as my squire. Have you a recommendation?"

She was tempted, but he would immediately find out those she named were most unsuitable.

"Sir Garrett would know better than I."

"A wise man, Garrett. I am pleased he has agreed to remain as a member of my council." Then he bowed slightly. "Begging your pardon, my lady, but I should be off."

With that, he took the last few steps to open the door to the lord's bedchamber and disappeared into the room.

Her father's chamber no longer. All belonged to Alberic now.

Even, it seemed, the people. Sedwick as steward. Garrett as counselor. Guards soon to be squires.

The swiftness and thoroughness of Alberic's conquest set her teeth on edge. She wanted to kick someone into organizing a rebellion. Except without Sedwick or Garrett to lead them, who would dare? Nor did she wish to put anyone at risk.

Besides, she wouldn't be forced to witness this folly much longer. As soon as she had the ring in hand, she would leave.

Gwendolyn spun back into the room and shut the door to resume her task without further interruption. She made quick work of stuffing William's garments into two sacks. They'd be taken to the same storage room where Alberic had found the fabric, to wait until she and Emma decided how best to distribute them.

At the table, she looked over the items brought up on the dawn of the burial, when the guards had removed Father's and William's chain mail, when she and Emma had sewn shut their shrouds.

Their suits of mail had been taken to the armory. Their swords and daggers lay on the table; their shields leaned against the wall.

Alberic had the right to claim them, too, if he chose.

She shouldn't care if they were given the honor of hanging in the hall, but she did, and their disposition seemed important to Nicole, so tonight she would speak to Alberic about them.

Surely she would have her emotions under control by then, her courage back at its rightful level. She would start by thanking him for his kindness to Emma, then speak to him of the ring, perhaps ask him *nicely* this time instead of demanding he give it over.

She wouldn't tell him the truth of the ring's importance, of course. Perhaps she could explain it was a gift from her mother to her father, a keepsake handed down through the female line.

If he didn't give it over, then she'd have to find another way to take possession of the seal of the dragon from the man not meant to wear it.

Alberic didn't know a prime ox from a decent ox. If Sedwick claimed the two oxen pulling the plow through the field were prime, he had no reason to disbelieve the man who'd been steward of Camelen for more than a decade.

Just as he didn't doubt the man's knowledge of how many sheaves of wheat and sacks of barley and oats were harvested each year; how much was kept for the lord's use and how much could be sold at what price.

He would understand all this eventually, but for now Alberic took contentment in sitting atop a quality horse, watching the work being done.

Lords might come and go, but the tenants' work didn't halt, each task to its season. Given, of course, that some army didn't come along and burn their homes and crops. He'd seen plenty of blackened timbers and scorched fields these past years, but hadn't contemplated the effect of the war on the common people until now, when they were his people. His crops. His livelihood.

The risk of harm came from directions other than an attacking army. Either lack of or an overabundance of rain. Pestilence. Early or late frost.

But then there were the sheep. Hale and hardy Shropshires. One needed only meadows and freedom from disease to make a success of raising sheep, or so he thought. And this lovely corner of Shropshire provided an abundance of grazing land upon its gently rolling hillsides.

The streams ran thick with trout and salmon. Hart and hare populated the woodlands. And he could hardly wait to fly the gyrfalcons against the herons and cranes.

He watched the oxen make their turn at the end of the long row, then wheeled his horse southward. Sedwick and Odell fell in with him. The other guards marched behind.

"Two villages?" he asked Sedwick.

"Two villages, three hamlets, and scattered settlements. All in all, between the castle and the rest, nigh on three hundred or so people are dependent upon Camelen. And we on them. Most are decent, hardworking folk. We have our troublemakers, of course. You will meet them soon enough in your court, I fear."

He'd never passed judgment before, not levied a fine or demanded added service, nor sentenced a man to the stocks or the gallows. Another thing he would learn by doing. A study of the judgments issued by Hugh would be of help.

"Craftsmen?"

"Blacksmith, tanner, dyer." Sedwick smiled. "God's truth, my lord, we have too many to name. We even have a bard who calls Camelen home."

Alberic vaguely remembered hearing the strains of a harp both before the vigil and after the burial. But what he remembered was very nicely done.

"Welsh?"

"The best kind."

Alberic had to agree, though his experience with Welshmen wasn't usually in a hall. Those who raided

Cheshire had been considered sword fodder, except when the earl needed troops. Then Chester wasn't above hiring anyone capable of wielding any type of weapon, including Welshmen.

"Have we many Welsh?"

"A few. Most came with Lady Lydia when she married Sir Hugh, or shortly thereafter. Rhys, the bard, of course. One of her ladyship's handmaidens married the blacksmith. There are a few others, among them soldiers in the garrison."

"And all is peaceful?"

"Oh, we suffer a raid here and there. A sheep or two go missing. But mostly they have left us alone, before out of respect for Lady Lydia, and now for her daughters."

The first village was in sight, but Alberic wasn't yet ready to visit. He reined in, and Sedwick halted.

"How does an English baron come to marry a Welsh princess?"

Sedwick thought for a moment, then answered, "Sir Hugh met her ladyship at court. Her father was among a Welsh delegation sent to petition King Henry for one thing or another. Hugh told me he took one look at the beautiful Lydia and lost both his heart and ability to speak. Apparently the father and daughter were amenable to the match."

"I gather the king did not object."

"Not that I am aware of."

Hugh had married for love? Alberic nudged his horse forward, mulling over the oddity.

Surely, for a Welsh prince and an English king to agree to the match, there had been considerations to the bargain other than a baron's attraction to a princess.

Normally, barons were given heiresses by their over-lords, either as a reward or to seal an alliance. Love deserved no place in a marriage contract between nobles, not when lands and wealth were at stake.

As with his own marriage; by marrying one of the de Leon daughters, Alberic sealed his claim to Sir Hugh's estates. Neither attraction nor love had aught to do with his decision of which daughter to choose.

That King Stephen had given Alberic the right to choose among the females might be an oddity, but that the king retained guardianship of the other two wasn't. In time, Stephen would exploit those rights in whatever way he saw fit.

Though Alberic hadn't yet decided which of the three would become his wife, he'd caught himself noticing Gwendolyn more than the other two. Of course, Nicole was too young to appeal. Emma's illness hadn't pre-vented her from attending to her duty toward her father and brother, but when her presence wasn't required, she'd taken to her bed. She struck him as a pale reflec-tion of Gwendolyn.

Gwen, as her sisters called her, certainly possessed a lovely face and a hardy constitution. The curve of her backside wasn't hard to look at, either. Aye, he'd have no problem with taking those lovely curves into his bed.

She'd been upset over his ring when they'd parted last eve. He'd half expected her to take him to task over it when he'd come across her this morn.

Perhaps she'd come to terms with his possession of the seal of the dragon, and thus his lordship of Camelen, for she'd not mentioned it. But then, he'd found her in the midst of a most unpleasant duty, and she'd been pre-occupied.

He hadn't lied when admiring her courage, and admired it even more when he'd walked into the lord's bedchamber and felt the emptiness. If the sparseness of the room had affected him, he could imagine how clearing it of her father's belongings must have affected Gwendolyn.

Still, she hadn't appeared overly distraught. And that, too, he had to admire. 'Twas no wonder Hugh left her in charge of the household in his absence.

Alberic rode into the village he'd been in briefly yesterday when putting Hugh and William to rest under the floor of the church at the far end of the village green.

As in most villages, the huts were constructed of wattle and daub, the roofs thatched. Geese and chickens pecked about in the yards, which sported patches of newly overturned earth, ready for planting gardens once the danger of frost passed.

Several women stood at the common well, buckets in hand, paying more attention to one another than the squealing children who chased around them.

As the children became aware of his approach, their squeals faded and the women turned to stare. He acknowledged curtsies and bows with nods, progressing slowly so all could get a good look at both him and the ring.

"Do you wish to stop, my lord?" Sedwick asked.

"At the church."

"I believe Father Paul is at the castle."

"'Tis not the priest I wish to visit."

Long ago he'd learned how deeply a show of piety could influence the peasantry. Ranulf de Gernons, the earl of Chester, might be a harsh and self-serving man, but a visit to church earned him approval. Alberic meant to stop only long enough to light a votive candle, allowing all to think he did so in honor of the old lord. If the pretense didn't aid his cause, for certes it could do him no harm.

He dismounted near the church steps.

The children's curiosity got the better of them, and when they gathered around to ogle the men in chain mail and to admire the horses, the women and the few men about crowded around, too.

Alberic smiled down at one particularly grubby, flush-faced urchin, remembering his own early childhood spent in a village not unlike this one. Barefoot, garbed in a tunic of rough weave, he'd once chased with other children around a common well.

A hitch in his heartbeat accompanied the many memories.

Most of them were of his mother, scraping out a living as the village brewer. He'd never doubted her love for him, or that she did all she could to make them comfortable, and done very well. Not until near the end had she told him about his father, and of the few pence the earl sent each month to keep her from telling others of his youthful misadventure.

At times Alberic wished she'd kept her secret. At others, like now, he felt grateful. He'd endured much growing up at the fringe of Chester's shadow, but the final gain was well worth the hardships he'd suffered. He now had the means to prove himself worthy of the earl of Chester's acknowledgment, and he meant to make the most of the opportunity.

Alberic squatted down to face the boy nose to nose. "What is your name, lad?"

The boy's eyes went wide, likely surprised to hear English from his lord rather than Norman-French.

"Edward . . . milord."

"A good English name."

"Me mum says she named me after the great Confessor."

"Then you must strive to do justice to the name." He tilted his head. "Your nose met the ground today. Did it hurt?"

The boy rubbed at the smudge of dirt. "Nay."

A woman's work-worn hands landed on the boy's shoulders. Alberic looked up to see a short, round female, gray streaking her otherwise brown hair.

"Beggin' yer pardon, milord. Did me boy do somethin' he ought not?"

Alberic realized he probably shouldn't have given in to the urge to talk to the boy. Most lords didn't bother to notice a peasant child, much less deign to talk to him. In doing so, he'd frightened the boy's mother.

Alberic rose up. "He has done nothing wrong, mistress. Indeed, he seems a fine lad."

Relief and pride mingled in her toothy smile. "I believe so. If I can be so bold, milord, might I ask after the ladies of the castle?"

"All are well."

"Lady Emma, too?"

"I believe I heard someone say she recovers."

"Praise be. Poor dear. She suffers so. Would you be kind enough to tell Lady Gwendolyn—"

"Mistress Biggs, his lordship is not a messenger!"

Sedwick's admonition pricked Alberic's ire, hearing again the haughty Norman treatment of the English. He might look Norman, might speak English with the undertones of the Norman-French he'd been forced to learn and use after coming under Chester's influence. But Lord above, he couldn't bring himself to forswear his peasant roots, or treat this woman with less courtesy than he would a noble lady.

He shot Sedwick a disapproving glance before addressing Mistress Biggs. "What is it you wish Lady Gwendolyn to know?"

Unsure of herself, she pressed her lips together before gathering her courage. "That we miss her, milord."

"You are accustomed to seeing her often?"

The woman nodded. "Once a sennight, at the least. She . . . she brings out medicines and spare clothin', and bread what's got burned on the bottom."

"She tends to the villagers' needs."

Another bob of head. "Seems she does not mind tendin' the likes of us, like Lady Emma. Hard to say how we would get along without Lady Gwendolyn's care."

"What of Nicole?"

Her smile returned. "Betimes she comes with Lady Gwendolyn. The girl likes to play with the children."

What manner of noble child played with peasant children?

"Nicole chases with them?"

"Oh, heaven forbid, no, milord! That would be undignified!"

He almost laughed at her horror, but managed restraint.

"Then what do they play?"

Wariness replaced her horror. She waved a dismissive hand. "Oh, this and that."

Which was no answer at all.

"We play empress and earls," Edward blurted out, supplying the information his mother hesitated to reveal.

Everyone went still, and Alberic wished he'd had the good sense not to pursue the matter. Certes, he didn't have to ask who assumed the role of empress.

In Alberic's opinion, Nicole had chosen her role poorly.

Though she preferred to be called empress, Maud had lost the title upon the death of her first husband, the emperor of Germany. Her father had then given her in marriage to Geoffrey, the count of Anjou, a hefty step down in her eyes. Nor did she rule over the earls loyal to her, for she possessed no true ruling power in England.

Several years ago, with King Stephen captured, Maud had been given a chance at obtaining her goal. She'd proved so arrogant and greedy that her support in London quickly vanished, leaving her vulnerable to forces raised by Queen Matilda. So had ended her reign as Lady of the English, with a hasty, undignified retreat.

Why Nicole would wish to liken herself to such a woman Alberic couldn't guess.

"Are you an earl?"

The boy had caught his mother's wariness, but he also knew he must answer. In a very small voice he admitted, "Reginald, earl of Cornwall."

One of Maud's half brothers and one of her staunchest allies.

"I fear you must give up your earldom, Edward. Perhaps on Lady Nicole's next visit, she can be Queen

Matilda and petition the king to grant you the earldom of York."

The boy's nose scrunched in confusion. "But who shall be king?"

"One of you lads must prove himself worthy of the title."

He shook his head. "Nicole will loathe having to ask one of us for permission to name her earls. She likes givin' orders on her own."

Alberic bit back another laugh and ruffled the boy's hair. "Such are the fortunes of war, lad. King Stephen is now our overlord, and I cannot have Maud and her earls mucking about in the village now, can I?"

Knowing a retreat was in order, and allowing himself to regroup and the villagers to breathe easier, Alberic turned to go into the church. He had no more than put a foot on the bottom stair when an arrow whizzed past his head and bit deep into the church's solid oak door.

"Attack!" one of his guards shouted. "Get down, my lord!"

Alberic paid the order no heed, spinning around to look in the direction from which the arrow must have come. He saw no one with a bow in hand. Indeed, he saw few people at all.

Already the villagers had scattered, fleeing to the safety of their homes. 'Struth, he didn't suspect any of the group of treachery. The arrow had to have come from the edge of the woodland.

He started for his horse. Sedwick caught him by the sleeve.

"Nay, my lord. You must not give chase. The risk is too great! Pray return to the safety of the keep."

Prudence demanded he heed Sedwick's advice, no matter that he didn't like it. He was lord of Camelen now, and lords didn't go chasing in the brush for rogues when he could send others. Lords didn't put themselves in danger for less than excellent reasons. He wished he could think of an excellent reason for getting himself shot at a second time. None came to mind.

He nodded his reluctant consent, and a moment later two men galloped off in pursuit of the archer, who was probably long gone.

Alberic climbed the church steps and tugged on the arrow. It failed to budge. The damn thing would have to be dug out.

"My lord, we should be off."

He heard the nervousness in Odell's suggestion, knew the man made as much sense as Sedwick, but couldn't stop staring at the slender rod of yew that had been aimed at his head and damn near found its mark.

The warning was all too clear. Someone took exceptional umbrage to Alberic of Chester's lordship over Camelen and intended to do something about it.

Chapter Four

"G WEN, CEASE PACING! Have you naught at all to do?"
She acquiesced to Emma's request by plopping
down on the bed the two of them had shared since their
youth, and in which Emma no longer suffered. With her
headache gone, Emma apparently felt well enough to
express displeasure at her restless sister. She certainly
looked better, her color more normal and her disposition
less troubling. Gwendolyn still didn't understand why
Emma had declared her headaches a penance, and had
decided not to bring the subject up again, blaming grief
for marring her sister's usual good sense.

But then, if Emma was so overwrought, how could
she calmly sit in the chamber's ornate chair, embroi-
dering the hem of a garnet tunic's sleeve with gold
thread?

A tunic meant for Alberic.

"Nay. Now all look to Alberic or Sedwick for instruction." To Gwendolyn's own ears she sounded petulant,
and admitted the lack of duties wore on her nerves.

Alberic's very presence wore on her nerves. She
found his sitting in her father's chair at the dais at meal-

times irksome. To know he slept in the lord's bed-chamber was so bothersome she could barely sleep. If one more servant remarked on how handsome and gallant and brave was the new lord of Camelen, she might be tempted to scream.

True, Alberic was both handsome and gallant. While she'd felt a kinship with him during their short talk yesterday, and admired the clean-shaven, rugged cut of his chin, she preferred not to be reminded of her enemy's qualities. As for brave, he'd returned yesterday from the village and stuck the offending arrow into a pillar, announcing his intention to capture the man responsible for its flight. This morning, he'd taken out one of her father's prize falcons to hunt, and all wondered what game he truly meant to bring back.

"Surely Alberic would not begrudge you overseeing the garden, or seeing to the needs of Camelen's people," Emma suggested. "Perhaps a walk out to the village would calm you."

"The ground is still too hard for planting, and we are not allowed outside the walls without guards. And until Alberic returns from his hunt, there are no guards to spare from their duties. I feel a prisoner in my own home."

Emma looked up from her stitching. "You are usually the calm pool, not the boiling river, and your ceaseless discontent is putting everyone on edge. You had best find *something* to do before you push us all to madness."

"I fail to see how you can be so tranquil and accepting. We have been as good as conquered, and with the exception of a lone archer, everyone seems willing to serve the conqueror! Do you not find that disquieting?

Nor has he seen fit to tell us of the king's plans for . . . us. How long are we supposed to wait?"

Not that the king's plans for them affected her. She would be gone soon, depending upon when she convinced Alberic to give up the seal of the dragon. However, her sisters' fates were of great concern.

"Perhaps Alberic does not know of the king's plans because none have yet been made. And all considered, the conquest could have been worse. We were not forced to suffer a siege, nor has his lordship made overbearing demands. Lord Alberic may have conquered, but he did so in civil, bloodless fashion. Indeed, he can be a pleasant man."

"Oh, Emma, has he charmed you to complacency, too?"

Emma smiled. "Would you rather him a beast? Should he allow the king's soldiers to rape and loot and pillage?"

"Nay, but 'tis unnatural for all to bow down so willingly." Gwendolyn's eyes narrowed. "How do you know he is pleasant? You have been ill most of the time he has been here."

"Not too ill to observe. And I talked to him a few moments this morning, to ask his preference on the embroidery." Emma secured the needle in the fabric and held it to the side; Gwendolyn sensed an oncoming lecture. "You should truly make an effort at courtesy, Gwen. We do not yet know how Alberic intends to deal with us, and after what happened yesterday I shudder to think of what action he might be forced to take if the villain is not found soon." She wagged a finger. "While we speak of courtesy, you must also be kinder to Garrett. None of this is his fault."

"He brought Alberic here, did he not?"

"Garrett had little choice if he wanted to return to his wife and children. 'Struth, Father knew the risks when he sided with Empress Maud. And he lost all. If you persist in raging against the inevitable, we may suffer more."

Emma's complacency rankled. All might not be lost.

Gwendolyn leaned forward. "Several of Camelen's men who survived Wallingford chose not to serve Alberic. Do you think any of them might have gone to Bristol? Is it possible the Empress Maud or the earl of Gloucester might send troops to liberate us? Perhaps the archer is an assassin sent to rid us of Alberic."

Emma shook her head. "Be sensible, Gwen. I am sure the empress has more urgent battles to fight. If she has not the troops to send to Wallingford's aid, then certes she has not the means of laying siege to Camelen to overthrow Lord Alberic."

So Gwendolyn had feared, but couldn't help but hope.

So be it, then. She would do as Emma suggested and be sensible, but not in the way her sister hoped.

'Twas time to retrieve the ring and arrange to leave Camelen, going first to her uncle's stronghold, and from there to Madog ap Idwal in Powys.

She knew little of her betrothed beyond that he possessed a good deal of land, and her father judged him well suited to be her husband and a partner in the legacy. To him she would give herself and the ring.

But first she had to get the ring.

Gwendolyn heard someone running in the passageway. Thinking Nicole must be done with her morning lessons, she paid no attention until the door opened with a bang.

"My ladies, you must come down to the hall quickly!" a serving wench demanded. "Lady Nicole has tried to murder Lord Alberic!"

Heart pounding, Gwendolyn slid off the bed and scurried down the passageway and stairs, Emma at her heels.

In the hall, Odell stood behind Nicole, holding her by her elbows. Alberic stood a few feet in front of the girl, studying a dagger Gwendolyn recognized as William's, which she'd left on the table in his chamber.

She allowed herself to breathe when she saw no blood on either attacker or victim. Still, Nicole's attempt to draw blood could reap harsh punishment.

Emma rushed past Gwendolyn. "My lord, you have my sincere apology for my sister's—"

"Silence!" he shouted, bringing Emma to a halt, his ire focused on Nicole. "Are you aware I could hang you for your treachery?"

Nicole paled, but her defiant expression didn't waver.

Horrified, Gwendolyn cried, "Nicole is merely a little girl! We give you our oath she will never try this again."

"You are right, she will not," Alberic agreed, then turned to another of the king's soldiers. "Find Garrett. Have him join me and the ladies in my bedchamber."

Then he pointed the dagger toward the stairs. "Up."

"Murderer!" Nicole spat out. "You should hang, not me!"

"Up!" he shouted again.

Odell pushed Nicole toward the stairs. Gwendolyn followed close behind, remembering how she'd tried to explain to Nicole that death in battle wasn't murder, and that every king's man shouldn't be blamed for their loved ones' deaths. Apparently she hadn't convinced the child, who now might pay a high price.

My fault.

Guilt battered Gwendolyn with each step, wondering what she could have said differently. Yesterday in William's chamber, if she'd paid more attention to Nicole instead of shooing her out of the room, given the girl more hugs and chances to speak her mind, this horrible situation might not have come to pass.

Sweet mercy, she couldn't imagine Alberic would truly hang Nicole, but neither could he allow an attempt on his life to go unpunished, no matter that his attacker was a mere slip of a girl.

Gwendolyn entered the lord's bedchamber directly behind Nicole and Odell, who still held tight to his captive. Behind her she heard Emma, and farther behind the sound of heavy boots.

Knowing she had but a moment before Alberic entered, Gwendolyn scrunched down to confront Nicole, whose face had gone paler still. Unshed tears glittered in her eyes, yet she fairly glowed with rebellious anger.

Gwendolyn had to admire Nicole's bravery. However, now was the time for a bit of humility and admission of wrongdoing if the girl expected any mercy from Alberic.

"Nicole, we talked about the difference between death on the battlefield and murder. I thought you understood."

"He killed William."

Emma gasped. "Dear heaven above!"

A chill ran down Gwendolyn's spine, dread nearly overcoming her ability to speak. She managed to blurt out, "What?"

Nicole's bottom lip trembled. "I overheard a kitchen scullion tell Cook. Lord Alberic killed William."

Gwendolyn clung to shards of reason. "You know better than to listen to servants' idle talk."

"Ask him. If he denies it to you, he lies!"

She heard the snick of the latch, knew Alberic had heard Nicole's accusation. When she finally gathered the courage to look up, she needed only to see his grim expression to know Nicole told the truth.

Alberic was responsible for William's death.

❦

Alberic had known this day would come and was prepared for the sisters' shock and horror and anger. What he hadn't seen coming, not in his wildest dreams, was the youngest of them getting her hands on a dagger and daring to attack him.

He'd disarmed her easily enough, but if she hadn't shouted at him, reviling him, giving him ample warning, he might now be prostrate on the hall's floor with a dagger stuck in his belly.

This second attempt on his life was far more unsettling than the first. A man letting loose an arrow with intent to kill an enemy, he understood. A girl wielding a dagger with murder in her heart defied all sense.

Unlike the rogue archer, Alberic doubted he could hang Nicole, but wasn't sure what else to do with the child.

Gwendolyn rose slowly, her condemning glare feeding the unwarranted guilt he thought he'd put aside at the vigil. He was very careful not to let it show now.

"You killed William."

An accusation seeking confirmation.

He crossed the chamber and tossed the dagger on the heavy oak pedestal table, then poured himself a healthy dose of wine, trying to decide how to answer her, or if he should answer at all. 'Struth, he owed the sisters no explanations or apologies for all that had occurred at Wallingford.

"I happened to be the last man to cross swords with William, is all. No more, no less. Your brother died, I did not."

Gwendolyn's bosom rose and fell in indignation, a movement so sublime he couldn't help but appreciate the upward thrust of those softly rounded mounds.

"Is that why the king awarded you Camelen, for slaying William?"

Of all the fool notions. "Nay. There were other reasons."

Which he didn't intend to reveal just now, if ever. He saw no good reason to inform Gwendolyn of the king's mistaken notion that awarding a barony to the earl of Chester's bastard would warrant Chester's loyalty. Best to keep focus on why they were all gathered in his bedchamber.

"Odell, you may release Nicole if I have her assurance she has no other weapon on her person."

"Wish I did," the girl muttered.

Emma stretched out a hand. "Be thankful you do not."

Freed, Nicole went to her elder sister just as someone rapped hard and sharp at the door.

"My lord? 'Tis Garrett."

"Enter."

The knight did so, his gaze flickering to each of the females in turn, then landing for a long moment on Nicole. Assuring himself she hadn't yet been beaten? Likely.

Garrett finally closed the door. "My lord, I have been informed of the events in the hall. I ask you to consider that Nicole is a mere child."

"A willful, malicious child."

"Not usually, though she does tend to act before she considers the consequences. These past days have been very hard for her, as they have for us all. The girl needs time to adjust."

Alberic had known from the beginning that everyone at Camelen needed time to grieve for the old and become accustomed to the new, especially the daughters of Hugh de Leon. He'd tried to accommodate them, hold them on a loose rein. Too loose, apparently, for Nicole.

"Nicole's actions cannot go unpunished."

"I agree, my lord. I merely ask you to consider her sex, youth, and noble birth."

So what did one do with a young noble female who'd attempted to stick a dagger in his gullet?

Send her away.

One to marry, one to court, one to a convent.

Alberic downed the last of his wine. He'd planned to put off deciding on the dispersal of the sisters for another fortnight or so, using that time to best judge which would suit as his wife, and which of them would be best suited for convent or court. But at the moment, the answer seemed so clear.

He dare not trust Nicole to behave in reputable fashion. If he sent her to court, when surrounded by the king's men she detested, she might well find another dagger and target another victim. The girl would surely benefit from the peace and discipline of a convent.

While Emma seemed a pleasant enough woman, he didn't want a sickly wife. She might do very well for herself at court, and perhaps the physicians there could find a cure for her ills.

Which left Gwendolyn to become his wife. Not that he trusted her, either, but she was certainly the prudent choice.

He'd heard her name several times during his inspection of the castle, each time said with fondness and respect, as with Mistress Biggs when visiting the village. Gwendolyn knew the workings of the household, got on well with all. Good wifely qualities.

Nor would he find her abhorrent to take to bed. Indeed, peeling off her surcoat and chemise to unveil the swell of her breasts and softly rounded rump might give him a great deal of pleasure. The stir in his loins confirmed her physical appeal.

Alberic put the empty goblet on the table. Arms crossed behind his back, he faced the females.

Not a one of them would be pleased with what he was about to tell them, but not a one of them was disposed to like him anyway. At the moment, all considered him lower than a worm for his part in William's death.

United against him, they might never fully believe he'd come by Camelen honorably, even if Garrett confirmed the tale. Separated, he would have a chance to convince one, Gwendolyn, that he wasn't the devil incarnate.

"This seems a fitting time to tell you the whole of the

king's orders. When he gave me Camelen he bade me to hold it in his name, then gave instructions on what to do with Hugh de Leon's remaining offspring. I will assume you are aware that on your father's death you became royal wards."

Nicole's eyes narrowed, ready to disbelieve whatever he was about to say. In Emma he saw a hint of curiosity, a spark of the adventurous he wouldn't have attributed to her before.

Gwendolyn crossed her arms, preparing to bend to the ill wind she sensed coming.

"He bade me take one of you as my wife, send one to his court, and give the last to the Church. Today's events have convinced me it is time to follow through on those orders."

"That is outrageous, my lord!" Emma declared.

"I do not believe you!" Nicole stated.

Gwendolyn looked to Garrett for salvation. "Did you hear the king give this order?"

"Nay, my lady. I was not close enough to hear all that was said, but I doubt not that such an order was given."

Emma waved a hand in Alberic's direction, though she spoke to Garrett. "You believe this outrage?"

"I have no reason not to, Lady Emma, especially when it is easily confirmed."

"As you will do, Garrett, when you take Lady Emma to court."

Emma rounded on him. "Court? The king's court? Me?"

"I am sure the king has already informed Queen Matilda to expect a new handmaiden. Once you have confirmed the king's orders, you may send word to your sisters." Alberic then focused on Nicole. "Though just where this little one might be must still be decided. If any of you have preference for one abbey over another, pray let me know."

Nicole's eyes went as wide as platters. "Nay, not a nunnery," she whined, then turned to Gwendolyn. "Do not let him send me away, Gwen! I swear I shall never touch another dagger in my lifetime!"

Gwendolyn must have heard her sister's plea, but ignored it in favor of staring hard at him, having figured out she was to remain at Camelen, as his wife.

"Your plan is flawed, my lord. I cannot marry you because I am already betrothed."

Damn. He hadn't expected a complication, and a prior betrothal bargain might well complicate matters.

"Betrothed to whom?"

"Madog ap Idwal of Powys."

A Welshman? True, Gwendolyn was half Welsh, through her mother, a princess of Wales if the king's tale was to be believed. But Gwendolyn was also half Norman; her father could have done far better for her.

Probably better than a Norman-English bastard.

Except the bastard was now a baron, and so of a rank worthy of her. Better than worthy.

The thought struck him that through the betrothal Hugh de Leon might have gained the support of a group of Welsh in the war against the king. But Alberic had never heard of ap Idwal, so he couldn't be a high chieftain, and was therefore of little consequence.

"I have been through all of your father's documents and saw no betrothal agreement."

She seemed taken aback, but rallied quickly.

"Whether a document is drawn up or no, I am certain my father and ap Idwal came to an understanding. The nuptials are to take place at summer's end."

Not an official bargain, then, and therefore not a complication.

"When the king gave me Camelen, all agreements your father might have made became void. Only those I care to keep are valid. Understanding or no, you will not be marrying ap Idwal."

"But all is arranged! You cannot blithely disregard my father's wishes!"

He most certainly could. Alberic dismissed a pang of ire that Gwendolyn protested so forcefully because she might care for this ap Idwal.

"Your father is dead, Gwendolyn. His wishes no longer matter." She winced at his harshness, but he knew of no other way to force her to face the reality of her changed circumstances. "I am merely following the king's orders and will brook no more argument!"

She dared open her mouth as if to do exactly that, then remained silent. But her expression spoke loudly; he hadn't heard the last of her protest.

The large bell that hung in the bailey called all to the noon meal. He silently thanked the cook for her timely intervention.

He waved a dismissing hand. "Go for your meal. Tell Cook to begin serving. I will be down in a moment."

Silently, all left except Gwendolyn. She stared at his hand, or rather his ring, for long moments before looking away.

"Gwendolyn, 'tis mine now."

"So you told me the other night."

"I wish to have the nuptials performed as soon as they can be arranged."

She crossed her arms, making no secret of her displeasure. "A wedding ceremony and feast are already arranged for the end of summer. Will that do, my lord?"

He almost smiled at her attempt to delay the ceremony for months.

"I believe a sennight will do."

Her already wide brown eyes widened farther. "A sennight? My gown is not yet begun, and there are invitations to send, and food to be purchased and prepared for the feast. Not possible."

"Any one of your gowns would do. The storerooms are full. And I will allow no one inside the gate who is not loyal to either Camelen or the king."

She huffed. "That does limit attendance, does it not?"

He knew he'd probably eliminated the whole of her relations, particularly those in Wales, but Camelen's security must be maintained. Especially with a rogue archer on the loose.

"Limited attendance means less food to prepare."

She tossed a hand in the air. "What of your family? Should you not be more considerate of them?"

His only "family" likely wouldn't attend even if invited, so he wouldn't bother.

"There is no one to invite."

Her hand lowered slowly. "No one?"

"Not a one. Convenient, is it not? There is nothing to prevent us from exchanging vows one week from today."

"Two weeks."

"One."

Several heartbeats passed before she asked, "Why me?"

"You have many qualities of a suitable wife. You are young, but not too young. Nor are you sickly, which—"

"You chose me because I am *healthy*?" she asked, incredulous.

"Well, that is important, but . . ."

Gwendolyn flounced out of the bedchamber, not bothering to hear the rest of his answer. Not that his other reasons would make her any happier.

Alberic splashed wine into the goblet, thinking all had gone well enough, under the circumstances. Emma seemed intrigued with the idea of going to court. Nicole was upset, but she was young and would adjust.

Gwendolyn wasn't thrilled with the idea of marrying him and objected to the haste, but surely she would come to accept the marriage. After all, noble females were raised from the cradle to accept the decisions of the men who held authority over them, especially in the matter of marriage. Too, she hadn't refused outright. Offered excuses, but not refused. A good sign.

And 'struth, he'd done his best to convey to servants, tenants, and soldiers alike that he planned to make Camelen prosper, calming many fears.

Aye, he intended Camelen should prosper. Gwendolyn was best equipped to help him. All he had to do was convince her.

Alberic smiled as he downed the wine, thinking of various persuasions a man could employ to win over a woman. Charm. Flattery. Gifts. Passion.

'Twould be a challenge and a joy to discover Gwendolyn de Leon's weakness, exploit it, then have her melt into his arms.

Chapter Five

GWENDOLYN FLED ALL THE WAY up to the battlements. She took a deep gulp of brisk spring air to clear Alberic's absurd demands out of her head, and wipe the loneliness in his eyes from her memory.

He'd told her yesterday about losing his mother, and she allowed both of his parents might be . . . gone, as were hers. Had he no siblings? No uncle, aunt, or cousin? No friend to whom he wished to show off his new barony? No peer he considered worthy of an invitation?

Not a one.

Having grown up in the midst of a loving, boisterous family, Gwendolyn couldn't imagine her life without them. She had myriad relatives, too, most of whom she hadn't seen for some time because of the war. Still, she hadn't felt the lack of their company too greatly because of the castle folk's and tenants' kindness to her.

No matter when and where she wed, she would be surrounded by people who cared for her and wished her well. That Alberic had no one . . . *bah!*

There would be no wedding between Alberic of Chester and Gwendolyn de Leon, and so no cause for him to bemoan his lack. No cause for her to feel sorry for him, a softening toward the enemy that she could ill afford.

Whether a formal document existed or not, she was betrothed to Madog ap Idwal, the man chosen for her by her father, the man she would wed as soon as could be arranged.

Father had known the importance of her marrying a man she could love, and whose heart would be faithful to her in return. He'd been utterly convinced Madog ap Idwal suited Gwendolyn perfectly. The seal of the dragon was meant for such a man, not for an upstart knight chosen by the usurper king of England!

So why hadn't her father and Madog made the betrothal bargain formal, put the terms of the agreement to parchment, or set the wedding date earlier? Had they done their duty, she wouldn't now be fretting over marrying the wrong man and thus endangering the legacy. Neither of which she could allow to happen.

Why me? God's truth, she wished she hadn't asked!

Alberic's passing over Nicole as a wife she understood. Not only was Nicole very young but, sweet heaven above, she'd tried to kill him. But Alberic should have chosen Emma, the eldest of them, as his wife! Emma was pretty, and bright, and far more suited to be a baron's wife despite her horrible but infrequent headaches. The insult couldn't be borne!

Sweet mercy, she dare not feel compassion for the man who intended to send her sisters away from Camelen; who'd brushed off her betrothal as if a crumb of bread on his tunic.

The man who'd killed her brother. For that reason

alone she must steel her heart against any sympathy for Alberic.

"My lady."

Garrett's softly spoken greeting startled her. So deeply had she been lost in thought she didn't hear his approach.

"Garrett."

He leaned against the cold stone, ignoring the lovely view in favor of studying her. "Lady Emma wonders where you are."

"Has Nicole left off her wailing?"

"Mostly."

"Then perhaps I will go into the hall . . . later."

But not to eat. Given her upset, whatever she might put down would surely come up again.

They stood side by side in silence, Gwendolyn cognizant of how faithfully the elder knight had served her father, and aware of his many courtesies toward her and her siblings. Then he'd brought Alberic to Camelen, even agreed to serve as the usurper's counselor, and betrayed them all thoroughly.

Her anger and frustration spilled over. "Nothing is as it should be!"

"Nothing has been as it should be since King Henry died and Stephen stole the throne. Why he believed he could take the kingdom without suffering resistance—"

"I care not for the kingdom! I mean here, at Camelen. Father and William are dead and now we have our own usurper! Dear God, Garrett, could you not have lost Alberic along the way?"

"I could have, but then we might have the king himself to deal with, and angry kings cause great havoc."

"Alberic is no better. He killed William, did he not?

And he proposes to dispense us without our consent, and expects us to obey like . . . like sheep to the shearing!"

"He has no choice."

"So he says!"

Garrett's deep sigh reflected her own feelings of powerlessness.

"Gwendolyn, I know you hurt. You all hurt, as do I. But you must know that Alberic did not set out to take William's life. Your father . . . aw, hell."

His hesitation gave her pause. Garrett didn't want to tell her something he felt she should hear. To spare her further agony? So like Garrett. Emma was right; she shouldn't be blaming him for their current coil.

"I beg pardon, Garrett. I know you are not responsible for the actions of others. Pray tell me, what of my father?"

Several heartbeats passed before he answered. "Sir Hugh was determined to break the siege, and thought eliminating the earl of Chester the best way to begin. He was sure that with Chester dead the three hundred knights in his force would go home, leaving the king's army weakened. Hugh might have been right, but his obsession with killing Chester himself blinded him to all else. When he should have surrendered the field, he fought on, and when he fell, William took up his standard and refused to yield. God's truth, Gwendolyn, Alberic happened to be the last to cross swords with your brother. He merely defended himself while protecting the life of . . . the earl, just as several of our men died trying to protect Hugh and William."

He sounded so reasonable. In her head she understood, had even used the same reasoning with Nicole.

Death on the battlefield wasn't considered murder. Even if her father had taken a bullheaded approach, leading to his own death and many others, her heart yet cried for the unfairness of it all.

"That may be, but I cannot bring myself to forget it was Alberic who took William's life. Whether on purpose or no, it was his sword that cut William down. You cannot ask me to accept the man as my lord."

"You have a generous heart, Gwendolyn. Perhaps in time you will find forgiveness."

Gwendolyn saw no need to tell him she doubted she could forgive Alberic anytime soon. Indeed, even before she'd known of his involvement with William's death, she hadn't been unhappy that some unknown archer had taken umbrage at Alberic's lordship.

She couldn't allow her heart to soften. She couldn't weaken. For her sisters' sake, for her own.

"You truly believe the king ordered Alberic to separate us?"

"As I said before, I have no reason not to believe."

"Is there no way to counter the order? If we petitioned the king to reconsider, would he?"

"Possibly. When at court, Emma will be in a position to do so."

In a position, aye, but would Emma want to? From her sister's reaction, Gwendolyn didn't think Emma was particularly upset about being sent to court. Still, Emma might petition the king on Nicole's behalf. The girl definitely did *not* want to enter a nunnery.

So many questions, too few answers.

"Might I suggest you speak with Lord Alberic this eve," Garrett said gently. "He has not yet issued orders for me to leave for London, nor has he decided where to send Nicole. As his future wife, you might have some influence over him. Perhaps, if you can warrant Nicole's behavior, he may let you keep the girl here."

Except Gwendolyn wasn't to be Alberic's wife, so she wouldn't be here to take care of Nicole. She might not have time to come up with a solution, either, depending upon how long it took her to convince Alberic to hand over the ring.

"Is Alberic easily influenced?"

Garrett thought that over for a moment. "During the journey from Wallingford we discussed much. I noted that he listened intently to all I told him, then formed his own judgments. In truth, I would say he is far more patient and tolerant than many of the men to whom the king might have entrusted Camelen. 'Tis my opinion that if given the chance he will make a good lord, might even make you a fine husband."

Garrett's full acceptance of Alberic was irritating. That she agreed with some of his statements was irksome, particularly when she remembered Alberic's patience and tolerance when dealing with Nicole. But just because Alberic might make a good lord didn't mean he'd make her a good husband!

No matter. There would be no wedding.

Still, it wouldn't hurt to ask Alberic about his plans—especially about when he intended to send off Emma and Nicole. Surely he would allow them to stay for the "wedding," which would give her a week to sort things through.

And she still had to get the ring, which might be the hardest task of all. He'd refused it to her twice already.

But persuade him she must, using whatever influence she possessed with the lonely man occupying the lord's bedchamber.

◇

Knowing her sisters were taking supper in their bedchamber, Gwendolyn slid into Emma's chair at the high table, confident in her plan to convince Alberic to give over the ring.

All she needed was for the man to appear.

The tables were readied for supper, each covered in white cloth. Baskets of fragrant bread and bowls of sweet butter awaited the diners. A spoon, tankard, and bread trencher had been laid at each place.

More people gathered for supper than in past days. All of the household knights had now sworn allegiance to Alberic and were allowed their weapons and the freedom of the castle. And tonight the villages' officials, the bailiffs and reeves, had been summoned to sup with their lord.

If not for the arrow Alberic had stuck in the pillar yesterday, one could hardly tell anything had changed from when Sir Hugh de Leon was lord. However, the arrow reminded all that not everyone was at peace with the change of lordship, and Gwendolyn was content to leave the arrow there to keep the memory alive.

Alberic came down the stairs, his expression puzzled when he spotted her. Odell took up his post behind the dais to watch for trouble.

Though it damn near killed her, she smiled sweetly when Alberic sat down next to her in her father's chair.

He smelled of soap, his facial hair freshly scraped with nary a nick on his rugged jaw. His dark blond hair was neatly combed. A new tunic of deep blue linen fitted him perfectly across his broad shoulders, the color striking against the sun-touched hue of his skin and the green of his eyes.

She hadn't been this close to him since the night of the vigil and had forgotten about those tingles of awareness she'd felt when first meeting him. She used the precious seconds during the priest's recital of grace to suppress the tingling's renewal.

"To what do I owe the pleasure of your company this eve, my lady? Is Emma ill?"

Even the deep rumble of his voice affected her more profoundly when this close. She commanded her pulse to slow and the fluttering in her stomach to cease.

Alberic might be a handsome devil, possessed of an enticing appeal, but she must consider him a sheep to be shorn. Except she'd never wielded the heavy, sharp shears. She would have to be careful, remain in command.

"Nay. We decided to allow all to have peace at their meal, so Emma sups with Nicole in our bedchamber. Wine, Sir Alberic?" Gwendolyn picked up the flagon and filled his goblet. "Cook tells me you requested dove. A fine choice."

He raised a questioning eyebrow. "A compliment, too? How intriguing."

Her false smile slipped a bit.

"I endeavor to put my troubles aside for an hour or two. Is that wrong of me?"

"Not at all, my lady." He raised a hand, signaling the

servants to begin hauling platters of food to the tables. "If a peaceful, pleasant meal keeps the smile on your face, then I shall endeavor to aid you."

He poured her wine, a dark, musky-scented red from Burgundy, then lifted his goblet toward her.

"Shall we drink to continued peace at Camelen?"

A sentiment she approved. No matter what the future brought, she wished Camelen peace. God's truth, she would miss her home and all the people in it when she left. In danger of becoming maudlin, she raised her goblet. "To Camelen."

The wine went down smoothly and tasted different. Her surprise must have shown.

"Like it?" he asked.

"I do. A new cask?"

"Nay. I merely asked the butler to add sugar and clove to that served at high table. I like my wine sweeter than most."

So he'd inspected the cellar, too. His cellar now. But she could hardly fault him for the change; the wine did taste better, more palatable.

For their first course he chose almond fish stew for their bowls, and figs stuffed with eggs and bits of baked salmon for their trenchers.

She'd never been fond of figs, so she used her eating knife to cut her portion into tiny pieces she could swallow whole and wash down with wine.

"A pretty knife," he commented.

"Did you not notice Emma's? They match. Nicole's, too."

"Nicole's, too, hmmm?"

She probably shouldn't have reminded him that

Nicole yet retained her eating knife. At least the girl no longer had the dagger. Alberic did.

"I meant to ask if you objected to our hanging Father's and William's swords and daggers in their place of honor. 'Tis tradition."

He glanced around the hall at the various weapons arranged in patterns. "Where?"

She knew exactly where they should be placed, and leaned toward him to point out an incomplete circle of swords. Her shoulder bumped his, and immediately she felt his warmth, somehow soothing and discomfiting at the same time. She instantly backed away.

"The swords should go there," she managed to say.

Gallantly ignoring her retreat, Alberic stared at the circle as if deep in thought. "I meant to ask Garrett about the weapons. Did they all belong to lords of Camelen?"

"The swords and daggers did. Of the others, some were given to my father as gifts, and some he bought because he admired them. A few belonged to my mother's Welsh ancestors. I fear I do not know which is which. Garrett or Sedwick might."

"Impressive." He took a healthy swallow of wine. "We will hang the weapons, but not until matters are more settled."

Not until the possibility of an organized rebellion was less likely, he meant. Until then, he apparently wanted no further honors done to Hugh and William. That might take months, too long for Gwendolyn's peace of mind.

"I had hoped to do so tomorrow, to have done with it. Would that not be best?"

"Tomorrow I ride for Shrewsbury. I need to visit the

abbey, the sheriff, and the king's castellan at Shrewsbury Castle."

She understood the politics of his plan, but not the timing.

"With the archer still on the loose? Is that wise?"

"I refuse to allow one misguided villain to trap me in the keep. I will take several men as guard, so if our rogue attacks again, we will catch him."

This made her wonder if he hoped to draw out the archer, using himself as bait. Was Alberic brave or reckless? She dismissed the concern for his safety as imprudent softening she couldn't allow. Especially when his leaving increased the urgency of her obtaining the ring tonight.

The first course finished, Gwendolyn dipped her fingers into the water basin. As did Alberic. Sharing wash water with a male partner had never bothered her before. With Alberic it somehow seemed intimate even though they never touched.

Hands dry, Alberic poured more wine, filling both goblets, then called for another flagon.

For the second course he chose the roasted dove he'd requested, rice with almond cream, and elderberry cakes.

She adored elderberry cakes, and the second goblet of wine went the way of the first.

"Have you lived at Camelen all of your life?" he asked.

"Aye. My mother preferred not to foster us, so I was raised here, though I have seen some of the kingdom. London and York. I fear I was too young to remember much of them. And several times we made the trip to Wales, most times to Snowdonia. What of you? Did you foster at Chester?"

His half smile took on that lonely quality she'd promised herself she wouldn't heed.

"Not in the usual way, but aye, I spent my youth in and around the castle." His smile then softened. "By the by, Mistress Biggs wishes you to know the villagers miss you."

The change of subject was abrupt, but the sentiment warmed her heart, even as she realized Alberic must speak English, a rarity for a Norman.

Her father never bothered to learn the language of the peasants, while Gwendolyn had been intrigued by the various words one could use to say the same thing. Norman-French, Latin, Welsh, and English. She could converse in them all, and the talent had served her well.

"Little Edward suffered from a nasty fever last fall. I feared we might lose him. His mother and I spent many an hour hovering over him."

"Ah, I met the lad. Adorable little urchin."

That he was. Cute and lively, he was the model for the little boy she would like to have some day. She would miss him, and the thought had her reaching for her third goblet of wine.

As she sipped, she looked out over the diners. Some ate with relish, others engaged in lively conversation with those around them. It was then she noticed the laughter, a lively sound that had been missing from the hall for several days.

When the platter containing cheese, dried fruit, and nuts was presented, and the wine in her goblet replenished for the fourth time, Rhys began to play his harp. Belly full, head fuzzy, feeling languid and peaceful, Gwendolyn leaned back in her chair to listen to the melody.

Alberic interrupted her peace. "Sedwick told me Camelen boasted a Welsh bard. What does he sing of?"

For a moment, Gwendolyn paid attention to the words. "He sings of a Welsh chieftain named Vortigen and his battles against the Saxons. That is how the Welsh keep their history alive, through the bards."

He nodded. "To appreciate the tales I shall have to learn the language, I own."

Taken aback, she asked, "You intend to learn Welsh?"

"Seems sensible to me. After all, you are part Welsh, and I should hate to have my wife tell me something I do not understand."

How odd, and very sweet that he should plan to undertake learning a language to please her. Or rather, to please the woman he thought would be his wife. A thoughtful gesture. Rare for a man. Would Madog ap Idwal be as gallant as Alberic? Perhaps. After all, her father would have chosen a thoughtful man as her betrothed, would he not?

'Twas disconcerting that she didn't know. Her father had only described ap Idwal, told her of the extent of his lands, then assured her of their suitability.

Surely her father's assurance should set her mind at ease over her betrothed's suitability.

Alberic stuck a finger in the air. "Which reminds me, I ought to quell the speculation I understand runs rampant from bailey to village."

"What speculation?"

He didn't answer, but stood up as the strum of the harp signaled the end of the song. When he lifted his goblet, the hall went utterly silent, and a shiver of apprehension banished Gwendolyn's languor.

"Good people of Camelen," he called out. "Some of you are wondering about an upcoming event. I hear wagers have been placed on the possible dates. All well and good. I wish you all good fortune."

The smattering of laughter didn't quell her misgivings.

He raised the goblet higher. "I know you will all join me in a salute to the lovely Lady Gwendolyn, who will become my wife seven days hence."

Cheers went up and her heart sank. Naturally the news had spread like butter on warm bread. Was nothing sacred? Given no choice, she nodded, graciously accepting Alberic's salute but inwardly seething.

When he sat, his smile was so self-satisfied she could have tossed her wine in his face. "Now, my dear, did you have a pleasant supper?"

She had, until he ruined it. The food and wine had been wonderful, and Alberic had been charming and attentive until he'd made his announcement and reminded her of what else she must accomplish this eve.

"Very pleasant. Lord Alberic, will my sisters be allowed to stay for the wedding?"

He thought that over. "The king ordered me where to send them, but did not say when. I see no reason why they cannot be present for our nuptials."

Then only one more task remained before retiring for the night. Except she didn't want to approach him about the ring in the hall. Too many ears around to overhear.

She put on what she hoped was her most charming smile. "Since you are in such an agreeable mood, I have yet another boon to ask, but not here. Perhaps . . . have you seen the garden?"

"Aye, but I am sure the garden will be much nicer when you show it to me."

More gallant flattery. Ye gods, the man surely had no trouble turning unwary women's hearts . . . heads . . . whatever he wished to turn.

He held out his hand to help her rise. Since they were supposed to be betrothed, everyone would be aghast if she refused. Besides, she wasn't sure of the steadiness of her legs.

His hand was large, and warm, and encompassing. Heat snaked up her arm and down her torso, pooling in the depths of her woman's places. Her reaction to his touch was most unwelcome, and she blamed her body's response on the amount of wine she'd consumed. Surely, if she were dead sober she would be repulsed.

They passed Odell on the way out, and Alberic gave him a small hand signal to remain where he was, so they would be completely alone. Perfect for her purpose.

The night air proved chilly, but the garden, graced by moonlight, had always been one of her favorite places no matter the season. Quiet and secluded, it would soon be green and lush with leaves, and then flowers. This spring she wouldn't be here to watch the blooms open.

Alberic led her to a bench near the grapevines before finally letting go of her hand. Unfortunately, he sat down next to her, so close their arms touched. She had to get this over with before she completely lost her reason.

"I know you are very fond of my father's ring, and I think I know why. However, I think you should know it has not been handed down from baron to baron as a symbol of lordship over Camelen, but was merely a gift from my mother to father."

"If one is to judge by the woman's lovely daughters, then your mother must have been a beauty."

Not the comment she expected.

"She was." Lovely and fragile. Too fragile to have borne four children, one of them long after she thought her childbearing years done. "She died three days after Nicole's birth."

"You lost your mother young, too."

"Ten. The same age as Nicole is now."

Gwendolyn tried to stop the memories from flooding in and a single tear from falling, but failed.

Alberic put an arm around her shoulders. "You still miss her. I beg pardon, Gwendolyn. I did not mean to make you cry."

She missed her mother, and father, and brother, and she didn't bother to move away, taking the comfort offered. She hadn't been held in so very long, and the solace felt too good to give up quickly.

She did notice, however, that he sought to distract her from talking about the ring. 'Twas bad of her, she knew, but perhaps her unexpected tears would serve to soften his heart further.

"The ring is an heirloom, passed down from mother to daughter. My father should not have worn it to Wallingford where it might be lost. I should like to put it away where it will be safe for my daughter."

He was silent for a moment, then asked, "Should the ring not go to Emma, the eldest, for her daughter?"

Gwendolyn realized her mistake. She'd given him too much information and must be more careful.

"The ring goes to the daughter of the mother's choosing. In any event, it should be put away."

"For your daughter's husband to wear."

"Only if she wishes him to wear it."

He pulled her closer, and Gwendolyn didn't object.

"Truth to tell, I knew about the ring," he said softly. "When King Stephen bade me put it on, he said your father wore the seal of the dragon in honor of his wife, a Welsh princess. Was she truly of the house of Pendragon?"

Oh, worse and worse! How had the king known the name of the ring? Her father must have bragged at some point. *Damn.*

"So her family claims."

"Then is it not fortunate that you and I are to be married, so I can wear the ring in honor of my Welsh princess, just as your father did? We will be good together, Gwendolyn, for Camelen and for us. I feel it in my bones."

He gave her no time to protest. With a finger under her chin, he tilted her head back and kissed her.

His moist lips claimed hers, and the heat in her nether regions burst into flame. She couldn't breathe, couldn't move, and didn't care. Everything she'd heard about a man's kiss paled in the face of the reality.

Gwendolyn leaned into the passion she'd not known existed, kissing him back and hoping she did it right, not wanting to give up the exquisite sensation of being fully alive and utterly female.

A niggling voice warned her of her folly, that such desire induced otherwise sensible women to go astray. Sweet mercy, at the moment she was willing to be led, to follow wherever he wanted to go.

Alberic took a big gulp of air as he backed away,

leaving her bereft and shaking with the enormity of what she'd allowed.

"Come," he said, his voice none too steady. "I do not want you to catch a chill."

She was so warm she might never again be cold.

He led her into the hall and on to the stairs, where he stopped. "Pleasant dreams, my dear," he whispered, and released her hand.

With what little dignity she could muster, her hand sliding along the stone wall, Gwendolyn climbed the narrow circular stairs to the upper floor and the safety of her bedchamber.

Between the effects of the wine and the kiss, her head spun.

But she knew her plan had failed miserably. All she'd done was give Alberic further excuse to wear the ring and to claim her as his wife—neither of which she could allow.

Nor dare she try again to wheedle the ring from him. After Alberic returned from Shrewsbury she would have to steal it. A daunting task, but the only choice left to her.

Then she must find Madog ap Idwal and sample his kiss. Surely her betrothed's kiss could wipe out the taste of Alberic on her lips.

She touched a mouth warm and swollen.

Admittedly, it would have to be one very powerful kiss to overcome the taste of Alberic.

Chapter Six

FOUR NIGHTS LATER, Gwendolyn lay in bed, muscles taut and innards churning.

Tonight she would steal the ring and be on her way to Wales.

She'd done all she could to ensure her success, carefully planning both the theft and her escape route. What few possessions she intended to take with her were packed in a satchel and hung on a peg beneath her cloak.

All was ready. All she need do was wait for the sleeping potion she'd added to Alberic's and Odell's ale to take effect before she snuck down the passageway to Alberic's bedchamber.

Only one thing yet bothered her about leaving—not being able to say farewell to her sisters and tell them where she was bound and why. But her mother had been most insistent on the need for silence, and over the years her father had supported her mother's instruction. Beyond those intimately involved—the couple who wore the ring and pendant, and ultimately their daughter—no one must learn of the legacy. The risk of abuse by the unscrupulous was too great.

She felt guilty about abandoning Emma to deal with Alberic and the king's orders, but then, Emma wasn't dull-witted. She could capably handle any situation when her head didn't hurt, and Gwendolyn prayed for Emma's good health for many weeks to come.

Alberic would demand a search, of course. Not because he wanted her as his wife but for the ring he valued so highly. She never doubted he would know who had stolen it, especially when he learned she'd fled the castle.

She planned to be well into Wales and out of his reach before he even thought to look in that direction.

When he couldn't find her, would he then decide to take Emma as his wife, ruining her chance to attend court? Would Emma care about attending court after experiencing the nearly overpowering force of Alberic's kisses?

Gwendolyn would have groaned aloud if she didn't think she would wake Emma, sleeping soundly next to her, or Nicole on her pallet on the floor at the foot of the bed.

For four days Gwendolyn had done battle with her reaction to Alberic's kiss. She might have drank more wine that eve than she usually consumed, and thus become overly susceptible to his advances. But an abundance of wine usually dulled her senses, and the force of his kiss had been far from unmemorable.

She warmed every time she thought about his kiss, and she thought about the disturbing melding of mouths far too often. Worse, the kiss aroused her curiosity about coupling, and even worse, she feared coupling with Alberic would prove more tempestuous than his kiss. If she stayed, became his wife . . . but she couldn't stay.

Gwendolyn eased over onto her side, facing the wall, bringing up her knees in a vain effort to ease the ache low in her belly, to banish the unwanted desire for a man she dare not soften toward even though Alberic had done much to wheedle his way into her affections.

He'd returned from Shrewsbury yesterday, and ever since had insisted she sit next to him at meals where he served her the choice pieces of meat and avoided figs. He kept the conversation lively, and employed flattery, making an obvious effort to be likable.

While he may have done all he said he needed to do in Shrewsbury, he'd also visited the merchants. Alberic had first presented her with a handful of lovely hair ribbons. Then this morning he'd gifted her with the softest, most beautifully fitting kidskin gloves she'd ever worn. Naturally, she'd smiled and thanked him kindly as a betrothed wife should, not having to pretend her delight at the gifts.

She'd never been courted before and, heaven help her, she liked it. Madog had never seen fit to court her, never sent her a gift. She excused the lapse as unnecessary because they were already betrothed.

But she wouldn't take the ribbons with her, for fear of crushing and thus ruining them. The gloves, however, she wouldn't leave behind. Not only were they wonderful, but practical. She saw no harm in being practical.

At last she heard the signal she waited for: the bell in the village church ringing matins. Midnight. The sleeping potion should have taken full effect by now.

Gwendolyn eased out of bed and, by the light of the night candle, slipped on the linen chemise she'd earlier hidden under her bolster. Emma never moved; Nicole rolled onto her stomach and then went still.

Her purpose uppermost in her mind, Gwendolyn slowly opened the chamber door far enough to peer down the hall. In the dim light provided by a single rush torch at the top of the stairway, she could see Odell sitting on the floor near Alberic's door, his head tilted back against the wall, his eyes closed.

Gwendolyn took a fortifying breath, closed her bedchamber door behind her, and padded down the passageway.

Odell seemed sound asleep, so she slowly lifted the latch and pulled, wincing when the leather hinges creaked.

She held her breath and stood very still for several moments. When Odell didn't move, she peeked inside the bedchamber. She saw the bed, and the large form of a man under the coverlet. Alberic hadn't heard, either.

Relieved, she quietly entered and shut the door.

The flickering night candle cast eerie shadows throughout the room, the silence almost deafening. Her heartbeat sped up, her breath became loud enough for her to hear. Chiding herself for foolish unease, Gwendolyn headed for the table.

She circled the chair on which Alberic had tossed his breeches and one of his new tunics, this one the color of the deep green of a summer forest. On the large oak table sat a flagon and a goblet, and beside them lay the leather girdle that wrapped so snugly around Alberic's trim waist. Next to the girdle rested his chatelaine, the small pouch in which he kept his eating knife and a few coins. And a ring?

Gwendolyn patted the leather pouch, feeling the edges of the knife and coins. No ring. Damn. She'd been hoping he took it off at night as her father had done in later years.

Which meant the ring was on his finger.

Disappointed but undaunted, Gwendolyn reasoned that if she was quiet and very careful, she should be able to get the ring off his finger without him being any the wiser.

Alberic slept in the middle of the bed, facing her, his handsome visage in peaceful repose, his breath even and soundless. His right arm was tucked up under the bolster, but his left lay atop the coverlet in front of him, the ring in plain sight.

She tried not to notice how the candlelight fluttered along the width of his bare shoulders and hair-sprinkled chest, and danced along the length of his muscled upper arms. The temptation to follow the light's path, to rake her fingers through his chest hair . . . she swallowed hard, steeling her determination to see this night's mission through.

Standing at the edge of the mattress, careful not to bump it, her attention flickering between his closed eyes and the ring, Gwendolyn reached out to snare the prize.

Beginning to sweat, her pulse pounding in her ears, with thumb and forefinger she squeezed the gold dragon claws on each side of the ring. Slowly, gently, she worked the ring to his knuckle, where the skin bunched and hindered further progress.

"Pull harder."

Gwendolyn yelped as she leaped away. With her hand covering her thundering heart, she stood motionless, her sudden fright giving over to rising panic.

Caught. Run! Except she couldn't move, frozen in place by wide-open green eyes that held no hint of sleep.

"Pull harder, Gwendolyn. Remove the ring."

His flatly delivered command confused her. Why was he not angry at her attempted theft? Did he truly mean to let her have the ring? Why didn't he move so much as an eyelash? A niggling sense of something amiss caused her to hesitate.

Wary, she asked, "Remove it?"

"Want of the ring is why you braved my chamber in the middle of the night, is it not?"

He knew it was. "You denied me the ring before. Why relent now?"

"Gwendolyn, remove the ring."

A hint of impatience colored the repeated order. Sweet mercy, why did she question her good fortune that he'd changed his mind? This time she leaned against the edge of the mattress and put a hand atop the coverlet to brace for balance. Nor was she so careful not to touch his hand.

She gripped the ring firmly and pulled hard, twisting it when she thought that might help. Again it refused to slip over the bunched skin at the joint. Soon his finger reddened and began to swell from the harsh rubbing of gold against skin. When she feared she might hurt him, she let go.

"You will have to take it off and give it to me."

With a deep sigh he rolled onto his back, exposing more of his broad chest than she cared to see, bringing his right arm from beneath the bolster. The muscles in his arms tightened and strained with his effort to remove the ring, but it remained stuck.

"I cannot get it off, either. Care to try again?"

No, she didn't. "Your finger swells. Perhaps if we put it in cold water for a bit?"

"I tried that. It did not work."

The hair on the back of her neck itched, but she dismissed the unease over the stubborn ring as unwarranted. She then forgot to think at all when Alberic tossed the coverlet aside and revealed . . . everything.

Sweet Mother Mary! Her hands flew to cover her eyes. Beneath her palms her face grew overly warm with a ferocious blush.

Alberic had the gall to chuckle over her embarrassment.

"Come now, Gwendolyn. In two days' time we will be husband and wife. Are you not even a wee bit curious?"

She refused to peek between her fingers. "I have already seen more than I ought."

The ropes supporting the mattress groaned. Gwendolyn took a healthy step backward as his feet hit the floor, then took another prudent step back when she sensed him rise up before her. Though what good so little space would do her should he decide to grab hold of her, she couldn't say.

"Odell?" he called out.

"My lord," came the answer from beyond the door.

Almost, her hands slipped from her face. Odell awake, too? Obviously the sleeping potion she'd given both men hadn't been strong enough. But it should have been; neither man should be so lucid.

Damn. Had she not used enough of the potion? Or worse, had she used too much and turned the ale unpalatable so they hadn't drank it all?

"Relieve the extra guards at the postern gate," Alberic ordered. "Their services are no longer necessary tonight."

"Not good that I should leave my post."

"I will bar the door. I doubt I am in any danger from Gwendolyn. She wants the ring, not my blood. Let me know when you return."

"As you say, milord."

Alberic moved toward the door. Feeling a bit ill, Gwendolyn allowed her hands to drop away, astounded by the implication of his order to Odell. For two nights she'd observed the postern gate, knew only one guard was normally posted there. If extra guards had been posted, then someone had expected something to happen tonight.

Her escape. Alberic knew! But how?

He hefted the heavy plank from beside the door. The muscles in his back showed no sign of strain as he slid the bolt into the iron holders.

Locking all out; locking her in.

He turned around. She averted her gaze, choosing to stare at a spot on the wall. He said nothing when he passed by her on his way to the table. From the sounds she knew he poured a goblet of wine.

"When in Shrewsbury, I thought to purchase a pair of gloves for myself. Knowing they would be snug, I tried to take the ring off before putting them on. The ring stuck. I thought that odd, so that night I tried cold water and soap, then goose grease. The ring will not come off."

Gwendolyn groped for a reason other than the one she refused to consider. "The ring is too small. It was not made for you."

"One would think it was. It fitted perfectly until I tried to slide it beyond the knuckle. Short of cutting off my finger, I fear it must stay where it is. And no, Gwendolyn, I am not slicing off a finger, not even to please you."

Ire touched his declaration, but she didn't know if it was directed at her for the pretense of having accepted her situation, or at himself for his gallantry and gifts gone for naught. Having no answer, she remained silent.

He placed the goblet on the table, and after a few moments of silence, said, "You may turn around now. I should no longer offend your sense of modesty."

Alberic wore only his forest green tunic. He leaned against the table, his arms crossed over his chest, his long, bare legs crossed at the ankles. Truly, the man was a fine specimen of a hardy, healthy male and, completely against her will, her woman's places warmed at the sight of all that male flesh on display.

His sensuous perusal of her own state of undress tingled along her bare arms and at the hardened tips of her breasts. She folded her arms over her chest, which only encouraged him to lower his gaze and linger overlong on one particular spot. The light was dim. Surely he couldn't see much. But maybe he could. Her chemise was thin, and she didn't have enough arms and hands to cover *everything*.

She desperately needed a distraction and to divert his attention.

"You knew I planned to leave tonight."

He shrugged a shoulder. "You were seen where you

ought not to be at strange times. I also assumed you would try to procure the ring before you attempted your escape." His smile was neither apologetic nor friendly. "I beg pardon, Gwendolyn, but I cannot allow either. You do understand."

She understood too clearly that someone at Camelen had observed her movements and informed Alberic, most likely a guard she hadn't seen. She also understood that two days remained before the wedding, not much time to make other arrangements to escape.

None of which mattered if the ring didn't come off Alberic's finger. She dare not leave the ring behind.

"You have kept the ring on since the king gave it to you?"

"Aye. Almost a fortnight now." He frowned and turned the ring in circles. "The ring slid on easily and is not tight or hurtful. I do not understand what hinders me from removing it."

Gwendolyn was beginning to, and the possibility sent a cold chill through her that had nothing to do with her thin chemise and the lack of a fire in the hearth.

For a moment, again her father sat at the table, distressed, sliding the ring off and on his finger. "From the moment your mother's father gave it to me until the moment of her death, I could not escape its magic. Now your mother is gone, the magic has escaped, and I would do most anything to get it back." He'd sighed then. "You see, Gwen, that is why we must find the right husband for you. The magic will not work unless you are mated to a man you can love."

"Perhaps I should put the ring with the pendant," she'd offered.

"Nay. 'Tis my duty to pass it on to whomever you wed, nor can I bear parting with it just yet."

Father had never parted with the ring. He hadn't passed it on to Madog ap Idwal as he should. Instead, the ring now sat hard on a hand not meant to wear it, attached to a man she could not love.

Was there magic involved? If so, that might explain her forcefully wanton reaction to Alberic, though she didn't understand why ancient forces wished her to mate with the man who'd killed her brother. But that was absurd. If anything the magic should work in the opposite manner, by inducing the man to fall in love with her, which she allowed might be happening because he'd chosen her to be his wife.

She wished she knew more about the magic. Mother had died mere hours after handing over the artifacts with the barest of explanation and no training in their use. Father had known no more than she'd learned from her mother.

Sweet mercy, if the magic had gone awry she didn't know how to force it right again.

"Perhaps tomorrow it will come off."

"Mayhap, but truly, it matters not. The ring may stay on my hand, and you, Gwendolyn, will remain at Camelen. I assume you meant to seek out this Madog you spoke of."

His obvious dislike of Madog raised her chin. "He *is* my betrothed."

"No longer." Alberic pushed away from the table and sauntered toward her, challenging her resolve to avoid retreat. "You must accept that I am now your betrothed and we will be wed in two days."

"Even over my refusal? You cannot force me."

He cupped her face with warm palms, and she felt the power in his light touch clear down to her toes.

"I can," he said softly. "Believe me, I prefer not to use force, but you continue to resist what you cannot prevent. Our fates are sealed. Yield, Gwendolyn."

"Never."

She expected anger but received an unnerving smile.

"Never is a long time."

His kiss was whisper soft against her lips, and only the power of magic could turn it all-encompassing, banishing her resistance and common sense so thoroughly. Every part of her became aware of how closely they stood, how little fabric covered either of them. Too easily she could grab his tunic and pull him closer yet, feel the heat of him against her. Too easily she could melt into a puddle at his feet.

"Perhaps we should not wait until the wedding night," he suggested, his voice rumbling with desire.

She couldn't yield, couldn't let him win. She gained sensibility in a hasty retreat.

His hands spread in a gesture of resignation. "I am willing to wait until after we say our vows, but no longer. On the night after next you will be mine."

Gwendolyn headed toward the door, not all that sure of her relief at the reprieve. She reached for the latch and found the bolt. She didn't struggle long with the heavy plank. Alberic came up behind her and lifted the bolt from the holders.

"I will not confine you to your chamber," he said, "but you will be watched."

A prisoner in her own home, as she'd been since his

arrival. Only now Alberic was on his guard. Truly, she'd failed miserably this night.

As soon as the bolt cleared the door she was out of the chamber and rushing to the security of her own.

She wasn't quiet enough while entering. Emma opened her eyes and rose up on an elbow.

"Are you all right?" Emma asked quietly.

Gwendolyn slid under the coverlet. "Aye. Sorry I woke you."

"You are sure?"

"Let it be, Emma."

Emma closed her eyes, and Gwendolyn snuggled deeper into the feather mattress, knowing sleep impossible.

What a disaster! First she'd been caught and then she'd been kissed. Disasters both. To keep from thinking about the latter, she focused on the former.

What a fool she'd been, thinking herself clever enough to escape. She'd been discreet in filching food. For the life of her she couldn't imagine how a guard might have seen her near the postern gate. Even when stuffing the small satchel with the artifacts and clothing, she'd done so when neither Emma nor Nicole was present in the chamber.

Over and over she examined her movements, her observations, and couldn't figure out how she'd been found out.

"You are not all right," Emma complained. "You flap around like a fresh-caught fish."

"Beg pardon."

"Care to talk?"

She couldn't possibly tell Emma now, her failure too

fresh and Alberic's taste still on her mouth. "Perhaps tomorrow."

If Gwendolyn hadn't been looking directly at Emma, she might have missed her sister's quick glance at the clothing pegs, at Gwendolyn's cloak.

The thought came in an agonizing rush that Emma wasn't sure Gwendolyn would be here tomorrow.

Nay, not Emma! But it all made sense. Of everyone at Camelen, Emma knew her best. Who better to notice Gwendolyn's absence in the middle of the night, and be aware the small satchel wasn't in its proper place in the trunk?

Damn. Damn. Damn.

"You knew." The statement came out as an accusation, and Emma again tossed a glance at the cloak, this time so guilt-laden it tore Gwendolyn's heart in two.

"I suspected."

"You warned Alberic."

"You were about to do something dangerous, Gwen. I knew no other way to stop you."

Aghast, she asked, "You did not think to speak to me first?"

"Would you have listened had I told you to desist? Sweet mercy, you are so set against this marriage, you planned to sneak out of the castle in the middle of the night! I would wager you still are."

Gwendolyn turned away, unable to tell Emma the true reason for her need to escape.

Emma continued. "Bandits and wolves roam the forest, and the rogue archer has not been caught. I also feared if you succeeded then Nicole might take it into her head to follow your example. And—"

Gwendolyn ruthlessly cut off her sister's excuses for delivering her up to Alberic. "And you feared that if I left you might be forced to marry Alberic and thus lose your chance to go to court! Well, you need no longer fear, Emma. Any hope of my escape has been thwarted."

Emma's eyes narrowed. "Think what you will, but my reasons were not selfish. I could not bear the thought of you lying dead in the forest."

Nicole's head appeared above the end of the bed. "You were planning to leave, Gwen? Without taking me along?"

"Do not be foolish," Emma snapped at the girl. "Gwendolyn is going nowhere. Now go back to sleep. Let us *all* go back to sleep."

Nicole's head sank down below the mattress, and Gwendolyn knew naught else to do than to close her eyes.

The magic had most definitely gone awry.

First Father and William had abandoned her. Then Alberic wielded his authority to decide her future. Even the ring seemed to have turned against her.

And now Emma had betrayed her, and Nicole felt betrayed *by* her.

Anger warred with sorrow and panic for dominance. With her escape thwarted and no possibility of rescue, Gwendolyn glanced down the path of her life and saw naught but bitter mud and soul-jarring ruts.

Nothing was as it should be and might never come right again.

Chapter Seven

As was the custom at Camelen, on Sunday morning the castle folk celebrated Mass in the village church instead of the castle's chapel. As lord, Alberic attended, as did Gwendolyn and her sisters and a host of tenants from leagues around. The tension in the nave was as thick as the fog outside, and Alberic's thoughts were far from pious.

He shifted his weight from one foot to the other, wishing Father Paul could slide over a prayer or two. But since that wasn't to be, he glanced again at Gwendolyn's beam-stiff back and wondered how the devil he could convince her to bend.

She showed not a dram's worth of submissive pretense this morn, her distress displayed to all and sundry. Many would assume her sorrow caused by her presence in the church where her father and brother now lie interred under the floor.

Alberic knew Gwendolyn also mourned the loss of her freedom, bemoaned her inescapable fate. He'd tried gallantry, flattery, and gifts in his effort to win her over. Courting her hadn't gained him any favor, and he was at a loss over what to do next. Or even if he should.

Perhaps time and familiarity would work a miracle, turn her despair into contentment. Except he didn't believe in miracles, and sometimes allowing fate to rule could be a grave mistake.

He shouldn't allow Gwendolyn to affect him so. Not her moods and not her kisses, especially not her kisses.

She wasn't indifferent to him. Her physical response to his kiss and touch was all he could hope for, which boded well for the marriage bed and the begetting of heirs. Yet she'd played him false, leading him to believe she was resigned to their marriage while defiantly plotting her escape.

Praise heaven Emma had been concerned about her sister's odd actions, become suspicious of her purpose, and given him warning, or this morning he might be out scouring the countryside for Gwendolyn.

More dangers existed in the forest than bandits and wolves. Patrols had found no trace of the rogue archer, but Alberic couldn't assume the man no longer lurked in the area, though he dearly hoped the coward had taken the one shot at him and then fled. To where, Alberic no longer cared, considering himself fortunate to have survived the serious attempt to murder Camelen's new lord.

The second attempt, Nicole's, he considered an aberration, the action of a distraught child who lacked discipline. On the day after the wedding, on the same day Garrett escorted Emma to court, Sedwick would take Nicole to Bledloe Abbey and leave her to the strict care of the nuns, which the girl considered an unholy fate. Punishment enough.

Emma's and Nicole's absence would leave him alone with just one female to tame. Gwendolyn.

While he hated to think Gwendolyn might never be at peace with him, it truly didn't matter if she found contentment as his wife. His wife she would be. 'Twould be nice not to be at odds with her and be assured she would remain at Camelen without his placing her under constant guard.

Nice, but not required.

But damn, he liked the woman. Aye, she'd tried to escape, and given her circumstances he might have done the same. Her attempt might have been foolhardy and dangerous, but showed spirit and bravery he couldn't help but admire.

He'd like to make that woman happy if she would let him. A contented wife, a willing lover. Did he ask too much?

Adding to the tension, something had caused strife among the sisters. Though Emma and Nicole stood near Gwendolyn, they held themselves a bit apart, and the looks they gave one another signaled discord. He'd not told Gwendolyn of Emma's involvement in thwarting the escape, but now wondered if the truth had been revealed after Gwendolyn's return to the ladies' bedchamber.

"Amen" rang through the small church.

Alberic quickly crossed himself and turned to leave. The crowd parted like the Red Sea for Moses, allowing him and the ladies to pass through. He waved Emma and Nicole ahead of him, then took his place beside Gwendolyn, who didn't acknowledge him, but neither did she speed off.

He considered it a good omen.

Outside, the fog had given way to a light mist. Beside him, Gwendolyn flipped up the hood of her beaver cloak to cover her veil and circlet, effectively shutting him out of her sight. Silence reigned during the long climb up the steep hill to the gatehouse, and across the bailey to the stairs leading up to the keep's great hall.

Just inside the door stood a man garbed in royal livery, who must have arrived sometime during Mass. For a moment Alberic suffered the vision of being informed that the king and earl had finally come to a falling-out, and the king now recognized his error in gifting the earl of Chester's bastard son with a barony, and intended to remedy the mistake.

The messenger bobbed his head. "Good morn, Lord Alberic. I bear tidings from His Majesty and news from Wallingford."

At the words, Gwendolyn flipped back her hood and altered her steps, coming to stand beside him instead of crossing the hall. She was hoping for the worst of news, Alberic was sure.

"All good, one hopes," he told the messenger, expressing his fondest wish.

"For the most part, my lord. Brian fitz Count yet holds the castle, but the king's forces have succeeded in sealing off Wallingford. With both supplies and communication cut, we are now hopeful of the castle's quick surrender."

"Good news, indeed."

The messenger's smile concurred. Gwendolyn's frown reminded Alberic that while he might be a king's man, most folk at Camelen had supported Empress Maud for many a year, even if they now did so in silence.

"The king also wishes to know how you fair."

Alberic almost smiled at the messenger's attempted diplomacy. "You mean the king wishes to know if I am in a position to send back his soldiers."

"He made no direct request, but I believe he would be most appreciative."

This wasn't a decision to be made lightly. The presence of the king's soldiers had given Alberic the time necessary to exert his authority over Camelen. Enough time? If he now allowed the soldiers to leave, did he court the possibility of an uprising?

Given the events of last night, the woman at his side might joyfully condone a revolt, if not take up arms herself. He was a bit more sure of the garrison than Gwendolyn, but obtaining the opinion of his council couldn't hurt.

"Lady Gwendolyn, would you see that the messenger is fed while I consult with Garrett and Sedwick?"

Alberic considered it a mark of Gwendolyn's training that she yielded graciously. If only she would be as obedient in other areas . . . He shook off the wish as premature, admiring her grace as she showed the messenger to a trestle table, seating him below the knights but above a group of soldiers.

Loyalty. How was a man to know the measure of another man's heart and mind? Alberic was fairly sure of Garrett. Sedwick certainly did and said all that was proper of a steward to his lord. Though the knights and soldiers of the garrison had all sworn oaths of homage and fealty, he could hardly expect to have gained their complete trust in so few days.

What must it be like for a king to know that many of his former supporters, all of whom had given him the same oaths, now fought to toss him from his throne? A fragile thing, loyalty.

Alberic breathed a sigh of relief that the messenger hadn't uttered Chester's name. Apparently the earl hadn't yet left the king's service so, for the nonce, Alberic needn't worry over a royal change of mind. Camelen was still his, but for how long? If for some reason he were forced to take up arms to defend his right to the holding, would the men of Camelen fight beside him?

He glanced up at the circle of swords Gwendolyn had pointed out to him the other day, where she wished to hang Hugh's and William's swords. He noted the gleam of the weapons, knowing they'd belonged to former lords of Camelen.

Would his sword someday hang in that circle of honor, or would he be too small a part of Camelen's history to be considered worthy?

Time to hang the swords.

Alberic generally heeded the prodding of instinct, and the more he considered the action, the more it made sense.

Of course, the swords of Sir Hugh de Leon and his son deserved their place among the others, and by hanging them he might earn a further measure of respect from the men who'd fought by their sides.

Too, and not an insignificant argument in favor of honoring Hugh and William de Leon, the ceremony would formally mark the end of one lord's rule and the beginning of a new one.

Another possible result hit him upside the head and turned him around to stare at Gwendolyn, now seated in her chair at the dais, breaking her fast. He tried not to gloat as he crossed the hall and halted before the high table to gaze up at the lady he hadn't yet been able to please.

Her spoon, filled with porridge, halted halfway to her mouth. Her somber, self-absorbed expression turned warily quizzical as she looked down at him.

"We spoke the other day of hanging your father's and brother's swords and daggers in the hall. Do you know where the weapons are stored?"

Her spoon lowered to the wooden bowl. "Aye."

"Then send messengers to the villages and hamlets. Invite all to a feast and ceremony this noon to honor the fallen lords of Camelen. Can you make the arrangements within so little time?"

He'd stunned her, but she recovered quickly.

"I can."

"Need you my assistance?"

She shook her head.

He nodded, then turned and strode toward the stairs.

Gwendolyn hadn't reacted beyond surprise, but his intent to honor her father and brother surely must please her. She might not fall to her knees in gratitude, but he hoped they had taken a first step on the path to harmony.

And if not? Then perhaps no path existed and harmony was beyond them. The thought made him sad but no less determined to make Gwendolyn de Leon his wife.

He'd astonished her with the abrupt and thoroughly hopeless task of preparing a grand feast and fitting ceremony within the short space of four hours.

The man clearly didn't comprehend the amount of time required to properly plan events, and Gwendolyn had almost told him so. Instead, part angry and part elated, she set out to accomplish the impossible.

Sending out messengers with the announcement had been easy. Accommodating a great number of people on such short notice proved taxing.

The poor baker had paled to the shade of his finest white flour, but he fired the ovens and rousted his helpers to provide enough loaves of bread for trenchers. The cook had nearly fainted. For several minutes they'd commiserated on the unfair, unimaginable task of cooking enough food in time to feed so many and then decided what to feed the tenants and what to serve at the upper tables. What the meal lacked in imagination and presentation would be made up in plentitude.

That they were using some of the supplies purchased for the wedding feast, now only two days hence and weighing heavily on Gwendolyn's mind, didn't bother her in the least. The ceremony to honor her father and brother was by far the more important to her. The other feast . . . well, she would deal with that later.

She'd set a lot of people to various tasks today, and now, standing next to Alberic beside the high table, garbed in her finest and listening to the strains of Rhys's harp, she could see they'd all done their best to please her.

The hall was nearly as crowded as on the day of the burials. Had it been only eight days? It seemed longer, somehow.

White linen covered the multitude of trestle tables, the goblets, bowls, spoons, and baskets of bread already in place. In the arrangements she saw Emma's deft hand,

and she would have to thank her sister for the assistance, which might help put them on speaking terms again.

Despite their harsh words of last eve, Gwendolyn still loved Emma dearly. Though she didn't like what Emma had done, she also realized her sister acted with the best of intentions, as was her way. Emma now stood with Garrett and Sedwick and Father Paul, all four awaiting their parts in the ceremony.

Nicole hovered near Emma, but she wouldn't participate. Intentionally putting a sharp weapon in the girl's hand might be too much for Alberic to tolerate.

On the wall, high up in the circle of swords, hung two new brackets, hurriedly and skillfully fashioned by the blacksmith and nailed in place by the fearless soldier who'd climbed the absurdly tall and creaky wooden ladder, and who must do so again to snug the swords into the brackets. Brackets for the daggers were also in place, but could be reached with a much shorter ladder.

On the table before her lay the four weapons, polished to brilliance by the two young men Alberic had chosen as his squires. Thomas and Roger had accepted the task as an honor, and not a hint of tarnish marred the blades or pommels. The squires now stood behind her and Alberic, officially replacing Odell, who, along with the king's other soldiers, would return to Wallingford on the morrow.

Even Rhys had outdone himself, composing the soulful melody he played. The song yet lacked words, but Gwendolyn was confident that soon the names of Hugh and William de Leon would be set to music, their lives' tale recorded for all time.

All was ready. The keep, the food, the people—and Alberic.

He wore the knee-length garnet silk tunic Emma had decorated with gold thread. He'd never before worn the girdle of gold links cinching his trim waist, nor the soft black leather shoes and the snug matching hose, all of which she assumed he'd purchased while in Shrewsbury.

He'd chosen his garb with care, and if Alberic had reasons of his own for a display of splendor, she didn't mind. His attire proclaimed that he considered the occasion one of importance, and for that alone she could hug him.

'Struth, she could hug him for simply granting this one wish of hers—to allow the weapons their place of honor—proving he possessed a generous heart.

Both Emma and Garrett had praised Alberic's virtues, and Gwendolyn had noticed many for herself. If not for her duty toward the legacy, she might not have been so set against the marriage.

Emma might believe Gwendolyn's resistance to the marriage the reason for last night's attempt to escape. And while Emma might have played a part in the thwarting, the stubborn ring had ended Gwendolyn's plans far more effectively.

She didn't know if she did the right thing or not, but it seemed that, for the moment, she must consider herself bound to Alberic by stronger ties than the upcoming wedding vows.

Rhys's harp went silent.

Gwendolyn's stomach fluttered, praying nothing would go amiss for the next few minutes.

"Father Paul, if you would," Alberic said softly.

The priest made his way to the dais and made a sign of the cross over the weapons. "Bless these weapons,

O Lord, that have seen their share of strife and bloodshed. May they now serve as symbols of the peace and joy Hugh and William enjoy in Your heavenly kingdom. We pray You look down in favor upon Camelen and its people in the days to come, grant us peace and prosperity. This we ask in the name of Jesus Christ, Your Son, our Savior. Amen."

Sedwick stepped up to the dais and picked up William's dagger. Holding it across his palms, he held it up for all to see. "We celebrate the short life of William de Leon, rich in fervor and glory, as befits a lord of Camelen. May we always remember him with fondness and pride."

He then walked over to the short ladder and climbed four rungs. With the dagger secure in the bracket, Gwendolyn couldn't help thinking Alberic must be relieved to see that particular weapon placed beyond easy reach.

Garrett then echoed Sedwick's actions, lifting her father's dagger with the reverence of a priest raising a chalice. "I served the baron for many a year, through peace and war, in times fair and foul. I am honored to place his dagger among those of his ancestors. May his lordship rest with God."

All watched as her father's most trusted knight placed the dagger within its bracket.

Emma lifted William's heavy sword and held the blade up as the men had the daggers. "My brother never had the chance to be a true lord of Camelen, but had he lived—" Emma's voice caught, and Gwendolyn tried to swallow the lump forming in her throat. "Had he lived, I believe he would have done the de Leon name proud."

Emma slowly walked over to the tall ladder and

placed the sword in the care of the soldier, who slid the weapon into a scabbard strapped to his back. Gwendolyn commanded her breath to a steady pace as the man hauled his burden up the creaky ladder, snugged it into the bracket, and made his way back down again, all without the mishap she'd feared.

Then Alberic picked up her father's sword and held it high. Pride mingled with grief, and the tears she'd managed to hold back before now slid down her cheeks.

"As we honor Hugh de Leon, so we continue a proud and fitting custom. May the souls of all the warriors whose weapons grace this hall look down on us in favor."

Gwendolyn's heart pounded when Alberic strode across the hall and waved aside the soldier. With only one hand to steady him, he climbed the ladder in careful steps, one rung at a time, each rung groaning under his weight. She almost cheered when he finally, blessedly, reached the top without falling.

Then he gave her a jolt when he half turned to look down on the crowd below and held out the heavy sword at arm's length. "Behold the sword of Sir Hugh de Leon. As we grant his weapon its proper place among those of Camelen's past lords, may also God grant him heavenly peace."

He snugged the sword into the bracket, and with both hands available, climbed down at a quicker pace.

Alberic's audacious maneuver completed successfully, her relief more overwhelming than it ought to be, Gwendolyn waited until he again took his place by her side before she lifted her goblet.

"To the lords of Camelen!"

To the crowd's cheer, she took a sip, then handed the

goblet to Alberic, who wore a soft smile that melted her insides. He tilted the goblet toward her in salute, then drank down the remainder of the wine.

As planned, Rhys began another melody, and servants bore in large platters of food.

She took her seat.

Alberic slid into his. "You did well, Gwendolyn."

"My thanks. So did you, except you were not supposed to climb the ladder. I had visions of your brain splattered among the rushes."

His smile widened. "Worried for me?"

More than she ought to be, though she saw no reason to admit that to him. "I also worried over the soldier who was assigned to climb the ladder, and he had two hands to use for balance. Your falling would have badly marred the ceremony."

"Ah," he uttered, completely discounting her denial, then made selections of fowl and fish and cheese from the platter set before him. "Dove. You remembered."

Of course she remembered, but hadn't taken his preference into consideration. "You gave me little time to prepare, and the dovecote is full and the birds roast quickly."

He laughed lightly as he filled her goblet, the timbre of it relating she hadn't convinced him. And she wasn't sure why she tried. Obstinacy? Perhaps. Confusion? Certainly.

This morn, when she'd put the pendant and scroll back in their hiding place, she'd been certain she would never use them, even though England suffered a time of dire need, with the war only getting worse and no end in sight. If the messenger was right, then the war wasn't going well for the empress. With King Arthur commanding her forces, Maud would be sure to win.

But now Gwendolyn wondered, as she had last night, if it mattered so much which man wore the seal of the dragon. Her father had maintained that he must choose her husband carefully, ensure the man was someone she could come to love.

She couldn't love Alberic. To give her heart to the man who'd killed her brother was impossible, just *wrong*.

But she might be true and faithful to him, as Merlin the Sorcerer had set down in the scroll as an essential condition between the man and woman considered partners in the legacy. Could Alberic be counted on to remain true and faithful to her, even if he didn't love her?

If she married him, and that fate looked more and more possible, she would have to tell him about the legacy, if only to impress upon him how carefully he must guard the ancient artifact stuck on his finger. As her father had not. And look what havoc his mistake had wrought.

Would Alberic believe or scoff? Did he need to believe for the spell to work? Perhaps not.

And perhaps she simply wanted a miracle to come to pass because she'd been miserably unsuccessful last night and wished to wash away the horrible feeling of failure.

Gwendolyn still hadn't made peace with her unruly feelings when the hall's doors opened and a young, very handsome man entered. Richly garbed in black velvet, the sword missing from his scabbard—safeguarded by the soldiers at the gate, no doubt—he glanced around as if looking for someone he might know. Then he ran his fingers through windblown, dark hair. The rough combing missed the lock that hung down the right side of his forehead to near his eyebrow. With a lithe, long-limbed stride he chose a path to the high table.

Blatantly noble and unmistakably Welsh, the visitor put one hand to his chest and swept the other outward before executing a courtly bow before Alberic.

"Forgive . . . intrusion, my lord," he said in halting Norman-French, with a lilt that put her in mind of Rhys the bard. "I learned . . . of Hugh de Leon's death and . . . offer sympathy."

Alberic didn't move a muscle, yet she could feel him tense and didn't understand why. The Welsh noble posed no threat as far as she could see. Indeed, she liked both his amiable expression and his attempt to express his sympathy.

"On behalf of the family of Hugh de Leon, I accept your condolences," Alberic stated so flatly as to be rude. "Who shall I say offers them?"

"Do I have the . . . honor of speaking . . . to Alberic of Chester?"

"Lord Alberic of Camelen."

"Of course. Must always . . . present oneself in best . . . manner. Do you, perhaps . . . speak English or Welsh?"

"English."

The man's relief was visible.

"An honor to meet you, my lord. I am Madog ap Idwal, betrothed of the Lady Gwendolyn."

Chapter Eight

BESIDE HIM, GWENDOLYN GASPED but didn't jump up and leap into the arms of her *former* betrothed. Alberic considered that another good omen, though he didn't dare look at her. If her eyes shone with admiration for the Welshman, he didn't want to see it. And what woman wouldn't admire the dashing noble with a courtier's manners and an engaging smile?

Alberic put down his goblet to prevent bending the stem.

Ap Idwal hadn't come merely to pay his respects to Sir Hugh, but to claim Gwendolyn—a journey that could have been avoided if Alberic had thought to send a messenger to inform the Welshman of the change in wedding plans. Reluctantly admitting he might bear part of the blame for ap Idwal's appearance, he decided to show the man a measure of courtesy.

But not overly much.

"On behalf of the daughters of Hugh de Leon, I accept your condolences. You may dine with us before you visit the church."

Ap Idwal's smile faded when he realized he wasn't

being offered the extended hospitality to which he right-fully felt entitled.

"I realize you have a full hall, my lord, so I will not press for hospitality, though I did hope that, perhaps later this afternoon, you might find the time for us to speak at length. I also request permission for a few moments with Lady Gwendolyn."

Never. The faster the man left, the sooner Gwendolyn would give up hope of a rescue.

He'd thwarted her last night, and he would again now. She was his, damnit! The thought of her in this Welsh noble's arms set his stomach churning.

"We have naught to speak of, ap Idwal. Nor is there reason for you to speak with the Lady Gwendolyn. I heard of your betrothal, but find no evidence of it among Sir Hugh's documents. Since no formal bargain was signed, no betrothal exists."

"But the bargain does exist," he insisted. "Sir Hugh and I discussed the terms at some length, and set a date for the wedding. I can provide witnesses, if you like, from among my family and Lady Lydia's kin. I realize the situation has changed with Sir Hugh's death, but I stand ready to abide by the betrothal bargain we agreed upon."

At the edge of his vision he saw Gwendolyn clasp her hands together tightly in her lap. She'd not said a word as yet, her initial gasp of surprise her only utterance. He dare not hope she would keep her peace much longer, making her identity known to the swain before them and add her pleas to ap Idwal's arguments.

It struck him then that since the two had obviously not met and therefore never developed an affection, ap Idwal must want something within Gwendolyn's dowry. A piece of land? The rights to collect a fee or toll? Whatever it was of Camelen's the Welsh noble wanted, he couldn't have that, either.

"Upon Sir Hugh's death, his daughters became wards of King Stephen, and I have acted upon the king's instructions. Lady Gwendolyn will be wed to another."

He sensed Gwendolyn's head turn, felt her stare at him. Comparing one *betrothed* to the other? Did she prefer ap Idwal's dark hair to his blond? The Welshman's wealthy heritage to Alberic's poor one? Did she see ap Idwal as her chance at freedom from marriage to a man who held her under guard?

Certes, she must. What woman would not?

"The king, hmmm? Then it is to him I must address an appeal."

What a perfect solution!

Alberic smiled down at ap Idwal. "You are certainly welcome to state your grievance to King Stephen. He is camped outside of Wallingford. As fate would have it, a king's messenger is here who can act as your guide. You and your men—I assume you did not come alone?"

"A small retinue only."

So Alberic had thought, because no guard had rushed in to inform him of a threatening force beyond the gate.

"Then you and your men may camp in the field beyond the village until morn. I bid thee good journey."

Ap Idwal frowned deeply, likely realizing he still didn't rate a pallet in the hall.

Gwendolyn's slippered foot nudged his boot-covered ankle before she leaned toward him. He braced for her objection to his treatment of ap Idwal.

"He deserves the full truth," she said, just above a whisper.

Unable to judge her mood from those few words, he glanced sideways and, for a moment, became transfixed by her wide, enchanting brown eyes. He gave himself a mental shake to avoid becoming distracted, to pay full heed to the matter at hand.

Gwendolyn was serious, but not upset. A good day for good omens.

He lowered his voice to match hers. "Why?"

"Because he came all this way to make good on a bargain with my father. His attempt is honorable, so he deserves a strong measure of consideration."

Before he could disagree about ap Idwal's sense of honor, she shrugged a shoulder. "Besides, my Welsh kin must be told of what will happen to me and my sisters. Madog could carry back the news."

Her reasoning made sense, but Gwendolyn seemed too accepting, too calm, given her upset of this morning. He'd known the ceremony to honor her father and brother would please her, but he hadn't dared hope to fully placate her and now mistrusted her apparent capitulation.

True, her relatives must be told, but when done, would they show up in force demanding her release? And did they not already know?

"You did not invite your kin to the wedding?"

She shook her head. "Until this morn I did not believe the ceremony would take place. Besides, you told me that no one who did not support either Camelen or the king would be allowed through the gate. Since I am unsure of their current stance, I did not want to chance your refusing them entry."

So none of her family knew and so wouldn't be here to see her wed. Guilt niggled at him. After all, he had told her to invite them. That she hadn't was her decision. Their absence wasn't his fault.

"Gwendolyn—"

"You are Lady Gwendolyn?"

The Welshman's interruption didn't sit well, and Alberic could have kicked himself for raising his voice loud enough for ap Idwal to overhear.

"I am," Gwendolyn answered.

Ap Idwal bent over in what Alberic considered an overblown bow.

"'Tis my greatest pleasure to at last set eyes upon you, my lady."

Gwendolyn wasn't ap Idwal's "lady," and he'd paid her utterly no heed until learning her identity. The dolt.

"My thanks," Gwendolyn answered simply.

"On my oath, I shall do all that is possible to convince the king to honor your father's wishes in the matter of our betrothal."

Gwendolyn gave the man a sad smile. "I fear 'tis too late for that, Madog."

"Surely, until vows are exchanged, there is hope."

Alberic decided ap Idwal's hope begged dashing. "You are mistaken, ap Idwal," he said, drawing the man's gaze from Gwendolyn. "Lady Gwendolyn will make a fine lady of Camelen, do you not think?"

Ap Idwal's affability disappeared, instantly replaced by irritation. His gaze darted to Gwendolyn and then back again.

"She is to marry you?"

Alberic flashed an affirming smile as his answer.

"By order of the king?"

"With his permission."

Ap Idwal tossed a hand in the air. "So you intended to send me on a fool's errand."

The man's wits were far from slow.

"You seemed so set on it."

Irritation flared to hostility.

"Does Norman audacity know no limits?" ap Idwal shouted. "You show no respect for the rights of others. You see a thing you want, you set out to obtain it. What you cannot obtain by legal means, you seize as if that possession were granted you by divine right!"

"I seized nothing," Alberic rejoined. "Camelen was lost to the king at Wallingford. 'Twas within his rights to grant the barony to whomever he chose."

"And the daughters, too, no doubt."

"Upon Sir Hugh's death, the daughters became the king's wards. Aye, he has the right to decide their fate."

Ap Idwal drew himself up to a haughty stance. "'Tis my fondest wish that your King Stephen falls, and the Empress Maud along with him. Neither of them deserves the power they fight over. Perhaps with them gone, the next man who wears the English crown will be one of reason and compassion, and recognize that people are not his personal pawns."

With that, he spun on his heel and strode toward the door.

Good riddance.

Gwendolyn grabbed his sleeve. "I must have a word with Madog before he leaves."

"Whatever for?"

"I wish him to carry a message to my kin!"

Not a good idea. "In his present mood he may refuse."

"Please, Alberic. A moment only."

The Welshman stormed out the door. Within moments he would pass through the gate and out of their lives.

But Alberic couldn't bring himself to refuse Gwendolyn's request outright. She seemed resigned to their marriage, and he couldn't lock her away until the morning she became his bride to ensure her cooperation. He had to begin trusting her sometime, but trust came hard and with serious reservations.

"You will give me your oath you will not try to leave Camelen with ap Idwal."

She didn't hesitate. "You have my oath."

He probably shouldn't believe her. She'd certainly given him reason not to trust her word. But he couldn't resist the plea in her eyes and voice.

"You had best hurry if you hope to catch him."

She flashed him a smile before she bolted out of her seat and scurried across the hall.

Still leery, he waved a hand at Roger. "Follow her ladyship. Give her a measure of privacy, but ensure ap Idwal leaves—without the Lady Gwendolyn—the moment they are done talking."

Gwendolyn caught her prey halfway across the bailey.

Anger flowed from Madog ap Idwal like heat from an open flame.

"My apologies, Madog," she said, choosing her words carefully. "You came a long way for naught. I would have had it otherwise."

His ire faded somewhat. "So would I, my lady." He tilted his head. "What brings you out here? Dare I hope his lordship has changed his mind?"

She gave him a small smile. "Nay, but he did grant me permission to speak to you before you left."

"How generous." Then he put aside his anger and sarcasm. "I truly am sorry for your loss, Gwendolyn. Losing loved ones, no matter how, is hard to bear. I did not know your brother, but your father was a good man, despite his being Norman."

"I thank you for that." Gwendolyn decided not to remind him that she was half Norman. The man's dislike ran too deep for her taste. Hoping to lighten the mood further, she continued, "And I do wish you better fortune with your next betrothal. Perhaps a dark-haired beauty with a hefty dowry."

He smiled, as she hoped he would, but something in the twist of his mouth gave her pause.

"You have no cause to rank others above you, my lady. The size of your dowry had naught to do with my agreement to the bargain your father offered. He sang praises of your charm and grace, and I developed an affection for you before he finished speaking. I feel the loss of you far more than the loss of your dowry."

What lovely words, and Gwendolyn recognized each one as a falsehood. Had Madog developed an affection for her, he would not have insisted on a yearlong betrothal, and surely would have come to meet her before now.

His inconstancy made her wonder at what sort of man he truly was, for now she saw the insincerity in the mannerisms he'd displayed in the hall. And that flaw made her wonder if her father had chosen her husband with as much care as he should have. She might not be inclined to marry Alberic, but she didn't think she wanted to wed Madog, either.

This truly confused her. She had always imagined she would fall deeply, rapturously in love with her betrothed at first meeting, instinctively recognizing him as her heart and soul's mate. How terribly disappointing to discover she'd made a grave error.

Not only did Madog fail to engage her heart, she felt no physical attraction as she did with Alberic. No heat. Not a tingle. No appeal whatsoever.

Disconcerting, but of certainty.

"My thanks," she said, hoping her insincerity didn't sound so blatant as his. "Might I ask you to do me a small service?"

"My time and life are yours to command."

Gwendolyn resisted the urge to roll her eyes. "My uncle Connor and other Welsh kin may not yet know of my father's and brother's deaths. I am sure they do not know of the fate of my sisters or of my wedding. May I impose upon you to inform Connor, who can spread the news?"

His brow furrowed. "You have not notified him as yet?"

She'd seen no need to send a messenger when she'd planned to tell Connor after she arrived at his manor. If she'd managed to escape last night, she would be far into Wales by now.

"Up until this morn, I had planned to journey into Wales and tell him myself. That is no longer possible."

The furrows in his brow deepened. "By yourself?" he

asked, then his eyes widened in surprise. "You intended to escape! Can you still? I am willing to aid you in any manner possible."

The offer proved tempting, but leaving was no longer one of her choices. Even if she could slip by the guards, and she knew Alberic must have sent Roger out to watch over her, she couldn't leave Camelen without the seal of the dragon.

She shook her head. "'Tis too late. My guards are many and on alert. Escape cannot be arranged."

And it came as a surprise that she felt a measure of relief in the finality of her fate. She would marry Alberic, and for reasons she couldn't name, her situation no longer seemed unbearable.

Madog began to pace. "Surely there is a way to secure your release before the wedding. I could appeal to the king, or execute a rescue. How much time do I have?"

"There is no time. We will be wed on the morn after next."

"So soon?"

She had to put an end to his speculation. She didn't want him to save her. How utterly odd she should feel this way.

"I beseech thee, Madog, to leave matters as they are. Any upheaval will only make matters worse. I will wed Alberic on the morn after next. On the day after the wedding Emma will leave for the king's court in London, and Nicole for Bledloe Abbey. All this is done on the king's order. Please, all I ask of you is to inform my uncle, and let him know I will send him a full report on our welfare as soon as I am able."

He stared at her a long moment before he relented, his

shoulders drooping slightly, his mouth set in a thin line. "This is how you would have it?"

"Nay, nothing is how I would have it, but this is the way things will be. If my father had lived . . ." She shrugged a shoulder. "But he did not, and so we pay the penalty for his support of Empress Maud. You should go now. There may be trouble if you linger overlong."

He glanced about as if deciding whether to leave at all, so she began walking toward the gatehouse, giving Madog little choice but to follow suit. Roger, naturally, followed closely behind.

"You will send for me if you think of a way out of this entanglement," Madog ordered.

A gallant offer, and not completely false. His own plans had been shattered, and Gwendolyn allowed that, for whatever his reasons, Madog had been prepared to carry through on his part of the betrothal bargain.

"I thank you for the offer, but entanglements are rarely unraveled. I wish you good journey, and pray give my regards to my kin."

She halted several yards from the gatehouse and allowed Madog to take her hand, bow over it, and wish her fare-thee-well. His hand was cold, his bow too courtly, and she was glad he was leaving.

Unsettled, she forswore immediate return to the hall.

"Where are we going, my lady?" Roger asked.

"Onto the battlements."

"For what reason?"

"Because I wish to."

He had no argument for that, so he followed along in silence.

At the top, she waved off the guard who offered her a

helmet, and looked down to see Madog ap Idwal, no longer her betrothed, cross the drawbridge to join the handful of men who awaited him. With fluid grace, he mounted his pony but didn't ride off immediately.

A hand waving in the air, he spoke to his companions, likely relating what had happened in the hall. She couldn't hear his words, but could imagine his tale.

As she watched Madog, a statement he'd made to Alberic came to the fore. He'd as good as wished both King Stephen and Empress Maud to the devil, preferring to see someone else, anyone else, sit on the English throne.

The thought struck her that King Arthur could be that someone else.

No one—not Norman, nor English, nor Welsh—could deny Arthur Pendragon's right to wear the crown. Nor was there anyone who could unite the kingdom as could King Arthur. All would bow before him. All would welcome his rule.

Was it possible Madog had been hinting to her that he knew of the legacy, that the two of them could give England a third and better choice of king?

Sweet Jesu! Had her father told Madog of the legacy? Would Hugh de Leon have felt compelled to ensure the man who was to marry the keeper of the pendant a willing partner as guardian to the legacy?

Possibly. And the thought made her shiver.

"My lady, the man on the black pony."

Wrenched from her disturbing musings, Gwendolyn glanced down at the man Roger spoke of. "What of him?"

"Do my eyes deceive me, or is that not Edgar?"

Gwendolyn looked harder. "Aye, it is," she said, very surprised to see one of Camelen's former soldiers in Madog ap Idwal's company.

Roger studied the man intently. "At Wallingford, Edgar was among those who chose not to accept Alberic as lord, so he did not return to Camelen with us. Now we know where he went."

To Madog ap Idwal.

Gwendolyn remembered asking Emma if she thought one of the soldiers who chose not to swear fealty to Alberic might go to the Empress Maud or earl of Gloucester to inform them of Sir Hugh's death and the loss of Camelen to a king's man. Never had she imagined one of the soldiers might journey into Wales to inform Madog.

"I wonder why he went to Madog."

She realized she'd voiced the thought aloud when Roger answered.

"I know not, my lady." He straightened up and his visage darkened. "But I do know that Edgar is skilled with a bow. We must return to the hall and inform Lord Alberic."

Within a heartbeat she realized Edgar could be the rogue archer! He could very well have made an attempt to murder Alberic, and upon failure, hurried into Wales and to Madog.

Why to Madog instead of her uncle? It mattered not at the moment.

"Go," she told Roger. "Quickly, before they leave."

Roger hesitated.

"Go! I am right behind you."

Roger nigh flew down the stairs and had nearly

crossed the bailey when Gwendolyn reached the last step. By the time she entered the hall, Roger and two others were rushing out, to haul Edgar back in, no doubt.

Alberic sat alone at the high table, both hands wrapped around his goblet, staring at the door. Watching for her to come in, she was sure.

It must have been hard for him to wait, likely thinking about her attempt to escape last night and wondering if she might try again. Her oath notwithstanding, he had reason not to trust her.

As she could trust him. Astonishing, but true.

Not once had he told her a falsehood. Certes, he'd delayed confessing his part in William's death, but when confronted, he hadn't denied his involvement or made excuses. To her knowledge he made no false promises to anyone at Camelen, and made a valorous attempt to ensure the change in lordship was peaceful and without undue hardship.

Aware he'd watched her since she entered the hall, Gwendolyn made her way to the dais and took her place beside him.

Her place? Aye, she supposed this chair was now hers as lady of Camelen, a position she'd never dreamed to claim.

"Did ap Idwal tell you what you wanted to hear?"

She heard the derision in his question, so assumed Alberic had sensed Madog's inconstancy, too.

"Aye. His holding is not far from my uncle's, so they are likely to see each other soon, if not as quickly as I might wish." She sighed. "I should probably send a messenger to ensure my kin are informed in a timely fashion.

And I should also send a message to a cousin on my father's side to inform them of recent events."

"You have a large family."

"Large and scattered over the kingdom."

While Alberic had no one.

Except me.

On the morn after next she would be his wife, his only family. How horribly sad.

More than ever Gwendolyn wished her mother had lived, if only to give her counsel about how to be a wife to a man who wasn't of her choice, but to whom her heart softened even as her head urged caution. Would there ever come a time when she could look at Alberic and not remember he'd slain her brother? She had her doubts.

Too, she wished another soul yet walking the earth could advise her about her responsibility to the legacy. She understood that the fewer people who knew, the more protection afforded the artifacts and the less chance someone might try to use them for unsound reasons.

But 'twas very possible Father had told Madog about the legacy, perhaps given him the choice of whether or not to accept the obligation.

She'd rarely given the man's involvement a thought, had always assumed that when the time came, her father would give her husband-to-be the ring and explain the weighty duty as, perhaps, her mother's father had explained the duty to Hugh de Leon.

With both parents now gone and beyond advising a confused daughter, Gwendolyn had only one person with whom to share her concerns—the man who wore the ring.

Alberic.

Was it best to tell him of the legacy before the wedding or wait until after? Did the timing truly matter? The ring held tight to Alberic's finger. He was now as involved in this legacy as she, whether he wanted to be or not.

The meal was finished, the people leaving to return to their homes. Emma and Nicole stood by the door, accepting good wishes and issuing fare-thee-wells, so they would be occupied for some time. She could take Alberic upstairs and not worry about interruption.

Gwendolyn shoved her concerns aside and gathered up her courage.

"Finished with your wine?" she asked Alberic.

"Aye. Want more?"

Wine did not make for a clear head, which she needed to do what she was about to do.

"Nay. If you have the time now, I have something I would like to show you. Upstairs. In my bedchamber."

His slow, sensuous smile told her where his thoughts wandered, igniting her own imaginings, which lit the now familiar yearning deep in her woman's places.

'Twas disconcerting to note that when it came to the physical aspects of their marriage, she would be an eager and curious participant.

Unfortunately, Alberic's ardor might cool completely when she told him why he couldn't remove the ring from his hand.

Chapter Nine

FOLLOWING GWENDOLYN up the narrow, winding stairway, Alberic managed to keep his hands to himself, even though the sway of her lovely backside tempted him nigh beyond endurance to touch the supple curves.

He knew damn well the invitation to her bedchamber didn't include bed sport. Whatever she intended to show him wouldn't involve glimpsing some portion of her uncovered body.

Still, a man was entitled to a fantasy or two, especially when the woman whose sweet scent he breathed in with each inhale would soon be his for the taking. In a mere two nights he could touch whatever part of Gwendolyn he wished whenever he wanted.

True, he possessed that right now, as her lord and betrothed, but prudence warned him to wait for full intimacy until after vows bound them. He'd never been a man of uncontrolled passions, and given Gwendolyn's reluctance to become his wife, much less his lover, his control might be the key to unlocking Gwendolyn's surrender.

A challenge to be sure. One he intended to meet head-on, armed with gentle touches and rousing kisses. And win.

Alberic bolted the door to the one chamber in the castle he'd not yet ventured into. Sunlight streamed in from a tall, narrow window overlooking the bailey, lighting up a small table holding combs, ribbons, jars, and tiny bottles sparkling with variously colored liquids.

Four trunks lined the far wall. Several cloaks hung on the pegs beside the door. He was just beginning to inspect the bed when a tapping noise drew his attention to the hearth where Gwendolyn knelt off to one side. Tapping on one of the bricks?

"What are you doing?"

"Sit, if you like," she said absently. "This may take a few moments."

He glanced at the single chair across the room, then took the offered seat on the bed he knew Gwendolyn shared with Emma.

For one more night Gwendolyn would sleep next to her sister under the green velvet coverlet. On the night after, she would share his bed.

On the night after that?

With her sisters gone, would she then occupy this room alone, following the practice of most noblewomen to sleep in a chamber separate from their lords'? He supposed she might, and like many a nobleman before him, he would be forced to visit his wife's bed, or arrange for her to visit his, when he desired intimate company.

Which seemed a waste of time and effort, but to maintain marital tranquillity, he supposed the decision must be Gwendolyn's. Alberic smiled to himself, considering which methods might sway her thoughts on the matter, those lusty images stirring his loins and urging him to begin his campaign now.

Finally, she wiggled the brick out of place and set it down next to her. Then she reached into the hole and pulled out a long, narrow sack of black velvet with a short length of silver cord wrapped around the top to secure the opening.

Valuables? Jewels, perhaps? Whatever the sack contained must be a treasure of some sort to warrant such a hiding place. He took it as a measure of her trust that she allowed him to witness the hiding place's unveiling.

Then Gwendolyn came toward him and his thoughts again wandered to an unveiling of a different sort, and the treasure he was sure to find hidden beneath layers of silk and linen. She halted abruptly, the rosiness on her cheeks revealing her awareness of his desire.

He willed her to join him on the bed. She retreated to the table where she put down the sack.

Disappointed, his male parts aching, he rose from the bed and crossed to the table, where she unwound the cord from the sack.

"What I am about to show you few men have ever seen. My father was the last. My mother's father before him. I must ask for your oath of secrecy before I open it."

"You have my oath."

She nodded acceptance, and again he felt privileged.

"I know why you cannot get the ring off," she said, catching him completely off guard. What the devil did her treasure have to do with his ring?

Thoroughly confused, he shrugged a shoulder. "The ring will not come off my finger because the skin bunches at my knuckle too much for the ring to slide off."

"You tried several methods to aid its removal. Do you not believe one of them should have worked?"

"Aye, but they did not. I have decided it does not matter." He pointed at the sack. "What does my ring have to do with your treasure?"

"Everything. When King Stephen gave you the ring, did he tell you its history?"

Realizing she wasn't about to reveal the sack's contents until he answered her questions, he gathered up his patience and recalled the day at Wallingford when his life changed in startling fashion.

"He told me your father called the ring the seal of the dragon, and that he wore it in honor of his Welsh princess, your mother."

"Nothing else? Either of the ring or of my mother?"

One other thing that had surprised him. "He said your mother came from the line of Pendragon. Did she?"

"So the tale goes."

Gwendolyn opened the sack from which she pulled a long, delicate gold chain. Fastened to it was a bold, stunning pendant—a trefoil fashioned of gleaming gold. The pendant caught the light coming through the window and spun rainbows to dancing through the chamber. A delightful spectacle.

"The ring you wear has belonged to several men before you," she said, drawing his attention away from dancing rainbows. "All were married to women in my mother's line. Always the couple married for love. You and I may be the first pairing in the history of these artifacts not to do so, and that concerns me greatly."

Alberic scoffed at the notion. "All of them? I find that impossible to believe. Noble pairings are made for reasons other than mere affection."

"I know. But my parents, a Norman baron and a Welsh princess, were allowed to marry because of their affection for each other. And my mother's parents were said to share a great love. I believe if I were to ask anyone who knows the old stories of my family, they would say my grandmother's parents were heart-bound, as well. The pendant has been passed from mother to daughter, and the ring to their husbands. The legacy binds us all."

He meant to argue further about her notion of generations full of love-bound couples. That Hugh had gained protection from Welsh raids would be among the worthiest of reasons for him to marry Lydia. He should correct Gwendolyn's naïveté, but this legacy business poked sharply at his curiosity.

"What legacy?"

Gwendolyn put down the pendant and drew a parchment scroll tied with bloodred ribbon from the sack.

"This one," she said, holding it out.

He dismissed a small shiver of apprehension as foolish. Gwendolyn might have demanded an oath of secrecy and woven a web of mystery around the pendant and scroll, but certes, there was naught to fear.

He untied the ribbon and unrolled the parchment. "This is written in Welsh. I cannot read it."

"It is written in *ancient* Welsh. I cannot read more than a few phrases, either."

"Then how do you know what it says?"

"From what my parents told me."

Becoming impatient and still pointlessly nervous, he wondered at Gwendolyn's reasons for bringing him up to her bedchamber to look at a scroll neither of them could read. Unless . . . *mon Dieu* . . . she implied that because of something written on this scroll, she couldn't marry a man she did not love. If she schemed to change his mind on his choice of wife, then the scheme fell short of its goal.

Or perhaps her attempt to escape last night was still too fresh and worrisome, causing his musings to run amuck. Best he knew what her parents said the scroll proclaimed, the better to prepare . . . for what he must prepare, he had yet to learn.

He sat in the room's lone chair and put the parchment on the table next to the pendant.

"Go on."

Gwendolyn's visage darkened. "When my mother realized her life was coming to an end, she had to pass on the artifacts to one of her daughters. Nicole was a newborn babe. For some reason Mother chose me over Emma. She told me of the legacy, and of the need to keep the artifacts hidden away until such time as I must wear the pendant."

He could think of only one reason why she'd pulled the pendant out tonight. "So on our wedding day you will wear the pendant?"

"Oh, no. My mother never wore it, so I do not think I may wear the pendant unless we are invoking the spell."

Spell? We? Every fiber of his being tingled in warning. Spells. Magic. Witchcraft. He might believe them nonsense, but the mere thought that one could invoke mystical powers sent his senses shivering. To hear Gwendolyn speak as though the two of them could somehow invoke those powers . . . impossible.

And yet, the woman was utterly serious.

"What spell?"

"To summon King Arthur from Avalon."

Stunned, he surmised either Gwendolyn had gone witless or his hearing had gone weak. "Summon King Arthur?"

With the same conviction she'd shown all along, she went on. "This scroll was prepared by Merlin the Sorcerer, and given into the keeping of a Welsh princess, a niece of Arthur Pendragon. You have heard the tale of how Merlin predicted that at England's time of most dire need, King Arthur will return?" She waved at the scroll. "These are Merlin's instructions on how the woman who possesses the pendant and the wearer of the ring are to summon King Arthur."

Gwendolyn possessed the pendant. The ring he couldn't remove from his finger suddenly felt heavy on his hand.

Nonsense. All of it. Insufferable nonsense.

"Gwen, do you truly believe what you have told me?"

"Yes, with all of my heart."

Likely because she received the artifacts from a mother who lay dying and Gwendolyn, a mere child, had been both impressionable and vulnerable. Gwendolyn wanted to believe the ridiculous tale because not to believe meant her mother had lied to her. Lady Lydia had done Gwendolyn a grave disservice for reasons known only to the dead woman.

Alberic strove to be gentle. "Gwendolyn, this cannot be possible. One cannot recall the dead."

"King Arthur is not dead. He resides in Avalon and awaits a summons."

Alberic tried to remember everything he'd heard of King Arthur's last battle, fought against his son, Mordred. Of Arthur's wounding, mortally wounded if he remembered the tale aright. He'd been carried off to Avalon by . . . someone. True, Merlin was supposed to have prophesied that Arthur would someday return, but *sweet Jesu,* even if Arthur had lived, he would be hundreds of years old by now.

Spell or no, prophecy or no, King Arthur wasn't coming back to England. Ever.

"I beg pardon, but I simply do not believe in sorcery."

"But you are part of this whether you believe or no," she said earnestly. "You have no choice. You wear the ring."

He looked down at the seal of the dragon, the gold claws grasping the onyx stone topped by a garnet.

"'Tis merely a ring. No more."

"Is it? My father wore the ring. He could not take it off, either, until after my mother's death. I suspect you will not be able to take it off until my death."

That absurd speculation brought him to his feet. He knew better than to try to remove the ring to prove her wrong, but somehow he must force Gwendolyn to see sense, or to at least have doubts.

Mon dieu, if word of her unnatural beliefs spread, people would think she had lost her wits or, worse, accuse her of practicing witchcraft.

"Let us say what you believe is true. If you cannot read the scroll to discern the spell, then what good is it?"

"I believe Rhys can read it."

"The bard?"

"How many English castles boast a resident Welsh bard?"

"None that I know of, but—"

"Rhys arrived in Camelen shortly after my mother came here as a bride. The bards know all of the ancient tales, both the ones they sing and, in this case I suspect, those they keep secret. If anyone can read the ancient language, it would be a bard."

"Have you shown it to him?"

"Nay. I do not believe Mother did, either. She just accepted his presence as an assurance of aid should it be needed."

"Then perhaps we should show this to Rhys, have him read what it says." And thus prove to Gwendolyn that her belief lacked merit.

She shook her head. "Not unless absolutely necessary, and 'tisn't necessary unless we decide the time is right to summon King Arthur." She pointed to words on the parchment. "Of the few phrases that seem familiar, I am certain the summoners must be of faithful hearts"—she moved her finger—"and their purpose honorable."

An honorable purpose spoke for itself. The spell wasn't to be cast for personal gain. Faithful hearts? Gwendolyn interpreted the phrase as a couple in love.

"So you are concerned that even if we did decide to summon King Arthur, the spell would not work because we do not marry for love, as did your parents and grandparents."

"I am not sure."

Alberic's patience came to an end. No matter which argument he presented, he'd not budged Gwendolyn's belief.

He put his hands on her shoulders, stared hard into her wide brown eyes. "Gwendolyn, maybe you believe this tale, and perhaps your mother and her mother before her believed it, but have you ever seen anyone perform magic? Have you ever heard of someone reciting a spell that worked?"

"Can you remove the ring?"

He'd tried soap and water, and goose grease, which hadn't worked. But there must be a way to ease the ring over his knuckle. All he had to do was find it, believing the ring's removal the only way to disabuse Gwendolyn of this absurdity.

"I do not for a moment believe an ancient sorcerer uttered some spell that fastens it to my hand. Put the scroll and pendant back in their hiding place and tell no one else of this foolishness."

She pursed her lips. Was she about to argue?

"Gwendolyn, there is no such thing as magic. Never was, never will be. And if there were a way to summon King Arthur from Avalon, do you not think someone would have done so long before now? England has suffered other periods of strife."

"Perhaps."

He settled for the small concession. "Now, I must go down to see if Roger has brought our rogue archer inside. Will you be all right?"

"Of course."

She wasn't, not yet, her upset visible in the set of her

jaw. But surely, eventually, Gwendolyn would come to see sense. 'Twould help greatly when he removed the ring.

∽

The following morning, a seamstress pinned up the hem of the surcoat Gwendolyn had never planned to wear. She liked neither the color nor the cut, but wear it she would on the morrow. At her wedding.

The distressing thought begged distraction.

Careful to keep her body still, Gwendolyn glanced over at Emma, who smoothed a chemise into her trunk, readying it for the journey to London. As was Emma's way, she'd piled all of her belongings on the bed and now sought to pack each item in the neatest, most efficient arrangement.

'Twould take her hours, keep her hands busy, and her thoughts ordered and calm.

Gwendolyn's feet itched to move, and she was far from tranquil. Yesterday's calamity lurked at the edge of her thoughts, and no matter how hard she tried to push them away, they intruded unmercifully.

She would have been better served to shed her garments and join Alberic on the bed. The invitation in his eyes had been unmistakable, and she'd definitely suffered temptation. Her curiosity over coupling with Alberic had swollen her nipples to hard nubs and caused her heart to race. Even now her body stirred, the yearning painfully centered in her most private woman's places.

But she'd resisted, admonishing herself for her physical weakness where he was concerned and believing she served a higher purpose by telling him of the legacy.

How wrong she'd been. His disbelief had left her reeling, torn between horror and fury.

She'd put the horror to rest, at least. Alberic had adamantly warned her to tell no one of her "foolishness," so she highly doubted he would spread the tale.

Fury at his utter refusal to consider the legacy legitimate had lessened to anger, and finally, in the hours since dawn, to resignation. Alberic didn't believe in sorcery. He spurned the possibility of magic. Clung fiercely to the belief that the ring held tight to his finger because the skin bunched at his knuckle, preventing it from sliding off.

Gwendolyn knew better. Alberic's finger could shrivel to half its present size and still the ring would stay put. Somehow the magic had gone awry. The ring clung to the hand of a man who wore it by chance, not the hand chosen for it. Not that she was sorry, precisely, that she wasn't marrying Madog. Still, she would somehow have to accept the ring's choice of wearer.

Convincing Alberic now that the ring bore magic, however, was impossible. Perhaps, someday, his stubbornness might abate. For now, she could do naught but allow him his defenses.

She'd scared him nigh on witless. True, he'd shown no sign of fright. No widened eyes or shaking hand. A true warrior kept his fear hidden away from sight, for good reason.

Only fear, she'd reasoned, could account for Alberic's denial of the legacy and his refusal to accept responsibility for an awesome power no other man in her lifetime could possess.

When she died, and the ring slipped from his hand, perhaps then he'd believe! A morbid and uncharitable thought, but at the moment she thought she could be excused for her lack of charity.

But then, so could he be excused today from further discourse on the matter. Roger hadn't returned as yet, and Alberic fretted over the welfare of his squire and the four soldiers he'd sent to capture Edgar. After seeing the king's soldiers off at dawn—and Gwendolyn ruefully admitted she might miss Odell a bit—Alberic ordered a patrol to search for Camelen's men. As yet there were no results.

From across the room, Emma sighed. "I fear I shall appear the veriest pauper at court."

Grateful for the interruption, Gwendolyn allowed herself a smile at Emma's unwarranted lack of confidence. The woman could garb herself in surcoats of the roughest peasant weave and not be mistaken for a pauper. 'Struth, no one of any sense would notice what Emma wore upon seeing her lovely face and hearing her speak. And if some half-wit noble disdained Emma for the fabric of her surcoat, the dolt didn't deserve the rank of noble.

"Your chemises are made of the finest linen, and your surcoats fashioned of silk and tight-weave wool. Surely that places you a rank or two above beggar."

"Perhaps."

Gwendolyn's smile widened. "Is there aught of mine you wish to take?"

In less than a heartbeat, Emma answered, "Would you be willing to part with the saffron?"

No decision was easier. "I have never been partial to the color, so feel free to take it."

The seamstress rose from her knees and pronounced the pinning finished. Relieved, Gwendolyn slipped out of the surcoat and handed it over.

The seamstress curtsied, then smiled. "'Twill be ready within the hour, milady."

Gwendolyn managed to smile back. "My thanks."

As soon as the seamstress closed the door behind her, Gwendolyn turned to Emma. "You may also have that one, if you wish."

Emma didn't misunderstand which surcoat Gwendolyn willingly parted with. She looked horrified. "Your wedding finery? I could not possibly."

"I see no reason why not. 'Tis close of a shade of the other, so I doubt I would wear it much."

"Then why did you choose that piece of silk?"

"I let Nicole choose it, not caring what she chose. Until yesterday I did not think I would wear the surcoat, ever, most especially not as wedding finery."

Emma frowned at Gwendolyn's unintended petulance.

"You have not forgiven me for warning Alberic. I do wish you would. I should hate to leave with ill feelings between us."

The wedding was now only one morning away, with Emma's and Nicole's departure set for the day following. While Gwendolyn stood for her surcoat's final fitting and Emma packed her trunk, Nicole was spending time with Father Paul, who was telling the girl about life in a religious house; both what she could expect and what was expected of her. Gwendolyn didn't want to part with ill feelings between herself and her sisters, either, but she doubted Nicole would quickly forgive her or Emma for allowing Alberic to send her off to a nunnery. Just as Gwendolyn was having a hard time forgiving Emma for alerting Alberic to the escape plan.

But in the end, 'twas not Emma's warning that had thwarted an escape, but the stubbornness of the seal of the dragon.

"You must have patience with me, Emma. I am not as reconciled to the fate chosen for me as are you."

"Alberic is a good man, Gwen. You could do far worse."

True enough. She knew of other brides who'd not been fortunate in their husbands and had always been certain she would escape their misfortune, sure that the legacy assured her happiness in marriage. Instead, it had brought her misery.

For now, she'd done as Alberic ordered; put the scroll and pendant back in their hiding place. If this war lingered on, with more lives lost, more crops destroyed, more castles and villages set to ruin, England would surely suffer its time of most dire need. Until she could convince Alberic of the truth, the legacy was useless to all and sundry.

Unless she could tell Alberic what was written on the scroll. Should she ask Rhys to read it? Nay, not unless absolutely necessary would she show it to anyone else. Best just to get on with life and try not to fret over all that had gone wrong. What else could a body do?

Gwendolyn took Emma's hand. "You are my sister, and so I love you and always will. My anger will pass. How do you on your packing?"

Emma's arms came around her, and Gwendolyn felt better for the brief hug.

"I love you, too," Emma whispered, then released her. "As for the packing, I am nearly done. I suppose it is silly of me to worry about clothing anyway. I will not be a popular member of the court because of Father's support of Maud, so will have no need for more than a few garments. Still, I want to do our family name proud."

"You will, Emma. Of that I have no doubt."

Emma's mouth thinned. "I hope I do well enough so the king grants our petition to have Nicole released from the abbey. She is terribly unhappy and hasn't yet set foot inside the place."

"Nicole knows you will do your best by her, and if you find court not to your liking, you are welcome to petition to return home, too."

Emma smiled. "And what would Alberic say if both sisters he thought himself well rid of show up at his gates begging admittance? But I thank you for the invitation all the same."

If her sisters came begging, would Alberic allow them to return? She didn't see how he could object, but then she hadn't anticipated his reaction to the legacy, either.

Sweet mercy, she was about to marry a man she barely knew. On the morrow she would take vows to cherish and honor Alberic, vows she would be honor-bound to keep—somehow.

And tomorrow night?

She nearly shivered with the anticipation. She didn't have to close her eyes to envision Alberic sitting on her maidenly bed, his eyes alight with desire. Nor was it hard to remember how hard she'd struggled not to accept his invitation. Tomorrow night she would be his wife, share his bed, with no choice but to lie with Alberic.

That should bother her, she supposed, but heaven help her, the prospect of coupling with Alberic bothered her not at all.

She'd overheard maids speak of the union, teasing and jesting with one another about "sharing blankets" and "taking a tumble." She even knew which maids "lifted her skirt for any prick gone hard." Vulgar terms, all, for coupling with a man.

Unfortunately, sometimes sharing blankets led to trouble for a maid if the man's "seed took root."

Trouble, Gwendolyn didn't worry over. Bearing children was the duty, and some said the joy, of being a wife. All lords needed heirs, and even though her mother had died as the result of childbirth, Gwendolyn had always accepted that she must strive to give her husband an heir.

Except she didn't have a notion of how to take a tumble. Once she lifted her skirt, Alberic would have to show her what to do with a prick gone hard.

Chapter Ten

ALBERIC PACED THE HALL, waiting for Gwendolyn and her sisters to come down the stairs so they could begin the procession to the church, when the squire he'd worried over most of the night walked in.

Roger looked haggard and worn, as if he'd been in battle. The hair on Alberic's neck rose, his warrior's instincts coming alert.

"Good God, man, what happened?" Alberic asked.

"Ap Idwal must have realized we were following him. They attacked our camp in the middle of the night and stole our horses. If not for the patrol you sent out to find us, we would still be walking back to Camelen." Roger took a fortifying breath. "We lost two good men, my lord, with naught to show for it."

Alberic's immediate reaction was to mount a large force and go after ap Idwal, to avenge his fallen men and retrieve his horses. Except he was getting married within the hour, and securing his lordship of Camelen must come before all else. Retaliation would have to wait.

"Did the men have families?"

"One of them. Oscar Biggs."

Alberic didn't have to think hard to remember the child he'd met on his second day at Camelen. Little Edward, who'd played the earl of Cornwall to Nicole's Empress Maud.

The widow must be informed. Alberic knew he could send someone else to do the deed, but considered it his duty. Along the way to the village he would decide when and how to strike back. 'Twould be unwise to allow the attack to go unanswered. Ap Idwal would see it as a sign of weakness, and so might others.

And damnit, he wanted his horses back, as well as a piece of ap Idwal's hide.

"Tell Gwendolyn I will meet her at the church," he told Roger. With a heavy heart, he headed for the village.

∽

Gwendolyn walked behind the priest, Nicole and Emma at her sides, too upset over the death of Oscar Biggs to fret over the imminent wedding.

Alberic had taken on the onerous task of informing Mistress Biggs, but she wished he had waited for her to go with him. No matter if Alberic related the news in a gentle manner, which she didn't doubt he would, the blow would be harsh for Oscar's wife and son.

Not only had they lost a husband and father, but their livelihood as well. Gwendolyn had no notion of what the widow would do for income without Oscar's soldier's pay.

As the small procession neared the church, she spotted Alberic standing at the top of the steps, waiting for her. He looked every bit the lord of Camelen: straight and tall, shoulders wide and square, garbed in garnet and gold.

His somber expression hit Gwendolyn in the heart. She knew facing Mistress Biggs and Edward hadn't been easy for him, and she very much wanted to console him.

She shouldn't feel his pain or want to ease it. Because of Alberic, nothing was as it should be. She suffered a moment of grief that her father wasn't present to place her hand into her husband's. She mourned the lack of her kinsmen and the joy that should mark a wedding day.

And yet, as Gwendolyn climbed the steps to join Alberic, she couldn't imagine herself standing there with any other man. So much was wrong between them, but as she looked into the green eyes of the man fate decreed would become her husband, she couldn't douse the flicker of hope in her heart that they could somehow make most things right.

"In the name of God the Father, we invoke divine blessings this morn for Lord Alberic of Camelen and Lady Gwendolyn de Leon. May He look upon this marriage with favor."

Aye, Lord, if You please!

Gwendolyn added her fervent prayer to the priest's, sure that she and Alberic would need all the divine aid they could get in order to make this marriage succeed.

Alberic clasped his hands together to keep them from trembling. He'd never truly planned on taking a wife. Given his illegitimate birth and his lack of rank, wealth, or land, he'd had nothing to recommend him to any woman. Events at Wallingford had changed that, the king giving him everything necessary to make a good living, even to take his place in the king's court should he choose.

At the moment, he couldn't think that far ahead.

The visit to Mistress Biggs's had shaken him more than he'd thought it would. She'd been almost inconsolable, her grief expressed in the wails and tears of a woman who'd deeply loved her husband.

During his attempts to give her and her son comfort, assure them that all would be well, he'd wondered how Gwendolyn would react to news of his own death, if it occurred. Would she shed a tear or two, or celebrate her freedom?

"Lord Alberic, you have freely given your consent to this marriage?"

"So I have given."

Alberic held his breath when the priest asked the same of Gwendolyn, and his heart skipped a beat when, in a clear, strong voice she answered, "So I have given."

"Lord Alberic, know you of any impediment, either of body or of spirit, which prevents you from fulfilling your duties as husband?"

Feeling a bit more sure that Gwendolyn was resigned to their marriage, he couldn't help but grin.

"Oh, nay, nary a one."

She blushed, a rosy hue brushing her high cheekbones, the color deepening when the priest asked if any impediment prevented her from fulfilling her duties as a wife. Her voice wasn't quite as strong when she admitted, "Not that I am aware of."

Relief flooded him. He had her consent, her disavowal of impediments. He saw no joy in her wide brown eyes, and in that moment he silently vowed to bring that about.

"The church's ruling on consanguinity decrees that a husband and wife may not be related within seven degrees. Lord Alberic, have you any such relationship to Lady Gwendolyn?"

"I have not."

"Hold out the ring."

Alberic extended his right hand, over which Father Paul made a sign of the cross, blessing the band of gold Gwendolyn would wear as the physical proof she belonged to him alone.

The priest then grasped Gwendolyn's hand. "In the absence of Lady Gwendolyn's male kin, I give you her hand, entreat you to accord her honor and affection, provide her with shelter and sustenance, and protect her from all harm."

The priest placed Gwendolyn's hand in Alberic's and stepped back, his part in the ceremony finished.

A sense of awe held him in thrall. The feel of her smaller hand resting so trustingly in his made him nervous again. He fumbled slightly with the ring before he slipped it into place, then found he had to clear his throat before speaking.

"With this ring I thee wed," he stated, evoking an odd smile from Gwendolyn that he didn't understand, nor could he take the time to now. He had to get the rest of his speech out before he forgot what he was supposed to say.

"As lady of Camelen you are entitled to income sufficient to maintain your wardrobe, reward your servants, and bequeath to charity. For this I grant you the tolls from the ferry and the profit from the gristmill. As your dower, you are entitled to one-third of any estates I may possess on my death to support your widowhood. Should

I die without heirs, all is yours, given the blessing of King Stephen and Almighty God."

With all requirements met and duly witnessed, Gwendolyn de Leon became his wife. As he turned her to go into the church for Mass, a calm settled in his heart and soul, believing himself the most fortunate of men.

Their hands remained joined, and Gwendolyn took strength from Alberic's warm, firm grip. All through Mass, she could feel the ring he'd slipped on her finger: a wide band of gold set with three sparkling amethysts. 'Twas simple and utterly beautiful, so perfectly in tune with her tastes she might have chosen it for herself.

Apparently, Alberic had done a good deal more shopping in Shrewsbury than she'd first imagined. The hair ribbons, the gloves, and now this ring. He'd been very generous in her marriage endowments, too; her allowance more abundant than she expected or needed.

No gift was expected of the bride for the groom, but she wished she had one for him anyway, because he'd given her another gift she doubted he knew anything about and had touched her deeply.

All through the ceremony he'd seemed so self-assured, so rock-solid. Not through word or action had he expressed a single doubt, a hint of misgivings. Then his voice had trembled slightly as he'd slipped the ring on her finger, and she'd become aware that his insides churned as hard as hers, that he was just better at hiding his turmoil.

With a final blessing the priest turned them loose. Alberic led her out of the church and into the sunshine. The people cheered as they came down the steps, and fell in after them on their way across the village green.

Alberic squeezed her hand, a hand he hadn't relinquished since he'd put the ring on her finger. "You made a beautiful bride, my lady."

"All brides are beautiful."

"You shame them all. None could be more lovely."

Flattery, but said with a sincerity she couldn't deny, and her heart felt lighter—until she spotted little Edward, grief in his eyes but putting on a brave face. She wanted to hug him, but feared doing him a disservice.

Instead, she held tight to Alberic's hand. "I am sorry for your loss, Edward. How does your mother?"

"Well enough. She asked me to thank his lordship for his kindness this morn, and to give you her good wishes on your marriage, milady." His half smile nearly made Gwen weep. "I am glad you did not go off to live in Wales. We would have missed you."

Gwendolyn allowed herself to ruffle the boy's hair. "I believe I would have missed you, too. Are you coming to the hall for the feast?"

"Nay, I had best get back to me mum."

"Then we shall send food out to you. Give your mother my love, and tell her I shall visit her on the morrow."

Edward scampered off.

Gwen took a deep breath to compose herself. "Might I take advantage of your generosity today and ask a boon, my lord?"

"Certes."

"May we forgive Mistress Biggs her merchet?"

He shook his head. "'Twould be bad practice to forgive the death tax. Mistress Biggs must give Father Paul her best blanket and forfeit the cow owed her lord."

"But she has so little already, and without Oscar's pay I do not know how they shall feed themselves."

He tugged on her hand and they began walking again. "You must not take every peasant's troubles to heart, Gwendolyn."

"Would you have them starve?"

"Nay, which is why I proposed to Mistress Biggs that her son might do as a page."

"Edward? A peasant child?"

"'Tis not unheard of. The boy is nimble and bright and would learn his duties right quick, I should think. Have you an objection?"

A page didn't earn the same wage as a soldier, the son yet unable to command a pay equal to the father's. Still, what coin he took home to his mother would be welcome, and Gwendolyn didn't doubt she could occasionally slip an extra loaf of bread or length of fabric into Edward's hands.

Alberic's solution proved more than satisfactory.

"No objection at all, my lord."

✑

At the age of four and ten, along with the rest of her family, Gwendolyn had attended the wedding of her cousin Danielle. She'd observed the marriage rites and rituals and decided upon several things that day.

First, her groom would *not* mutter his vows so softly that even the bride was unsure of what he said. Alberic had already passed that test—in a clear, strong voice, making her rights and grants known to all.

Second, noblewomen could be as bawdy and vulgar as a scullery wench. Old enough to join in the ritual of putting the bride to bed, Gwendolyn had been shocked by her aunt's and cousins' advice to the bride, even though she hadn't understood all of what they'd referred to until years later.

Most important, Gwendolyn had vowed she would not await her groom naked in bed. Some drunken dolt had teasingly tugged at Danielle's coverlet and managed to pull it off the bed, exposing the bride's nakedness for all to see. Gwendolyn had nearly died of embarrassment while others tittered or laughed so hard they cried.

Emma had attended that unsettling bedding ceremony, too, so she understood why Gwendolyn sat on a stool to have her hair brushed with her cloak at hand, ready to cover her chemise when she heard the smallest sound at the lord's bedchamber door.

Her father's bedchamber.

Alberic had not changed much in the room. She'd expected trunks of his possessions and possibly servants to arrive from Chester, but they never had. Nor had Alberic acquired furnishings or ornamentation for the room when shopping in Shrewsbury, only gifts for her.

She again admired her beautiful wedding band, the sturdy gold and sparkling amethysts, the gift she would wear all her days as proof of her wedded state. To Alberic.

"So what happens now?" Nicole asked.

Gwendolyn kept her mouth closed, hoping Emma would answer because Gwen wasn't at all sure.

Emma put down the brush and sat in the other chair, holding her arms out to Nicole, who promptly accepted the invitation to cuddle on her sister's lap.

"The men will come up and make bawdy remarks, which you must neither listen to nor try to comprehend. Then Father Paul will bless the bed and we will all leave, except Alberic and Gwendolyn, of course." Emma pulled Nicole in for a hardy and loving hug. "And then I believe you and I shall retire. We each have a long day of travel tomorrow."

Gwendolyn's throat closed up at the reminder of their leaving.

"May I sleep in Gwendolyn's place tonight?"

"If you promise not to seize more than your share of space."

Nicole readily agreed, and Gwendolyn's resolve not to cry fractured, but didn't wholly split apart. She quickly brushed away the single tear before either sister could notice.

Loud voices in the passageway saved her further agony, tossing her from painful thoughts back to those of confused anticipation. As she stood up to greet the men, she remembered to wrap her cloak around her just in time.

The door burst open and several men entered, all of them grinning and, Gwendolyn suspected, all the worse for the amount of ale and wine they'd consumed during the feast and festivities of the afternoon.

Sedwick and Garrett performed exaggerated bows, comically mocking Madog ap Idwal's overblown obei-

sance. Thomas and Roger aped the older men. Alberic
stood behind them, taking in their antics with good-
natured humor. Father Paul didn't look amused at all.

Then Thomas offered her a goblet of wine. "Fortifica-
tion, my lady." He winked. "His lordship looks forward
to a long, lusty night. Most of us are of the opinion that
a de Leon can not only endure but outlast him."

She raised a surprised eyebrow at the implication.
"You wagered against your lord?"

Roger's smile faded, his expression turning serious.
"Nay, my lady. We merely wagered in your favor."

Careful to keep her cloak mostly closed, she eased a
hand out the front to take the goblet. A contest, then?
One she was expected to win without knowing the rules
or what determined success or failure. And if she learned
enough during the course of the night to fully engage her
sparring partner, on the morrow could she summon the
audacity to announce victory or loss so the men could
settle their wagers?

The squires' confidence bolstered her resolve to give
good account of herself, win or lose. She took a heathy
swig of the robust red wine, then tilted the goblet toward
Thomas. The teasing and yet proud twinkle in his eyes
brought on a wry smile.

"I shall endeavor to ensure your faith in my meager
talents not misplaced."

Accompanying the men's laughter, the squires now
honored her with a truly respectful bow before stepping
aside. Her bravery floundered at the sight of Alberic's
wicked smile, as if he knew of an unfailing method to
ensure her defeat. He probably did, and the prospect
forced the goblet to her lips once more.

"Shall we?" Father Paul asked, his tolerance for the men's mischief clearly strained.

"Do proceed, Father," Alberic said. "Bless the bed well, but quickly. I want you all out of here within a trice."

Gwendolyn swallowed hard, barely hearing the priest's invocations for God's grace and mercy for the couple about to share the mattress and blankets . . . and their lives. And within Alberic's trice, the room cleared of all but her and the man who was now her husband.

He slid the bolt to ensure their privacy, and the ensuing silence held both frightening and promising possibilities. She took another gulp of wine when Alberic came toward her, the wicked gleam yet shining in his eyes, his unmistakable intent clear for any dolt to perceive. She clutched at the cloak more tightly.

He took the goblet and set it on the table. "Going somewhere, my lady?"

His voice was rough, not as teasing as before. Did he truly fear she might try to escape him again, leave him alone in the marriage bed? She'd given him her vow, and intended to honor it.

"Nay, my lord. I go nowhere tonight."

He tugged at the cloak's ties. "Then you have no need for this now."

None at all. Not for modesty's sake, for already her body yearned for his touch. Not for warmth, for effusive heat bloomed on her cheeks and raced down to her curled toes. Slowly, gently he unwrapped her, and without forethought or hesitation she released the fabric she'd clutched in her fist.

Alberic's mouth went dry. He'd seen Gwendolyn in

this state of undress before, had enjoyed the sight of her generous breasts and rounded hips beneath the sheer veiling of her chemise. While he'd routed temptation that night, now he could look and touch his fill.

Her long hair hung forward over creamy shoulders to flow between her breasts, which rose when she took a steadying breath. He licked his lips in anticipation of taking the hardening tips into his mouth and suckling as long as he pleased.

He tossed the cloak toward the table, not caring about his accuracy. Despite her bold answer to Thomas's teasing, and no matter how much she'd been told about coupling by female kin or gleaned from scullery maids, her inexperience must be taken into account.

Vowing to gradually accustom her to his touch, he ran a finger along her collarbone. To his delight she shivered, though he doubted her chilled.

"Did you enjoy the celebration?" he asked, working his way across her shoulder.

"Aye. We need to improve your dancing."

And here he'd been proud that he'd smashed no one's toes. "I admit to little practice. Perhaps you can teach me."

She tilted her head, her eyes narrowing slightly. "Now?"

"Later. Much later."

"Good."

So much relief expressed in one word.

Tentatively, as though testing boundaries, she placed her hand on his chest. Warmth seeped through the silk tunic he wished he'd discarded sooner.

She smiled. "Your heart beats hard. Perhaps you should lie down."

Wonderful suggestion. "Perhaps we both should."

"In a moment. I believe I will finish my wine first." She backed away, snatched up the goblet, and sat down in the chair. "Thomas's offering should not go to waste."

What was this? He'd sensed no fear or even hesitancy on her part. Indeed, a moment ago he would have sworn Gwendolyn's desire for the coupling rose at a pace with his now aching arousal. But then, she'd not been awaiting him already abed, as was usual for a bride. Perhaps she needed more coaxing, more assurance.

Patience. His randy prick objected to the caution, but this was Gwendolyn's first experience with coupling, and getting it done right must rule over getting it done according to his body's wishes.

All well and good, except the lady didn't appear as if she needed coaxing. The sparkle in her doe-brown eyes suggested she'd backed away from him for another reason entirely. She made no attempt to hide any part of her lovely form from his view. She lounged in the chair, the goblet dangling from her fingers, her gaze open and focused on . . . oh, heavenly day.

Several nights ago she'd covered her eyes to avoid viewing his nakedness. Tonight she wanted a good look.

Quite willing to oblige her curiosity, Alberic unbuckled his belt. "I gather you have lost your sense of modesty."

"Not entirely," she admitted, though her tone of voice didn't reveal the extent.

His tunic joined the belt somewhere on the floor. "Ever seen a man's private parts?"

"Certes," she asserted, then acknowledged, "Well, not a man's, but a boy's. I imagine a man's is . . . larger."

Alberic stifled a smile and sat on the other chair to toe off his boots. "You were not tempted to peek through your fingers the other night?"

"Nay!"

He knew she was lying. "No curiosity at all? How very virtuous of you, my lady."

"Now you mock me."

He stood up to shove down his final piece of clothing, and her already wide brown eyes grew huge as she beheld his boffing-ready prick. "I only call you on your . . . untruth. You suffered temptation. Even then you wanted to know, but since you did not plan to wed with me, you averted your eyes. Now we are husband and wife, and you have as much right to my sword as I to your sheath. What say, Gwendolyn? Shall we make ours a match in truth?"

Gwendolyn looked up, slowly, allowing herself the pleasure of fully appreciating Alberic's finely sculpted body, from the hard rod between his thickly muscled thighs, up over his taut stomach, and wide, magnificent chest.

Sweet mercy. This incredibly built male was all hers. His impressive sword to her now wet and burning sheath. All she had to do was lift her skirts, and he would ease her deepest aches.

She put the goblet on the floor and grabbed hold of the chemise's hem, raising it to uncover her ankles, and calves, then knees and—

"Halt. Stop there." His demand came in a deeper than normal voice, his gaze transfixed on her mostly bared thighs. "I have thought of your unveiling often, and always I did the honor of uncovering you. Selfish bastard that I am, I would have it be my hand that reveals you to my sight."

He didn't wait for an answer, but knelt before her and ran his long-fingered, warm hands along the whole length of her inner thighs. Surely he could hear her heart thud against her ribs as he pushed the fabric upward and bared her lower body fully.

She nearly came up off the chair when he brushed the hair there with his thumbs. She grasped his shoulders to steady herself, wishing he'd do it again.

"You glisten already," he said with awe, then as if he'd heard her silent wish, repeated the caress.

She hissed his name. How he managed to pick her up, strip off her chemise, and carry her to the bed she would never be able to say, for from that moment forward the sensations waxed and waned, often too stunningly for coherent thought.

Just when she was sure his kisses were the most magnificent part of coupling, he shifted his attention downward to nuzzle the breasts he'd stroked and fondled until swollen, the tips hard and erect. Then his mouth suckled at her breasts while his hands moved lower yet, to pet her inner thighs.

With one finger he seized total command. Firmly yet gently he slid through the wetness from the sensitive nub at the apex to the weeping, wanting pathway to her womb. With each caress she breathed more raggedly, and when his finger glided into her she forgot to breathe at all.

Alberic gave up trying to slow down. Gwendolyn responded so rapidly and heatedly to the lightest touch that she put his every other experience with a woman to

shame. He'd wanted to make love to her for hours. Enjoy
the feel of her silken skin. Allow his hands to memorize
the shape of each full, womanly curve.

But he'd barely begun his seduction when he realized
she'd gone from willing and ready to the sharp edge of
release within a flash.

He withdrew his hand, wet with her woman's dew.
She groaned in frustration. Only a cad would leave her
near the peak without taking her over the edge. Nor
could he ignore the plea in her eyes for release.

She wanted him inside her, desperately, and the real-
ization that he would be her first lover proved both humbling and exciting.

He moved over her, watching her eyes for any hint of
fear. All he saw was passion and need. When he entered
her, a heated velvet glove closed around him, and
squeezed.

The sensation was pure bliss.

He pierced the virginal barrier he'd never doubted he
would find. She rose up and hissed. Within moments she
eased back down, her muscles still taut but not tense. She
squeezed again, the intimate embrace encouraging him
to resume. Hoping her pain fully subsided, he tested with
a slow stroke, then another.

Gwendolyn's hips rose again, but this time seeking a
deeper, faster thrust.

Alberic obliged, and the control he'd been so sure he
could maintain slipped with each lunge into her depths.
He began to sweat, and to worry that he might not last the
distance. Never before had he suffered concern over his
prowess, but never before had the lady's satisfaction
been so vital.

Each thrust and withdrawal brought him closer to the end of his endurance. Each of Gwendolyn's throaty moans, the quickening of her breaths, assured him that she, too, neared completion. Just as he lost his grip on reason, she cried out and released him from his fears.

The pulse of her bliss sent him reeling. Her shudders inflamed his passion to beyond mastery. With a last, deep thrust he gave himself up to his body's screaming need.

Gwendolyn had, without a doubt, ruined him for all others. But then, he didn't need others anymore; Gwendolyn was his wife. His alone.

He kissed her face, her neck, and nibbled on her ear as their breathing returned to normal. Then he gloried in the oh-so-fulfilled smile she gave him when she finally opened her eyes.

"Sweet mercy, Alberic. I had no notion . . ."

"Ah, but we are not finished yet."

"There is more?"

"Much more. I shall be away for two days, perhaps three, while Roger and I retrieve our horses. I want you to think of me while I am gone."

"You think my memory so poor?"

"Nay, I wish to ensure your memory of our coupling so satisfactory that you will welcome me back into our bed when I return."

And so he did, this time more slowly but with the same exquisite results.

Afterward, Alberic slept soundly, nearly missing the dawn. He hated leaving, would much prefer to linger in the warm bed and arouse his beautiful, enticing wife to make love once more.

Her day wouldn't be an easy one. Her sisters were

leaving this morning. In the afternoon she would attend the burials of the two soldiers lost to ap Idwal's attack. He wished he could be there for her, but the duty demanded of his lordship didn't allow him the luxury.

Roger awaited him. The need to retaliate against ap Idwal beckoned him out of the bedchamber and onto a horse. As the sun breached the horizon, Alberic and his squire rode toward Wales.

Chapter Eleven

GWENDOLYN WOKE TO SILENCE, an oddity that snapped her eyes open to see what was amiss with her sisters.

Within a heartbeat she realized she was alone in a bed she'd never slept in before, in a bedchamber she'd never dreamed to occupy.

Memories of the night bore down on her conscience, her aching muscles serving as penance for reveling in Alberic's carnal possession. Surely what they'd done was sinful, for nothing holy or sacred could possibly prove so delightful. No wonder the scullery wenches sought out whatever hard rods they could find.

Gwendolyn giggled at the wanton, wholly wicked thought. While she tried to admonish her waywardness, she grinned as she reached out to touch the bolster indented from Alberic's head.

He'd untangled their limbs somewhere near dawn and quietly slipped out of bed. He'd dressed in the dark and left without a word to meet Roger. Gwendolyn wasn't sure if she should be angry at him for not trying to wake her to bid her adieu, or pleased that, believing she slept, he'd considerately left her undisturbed.

Why she hadn't opened her eyes to reveal that she'd woken she didn't know, and refused to contemplate.

She snuggled deeper into the mattress, knowing the rest of the day wasn't going to be pleasant. There were funerals to attend, and Emma and Nicole . . . Panicked, Gwendolyn threw off the coverlet and frantically searched the floor for her garments. She tossed on her chemise, grabbed her soft shoes and surcoat, and raced to her sisters' bedchamber.

Her sisters' empty bedchamber. Nicole's pallet no longer lay on the floor at the end of the bed. The bed's coverlet lay smooth, the bolsters neatly arranged. Emma's trunk was missing.

Dread coiled in Gwendolyn's stomach, praying her sisters were breaking their fast. The thought that she might have missed their departure was simply too horrific to contemplate.

She tossed open the lid of her clothing trunk and grabbed the brown workaday gown on top. She forswore a veil and circlet, didn't even brush her hair in her haste. With her wedding surcoat in hand, she raced down the passageway and stairs to the hall.

Not there. Sweet mercy, if they'd already left she'd never forgive herself—and strangle Emma for not waking her to say fare-thee-well.

Heart in throat, she dashed into the bailey and, to her great relief, saw her sisters standing near a cart.

Emma's trunk hadn't yet been loaded. Nearby stood Nicole's pony, a satchel containing a few of her belongings tied behind the saddle. Nicole wouldn't need or even be allowed many personal possessions at the abbey, while Emma probably could use more than she had packed.

Gwendolyn shoved the surcoat into Emma's arms. "Why did you not wake me?"

Emma smiled at the harsh question. "Had you not come down, we would have come up. Are you sure you wish to part with this?"

Gwendolyn's bluster faded. "'Tis only a surcoat, and the color flatters you more than me."

Without further protest, Emma refolded the surcoat and placed it in the trunk before signaling the servants to load it into the cart. Gwendolyn watched the men heave the trunk onto the bed and tie it down securely with ropes.

The finality of her sisters' leaving hit Gwendolyn hard in the heart.

"I hate this," she spat out.

Emma's hands landed on Gwendolyn's shoulders. "None of us are happy, but your duty is to care for yourself and Camelen. All else will sort out, in time. We will be fine."

Nicole snorted. "So you say, but you need not suffer a cloister."

"'Suffer' is a harsh word," Emma admonished. "And you know I shall do what I can to procure your release."

Nicole kicked at the dirt. "I shall hate it, I know it. This is all Alberic's fault. If not for him—"

"Stop it, Nicole." Surprised by her swift defense of Alberic, Gwendolyn reined in her ire. Nicole was angry and frightened, needful of hugs and reassurance. She pulled the girl into a fierce embrace.

"No one can change the king's order except the king, and you know Emma shall do all she can to change his mind. Try to consider this an adventure. I dare say you might learn something at the abbey."

"I already know how to pray."

"Aye, well, we could all use your prayers." Gwendolyn tilted Nicole's chin upward. "Sedwick will explain your situation to the abbess, so she will know you are not called to a religious life, though I dare say the abbess would learn that on her own soon enough. So you might use your time there to improve upon your education. Perhaps read whatever is available in the library, or spend time in the infirmary and learn herb lore. Perhaps you can bring back ideas upon how to improve Camelen's garden."

Nicole sighed. "So Father Paul advised."

"Then you must listen and act upon such good counsel. You must write to me as soon as you are able. I wish to hear about all of the interesting things you find there."

Seeing Sedwick coming toward her, his sad smile a portent of his readiness to leave, Gwendolyn gave Nicole another fierce hug before releasing her to Emma's arms. In too short a time Nicole sat upon her pony, tears flowing down her cheeks. Sedwick took firm hold of the bridle and led the pony and an escort of four soldiers across the bailey.

"Dear God, Emma, she is a mere babe!"

"More a strong-willed minx," Emma retorted with choked affection.

By the time the company reached the gatehouse, Gwendolyn's throat had closed up so tightly she could barely breathe, and to make all worse, Garrett stood by the cart awaiting Emma.

The parting with Nicole was heart-wrenching. But Emma's leaving fair broke Gwendolyn's heart into tiny shards.

"You will write, too," Gwendolyn ordered in the midst of a parting embrace.

"Certes." Emma pulled back and narrowed her eyes. "*Tsk.* Look at you. I swear, Gwendolyn, you appear the utter hoyden. Go up and repair the damage before the people forget you are now the lady of Camelen."

Emma only half teased, and Gwendolyn managed a small smile at her sister's attempt to lighten the parting.

"Have a care who you order about at court. I should hate to have them toss you out too soon."

Emma laughed lightly before she climbed up into the cart and took the seat beside Garrett. Eight soldiers, split evenly between leading and following, provided escort.

Gwendolyn knew if she went up onto the battlements to watch both sisters until they were out of sight, she'd sob and wail and draw pity, so she returned to the hall.

Servants went about their chores as on other days. Gwendolyn took her chair at the high table to break her fast, as she had for many mornings, except today Alberic didn't sit beside her to provide distraction. Her sisters were no longer here to talk to. The bread turned dry in her mouth and the cheese clumped in her stomach.

Thomas stood not far off, likely ordered by Alberic to watch over her to ensure she didn't do something rash, like run off with one of her sisters. The mannerly tilt of his head in her direction reminded her of his offering of a goblet of wine last eve, and of the wager she had no notion of who had won.

Sweet mercy, both she and Alberic had endured for many hours, through two couplings; the first fast and hard, the second a slow, gratifying enjoyment of sight and taste and sound.

Surely the priest would admonish them both for enjoying each other so thoroughly, but Gwendolyn couldn't bring herself to care and hoped Alberic wouldn't mind enjoying her again when he returned.

'Twas hard to say how long he would be gone. Two or three days, he'd said. So she had best find something to do to pass the time or go witless.

Repair the damage, Emma had ordered, and so she would, not because of Emma's prodding but because as lady of Camelen she had duties to perform after nooning. Two soldiers would be put to their eternal rest, and 'twas Gwendolyn's duty to attend the burials.

The only bright spot she could see in the day was bringing Edward into the keep to be fitted for his livery and introduced to the other pages.

Surely that would take her mind off both her sisters' departures and Alberic's lovemaking.

If pride was truly a sin, then Alberic needed to confess the elation pulsing through his veins. Within site of Camelen, Alberic urged the two horses he led to a faster pace, noting Roger did the same with his charges.

While retrieving four out of five of Camelen's horses right from beneath Madog ap Idwal's nose certainly justified pride, 'twas the sight of Gwendolyn on the battlements that caused his heart to swell.

Garbed as on the day he'd first met her, a helm on her head and chain mail draped over her body, Gwendolyn had not only stayed at Camelen but now watched for him.

He'd done right to ensure her memories of their wedding night not only pleasurable but firmly fixed. He could hardly wait for a celebration of his successful venture into Wales and victorious homecoming.

Home. Ye gods. In the space of a fortnight the castle had become a home. And not only was it nice to have a home to return to, but a wife to greet him upon his arrival.

But still, the closer he drew to the gate, the harder Alberic watched the drawbridge for signs that not all was well.

He had reason not to trust Gwendolyn. The ecstasy of their wedding night aside, Gwendolyn might not be awaiting him as an eager bride. Too easily he could envision her ordering the gates shut against him.

He'd taken her father's place as lord of Camelen, and knew she blamed him for her brother's death. He'd forced her into a marriage she opposed then sent away her beloved sisters. Gwendolyn had reason aplenty to raise the drawbridge.

He held his breath until his horse's hooves hit the wooden planks. As he entered the bailey elation again claimed him when he saw Gwendolyn waiting for him at the bottom of the gatehouse stairs, her chain mail in place, her helm gone. She gave the horses a quick but assessing inspection.

"Only four?" she asked, sending his high spirits plummeting.

Alberic dismounted and handed over his recovered booty to the waiting stable lads.

"We never saw the fifth. When the opportunity arose, we took what we could and still escape."

"Ah."

So much for a joyous homecoming! He supposed he should be thankful she hadn't ordered the drawbridge raised, be glad she hadn't left Camelen in his absence.

Damn. He'd thought they'd reached an accord on their wedding night. Apparently not. Well, there was always tonight to try again. But first he needed food and drink, and a thorough washing. He smelled of his own sweat and horse droppings—odors not suited to the marriage bed.

Confident Roger and the stable lads would take excellent care of the horses, he led Gwendolyn into the hall, which seemed inordinately quiet.

No royal soldiers. No Sedwick or Garrett. No Emma or Nicole. They'd all left Camelen yesterday.

He'd known Gwendolyn would have to deal with her sisters' departure and the soldiers' burials on her own. Perhaps that explained her somber mood, her lack of appreciation for his success.

"Sit with me while I eat?"

Gwendolyn nodded and called out to the nearest page to fetch food from the kitchen, and sent another to the cellar for a flagon of wine.

Settled into his chair, he rested his head against the tall back, closed his eyes, and allowed himself a deep, calming breath.

"You seem all done in, my lord. I had thought you would immediately begin telling the tale of your adventure."

She made it sound as if he'd left because he'd wanted to and enjoyed himself all the while. The small act of retaliation against ap Idwal had demanded swift action.

To delay would have lessened his chance for success. Surely she understood he'd had no choice.

Or perhaps not. Maybe the strain and grief of the past weeks had simply caught up with her and burdened her heart.

"Later. First you must tell me how you fare. My apologies for leaving you to face all the sadness alone."

She pursed her lips hard, in her struggle to hold back tears. "Emma and Nicole departed without mishap. Both have promised to write as soon as they might."

Alberic didn't worry about Emma; she relished her chance at court. However, Nicole felt differently about the abbey.

"Did Nicole go quietly?"

"As quietly as is possible for Nicole."

My thanks, Nicole. Had the girl tossed a fit, Gwendolyn would be utterly distraught over their parting.

"The burials went as planned?"

"With nary a misstep, may God have mercy on their souls. Mistress Biggs is most distressed, naturally, but she does not give in to despair, partly for Edward's sake, I imagine."

"And Edward?"

Finally she gave him a small smile. "He is right fond of his livery, says it makes him look like new."

Alberic knew the feeling. New, fine garb would make the boy feel like a bright, shiny coin. He just hoped Edward's experience as a page at Camelen proved to be a better one than his own at Chester.

"You have him outfitted already?"

"Aye. He is utterly adorable."

Spoken like a woman prideful of her charge.

"Any trouble with the other pages?"

"I think not. Thomas gave them all a talking-to, so I expect no trouble."

Alberic knew better than to let it go at that. Boys could be mean to the newest among them, particularly to a boy who ranked beneath them. He would have to caution Thomas and Roger, whose new duties as squires included the supervision of the pages, to watch for signs of undue teasing or outright torture of the new page.

"Edward is in the keep?"

Gwendolyn glanced around. "He is . . . ah, there."

Two pages came toward the dais. One boy he recognized, the other he wouldn't have if Gwendolyn hadn't pointed him out. Bathed, his legs encased in tight hose and feet stuffed into unfamiliar leather shoes, Edward held his head high and spine straight, so obviously bursting with pride his chest strained his thigh-length tunic.

He carried two gold goblets as though they were made of precious, breakable glass, too new at his position to be entrusted with a flagon of wine.

In step with the other boy, Edward mounted the dais, and Alberic could hear whispered instructions from behind him. Soon a small hand set the goblet on the table at Alberic's right, and then at Gwendolyn's, without mishap. A slightly larger hand poured the wine and set the flagon down a bit forward and to the right of Gwendolyn's goblet.

She smiled fondly at both pages. "Well done, Edward. My thanks, Roland. You may step down."

Footsteps in unison, the boys walked to the end of the dais and stepped down, but not too far away. There they would wait until called upon to clear away the goblets and flagon.

Gwendolyn leaned forward. "Did I not tell you he is adorable?"

Sure that Edward wouldn't appreciate being called adorable, Alberic reached for his wine.

"As you say," he told her, and along with a swig of wine he caught a whiff of his sleeve. "I need a bath."

With mere hand signals Gwendolyn sent the pages scurrying to fulfill the request. Ah yes, he liked having a comfortable home and a wife who knew how to manage it and its servants.

"Did you have trouble retrieving the horses?" she asked.

"A bit." A vague answer would do for now. Likely she would hear the whole tale later, but he'd rather that be later. Her mood brightened apace with their conversation. Best he keep her talking. "Ap Idwal's holding is easily entered, and our horses stood out like giants among their ponies. We left him the saddles in our need for haste and in thanks for leaving the bridles and halters on the horses."

"A fortunate happenstance."

True, except it irritated Alberic that he and Roger had been discovered too soon to fetch the saddles.

"This is not the end of it, Gwendolyn. The man has yet to pay for the lives of two men."

"You intend to retaliate?"

"I must, or be considered soft, an easy mark." He smiled at her concerned frown. "But not tonight. Now that I have seen ap Idwal's holding, I can make plans for when Sedwick and Garrett return. Our garrison is too depleted for the nonce to take action."

She nodded her comprehension, but still frowned, which was understandable. He'd been a baron for all of two weeks, and here he was planning to lead a second raid on a Welsh landowner. On Gwendolyn's former betrothed, no less.

The king might not approve of the action, either, but by the time he received a report, 'twould be done and all peaceful again. 'Twas ironic that the earl of Chester would approve wholeheartedly.

'Struth, Chester merely waited for the right time to suggest to King Stephen that he join his royal forces with those of the Marches' earls in a united effort against Wales.

Such a war would cause mixed feelings at Camelen, with its mix of English and Welsh citizenry. Fortunately, as far as Alberic knew, the king was yet camped outside of Wallingford and entertaining no such notions.

As for a bit of retaliation against ap Idwal, Alberic felt sure the garrison would follow him willingly against the man who'd killed two of their own. As soon as Sedwick, Garrett, and the escorts returned, they'd make plans.

Right now all he wanted was his bath and, he thought wryly, for the lady of the keep to assist him. Already he could feel her soap-slicked hands wandering all over him.

"Think you my bathwater ready?"

"Not as yet. You have time to eat first."

"Time, aye, but the thought does not appeal. Whenever I lift my arm I catch the stench of horses. I should rather wait to eat until all I can smell is roasted meat and fresh-baked bread." He leaned toward her, envisioning his soap-slicked hands wandering all over her. "The tub is big enough for both of us, I think."

She blushed furiously. "Surely we would make a mess."

"Very likely."

She bit her bottom lip, her eyes lit with curiosity, giving the prospect of a shared bath serious thought.

He decided to help her decide. "I have other pleasures to show you."

She raised an eyebrow. "In the middle of the afternoon?"

"We shall toss open the shutters and allow in lots of light. We shall be able to see each other fully as well as touch and taste."

"The sun may shine, but the wind is chilled."

"I give you my oath I will keep you warm."

"The servants will gossip."

"Let them. 'Struth, Gwendolyn, we are newly wed. They expect us to be about the business of giving Camelen an heir, and will be proud of you for doing your wifely duty."

She seemed to have run out of objections, but hadn't yet come to a decision when the creak of the hall's door drew her gaze. He glanced that way, too, and smiled.

A parade of six youngsters—four pages and two scullery maids, each carrying a water-filled bucket—crossed the floor to the stairs. Behind them a little girl scampered to keep up, her arms loaded with towels. As the water bearers began to climb the stairs, he turned back to Gwendolyn.

"Our bath awaits."

She shook her head. "*Your* bath. We will not both fit in the tub. Come, before the water cools."

They followed a trail of water up the stairs and into the bedchamber. The two tallest pages had pulled the wooden tub out of its storage space and set it near the hearth by the time Alberic entered the room.

One by one the children poured the water, four buckets of hot and one of cold, into the tub. Gwendolyn then swished a hand through the water and pronounced the temperature acceptable. The children bowed out, leaving one bucket of hot water sitting off to the side. The littlest girl handed Gwendolyn the stack of towels, her blond curls bobbing while executing the cutest curtsy he'd ever seen.

He waited until all had departed before he allowed himself to grin. Closing the door, he announced, "Heaven help me, I want one of those. Preferably one with a pert nose and your color hair."

Gwendolyn clasped the towels to her chain-mail covered chest. "I thought all men wanted a son first."

He snapped open the metal latch on her shoulder, eager to get her out of her armor so she could divest him of his. "First, second, third, fourth . . . makes no matter to me."

Her widening smile turned him fumble-fingered. "You seem rather sure of your prowess. The siring of so many children may prove . . . an ordeal."

The latches open, he snatched the towels away and tossed them on the floor. "To be sure. But I shall endure and persevere. Raise your arms, my lady, and prepare to be ravished."

Light laughter accompanied the rattle of the metal links coming off over her head. "I thought you wanted a bath first."

"Get me out of this armor and then we will decide."

Gwendolyn had no more than opened the shoulder latches on his mail shirt when someone pounded on the door.

He cursed. Who would dare?

Gwendolyn put her hands on her hips and sighed.

Alberic threw open the door, prepared to strangle whoever was on the other side.

A guard stood at the threshold, his face pale as new flour, his eyes wide in terror.

"Beg pardon, my lord, but you had best come to the battlements. 'Twould seem we are under siege!"

Chapter Twelve

ALBERIC DIDN'T HAVE TO ASK who dared to lay siege to Camelen. He knew.

He and Roger had escaped ap Idwal's holding by a gnat's breath, arrows whizzing by their heads. The Welshman must have gathered his men immediately and marched them across the border at a punishing pace to have arrived so soon.

"Is the drawbridge up?"

"Aye, milord. We raised it when we saw a large force comin' at us."

"How many men?"

"Fifty or so."

"I want every man who can pull a bow up on the battlements. Lances in the hands of those who cannot. Ap Idwal must not guess that our garrison is at less than full strength."

The guard bobbed his head before racing down the passageway.

He lifted Gwendolyn's hand to his mouth and lightly kissed the back. "I fear we heated water too soon. Our bath shall have to wait."

"Go do what you must with the garrison," she said. "I shall ready the keep."

Her calm bolstered his confidence, until he wondered if she placed her faith in him, or in the solid thickness of Camelen's outer wall. Either way, if Gwendolyn showed no sign of panic, 'twould reassure the castle folk.

He hurried down the stairs, Gwendolyn following. At the bottom he nearly ran over Edward. The boy's eyes were wide and fearful.

"Me mum is out there alone," he said in a trembling voice. "You must let me go out to her."

Alberic understood the boy's need to protect his mother. Just as he'd once done all he knew how to keep his mother alive, so Edward wished to shield his mother from harm. 'Twasn't easy to deny the request.

"The drawbridge remains up and the postern gate bolted until I can fully assess our enemy's intent. No one goes in or out of the castle until the danger has passed."

Tears welled in Edward's eyes. Gwendolyn stepped forward and put her hand on the boy's shoulder.

"Edward, your mother does not lack wits. She was a soldier's wife and knows what she must do in times of danger. 'Struth, she would never forgive his lordship if he allowed you to leave the keep, where she knows you are safe. Your duty right now is to clear away the goblets from the high table, and allow his lordship to do his duty."

"Which is to keep us all safe," Alberic added, not exactly sure how he was going to do that as yet. Always he'd been on the other side of a siege, waiting outside the castle walls for those in command to order an attack, never on the inside wondering what the enemy would do next.

The bailey churned with activity as guards in battle array hastened to line the wall, and Alberic had to admire their adherence to duty and obvious good training, neither of which he could take credit for inspiring or causing. For both he had Hugh de Leon to thank.

Disgruntled, he crossed the bailey and climbed the gatehouse stairway, trying to ignore the little voice that chided him for his lack of knowledge. Up till now he'd learned a lord's duties by watching, and reading, and observing. For this calamity he had no time to learn at his leisure. Lives and property were at risk. He would have to rely on his instincts and pray that they were good enough.

Alberic looked out over the countryside and calmed some. The guard had reported a force of fifty, and that appeared correct. Too small of a force for a direct assault on Camelen's defenses, even with its depleted garrison, but too large a force for Alberic to consider a foray into the field.

Ap Idwal's small army consisted mostly of roughly garbed pikemen. A few bows peeked over shoulders. A handful of ponies were ridden by those Alberic assumed to be the invaders' leaders, including ap Idwal.

'Twas both outrageous and embarrassing that such a motley group could force him into a defensive stance. Surely they couldn't take the castle, but they could do a great deal of damage. Already they trod across newly planted oats.

And having been on the opposite side in a siege, Alberic was well aware of the havoc an enemy could wreak upon the villages and their inhabitants.

Ap Idwal signaled his men to halt just beyond arrow range. Soon ap Idwal, or someone chosen as his emissary, would make his way toward the castle to state what demands must be met in order to avoid a siege, and bloodshed, and loss of property.

Alberic knew damned well what ap Idwal wanted. Gwendolyn.

Never.

He'd send ap Idwal to his Maker before giving in to so ridiculous and offensive a demand.

As if his thoughts had called her, Gwendolyn appeared at the top of the stairway. She'd not put back on her chain mail. He thought to protest when she waved aside the offer of a helm from one of the guards, but decided the danger too slight to insist.

She joined him, leaning against the cold stone to look down and, likely, make her own assessment of the situation.

"Edward?" he asked.

"I put him to work filling buckets of water to spread out through the bailey in case Madog decides to send fire arrows our way."

"Not with you inside, he will not."

"Perhaps, but 'tis a usual precaution and all will feel better if the buckets are at hand. The heavy rains of the Easter season filled the well nicely, so we need not worry over water for some time. Cook is busy deciding on how best to use our provisions. The baker will keep the ovens in use for an added hour each day. We are low on game, but are well stocked with cheese. The seamstresses are tearing old linens into strips for bandaging wounds."

Her report and seeming unconcern about the prospect of a prolonged siege prompted him to ask, "Camelen has suffered through a siege before?"

"'Twas many years ago, but I remember the orders Father gave Emma and me to prepare."

For which he should be grateful, though it irked him that she knew how to prepare better than he did.

"Did the siege last long?"

"A fortnight. 'Twas long enough for me."

Alberic hoped he could bring this foolishness to an end within a few days, much less two weeks.

"Edgar comes," Gwendolyn announced.

Alberic watched the man who might have tried to put an arrow through his head approach the keep.

"I had hoped ap Idwal would make his own demands."

Gwendolyn's smile was wry. "I imagine he fears you might take advantage if he came within arrow range."

"'Twould be a temptation, I admit. But such dishonor I would not bring upon myself."

"Even though what he hopes to achieve would shame me?"

Alberic smiled. "Ap Idwal covets what is mine, and just as he was not allowed to keep my horses, he will find he cannot take my wife. I would defend this keep to the last man and down to the last stone to keep you."

She shot him a tight-lipped, sideways glance, wiping away his smile. Hadn't he just told the woman he would defend her to the death? Shouldn't such a compliment be taken with more grace?

Women. Who could understand their minds? Their bodies, aye. But their thoughts? 'Twas certainly beyond him.

"Hail on the battlements!"

Alberic pushed his confusion aside to deal with whom most assumed to be the rogue archer.

"Your new lord makes mud of my oat field, Edgar. He had best have good reason!"

The man looked a bit taken aback at the use of his name, but pulled his attention back to business quickly.

"Madog ap Idwal demands the release of the Lady Gwendolyn into his care."

"You may tell him that his demand comes too late. The ceremony has been performed, and the marriage duly celebrated and consummated to the satisfaction of all."

"Alberic," Gwendolyn whispered harshly.

"Well, it has. Did I state an untruth?"

"You add fuel to the fire!"

"Let him burn."

Edgar continued. "Ap Idwal contends that since the Lady Gwendolyn was forced into marriage, a case can be made for an annulment." The man had the audacity to smile. "Too, there is always the possibility she might become a widow at any moment."

Annulment? Highly unlikely. Widowhood? He would have be careful. Dismissing both, he called back, "Pray give ap Idwal our regards and wish him a safe and speedy journey back to Wales."

"There is also a matter of compensation for the horses you stole from the ap Idwal holding."

Alberic could hardly believe his hearing. "He expects me to pay for horses that are mine?"

"Your men trespassed on ap Idwal lands. The horses were taken as punishment for the offense."

His temper flared hot. "He also took the lives of two decent men who meant him no harm. Men with whom you once shared meals and duties. Tell me, Edgar, were their deaths worth your freedom?"

After a moment's hesitation, Edgar continued. "You have until dawn to satisfy the demands."

"The demand for Lady Gwendolyn's release is insufferable. The lady is now married, and ap Idwal dishonors her by asking her to disregard her vows. As for the horses, I am willing to negotiate. Tell ap Idwal I will trade two of them for one Edgar the archer, which is far more than you are worth."

∽

"Last of the hot water, milady." One of the serving wenches Gwendolyn had pressed into service poured a bucket of hot water into the tub. "Will you be needin' aught else?"

"Nay, this should do."

With a quick bob, the young woman left Gwendolyn alone in the bedchamber, contemplating whether or not to take off her clothing and avail herself of the steaming water before Alberic arrived.

He'd said he would be up straightaway, after he gave Thomas and Robert instructions on what to watch for in ap Idwal's camp that might signal a dishonorable move. Alberic obviously didn't trust ap Idwal not to move against Camelen before dawn, the limit set on Alberic's final decision.

Wise of him.

She doubted he'd been wise to taunt Madog with their satisfactorily consummated marriage, but also didn't think anything Alberic might have said—except agreeing to the ludicrous demands—would have persuaded Madog to quit the field.

This wasn't how she'd envisioned Alberic's home-coming. After two days of heart-wrenching sadness and nigh unbearable loneliness, she'd hoped for a bit of peace and a chance to get to know better the man the ring clung to so tenaciously, thus deciding the course of her life.

Not that she'd planned to bathe with him, and was rather shocked at how much the idea appealed.

Gwendolyn looked over the array of supplies on the table. Towels, French-milled soap, a small vial of scented oil. She'd dug clean garments out of his trunk and placed them on the bed.

Everything was ready. All she lacked was the man who'd ordered the bath, and the courage to close the door and slide into the tub to await him.

She'd faced the prospect of a siege with less trepidation. But sieges she knew about. How Alberic might view such a brazen action, she couldn't guess. Still, the water tempted, and the thought of the two of them naked and slick in the small tub enticed her even more.

His voice coming from the stairway brought her back to her senses. His appearance in the doorway ended her silly fantasy. Alberic's big body would barely fit into the tub all by itself, so she'd been wise to resist temptation.

He closed the door, and temptation took a different form when he immediately drew his tunic over his head to reveal the sprinkling of chest hair she remembered so well from their wedding night.

Desperate for a distraction, she turned toward the tub and again tested the wonderfully hot water, and searched for a safer subject than her disappointment in the tub's size.

"You spoke to Thomas and Roger?"

She heard the ropes holding the mattress groan beneath his weight.

"They are assigning every grown male in the castle to take a turn on the battlements. Many will not have a notion of what to do with a weapon, but right now the appearance of a fully armed garrison is more important than the reality."

She heard his boots hit the floor; one, then the other. She fussed with a towel.

"Do you believe Madog will attack before dawn?"

"'Twould not surprise me. He knows damn well I am not about to give in to his demands."

"Then you had best hurry and wash before you are needed."

He sighed, the sound telling her he'd padded silently over to the tub. "Aye, I suppose . . . Saint Stephen's bones, that is hot!"

His protest turned her around to view a truly admirable rump, which she promptly ignored the moment she saw his right side.

"Ye gods, Alberic. What did you do?"

"I stuck my hand in the water to test the heat and—"

"You have a large, ugly bruise on your side and back!"

He raised his elbow to glance beneath it at his side. "Oh, that. I fell. 'Tis nothing."

An absurdly male denial.

Irritated, she asked, "Truly?" Then she touched the bruise, making him hiss. "No pain at all, you say?"

"Well, you were none too gentle!"

"I barely touched you."

He glanced around the room. "Is there no cool water to add to the tub?"

"Nay. How far did you fall to bruise so deeply?"

"Off a horse. Gwendolyn, this water is too hot."

"'Tis perfect. Was the horse moving?"

"Rather quickly. I wish to bathe, not boil in my skin."

"If the water is not hot at the start, 'twill be cold long before you finish. I gather recovering your horses did not go without incident."

"We dodged a few arrows. This water will stay hot for so long that—" He smiled, an utterly wicked, self-satisfied upturn of his mouth. "You had planned for the two of us to make scandalous, leisurely use of water and soap, did you not?"

Gwendolyn bit her bottom lip and crossed her arms. "The tub is too small. I suppose I should rejoice that you were merely bruised and not pierced."

"Would that upset you?"

Yes, damn his bare-assed, seductive hide. "I dislike seeing any living thing suffer. Take your bath while I fetch a balm for your bruises."

In the blink of an eye his expression melted to one of concern. "Gwendolyn, where did you sleep last night?"

The abrupt change of direction confused her, but she saw no reason to not tell him the truth. "In here."

"In our bed."

Our bed. She supposed it was. What had once belonged to her parents now belonged to her and Alberic. They'd made it theirs on their wedding night.

"I could not sleep in the chamber I shared with my sisters. 'Tis . . . too empty. Better I spent the night in here than in the bed where I feared I would cry my eyes out for missing them."

He cupped her cheeks in his warm, encompassing hands. "Did you miss me?"

"I missed my sisters. We buried two soldiers yesterday. 'Twould have been nice to . . . have you hold me afterward."

"Ah, sweetling." His arms came around her, and Gwendolyn sank into the embrace she hadn't realized she needed desperately. "I am sorry you had to deal with so much upset and sorrow alone."

The simple acknowledgment of understanding nudged forth tears, so she closed her eyes against them, rested her cheek on his not-so-sweet-smelling chest, and absorbed the offered comfort. After several moments, her composure returning, she knew she should pull away.

Alberic *did* need to bathe. And she must fetch the balm for his bruise. But she was loath to seek release, and he didn't seem to mind indulging her in a moment of weakness.

"Gwendolyn?" he prodded softly.

"Hmmm?"

"My arse grows cold."

She couldn't help but smile at what she sensed was false distress. After a brief squeeze, more gently on his right side so she wouldn't hurt him, she backed up a step. "Then put your arse in the tub and I will fetch the salve."

He stuck a hand in the water. "It does not bite so hard anymore. What say, when we are rid of ap Idwal, we have the cooper fashion us a larger tub?"

"As you say."

He got in and sank down with a pleasured groan, his legs bent so sharply his knees nearly touched his chest. The comical sight widened her smile as she left the bedchamber and hurried down the hallway to her old room.

With her sisters gone, the chamber the three of them had shared felt empty, too silent. As she'd admitted to Alberic, trying to sleep in here last night had proved impossible. So she sought respite in the bed she'd considered her parents' until now.

Our bed.

'Twas only a bed, after all. A thick, comfortable, feather-filled mattress supported by strong ropes fastened to sturdy planks. The four corner posters were neither as big around nor as highly decorated as some she'd seen in other castles, but stoutly supported the rods holding velvet draperies. When let down, the draperies shielded the bed's inhabitants from drafts and created a cozy, private refuge.

If she intended to take advantage of that refuge, then it made no sense to leave her trunk and other belongings in here.

Gwendolyn took a deep breath, realizing the implications of the move she contemplated. Sleeping with Alberic, supervising his baths, eating her meals at the dais—those were all wifely duties expected of her no matter how she felt about the man. To give up her bedchamber and fully occupy his would be taken by many as an indication of affection for him, not just a move for convenience's sake.

She'd surprised herself when she defended Alberic's actions to Nicole. She'd expected to be thoroughly wroth with him on the day of her sisters' departure. Instead, she'd placed blame where it rightfully belonged: on the whim of a king who hadn't considered, or cared, what suffering his orders would cause.

If she were to be completely truthful, her father bore a part of the burden, too, for his single-minded and fool-hardy attack on the earl of Chester. As for William, he'd always been a follower, not a leader. Perhaps given time and guidance her brother would have made a fine lord of Camelen, but as it was, he'd followed his father to his death on the point of Alberic's sword.

Admitting Alberic hadn't been at total fault for William's death came hard. Knees weak, Gwendolyn sat down on the bed.

Both Garrett and Emma had tried to convince her that Alberic shouldn't bear responsibility for what had happened at Wallingford. That he'd been as much a victim of the king's whim as the de Leon sisters.

Gwendolyn wiped aside a grief-induced tear, banishing with it her stubborn refusal to fully admit William's faults. Nor did she have the right to bear ill will toward Alberic for merely defending himself.

Or did she grasp for excuses to soften toward Alberic? To justify her preference for him as her husband and legacy partner over Madog?

Since his arrival, Alberic had done all he could to ensure Camelen prospered and to shield its people from harm. He'd proved both generous of heart and willing to fight for his possessions. Though she'd been miffed that he'd likened her to his horses, she'd understood the meaning behind his words. Alberic considered her valuable, would protect her to his dying breath.

He cared for her and all she cared for, which was more than she could say for her former betrothed.

Madog intended to do Camelen grievous harm if his ridiculous demands weren't met. The surest way to force any besieged lord into the field was to burn a village hut or two, or harass the people.

'Twas hardly the way to win her respect or affection or cooperation.

But then, this siege truly wasn't about her, but about power. About who possessed her and a few horses.

And no matter which man she might prefer, Alberic wore the ring and so with him she must remain.

Shaking her head over the absurdity of the situation, Gwendolyn rose and fetched the jar of salve from the table. Alberic should be near finished with his bath. She'd rub some salve on his bruise before sending him back to the battlements to figure out how to thwart Madog. And while he was occupied, she would move her trunk and other possessions into the lord's bedchamber.

The artifacts, too?

There must be someplace in the lord's bedchamber to conceal them where they would be safe and out of sight.

Alberic surely didn't want to see them again anytime soon.

Could he be right about the legacy? Had her parents been fooled into believing in magic, making the claim of the power to recall King Arthur nothing more than fantasy?

She didn't believe it possible. Her parents hadn't been stupid people. And the ring stubbornly clung to Alberic as it had to her father. Alberic could deny the existence of magic all he wished, but until the ring slid off she had to believe some power greater than any lord's, any king's, ruled the ring.

Magic. Sorcery. Whatever one wished to call the force behind the legacy, it existed.

Proving that to Alberic, however, would be a daunting task.

The only way to know for certain was to conduct a test. A small test. Sweet mercy, she truly didn't want King Arthur to suddenly appear in the hall!

There must be a way to determine if the legacy was true or false. But how?

Wishing her mother had lived but a few hours longer, enough to give her a bit of training in the artifacts' use, Gwendolyn headed back to the lord's bedchamber, mulling over what very little she knew about magical spells.

Chapter Thirteen

THE ONLY TEST GWENDOLYN could think of was to put on the pendant and see what happened, if anything.

She held it in the palm of her hand, thinking the strip of gold shaped into a simple trefoil design, akin to a shamrock, was both heavier and sturdier than it looked.

The trefoil symbolized the number three, sacred to the pagan Celts and believed to hold power. 'Twas not surprising that Merlin the Sorcerer, who some thought to be among the first of the Druids, had used the trefoil in the workings of what might be his most powerful spell.

She'd never seen her mother wear the pendant. Indeed, she hadn't known it existed until a few hours before her mother's death. Not knowing what else to do with it, she'd obeyed the command to keep it hidden away behind the loose brick in the hearth. Only twice in those ten years had she taken it out to look at it and ponder its mysteries.

Her father became upset whenever her curiosity prodded her to ask about the legacy, so she'd stopped asking, aware that when she married and the ring must be passed on, he would be forced to explain. But now her father had died without divulging whatever knowledge he possessed.

Faced with Alberic's certainty that the spell wouldn't work because no magic existed, Gwendolyn wanted some sign that her parents hadn't been fooled.

She didn't think they had been, because the seal of the dragon clung as stubbornly to Alberic as it had to her father. But some other sign that she was right about the legacy, and Alberic wrong, would be welcome.

Conducting the test was one thing. Having Alberic know she did so was another.

Gwendolyn slid the delicate gold chain over her head and slipped the pendant beneath her chemise. The trefoil settled against her breastbone, the bottom circles touching the uppermost swell of her breasts. She placed her palm over the pendant, pressing the smooth gold against her skin, surprised at how lightly it pulled at the chain around her neck.

Lightning didn't strike her dead. Time didn't cease to pass. King Arthur didn't appear in the bedchamber—not that the possibility had worried her. Surely Merlin wouldn't have been so careless as to make the process so simple. Certes, there must be words uttered in a set order, in a ceremony performed involving certain actions, possibly to take place at a specific time. All of which were probably spelled out on the scroll she couldn't read and so couldn't inadvertently set the spell in motion.

Still, she stood motionless for several minutes, taking deep, measured breaths, opening her mind and senses to any subtle change in herself or her surroundings.

She noticed nothing unusual, confirming her reasoning that merely wearing the pendant wouldn't usher forth magical events.

The test would come when she got close to Alberic. True, the pendant and the ring had been near to each other before, but then she hadn't been wearing the trefoil.

Would she feel a stirring in the air? Perhaps the pendant would grow warm or cold. Or Alberic's ring might glow, which would likely frighten him again, but then, at the least, he would be forced to admit that the spell might work if they could determine what was written on the scroll.

Gwendolyn tucked the scroll into her clothing trunk, now settled in the lord's bedchamber beside Alberic's. She'd been forced to empty the trunk in order to drag it between the bedchambers, and when finished with the task, was disappointed with the result. Her simple trunk didn't belong in the room. Another trunk did—the mate to the one already there. Her mother's.

But that was a decision and task for another day.

With a flight of hands Gwendolyn ensured the chain was completely hidden under her chemise, and the pendant pressed flat so no one could detect its presence beneath her clothing.

Nervous, but determined to carry through, Gwendolyn headed down to the hall where preparations were under way for supper. This evening's meal would be light and cold, preserving both provisions and firewood. Though Gwendolyn doubted the siege would last overlong—surely Alberic would find a way to dispense with Madog in short order—the meager fare would impress upon all that the situation wasn't to be taken lightly.

All one had to do was look at little Edward's face to know lives could truly be at risk. His worry for his mother's safety shone as brightly as a beacon, though he went about setting trenchers on the table as if nothing were wrong.

Gwendolyn resisted the urge to hug the child, mindful of how both Edward and the other pages might react. Best to leave the boy to his duties and not call undue attention to either him or his distress.

So where was Alberic? On the battlements?

The moment she stepped outside, Gwendolyn wished she'd put on her cloak. Fog had settled in, depriving the afternoon of light and warmth.

With a start she wondered if putting on the pendant had caused the fog to descend. Nay, surely not. At the least, she would have had to be thinking of the weather for such a thing to happen. Dismissing her foolish thought, she spotted Alberic along the wall walk near the gatehouse, looking outward toward an enemy camp he probably couldn't see.

She climbed the stairs with a sense of apprehension and anticipation, torn between wanting her test to prove the legacy valid, and fearing it wouldn't.

Alberic absently noted her approach, his attention claimed by the threat from without. She halted several steps away, her senses again open to any change in the space between or around them.

The fog didn't begin to rise. No ethereal light appeared in the sky. Alberic's ring didn't glow.

Unwarrantedly disappointed, she continued on until they stood shoulder to shoulder, hands braced on the cold stone, to stare out over the fog-shrouded countryside.

"Any change?" she asked.

"Nay. Ap Idwal is still out there. I wish this fog would clear so I could see what the devil he is doing."

Given her silly thoughts on the fog, she couldn't help but smile. "He is probably staring at the keep, wishing the fog would clear so he could see what the devil you are doing."

He smiled at that, but kept his attention focused outward.

Gathering her courage, holding her breath, she put her hand over his, feeling the ring against her palm.

No angelic chorus sang on high. No dragon reared up out of the mist. No heat flared from the ring to singe her palm.

That her heartbeat sped up and her nether regions warmed signified naught but her usual reaction to Alberic's nearness.

"Is aught amiss?" he asked.

Nothing. Everything.

Gwendolyn swallowed the urge to tell him of her test. Instead, she let go of his hand and strove for a reassuring tone.

"I came out to ask that you not stay out here much longer. The chill cannot be good for your back, and supper will be served soon."

"All right," he said, studying her, his confusion and concern much in evidence.

Gwendolyn quickly returned to the keep. Disheartened, but unwilling to give up too easily, she decided to wear the pendant at least through supper.

When by early evening nothing out of the ordinary had occurred no matter how near Alberic's side she remained or how often she touched him, Gwendolyn conceded defeat. And when Alberic sat down at a trestle table with Roger and Thomas to ensure they knew what to do on the morn should Madog attack the keep, she made her way up to the bedchamber.

'Twouldn't do to wait too long to remove the pendant and risk Alberic seeing it.

Against the advancing night, Gwendolyn lit a wood taper from the fire a servant had laid in the hearth and carried it back across the room to light the candle near the door. The wick caught instantly, casting welcoming brightness around the threshold.

Encompassed within the warm, flickering glow, her mood lightened. Perhaps her test hadn't been a complete failure. All she'd proved, of course, was that the man and woman who wore the jewelry could be near each other without *something* magical happening. She hadn't known that before, so she had gained knowledge. Not a waste at all.

She then moved to light the candle near the bed, where tonight she and Alberic would again share blankets. Given his earlier suggestion that pleasures untold could be savored in a tub—said too-small tub having been emptied and removed from the room hours ago— she didn't doubt he'd be amenable to savoring those pleasures on a mattress.

Her breasts tingled at the memory of his hands cupping them, his thumbs grazing the tips, his mouth suckling in the most enjoyable manner.

He'd touched her everywhere, from the light kisses he'd placed on her forehead to the arousing skim of fingers along her legs and between her thighs. Her body fairly hummed with the desire to once more experience the wonders of coupling.

Tonight, however, she intended to give back what she'd received. Surely he would enjoy her hands on him as much as she enjoyed his on her.

Feeling more than wanton, remembering the ultimate pleasure of Alberic's thrusts flinging her into the heavens, Gwendolyn lit a third candle—and suffered cravings so sharp and deep that they took her breath away.

She trembled with need, so hard she nearly dropped the taper. The yearning for Alberic to take her, here, *now*, weakened her knees.

Even as she whispered his name, a plea she knew he couldn't hear, she felt heat against her chest.

The pendant.

Alberic squirmed on the bench, anxious to go upstairs and be with Gwendolyn. She'd been attentive all afternoon and through supper, and every time she brushed up against him or touched his hand his loins stirred. All the while he'd tried to concentrate on ensuring Camelen's defenses were in place for whenever ap Idwal chose to attack, he'd envisioned Gwendolyn in the lord's bedchamber readying for the night.

Would she, this time, play the bride and await him naked in bed? Or would her modesty again force her to leave on her chemise, giving him the delightful opportunity to remove it?

Either way, the night would prove a delicious diversion from the awkward and irritating problem of being besieged.

On the map spread in front of him, Alberic again stared at the area of the village, his biggest concern. The tenants and their homes were the most vulnerable. He'd seen what a besieging army could do to the countryside when intent upon capturing a castle. Ap Idwal's intent wasn't to capture Camelen, but to *rescue* Gwendolyn, so this was no ordinary siege.

Alberic reasoned that if he remained firm in refusing to hand Gwendolyn over, the man might eventually abandon his pointless cause and return to Wales. Maybe. Probably not. Which meant finding a way to force the dolt into seeing reason, because the heavens would rain sheep before Alberic released Gwendolyn into ap Idwal's care.

She was his wife, his lover. And at this moment she awaited his arrival in the bedchamber. Soft, warm, and welcoming.

Determined to focus on the task at hand, he turned to Roger, seated next to him. "The men know where they must be, and when?"

"Aye, my lord. Not all have weapons, but we can move armed soldiers into position once we know from what direction and in what form ap Idwal begins his attack."

"The postern gate is secure?"

"As secure as we can make it without nailing it shut."

Which wasn't a good idea. The back door to the castle might be needed to move people in or out as circumstances changed.

"The woodpiles are ready for lighting and cauldrons

are at the ready," Thomas said. "Should you decide we must use boiling oil in our defense, we can have it heated in a trice."

Not for the first time Alberic wished Sedwick or Garrett were present. Roger and Thomas were good soldiers, made excellent squires, but to test their command abilities with so much at stake didn't sit well.

Hell, he wasn't even sure of his own command abilities. Until now, he'd trusted his instincts and they'd served him well. But no lives had been at stake. While he accepted the responsibility of keeping all within his charge safe, he truly wasn't confident he did so in the best manner.

Not that he would confess his unease to anyone. A good commander showed no fear, not even the least doubt.

"We will go over this again before dawn," he told the squires. "If either of you see some flaw in our plans, I want to hear about it then."

Their chorus of agreement came at a good time, for he could no longer keep his thoughts from roaming toward the woman who awaited him upstairs.

A sense of urgency discomfited him, prodding him to wonder if something was amiss, and he suddenly found the need to see Gwendolyn and assure himself of her well-being almost overwhelming.

Long strides took him to the stairway. By the time he reached the chamber's doorway, his palms were sweating. He entered the bedchamber to see Gwendolyn seated on a chair, fully clothed, her hands clasped together.

Not serene, but not troubled, either. She raised an

eyebrow at his presence, and he chided himself for his discomfort.

But was her face too pale, or just oddly shadowed? Of the three candles in the room, she'd lit only the one by the door, its circle of light dimming before it reached her.

Unsure of what to do, he leaned against the closed door, wondering what he could say that wouldn't make him sound like a fool for rushing up here without cause. She would think he'd gone daft.

Still, his instincts gnawed at him, urging both caution and patience. Why that should be he didn't know yet.

Then he saw her trunk sitting next to his and knew what she'd been doing all this time. Alberic grabbed at what he hoped was a safe subject, like a drowning man thrown a rope he didn't have time to check for fraying.

"You decided not to keep a separate chamber."

Gwendolyn glanced over her shoulder at the trunks before she answered. "I probably should have asked your permission first. I know some lords prefer having a chamber to themselves. If you object—"

"Nay, no objection. I hoped you would choose to move in here with me. 'Tis a large chamber with a big bed. I saw no reason why we could not share."

She rose from the chair, her movement graceful, and as she came toward him he ignored the itch he wanted her to scratch. *Later,* he assured his unruly parts.

"My parents shared this chamber. I saw no reason why we should not. Truth to tell, I intend to have my mother's trunk brought out of storage and use it for my things. I think it fitting the matching trunks should once more grace the room."

"Fitting," was all he could say before Gwendolyn's

hands landed on his chest. She leaned against him, placed her head on his shoulder, and he could do no less than wrap her in an embrace.

Even as he held her tight, noting how right and good she felt in his arms, he felt her shaking. As much as he wanted to believe she trembled for want of him, he sensed otherwise.

"Gwendolyn, what is amiss?"

"Nothing, now that you are here. Have you decided what to do about Madog?"

"Mostly. You shake. Why?"

"The room is chilled. How does your side? Shall I rub more balm on your bruise?"

The room was cooler than usual. And darker. Not only had she lit just one out of the three candles, but the fire in the hearth wasn't as high as usual. Was she preserving supplies because of the siege?

"Later," he said of the balm. "If you are cold we can toss more wood on the fire. You need not take your precautions so far that you are uncomfortable."

"I am most comfortable at the moment. Do you think Madog might listen to reason if someone other than you spoke with him?"

His embrace had never before been deemed comfortable. Warming. Enticing, aye. But comfortable? He decided it wasn't a bad thing, especially when her trembling eased.

"I doubt Madog would listen to anyone who argues against rescuing you from me."

"I tried to tell him the other day to leave things be. Perhaps if I made my feelings on the matter clearer—"

"Nay. You are not to go anywhere near the man."

She sighed. "I do not intend to, but he might desist if I send him a message declaring I would not support petitioning the pope for an annulment. As you told Edgar, all of the conditions for a binding marriage, including consummation, have been met. We are bound by our vows and the legacy. Neither can be set aside."

He ignored her comment on the legacy. The vows were more than enough binding for him. "I believe ap Idwal would rather see you widowed."

Gwendolyn tightened her hold. "Which means you are not to go anywhere near the man, either. When the time comes to negotiate a peace, you might consider sending Rhys and Father Paul out to his camp. Madog would respect the priest and the bard, not harm them. I also believe the two of them might bring him to his senses."

He had no intention of promising not to go near ap Idwal. 'Struth, he would dearly love to take a chunk out of the man's hide. However, the bard and the priest would make good emissaries, and both were in the keep. Alberic vaguely remembered the priest saying grace before supper and the bard strumming his harp afterward. His mind had been diverted, both by ap Idwal's menace and Gwendolyn's attentions.

She still leaned against him, snuggled in for warmth—and comfort he suspected, though he didn't yet know why. Ap Idwal and his siege didn't worry her overmuch, as she'd proved to him earlier. So what else bothered her enough to prod *his* instinct?

"You may be right, especially if Father Paul threatens him with excommunication for coveting another man's wife. My wife." He kissed her forehead. "Still chilled?"

"Nay."

"Is the offer of balm still good?"

"Of course. Remove your tunic and I will fetch the balm."

A good start to what he truly wanted; both of them unencumbered by clothing and abed. As soon as she slipped out of his arms he felt the chill. More wood on the fire was definitely called for.

As he neared the wood box, he spotted what might have bothered Gwendolyn earlier. On the table lay the black velvet sack containing the scroll and pendant she'd shown him while telling him a fantastical tale of magic and King Arthur.

Alberic picked up the sack, confirming both artifacts were within. It shouldn't bother him that Gwendolyn had brought her treasure into the bedchamber along with the rest of her belongings, but her belief in their magical attributes made him shiver.

"Is there a loose brick in this hearth, too?"

Gwendolyn released the breath she'd held since he picked up the sack, fearing he'd be upset by seeing it. From the moment Alberic entered the chamber, she'd sought to distract him from noticing the artifacts, then become caught up in the comforting distraction. A second mistake on her part in the course of a very few minutes.

She'd recognized her first mistake almost immediately: lighting the third candle. She knew little of pagan rituals, but she did know they all included use of the number three. While wearing the trefoil pendant she lit three candles, provoking a reaction.

Had he heard her whisper his name while suffering sharp pangs of intense desire? Apparently not, or he would have made comment. Wouldn't he? She decided not to ask, fearful he would think she'd gone daft.

After recognizing her mistake, she'd swiftly blown out two of the candles, removed the pendant, and put it in the velvet sack. Alberic had come into the chamber before she had the chance to hide it away.

"I do not know," she answered truthfully. "'Tis possible a secret hiding place exists in here, too. 'Tis also possible my mother merely kept the sack in her clothing trunk."

He tossed the sack on the table, then reached into the box for a chunk of wood to add to the fire. "You should have a care with those. Promise me you will not wear the pendant."

He'd told her before to put them away, and now demanded further assurance that she not believe in the magic he refused to acknowledge.

"The pendant bothers you so much?"

He shook his head. "Nay. To me it is merely a pretty bauble. However, with a Welshman camped outside our gate, this might not be a good time to remind everyone that you are half Welsh."

She didn't need to remind anyone of her heritage. Likely they remembered every time Rhys played his harp. And though Alberic used a poor choice of words, he hadn't meant to insult her by associating her with the likes of Madog. Verily, he meant to protect her.

Now was not the time to chide him for his disbelief in magic or his ill-considered words. Indeed, the Welshman outside the gates preyed on Alberic's mind and affected his mood. He needed relief from his concerns, and sleep, before dealing with Madog on the morn.

Besides, now that she knew magic *did* exist, she was at a loss over what to do about it. She still couldn't read the scroll, and had no way of knowing if England suffered the time of its greatest need. Both matters to ponder over later.

"As you wish," she said, a comment too obscure to be considered a promise, but enough to placate Alberic for the nonce.

He pulled his tunic over his head, and Gwendolyn dismissed all else from her thoughts other than applying a balm to his bruise, which seemed uglier than before.

"Hurt?" she asked, spreading white cream over bluish-purple skin.

"'Tis worth a bit of pain to have you tend it. You have gentle hands, Gwendolyn. I am slave to your tender ministrations."

She smiled at the bit of gallantry, hearing an undertone she was coming to recognize. Alberic suffered other hurts he wished tended, and she truly didn't mind obliging. Her intense desire of earlier had abated but not left her completely.

"I have often wondered what it might be like to have a man as my slave, at my beck and call to do whatever I require of him whenever a fancy strikes."

"Have you a fancy?"

"Several," she said wistfully, putting the jar back on the washstand. "They would require my slave to be of superior strength and form, possessed of unrivaled vigor and matchless endurance. Know you such a man?"

He spread his arms wide, a truly wicked gleam in his eyes. "I am yours to command, my lady. Whatever your fancy, I shall strive to satisfy."

Gwendolyn looked him up and down, judging his merits. "Your arrogance is insufferable, for a slave, yet I believe you might . . . satisfy."

He raised an eyebrow. "Aye, well, this slave has yet to determine if his efforts are wasted on an undeserving master. Are the lady's charms worth expending my vigor?"

"How ungallant!"

"Insufferable."

She pulled off her surcoat. He sat down on the bed to remove his boots, yet watched her every movement.

On their wedding night, he'd helped her out of her chemise. Tonight he watched, unmoving, as piece by piece she removed her garments. With each piece cast aside, she felt more powerful, more desirable.

She didn't have to ask if she'd been found worthy. His worshipful expression and outstretched hand said all. She deliberately resisted his invitation. Not an easy thing to do, but he'd begun this game, and she intended to play it out.

"The lady seeks proof of her slave's superior form."

"A shameless command."

"Insufferable."

Alberic stood, straight and proud, the bulge in his breeches straining the laces, a most gratifying sign of his willingness to expend vigor.

The pounding on the door startled them both.

"Lord Alberic! Ap Idwal has set fire to the village!"

Chapter Fourteen

ALBERIC'S OATHS BLISTERED THE AIR.

Some of them Gwendolyn guessed were Norman-French, and though she'd never heard them before, she caught the meaning.

Having slipped on her chemise, she helped him dress, handing him pieces of clothing while he ranted.

"I will have that whoreson's head," he vowed, jamming a foot into a boot. "Send the wretch to hell. He had the audacity to complain about Normans, but were it a Norman knight beyond the gate who set the limit of dawn, then dawn it would be! 'Tis unconscionable of ap Idwal to move before then."

Gwendolyn agreed, but for entirely different reasons. This was the second time today ap Idwal had interrupted her time with Alberic, and she was damn tired of his interference.

"You could not have known for certain he would disregard the courtesy," she murmured, feeling she should say something soothing, though she doubted Alberic was in any mood for soothing.

He jerked on the second boot. "Well, I know now. I swear, if any of the villagers are hurt, ap Idwal will pay dearly."

He rose from the bed, strode toward his trunk, flipped up the lid, and pulled out his chain mail. "I shall need you to play squire."

"Certes."

Alberic whipped on the heavy shirt made of metal links as if it weighed no more than fine-weave linen, then sat on the chair.

Gwendolyn began securing the latches he couldn't reach. "What will you do?"

"Go out to the village to see how bad things are."

Her hands fumbled with a latch. She'd believed him headed for the battlements, not out into the fray.

"The villagers have been through a siege before, so they know what to expect. You should not wander beyond the wall. 'Tis no place for the lord of the castle. Send others out."

He snorted. "Thomas and Roger are too new to command. If Sedwick or Garrett were here, then I might. But they are not. And since my misjudgment put the tenants in danger, 'tis my place to make things right."

She moved to the other shoulder, ensuring each latch secure, doubting anything she could say would deter him from this lunacy. Lords didn't put themselves in danger without good reason. If they should fall, then everyone loyal to him suffered.

Only look at what happened when her father and brother . . . dear God, she didn't want to think of what would happen if Alberic . . . nay, he'd be fine. He wasn't facing well-armed troops. Still . . .

"If you insist on going out there, be sure to take several men with you."

"Naturally. They will be needed to fight the fires."

And they would watch their lord's back. 'Twas all the assurance she could ask for, for now.

The chain mail secured, he strapped on his sword, the same sword that had killed her brother. To keep her hands from shaking and her emotions from flying to the boughs, she crossed the room to fetch his helm. She had to remain calm, dare not allow him to see how badly the whole situation upset her. For his sake. For her own.

They came together at the doorway, and it struck Gwendolyn that he appeared as she'd first seen him: a battle-ready warrior who'd brought her father and brother home for burial.

She remembered wishing she'd not allowed Alberic of Chester to pass through the gate. Now, heaven help her, she didn't want him to leave.

She handed over his helm. "Is there aught you wish me to do?"

"Ready the hall for wounded, especially for burns."

Ready the salve and bandages. That she could do.

Fingers entwined in metal links, Gwendolyn pulled him down for a kiss, finding some comfort in his fierce response.

"Have a care," she whispered.

"I always do," he said, as if she should know that.

Then he shoved on his helm and was gone.

The silence in the room was deafening. Her stomach roiled and tears threatened. Unwilling to succumb, Gwendolyn finished dressing and grabbed the jar of balm, squeezing it so hard her hand hurt.

"Dear God, keep him safe."

The prayer brought no relief, but what more could she do than consign him to divine grace?

Slowly, she crossed the room to the table and picked up the velvet sack. If she knew more of magic, could she rid them of Madog with a well-placed bolt of lightning?

The thought made her shiver.

Perhaps such sorcery was beyond her, but surely she could invoke the protection of the pagan gods, too.

The priest would be appalled, but anyone born and raised in the Marches wouldn't be surprised or condemn her. Pagan beliefs mingled with Christianity, the rites of both honored.

Gwendolyn bit her bottom lip, debating the wisdom of her impulse. She took out the pendant and stared at the trefoil.

'Struth, she'd learned a bit from her test. Once she lit the third candle, she must carefully control her thoughts, remain peaceful and calm.

But she wasn't in a serene mood and might do great harm if something went wrong.

Chagrined, she admitted Alberic might be right about hiding the artifacts away and not wearing the pendant, at least until she knew how to use it properly and for the right reasons.

Still, she clutched the pendant and closed her eyes. "Oh, Mother Goddess, from whom all earth's bounty comes, I humbly ask thy protection for the man I— love."

Her head screamed in rebellion even as her heart embraced the notion that she might have fallen in love with Alberic. Her knees shaking so hard she couldn't stand, Gwendolyn collapsed onto the chair and stared at the pendant, blaming its magic for endangering her heart.

She couldn't love Alberic. Serve as Camelen's lady, aye. Be Alberic's wife and share his bed, aye. But love him?

Sweet mercy, she'd prayed for his protection when she should have asked for a divine shield for her heart!

But then, how could she not love the man who even now risked his own life to ensure the well-being of the villagers? Who blamed himself for not foreseeing their predicament when Gwendolyn knew damn well any other lord would place the blame where it belonged—on Madog ap Idwal.

How could she not be enamored of the man who'd done all he knew how to ensure the change of lordship was peaceful, who hadn't punished Nicole severely when he'd had every right, who'd brought a peasant boy into the keep and made him a page so he could support his mother?

The man who'd shown her that a piece of heaven was within reach when in his bed.

If that man didn't come back whole and hardy, she was going to strangle him and then tear ap Idwal in two.

Sighing at her own lunacy, Gwendolyn slipped the pendant back into the sack, then tucked it away in her trunk. Jar of salve in hand, she made her way down to the hall where she put her emotions aside and let instinct take over.

She ordered trestle tables set up and the bandaging and salve made ready. Cauldrons of broth were hauled in from the kitchen and kegs of ale brought up from the storage room.

In the midst of the turmoil she glanced about, looking for a boy she couldn't find. Edward. And she very much feared she knew where he'd gone.

❧

The fog had lifted and a bit of the moon shone in the sky. One couldn't see much beyond a few feet, but the flames in the village provided a guiding beacon.

At the open postern gate, Alberic chose several men to accompany him, Thomas among them. His other squire he would leave in charge of the keep.

"Roger, you are not to let anyone pass through this gate whom either you or another of the guards do not recognize. No one. Understood?"

"You expect treachery?"

An understatement. "This could well be a ploy to draw us out. I would not put it beyond ap Idwal to attempt to storm this gate. Have a care."

On the edge of his vision he caught movement among the soldiers, a form too short and stealthy to belong. Two long strides put him in striking distance. With a quickly flung arm he captured Edward by the scruff of the neck.

"No, Edward. 'Tis too dangerous."

"But me mum!"

"I understand your concern, but you will stay here." Alberic spun the boy around and took a firm grip of those young shoulders. "I shall make you a bargain. You stay here, and I will find your mother and have her brought into the keep."

Alberic could hardly blame the boy for hesitating to

agree. Why trust the lord who'd put his mother in danger?

Then Edward squared his shoulders. "As you say, milord."

Alberic desperately wanted to hug him, but refrained when he saw Gwendolyn running toward the gate. Her relief upon spotting Edward said all.

"Go to her ladyship. I believe she needs your help in the hall."

The boy dashed straight into Gwendolyn's arms.

"I should box your ears," he heard her say in such a loving tone he knew she'd do no such thing.

She will make a good mother.

Not willing to contemplate his abilities as a father, Alberic ran toward the village.

Already the hut nearest the church was beyond hope. The graveyard separating the two structures gave the church some protection, but flying sparks from the thatched roof had set a second and third hut ablaze. The fire would spread from rooftop to rooftop if not halted.

And Gwendolyn had the measure of the villagers. Every man and woman was employed in the daunting task of hauling water up from the well and passing the buckets down the lines, shouting encouragement at one another, until the one at the end tossed the water on the fire then ran the bucket back to the well.

Efficient and orderly. Unfortunately, they made little headway trying to put out all three fires. The first hut must be sacrificed to save the rest of the village.

But when he shouted the orders to alter their efforts, some looked at him as if he'd lost his wits, and others turned toward the soot-coated, crestfallen couple in the middle of the line.

The man came forward and waved a hand at the flaming hut. "My lord, this is all we own. If we save naught of it—"

The choked-off words speared Alberic's heart, but he stood his ground. "Come see me on the morn, but for now go help the good folk who tried to help you."

Then half the roof fell in, sending bits of burning wood and thatch upward and outward. People scattered, some screaming, to avoid the rain of fiery embers.

Alberic batted at a shard of glowing wood that landed on his arm, putting it out. His chain mail provided a barrier, but the tenants weren't so fortunate. Chaos erupted as clothing and hair caught fire, the buckets of water put to use now on people and not huts.

He felt so helpless he didn't know what to do next, until he saw a woman lying on the ground, her skirt aflame and her screams panicked.

He ran to her, as did others. He tore at the fabric, singeing his fingers. A bucket of tossed water doused most of the flames and turned the dirt to mud. For what seemed an eternity, they worked frantically. Only when the fire was out and the woman's screams subsided to deep sobs did he realize he knew her. Mistress Biggs.

Her legs were badly burned, but she would live. And by the gods, if he had his way so would everyone else. Huts could be rebuilt, but people couldn't be replaced.

He shouted for Thomas, who came running. "Get the older women and any child too young to heft a bucket into the keep. And tell Gwendolyn that when these fires are out I am bringing everyone else in, too."

Thomas raised an eyebrow but set about organizing the older women to round up the children. The able-bodied went back to work hauling water.

They wet down rooftops, turned cattle loose in the meadow, and shooed honking geese and flapping chickens out from underfoot. Voices grew rough with throats sore from both exertion and the sting of smoke.

By the time fire no longer threatened to consume the village, they'd lost two huts, a third was badly damaged, and a fourth would need repairs.

Alberic's fingers bled from both burns and abuse. His back and legs hurt, and his arms were too weary to lift.

"Gather whatever blankets and provisions you can carry and get to the keep," he told the bedraggled crowd gathered around the well.

No one argued, just drifted off to their huts, leaving him alone with the few soldiers he'd brought out with him. They all looked worse than if they'd been in battle, ready to fall where they stood. Many of them, Alberic knew, had not only fought the fire but made several trips back and forth to the keep, escorting to safety those who'd been burned or whose strength gave out.

"Well done, men. You have proved your mettle this night." A few smiles broke out, but most were too weary to bother. "Hurry the villagers along and herd them into the keep. I warrant our beds will have never felt so good."

With grunts of agreement, the men spread out to obey the order. Thomas took a few steps, then turned around.

"Coming, my lord?"

"Aye, as soon as I fetch my helm and sword." Which he'd taken off only God knew how long ago. "What word from the keep? Any sign of impending attack?"

"Nay. I do believe Roger is disappointed."

Alberic had to smile. "Well, I am not. How goes it in the hall?"

"Last I knew Lady Gwendolyn had all well in hand. She asked after you." The squire smiled sheepishly. "Beg pardon, my lord, but I told her you fared well but would need a bath upon your return."

Alberic couldn't help a bark of laughter. "That assumes my body will bend to fit in the tub."

But damn, a bath sounded good, and a bed even better. A glance at the moon's position said dawn was hours away, yet he felt he'd been exerting himself for days.

On his way toward the oak tree under which he'd placed his belongings, he again surveyed the damage. Guilt almost overwhelmed him.

So much lost. All his fault.

He could almost hear the earl of Chester remonstrate him for putting a dram of trust in the word of a Welshman. The judgment, of course, came from long years of sparring with the Welsh along Chester's borders. The judgment also came from a man whose word was suspect, his reputation little better than ap Idwal's.

Alberic strapped on his sword, and when he bent down to pick up his helm he caught a shadowy movement in the graveyard. A place no one should be. Father Paul was in the keep. The villagers surely weren't visiting the dead at this time of night.

He put on his helm, his anger flaring. The only one who might be skulking among the mix of monuments and Celtic crosses was the enemy. Possibly the very man who'd started the fires and then stayed to watch the huts burn.

The whoreson!

Anger boiled over into fury, the need to punish someone for tonight's outrage thrusting him toward the graveyard. A satisfied grin hurt his cheeks when he saw ap Idwal step out from behind a cross. That two others came out of hiding, too, didn't give him a moment's pause.

He advanced on ap Idwal, relishing the prospect of a punishing fight.

Ap Idwal sneered. "How nice of you to oblige me, Norman. We will not have to carry you far for burial."

"I will see you in hell first."

Alberic drew his sword, his arms no longer weary, every fiber in his being prepared. Behind him he heard Thomas's indistinct shouts, likely mustering the guards to the graveyard.

Ap Idwal gave no sign of retreat, merely stood by the cross he had hidden behind, a smug smile on his face, his sword at the ready.

Then Alberic's head exploded, his ears ringing and vision blurring. As he fell face forward into the dirt, he realized his error. He'd been so intent on ap Idwal he'd neglected to thoroughly study his surroundings.

Just as Sir Hugh de Leon had been so intent on killing the earl of Chester that he'd forfeited his life.

Gwendolyn!

He closed the eyes that refused to remain open, envisioning Gwendolyn in the arms of Madog ap Idwal. The earl of Chester stood beside them, shaking his head in disappointment at his bastard son's inexcusable misjudgment.

∾

Gwendolyn was nearly at her wit's end when Alberic's eyes finally opened.

Prone in their bed, Alberic stared up at her, his gorgeous green eyes clear and wide open—this time open for good, she hoped. He'd opened his eyes before and closed them again too soon.

"I must be in heaven," he murmured. "An angel watches over me."

She almost cried for joy that he spoke, even if his gallantry was misplaced. "You have not yet left this earthly kingdom, so your sight must be faulty." Then she considered the possibility that his sight might be affected by the head injury. "Have you trouble seeing?"

"I see you perfectly well, Gwendolyn. What confuses me is that I fully expected to awake in heaven . . . or elsewhere."

Gwendolyn sat down on the bed she'd hovered over for long hours. "You took a nasty blow to the head. If you had not been wearing a helm . . ." Best not to speak her worst fears aloud. Her voice might crack. "You have a lump the size of an egg. Does your head hurt?"

He reached behind his head, turning it slightly, and winced. "It does now."

"Well, now that I know you will live long enough to drink it, I will have Cook brew willow-bark tea. Stay still. I will not be gone long."

She started to get up; his arm shot out to hold her in place.

"Not yet. What happened . . . after?"

Unsure of which "after" he meant, she began with what she thought he most wanted to know.

"Thomas could not reach you before one of the bastards swung a club at your head from behind. By the time you went down, your soldiers and the villagers were rushing the graveyard." She smiled. "Madog must have realized how badly outnumbered he was and fled back to his camp. Thomas forswore pursuit and brought you back to the keep."

Muddy, soot-coated, his hands burned, and unconscious. With the help of his squires she'd cleaned him up and put him to bed and waited, and prayed to every deity she could think of, both Christian and pagan, to spare Alberic's life.

She didn't know which goddess or saint had answered her plea, but was so grateful she intended to send her thanks to all. Given Alberic's inclination to put himself in harm's way, she might need their goodwill in the future.

But that was for later; Alberic wasn't completely out of danger yet.

He sighed. "So now ap Idwal gloats in his camp."

"Nay, he is gone."

His eyebrows shot up. "Gone?"

"Since you thought the idea a good one, at dawn I sent Father Paul and Rhys out to the camp. As you suggested, Father Paul threatened Madog with excommunication should he persist in his folly, but I suspect that bothered him less than Rhys's threat to put Madog's dishonorable behavior to song and spread the tale far and wide. They also let him know in most explicit terms that I had no wish to be rescued. Within the hour they broke camp and went back to Wales."

His eyes closed briefly, and she almost wished he'd

kept them closed longer. Now within them lurked both sadness and a vulnerability she would never expected of him.

"I failed them, Gwen. I failed all of us."

Gwendolyn could hardly believe what she heard.

"How, pray tell? I grant you, you should not have gone into the graveyard alone. But how were you to know someone would sneak up behind you and swat your head? You had best not let Edward overhear such talk. You are his hero!"

"I allowed the enemy to fire the village, which injured his mother." His eyes narrowed. "Is she all right?"

"The burns on her legs will pain her for some time, but she is thoroughly enjoying her son's fussing. Sweet mercy, Alberic. Very few of the villagers have left the keep. They are awed that their lord would endanger himself on their account, and realize that more of the village, if not the whole of it, would have burned had you not been there. Most have not gone home. They remain in the hall to pray for your recovery."

"I nearly made you a widow. Ap Idwal almost won."

His failure to see sense irked her. "But he did not. You did! The siege is over, the enemy vanquished."

He closed his eyes then, not because of the pain in his head or weariness, but to shut out her arguments.

Gwendolyn refrained from tossing up her hands in frustration. Why he should feel so wretched when all had turned out so well, she didn't understand.

"I am going down for the tea and to let everyone know you have wakened. Shall I bring food up, too?"

"Nay, not hungry," he whispered.

His lack of appetite didn't surprise her. His head must

hurt as badly as Emma's did when gripped by a sick headache, and Gwendolyn had always known a headache was coming on by her sister's lack of hunger.

Gwendolyn left the bedchamber door wide open. As she suspected would happen, her announcement that Alberic had awakened and spoken lucidly elicited cheers loud enough to carry up the stairs and into the chamber.

She hoped the accolade would lift his spirt. True, he'd suffered a knock on the head tonight, but he'd also proved himself a capable and caring lord. Surely he would come to realize that, in time.

All the while she strode out to the kitchen to brew tea for his aching head, she wished she knew of a potion or balm to cure an ailing spirit, which she suspected might take longer to heal than Alberic's injury.

Chapter Fifteen

'TIS UNCONSCIONABLE FOR THOSE who profess to believe in Christ to participate in pagan rites." In obvious despair, Father Paul waved a hand at the Maypole. "To raise this . . . this reprehensible *abomination* within such short distance from the church door is . . . is heathen."

Alberic had heard the Church's position on the celebration of Beltane before. As for the Maypole, which some believed represented a male phallus, he thought the villagers had done a fine job with it. The ash tree had been harvested yesterday and installed in the village green last eve. The women had decked it with a huge crown of flowers and hung the long red and white ribbons that would later be woven around the pole by merry dancers.

He refused to have the Maypole removed, even for the priest partly responsible for convincing ap Idwal to end his siege.

"I understand your concern, Father, but the rites of spring are celebrated all over the kingdom. I shall not deprive Camelen's people of the pleasures of the tradition."

"*Pleasures,*" the priest said as if the word were foul-tasting. "If you do not, at the least, forbid the bonfire, the tenants will commence with pleasures at the lighting and not cease until the last ember dies. I warrant we will count fewer virgins in our midst come the morn."

No doubt.

Alberic remembered a Beltane or two when he'd snuck off with a lusty maiden, heady from the ale and the dancing, cavorting naked in the woods, and the inevitable, successful completion of the rites.

"Perhaps you should caution the fathers to keep a close watch on their daughters."

"Humph. More than a few fathers would not be upset should the girl swell with child and be forced to marry and move out. One less mouth to feed."

Alberic couldn't dispute the charge, though he thought the priest might be a bit harsh in his judgment. And while fire yet haunted his dreams, among other horrific memories, he'd not forbid the bonfire or the ale or the dancing.

"Come, Father, look around you. Given that we still have a village, and the repairs and rebuilding are going well, and the planting has gone on as scheduled, I think the people deserve a day of play. If that be Beltane, so be it."

The priest gave a deep sigh. "I suppose I could speak with the fathers."

"A good decision. I am sure God will look down on your efforts with favor."

The disgruntled priest wandered off, and Alberic continued on his interrupted quest to inspect the repairs and rebuilding. No work would be done today, of course.

Even those whose homes were only partially repaired, and who currently resided in the keep, had other plans for the day.

Gwendolyn had been up and out before dawn to lead a flock of women to the meadow to wash their faces in the first of May dew—why, he had no notion—and to gather armloads of flowers. Even now, she and a few others wove white-, purple-, and yellow-headed flowers into evergreen boughs to hang in the hall.

He'd escaped the nearly overpowering scents and, as he had each day for the past week since Gwendolyn finally pronounced him fit enough to leave their bed, he now stood before the new huts.

Not even the scent of flowers could banish the stench of smoke. Not even seeing stout oak center beams and patches of new thatch could obliterate the vision of flames and flying sparks.

His head no longer ached and the burns on his fingers were nearly healed. Paying most of the cost of restoring what was lost eased his conscience but didn't diminish his guilt.

Not a day went by he didn't suffer doubts about the quality of his lordship over Camelen, and not a night passed that he didn't awake at least once, sweating, terrified that ap Idwal had somehow won.

Only by curling around Gwendolyn could he go back to sleep.

Leaning on Gwendolyn for comfort, even though she never woke and didn't know, bothered him immensely. Never had he turned to another for succor, relying only upon himself. The dreams had to abate sometime, and that time couldn't come quickly enough to suit him.

Giggling alerted him to the return of the village women. From the oldest to the youngest, each wore a circlet of flowers. Many carried an evergreen bough to hang over her hut's door. Mistress Biggs wasn't among them, her burns too severe to allow her to walk much yet.

Alberic began the trek back to the keep, hoping that enough of the greenery had been carried out of the hall to allow breathing. Soon enough he learned that the scent of evergreen could be ignored when one beheld the festive look of the hall.

Gwendolyn hadn't taken down any groupings of weapons, merely hung the flower-dotted boughs over them, with the exception of two circles—those where her father's and brother's swords and daggers hung. The effect was astonishing, changing the whole feel in the hall from one of irrefutable power to one of . . . a home.

The woman responsible for the transformation stood at the dais, her finger tapping her chin, perusing the walls for one more spot to hang one more bough. She, too, wore a circlet of flowers in her unbound hair, a pagan goddess surveying her realm. The image struck his fancy, and 'twas suddenly easy to envision her in a moonlit woodland clearing, garbed in naught but her own skin, cavorting with fairies.

He shook off the fanciful vision and strode toward her, glad she was mere flesh and bone. "Perhaps we should remove some of the weapons."

Her eyes widened, and he could almost hear a protest skitter through her head.

"Not the circle of swords or daggers," he reassured her. "But many of the others have no special meaning and could be cleared away to make room for your boughs. Or a tapestry or two."

"Well, it is your hall now."

A quiet concession, but he could tell she rather liked the idea.

"'Tis merely a suggestion, and the hall is yours also. Make whatever changes you like, or none at all. Have you decided where to put the last bough?"

She smiled, and the room seemed homier yet. "If you truly do not mind removing a few weapons, then I believe the bough would look better over the door than the battle-ax."

"Down it comes."

For the next little while they discussed which weapons to take down, which to leave or move. Alberic decided the arrow he'd stuck in the pillar no longer served any use. He knew the identity of the archer, and someday Edgar would pay for firing the arrow, probably the same day ap Idwal suffered for his audacity.

Assisting Gwendolyn proved restful, the feeling lasting until one of the guards entered the hall to deliver a scroll tied with a red ribbon flecked with gold.

From Chester.

"The messenger was told not to await a reply, milord. He said you would understand why after you read this,"

Alberic sat down at a trestle table and untied the ribbon. He quickly perused the message, written in Norman-French in neat lettering and formal wording—a graciously issued command for Alberic and whichever de Leon daughter he'd married to visit the earl at his castle in Chester.

Gwendolyn eased onto the bench opposite him. "Ill tidings?"

"We are invited to visit Chester."

"The earl or the city?"

"Both. Apparently the earl is no longer at Wallingford."

Not a good sign, unless Wallingford had fallen to the king. Unlikely. Had such a prize fallen, some passing traveler or merchant would have disclosed the news. So either Chester had gone home for a respite or he'd broken from King Stephen, and Alberic very much feared the worst.

"Are we going?"

He heard the hope in her question, but damn, he didn't want to face Chester so soon after this latest debacle. And getting caught up in the earl's self-serving politics might be bad for his health.

"We probably should, but I must warn you the visit might be unpleasant." He leaned forward on crossed arms, searching for the words to explain the situation simply. "Chester does nothing without reason. This invitation means he wants something from me, most likely to take measure of where my loyalty lies if he renounces his support for the king."

"Chester would expect you to break with the king because he does?"

"He might." If he didn't tell her why, she would ask, and she might as well know why the decision would be difficult. "Chester is my father."

She stared at him for a moment, her brow furrowing. "Your father? But Chester is newly married and he has no . . . oh."

Oh. He'd let his illegitimacy be known and all she could say was "oh"?

"That I am his bastard does not bother you?"

She shrugged a shoulder. "Not particularly, perhaps because I am half Welsh. Legitimacy is not such a delicate issue with them. All children are treated equally under the law."

"Unfortunately for me, neither of my parents can claim a drop of Welsh blood. I am the by-blow of a Norman earl and an English peasant, God rest her soul. And no, I have no rights, legal or otherwise, unless Chester admits to his youthful lust for a woman so far beneath him and then grants me rights, which I doubt is his inclination."

Her mouth thinned. "Then why bother with him?"

"Because he is my father."

"Whom you did not invite to our wedding because you did not think he would lower himself to come." She rose from the table. "'Twould seem to me you owe him naught, not even a visit."

She flounced off, leaving him to gape after her. Then she spun on her heel and in high ire, hands on hips, she continued.

"The earls of Gloucester and Cornwall are both illegitimate. Does anyone think the less of them? Nay. A man's measure is in his character, not in his birthright."

This time when she left she kept going, clear out the door.

Gwendolyn had correctly assessed the situation and immediately passed judgment against the earl. He'd known she would find out about his bastardy sometime, and expected . . . what? Horror? Outrage? Fainting?

Her acceptance of his heritage surprised him, warmed him clear through. Smiling, Alberic decided he wouldn't remind Gwendolyn that both men she mentioned might be illegitimate, but they'd been born of noblewomen and sired by a king who'd taken pride in all of his children. Unfortunately, at the time of old Henry's death his remaining legitimate child had been a female—Maud.

Hence this war.

Nor would he chide his wife for using as examples men steadfast in their support of their half sister.

He tapped the scroll on the table, wishing he could dismiss Chester as easily as did Gwendolyn.

The earl was his father, and ever since King Stephen had bestowed Camelen on an undeserving soldier, Alberic had sought to prove himself worthy of both the honor and his father's acknowledgment. He certainly hadn't done so as yet. Still, personal feelings aside, Ranulf de Gernons was the most powerful earl in the northern Marches, not a man to be ignored. Declining the invitation might be a huge mistake, but disobeying the command might be courting disaster.

There was also ap Idwal to consider. The man had yet to pay for the deaths of two soldiers and for the burning of huts. Something must be done, and now that he'd healed, he must decide what and when.

But those decisions were for tomorrow. Today he had duties to attend, most notably the lighting of the bonfire. There were gifts to present and dancers to watch. And an adorable goddess with whom to cavort and engage in lusty spring rites.

❧

"'To my lovely and loving sister, Gwendolyn, who I pray will recommend me to her most excellent husband, Alberic, lord of Camelen, my greetings.'"

"Read that part again. Either you read it wrongly or my hearing is faulty."

Gwendolyn glanced up from Nicole's letter to smile across the trestle table at Alberic, unable to resist the urge to tease.

"My sister thinks I am lovely."

His arms crossed on the table, he leaned forward, the spark in his eyes a welcome sight. Perhaps the gaiety of Beltane had lifted his spirits, though she'd like to think her earlier outburst at the earl's unimaginable, unacceptable shunning of a baseborn son had brightened his spirits, too.

"Your sister's sight does her proud. 'Tis your attempt to alter her words that concerns me."

Gwendolyn turned the letter around and held it up so he could see she did no such thing. "'Excellent husband.' Clear as day. Satisfied?"

He leaned back. "Unbelievable. Go on."

Gwendolyn turned the letter around, admitting her surprise that Nicole deigned to mention Alberic, much less in good terms. Either Nicole suffered a softening of her heart, or the lessons on how to write a proper letter had prompted her courtesy.

"'On this fourth morning since God, in His wisdom, guided me to Bledloe Abbey—'"

"Wait until Sedwick hears he is divine."

Again Gwendolyn glanced across the table. "You interrupted me all through Emma's letter, making it impossible to comprehend the first time through. If you intend to do so again, I shall not read it aloud."

"Emma called me your most noble and honorable husband."

Gwendolyn narrowed her eyes. "Soon to be my most sorry husband if he does not keep silent."

Alberic rose from the table and snatched up their mugs. "I am off to refill these with ale. You may read and inform me if there is aught of import in it."

Gwendolyn suspected the amount of ale he'd consumed might also be affecting his mood, but said nothing as he strode off. He hadn't yet decided on whether or not to make the journey to Chester to see his father. A startling revelation, that.

What remained of her discontent over his part in William's death had now vanished. Garrett had told her, weeks ago, of how Alberic had stood between her brother and the earl. Now she knew Alberic had been defending his own father, a man who didn't deserve his son's defense. And before she could become outraged on Alberic's behalf again, which would do no good, she again turned her attention to Nicole's letter.

On this fourth morning since God, in His wisdom, guided me to Bledloe Abbey, my heart cries for joy that my fears were unwarranted. I share a cell with a sweet girl two years older than me. My cot is comfortable. Our meals are simple but filling. The nuns are kind. The garden is blooming and I am learning to discern a plant from a weed. If it is God's will that I must dwell in a nunnery, I do not think I shall mind overmuch if I may stay here. Mother Abbess says I must pray for the Lord's guidance and attend to my lessons. So I shall.

Blessings upon you and all the good people of Camelen. Your devoted sister, Nicole.

Uneasy, Gwendolyn glanced around for Alberic. He stood near the ale barrel speaking to Garrett and Sedwick, both of whom had returned in the past days, making it easier for her to convince Alberic to rest and heal. Apparently he wasn't in any hurry to either fill the mugs or return to the table.

She should be overjoyed Nicole had settled into her new surroundings so nicely, but something about the letter proved bothersome. Unable to identify the source of her unease, Gwendolyn made her way up to the bedchamber, where she put the scroll on the table beside the two others that had arrived today.

Three letters.

She shivered even though she wasn't wearing the trefoil pendant and she'd lit no candles. The letters numbered three, and all were troublesome.

Emma's letter had arrived shortly after the earl's, filled with news about her arrival, confirmation of the king's orders for the disposition of the de Leon siblings, and of her position at court. Imagine, Emma a queen's handmaiden! Unfortunately, since the war wasn't going as well as hoped, the queen had advised Emma that now was not the time to bother King Stephen with so trivial a matter as an unhappy little girl in a nunnery. Emma would wait for a better time.

But there might not be a better time soon. Emma had mentioned gossip of Chester leaving Wallingford, and that some were questioning the earl's loyalty to the king. Her sister had no notion, of course, of Alberic and Chester's relationship, and how interested Alberic had been in the gossip.

Perhaps because the day was Beltane, or because after reading Emma's letter the thought had crossed her mind that only King Arthur could force King Stephen and

Empress Maud to settle their differences civilly, receiving a third letter had seemed a bad omen.

Alberic came into the room carrying their ale. "How does Nicole?"

Gwendolyn thought to say nothing of her suspicions, but if she couldn't talk about them to Alberic, with whom could she share them?

"Something is wrong."

He put the ale down and picked up the letter. After a few moments he shrugged a shoulder and returned the letter to beside Emma's. "To me it seems as though she has made peace with the place."

"To me it sounds like another person wrote it."

"Do you recognize the handwriting?"

"Aye, but I fully expected a plea for someone to come get her, not this."

"Perhaps the experience has been good for her."

"Maybe. Still, I have half a notion to visit and see what demon has possessed her."

"Leave it be, for now. Likely Nicole wished to put a good face on it so you would not worry."

That would certainly explain the oddity; Nicole could be considerate when she wanted to be. Except Nicole rarely wanted to be considerate.

Gwendolyn placed her sisters' letters in her trunk, then glanced at the window. The light was beginning to fade.

"'Tis nearly time for you to light the bonfire."

"Nearly. What say we put the time before it to good use."

She didn't have to ask what he considered "good use."

"Every time we try during daylight we are interrupted." She tossed her arms around his neck, giving him access to the surcoat's side ties, which he immediately tugged. "Here I was so sure you would wish to wait until later this eve and drag me off into the woods."

"We can do that, too, but given the choice between a soft bed and the hard ground, I prefer the soft bed."

"I gather you know all about hard ground."

He chuckled. "'Twas Beltane, and the wench was more than willing and I am a weak man."

No, he wasn't. He might be vulnerable, which made him human, but never weak, not of body or of will.

Her surcoat loosened, she tugged open the ties of his tunic to expose his throat, planting a kiss at the hollow, eliciting a moan.

"Are you saying she seduced you?"

"With a saucy mouth and the thrust of her hip."

"For me Beltane always ended with the lighting of the bonfire. Then I was hurried off to my bed before I could participate in the debauchery. 'Tis not fair that I have had no other lover so cannot compare."

"Do I pleasure you?"

Silly question. Apparently he'd learned much from saucy-mouthed wenches. While Gwendolyn refused to thank his previous lovers, she could hardly be too upset because she benefited from his experience.

"You know you pleasure me."

"Then there is naught to compare."

She pulled on his tunic until it came off over his head. "Not all men are put together the same, or so I hear."

"Nor are all women." He removed her surcoat and chemise as one, and the desire darkening his eyes thrilled her to her core. "Were I to search the entire kingdom, I would find no woman I prefer to take to my bed over my wife. God's truth, Gwendolyn, you have ruined me for all others."

Sweet mercy, he'd turned her into a wanton, lusty wench, so hungry for the coupling she nearly broke the ties on his breeches.

With a flurry of hands they divested each other of remaining clothing, eager to make good use of the soft bed, or so Gwendolyn thought. But once in bed, lying skin to skin and limbs entwined, Alberic seemed content to lie still and merely hold her.

After long moments, she had to ask, "Is aught amiss?"

"Nay. I was merely thinking how well we fit together, how well suited we are. I fear to ask for more, but I cannot help hope our union will be blessed with a child or two."

Every man needed his heirs, and 'twas a wife's duty to provide them, a duty she'd given little thought to except in regard to the legacy. She, too, needed an heir. A daughter to whom she someday would entrust the scroll and pendant if she didn't invoke the spell herself.

She'd had her woman's time once since the wedding, coming on a few hours after Thomas hauled an unconscious Alberic in from the village, and lasting its usual five days. Considering her other upsets, she'd not given the weeping of her womb much thought.

With an inward grin she thought it utterly perfect if Alberic could get her with child on Beltane.

Gwen pressed hard against the source of life-producing seed. "Then you must plant often and deeply. Do you foresee a problem with that, my lord?"

"None at all," he said with enthusiasm, and proceeded to prepare her to receive him.

'Struth, she needed little preparation. She'd become wet during their disrobing, her yearning for the coupling becoming more acute with each garment tossed aside. But she didn't stop him when he insisted upon fondling her breasts, the nipples hardening under the skillful brush of his thumb. Nor did she object when his fingers slid up her thighs, seeking a particularly sensitive spot that when stroked drove her nearly senseless.

Greedy wench that she was, she allowed him to kiss and pet and fondle wherever he wished for as long as he wanted, until, on the verge of bliss, she gave him a shove to roll him on his back.

He didn't object, obeying her high-handed command instantly. He tucked his hands under his head and closed his eyes, giving her the same open and complete access to his body as she'd given him. With hands and mouth she roamed the wide plane of his chest, and smiled when his stomach quivered at her light touch.

She didn't linger there overlong, however. Though she might be a novice at bed play, she'd become aware of Alberic's preferences and discovered what he liked most. Kneeling between his widespread legs, Gwendolyn grasped his already hard penis and with slow, firm strokes made him harder.

The first time she'd done so, she'd been amazed and delighted at the rush of power she'd felt. Then later, some evil imp inside her had taken over and she leaned down to kiss the tip. He'd nearly come up off the mattress. Now she braced on both arms and, with the tip of her tongue, licked his hard, proud sex from base to tip.

He hissed. So she did it again. His inhale was hard and deep in an effort to maintain control. Her third long stroke was all he could take. He grabbed her upper arms and hauled her up to lay atop him.

"Have mercy, Gwen. Any more and I shall be done before I am started."

She squirmed against him. "Do I pleasure you, my lord?"

"You know damn well you do."

"Then might I suggest 'tis your turn again."

He didn't need to be told twice. He flipped her over, entered her, filled her. With slow strokes he took her to the brink of a precipice, and with swift thrusts tossed her over the edge.

In the midst of her fall she felt him throb within her, the planting complete and deep. 'Twould be weeks before she knew if the seed took root. If not, well, they would simply have to try again . . . and again. Not an unpleasant prospect.

He nuzzled her neck. "Now are you not glad I chose the bed over hard ground? You have no twigs tangled in your hair or rocks poking your back."

She smiled, running her hands over his broad shoulders. "Then I shall have to trust you will find us a patch of long, soft grass for our tryst."

He lifted his head. "You truly want to tryst in the woods?"

"'Tis Beltane, so we should participate fully in the spring rites. What better than to honor a long-standing tradition?"

"Not for the lord and lady."

"Especially for the lord and lady. Who better to beckon the blessings of the gods and goddesses of fertility?"

He tossed back his head and laughed. "Then so be it. If my lady wishes to cavort in the grass, I will not say her nay."

Still smiling, still joined with her, he shook his head. "I swear, Gwendolyn, I never dreamed marriage would suit me so well. 'Tis far more than I expected, and I thank you for making it so."

His kiss was soft and gentle, a peace-filled expression of contentment. Then he rolled over, relieving her of his weight, taking her with him to enjoy the aftermath of their exertions.

She, too, had found more in this marriage than she expected, the joys of the marriage bed merely one of them.

Never would she have expected to fall in love with Alberic. She loved the man who hadn't been carefully selected for her, whom she truly should dislike for coming into her life through violence and misery. Whom she married because she'd seen no way out of it.

She'd given up examining her unexplainable feelings and berating her heart for succumbing so easily. Still, she'd been raised to expect the man she married would love her in return. If Alberic never came to see her as more than a suitable wife, could she live with the lack?

'Twas disheartening to know in that, too, she had no choice. The king had ordered Alberic to marry one of Hugh de Leon's daughters, and Alberic had done his duty, choosing her because of her age and health. Affection played no part in his decision, just as emotion wasn't a consideration in most noble marriage bargains. Many husbands never came to love their wives. One couldn't bind a heart that didn't want to be bound.

But if the heart already held caring and affection, as did Alberic's, perhaps love could bloom. With a bit of a nudge, love might grow.

Snug against Alberic's side, Gwendolyn wondered if she dared try to provide that nudge—with magic.

Chapter Sixteen

ALBERIC WASN'T SURE why he felt the need to seek out Gwendolyn. Maybe because she'd been so quiet this morning. Or perhaps because she'd taken a furtive glance around the hall before heading up the stairs, as if ensuring everyone was occupied so they wouldn't miss her.

Come to think on it, she'd been rather preoccupied since their tryst in the woods on the night before last, which Alberic could hardly believe had happened. Imagine the lady of the castle dragging the lord out into the woods for Beltane debauchery. He'd felt lecherous and lusty, and had found that soft patch of long grass she'd expected him to provide.

He smiled, remembering how she'd lost a bit of her daring, unable to bring herself to disrobe. She'd lifted her skirts and he'd lowered his breeches, then they'd rutted like the beasts of the forest—secretly and silently with little finesse and all heady sensation. A fine, lusty way to celebrate the rites of spring.

Why she'd wanted to make love that way, he couldn't say. Perhaps merely because, as she'd said, she'd never had the opportunity to sneak off into the woods with a male before and wanted to satisfy her curiosity. Fine with him. Whatever curiosities she wanted satisfying, he'd be most willing to satisfy.

But right now his own curiosity nudged him toward the stairs and up to where he'd thought she'd gone. The bedchamber.

She stood near the trunks, her gaze rising from her clenched hand at his entrance. Chagrined, she glanced back at her hand, and the hair on the back of his neck itched. He knew what she held before she opened her hand to reveal the trefoil pendant.

"I shall have to be more careful next time," she said.

Tempted to rip the pendant from her hand, he closed the door and leaned against it. "Why do you have that out? I thought we agreed you should put it away and leave it be."

"Had I better control over my thoughts, you would not have known I took it out." She picked up the chain, allowing the pendant to dangle, the rainbows to fly around the room. "It appears I need no candles to unleash its powers."

Not sure if he truly wanted to know what she meant, he asked, "What powers?"

"I called you to me."

"Not that I heard."

"All the same, I did so."

"Nonsense!"

She arched an eyebrow. "Is it? My thoughts were of you, and so you came, as you did the other night. I thought I needed to light candles or say your name aloud. I was wrong."

Her belief in magic was deeper than he'd thought. Not only did she believe the two of them could summon King Arthur back from the dead, she now believed she could call him to her side by merely wishing on the pendant.

The very thought of the possibility that magic could exist bothered him. The notion of someone controlling his actions with a mere wish was terrifying. No such magic existed, of course. Unfortunately, Gwendolyn was not only convinced magic existed but that she could use it. He worried for her sanity, and that someone would learn of this silliness and brand her a witch.

Something had to be done, quickly and firmly.

"You did not call me, Gwendolyn. I noticed how furtively you left the hall and became curious over what you were about, that is all."

"But it has happened twice, now and the other night, just before the fire in the village. I called out your name and within moments you came upstairs!"

It took him a moment to realize what she was talking about. He'd been on the verge of a tumble with Gwendolyn when a guard interrupted them to announce ap Idwal's menace. Before that, he'd been down in the hall with Roger and Thomas.

He remembered the feeling of something being amiss, of his instincts urging him to find Gwendolyn. But at no time had he heard her call out to him.

"Coincidence. We were done discussing the preparations for the siege and I wished to spend some time with you in the hours before dawn. I heard no call that night, either."

He started toward her. She grasped the pendant tightly and, childishly, hid her fist behind her back, as if he couldn't take it from her if he didn't see it. She held out her other hand, palm outward, as if that would stop him.

"But I did call you!" she protested. "I wore the pendant for several hours the other day—"

That stopped him. "You *what*?"

"I wished to know what would happen if I wore it."

"I saw it not."

"I hid it beneath my chemise so you would not know." She tossed her hand upward. "You forced me to question everything my parents told me about the legacy. So I conducted a test to discern if you could be right."

His hand shook when he raised it to rub at his brow. "Dear God, Gwendolyn."

"Alberic, if you believe this pendant holds no magic, then I should be able to wear it as freely as you wear the ring, which you still have not been able to remove, have you?"

Aye, she should be able to wear the pendant and nay, he hadn't removed the ring, having given up trying. Nothing, however, would convince him that he wouldn't, someday, find a way to take it off.

"That you wear the pendant is not as disturbing as what you believe can happen when you wear it!"

She slipped the damn thing over her head. "Take my hand."

He stared at her outstretched hand.

"If there is no magic, naught will happen," she stated firmly, daring him to cooperate.

Nothing would happen because magic didn't exist. He knew that. So why did he hesitate to accept her challenge?

"You wore the pendant the other day and nothing happened, correct? So why bother now?"

"Because now you know I wear it and we are alone. Perhaps that will make a difference."

Chiding himself for cowardice, he took her hand. 'Twas warm, as always, and fitted perfectly in his, as always, and his loins stirred at her touch—as always. Normal feelings and reactions all.

She looked at him quizzically, waiting for him to tell her that he, what? Could feel some kind of power? He could, but not the kind of power she expected.

"I want you, Gwen. But that is not unusual, is it? Given that we are alone in our bedchamber, I should think the stirring in my loins quite normal."

He wasn't sorry to see disappointment. Then she slipped away, headed for the hearth and lit a taper. Though it was the middle of the morning, she lit a candle. Before she could light a second, he figured out what she intended to do. 'Twas time to stop this idiocy before she went too far.

He snatched the taper from her hand. "Enough, Gwendolyn. I will stand for no more!"

"You fear if I light the candles I will prove you wrong."

"I fear for your mind! If you light the candles and nothing happens, then what? Do we drink some nasty potion? Must we anoint ourselves with special oils? Perhaps we must stand on one foot, facing south. And if all those do not produce the results you wish, then what else will you decide must be done? Well, I am having none of it!" He stretched out his hand in demand. "Take off the pendant and give it to me. I shall put it away this time so it remains put away!"

She backed up a step. "You fear what you do not understand."

"Apparently you do not understand, either, or you would not be conducting these ridiculous tests!"

"At least I try to understand. You make no effort!"

"I have no reason to try! Gwendolyn, you cannot perform magic. You cannot summon me to your side simply by thinking of me. You will never be able to summon King Arthur from Avalon. The entire legacy is *nonsense!*"

She bit her bottom lip, hard, telling him how desperately she wanted to refute him. Wisely, she didn't try, but merely stood there looking hurt and disillusioned. Better that than her continuing to believe a ridiculous falsehood. Whoever had perpetrated this nonsense on her parents, and so onto Gwendolyn, should be hanged from a stout oak and left as carrion for the ravens to pick clean.

He extended his hand again, palm upward. "Give me the pendant."

The demand squared her shoulders. "'Tis mine, a gift from my mother. No matter whether you believe in the legacy or not, you may not have it."

Her outright defiance took him aback. "You are my wife, Gwendolyn. What is yours is mine."

She shook her head. "Not the pendant! I may give it to no other than the next guardian."

He lowered his hand, stunned. Short of ripping it from around her neck, which he refused to lower himself to do, she wasn't giving it over.

Next guardian? *Passed from mother to daughter.*

That he would never allow. To have Gwendolyn delusioned was bad enough without her passing on a false legacy to a daughter. They didn't have one yet and might never have, but he still vowed to protect her as a father should, even from her mother.

Somehow he had to save them both. Somehow he had to decisively convince Gwendolyn that King Arthur was dead, buried, and would never again walk English soil!

On his own, he couldn't. He'd tried and been rebuffed—defied! He needed help, and he knew where to find it. At Chester. Which meant facing his own demons, but he knew of no other way to put this legacy nonsense to rest. *Damn.*

"Several years ago, a man by the name of Geoffrey of Monmouth wrote a history of the kings of England. The *Historia Regum Britanniae*. Have you read it?"

"I have heard of it but not read it."

Neither had he, only heard parts of it discussed. But from what he'd heard, he was sure the book contained the answer to his dilemma.

"'Tis my understanding that the tome also contains the prophecies of Merlin. I believe 'tis time you read them."

"You have a copy of this book?"

"Nay, but I know who does. Prepare for a visit to Chester. We leave on the morn."

The town of Chester looked no different from when he'd left it for Wallingford.

On the palfrey beside him, Gwendolyn stretched this way and that in an effort to take in the sights along the dirt-packed streets. From those streets, people stared up at who most knew as the earl's by-blow, with his new wife and a small entourage in their wake.

Alberic wondered if he should have listened to Gwendolyn and brought a larger retinue. She'd argued that a baron should travel with no fewer than a company of twelve, six of those being knights. He'd balked, bringing only two knights, one of them Garrett. Roger, four liveried soldiers, the cart driver, and a maid for Gwendolyn made up the entire entourage. Until now, when no one raised an impressed eyebrow, did he admit he'd truly wanted to impress his father's people, allow them to remark upon how well the unacknowledged son had done for himself.

Too late for a show of rise in rank, wealth, and power. Too late to impress his father.

Only one bejeweled ring sat upon Alberic's hand: the seal of the dragon. He wore no gold chains around his neck, no showy brooch fastened his mantle. Instead of spending a portion of his newly gained wealth on flashy baubles, he'd purchased lumber and labor to repair fire-ravaged huts. All well and good, but the earl would dismiss the altruism as unnecessary because Alberic gained naught of import from it.

Peace of mind didn't have a place on the earl's ledger. Wealth and power were all that counted in his books, and he'd done a damn good job of ever adding to both.

Alberic spotted a few familiar faces. A bar wench, whom he ignored completely. The blacksmith who'd repaired his chain mail a time or two rated an acknowledging bob of his head. Two of his father's knights came out of an apothecary shop, and to their hails of greeting Alberic raised a hand.

He led the way through the gate in the thick stone wall that separated the castle grounds from the town that had grown up around it. Gwendolyn sat tall and erect in her saddle, her expression serene, though she must be impressed by the size of the earl's residence. She gave nothing of her thoughts away, however, as a proper, well-bred wife of a baron shouldn't.

But then, a proper, well-bred wife of a baron wouldn't have defied her husband over possession of a pendant, forcing him to make this journey to Chester! Alberic tucked away his ire as he had since their argument. If this journey turned Gwendolyn right-headed, then he considered the time and money well spent.

Naturally, a guard at the city gate had hustled to the castle to inform the inner garrison of Alberic's arrival. A bevy of stable lads and servants hovered near the steps to lend the company assistance, and with them, quite to Alberic's surprise, stood Lady Mathilda.

An honor, that. While he would like to think the honor all for him, he knew it wasn't. As the daughter of a Norman baron and Welsh princess, Gwendolyn was due consideration in her own right, and the wife of the earl well knew which personages in England were due consideration.

Young and pretty, fair and blond, and of royal blood, Mathilda had married Ranulf de Gernons several years ago in a political marriage arranged by her father, Robert, earl of Gloucester. How she managed to remain on good terms with both her empress-loyal family and her now king-supporting husband, Alberic didn't know.

But he knew her greeting smile for him was genuine,

and didn't doubt she would take proper care of Gwendolyn during those times when it proved necessary.

Alberic dismounted and aided Gwendolyn down from her palfrey, then led his wife to their beaming hostess.

"You bring me company, Alberic. How very sweet of you!"

Alberic took Mathilda's outstretched hand and bowed over it. "Lady Mathilda, you honor us with your greeting. I should like you to meet my wife, Lady Gwendolyn."

Gwendolyn dipped into a deep curtsy. "I am in your debt for your courtesy, Lady Mathilda."

Mathilda accepted the obiescense as her due and waited for Gwendolyn to rise before grasping her hand, too. "I am delighted the both of you accepted the earl's invitation. He knows you are here, Alberic, and awaits you in the solar. Your wife and I shall have a pleasant visit until the two of you join us for supper."

Alberic wasn't surprised the earl wished an immediate audience, and he had no excuse to linger, knowing Mathilda would see all in his company settled in short order.

"I beg a boon, my lady. Gwendolyn is most interested in Monmouth's *Historia*. Might she be afforded the honor of reading your copy?"

"Of course, Alberic. We shall have our visit in the library."

"Then I shall leave Gwendolyn in your most excellent care."

He bowed off, gathering his resolve to endure what was sure to be an uncomfortable meeting with his father. He'd taken no more than five steps when he heard Gwendolyn call his name. He turned to see her rushing toward him. She stopped a mere foot away, so close he caught her lavender fragrance.

She bit her bottom lip, a sure sign she wished to say something she wasn't sure she should say. Likely she wished to issue some order, which he preferred to think of as well-meant advice or suggestions. Just this morning she'd advised him to wear his scarlet-and-gold tunic for his visit with the earl. He'd done so, not bothering to tell her that he'd already made that decision.

He smiled down at her. "You rarely hesitate to speak your mind. Out with it, Gwen."

"Pray remember you need not court the earl's favor any further than you wish to."

Encouragement delivered as instruction. It struck him that in the past weeks she'd come to know him better than he knew her.

"You need not worry over me, Gwendolyn."

"'Tis part of a wife's duty, Alberic."

And with that, she spun on her heel and returned to Lady Mathilda.

Now dismissed by both women, he made his way up the stairs into the great hall, then up more stairs to the earl's solar. Not until he was outside the door did it occur to him that tonight he would sleep in a room on this very floor instead of out in the barracks. The notion that as a baron he now rated a bed in the castle amused him, so it was with a smile on his face that he knocked on the door, though he was careful to hide all emotion before obeying the earl's order to enter.

The earl of Chester sat behind a large, ornate desk of dark, highly polished wood. Several scrolls sat off to the side, with one spread out before him. The man needed to neither wear nor display any trappings of power. His very presence dominated the room, and Alberic knew better than to let his father know how very dominated he felt.

In that he wasn't alone. The earl intimidated most everyone, from the lowliest of peasants to the highest of nobles. Green eyes that perfectly matched Alberic's stared out of a face older but of similar cut and hue. He raised a hand to stroke his bushy mustache, the facial hair an oddity among Normans, who preferred to face the world clean-shaven.

"I rather expected you to arrive yesterday," the earl said in his deep, commanding voice.

Alberic heard both the admonishment and disappointment.

"I decided to delay a day," he answered, surprising himself by halting with the simple statement, giving no explanation or apology. Gwendolyn would be proud of him.

Chester waved him to a chair. "Have a pleasant journey?"

He removed his cloak and tossed it over the back of the chair, knowing the earl truly didn't care whether the journey had been pleasant or not. It had been pleasant because as efficiently as Gwendolyn ran his household, she'd packed for their journey.

He settled into the heavy, armed chair, allowing his hands to dangle over the ends of the arms, his ring in plain view. "Pleasant enough considering the weather."

"Do you find Camelen to your taste?"

He couldn't begin to tell the earl just how much he enjoyed Camelen. "It suits me well enough."

"Which daughter did you marry?"

"The middle daughter, Gwendolyn. She is currently with Lady Mathilda."

"Any problems on that score?"

The earl truly didn't care about that, either, and Alberic saw no sense in revealing his problems with Gwendolyn. Not that they were many. She no longer seemed to hold the death of her brother, or his possession of Camelen, or their forced marriage against him. At the least, she'd not mentioned them of late. If not for this nonsense about magic and King Arthur, he believed his marriage would be nigh on damn near perfect.

"She has accepted me and the marriage."

For that, Alberic earned an approving nod, and he found himself uncaring of whether or not the earl approved of his marriage. How strange, considering how many years he'd spent seeking Chester's approval.

"Do you know why I asked you to come?"

"I assume to discuss how the war progresses. Has the king made inroads at Wallingford?"

"He believes he has." The earl shrugged his broad shoulders. "If one can call isolating Brian fitz Count from the rest of the rebel forces progress, then I suppose he has. Unfortunately, in order to keep the man isolated, Stephen must commit troops he could use to greater advantage elsewhere."

From Chester's easy manner and offhand use of the king's name, Alberic assumed the earl remained the king's supporter. However, Chester would rather the king take a more aggressive route to winning the war, and thus take back the honor of Carlisle, held by King David of Scotland, a supporter of Maud's, and hand it over to the person whom Chester believed the honor belonged: the earl of Chester. 'Twas all Chester wanted as an end result of this war, and he would serve whichever royal personage he thought might give him Carlisle in payment for his loyalty. At present, that royal personage happened to be King Stephen.

"Your force is no longer needed?"

"I left two hundred knights at Wallingford and brought the others home. My presence is still felt, for now." His impatience with the situation clear, Chester spun the parchment on his desk and gave it a small shove. "Look at this."

Wary, Alberic rose to obey and found himself looking at a map of Wales. His heart thudded against his chest, very sure of what the earl was planning. Chester made no secret of his ambitions as far as Wales was concerned, either. Knowing Carlisle was beyond his reach for now, he'd decided to turn his sight in another direction.

"'Tis a map of Wales. I assume you wish to rearrange its borders."

Chester actually chuckled. "A fine way to put it. Truth to tell, I wish to do away with the damn border from here to here."

The line he drew with his finger was long. Chester craved almost the whole northern half of Wales.

"Ambitious."

"Less would make no sense. If the north falls, the south will follow in due time, but I care naught for it. Let another grab it if he can."

Alberic doubted Chester would feel that way if the north did fall and the south lay open for the taking. The earl would seize whatever he could manage.

"The commitment to such an endeavor must be total. Have you enough support?"

"If you ask if the king shows interest, nay, not as yet. But soon now he will tire of looking at Wallingford from the outside and seek new ventures. When that time comes, I plan to have the pieces in place to launch an invasion from here. Between the forces William and I can provide, and those of the royal army, we could sweep through a vast area before the Welsh know we are coming."

William de Roumare, earl of Lincoln, typically supported Chester's schemes. The half brothers could cause the Welsh more Norman trouble than they'd suffered in years, whether the king joined with them or not. Between the two earls, they commanded the greater part of the north of England and ruled it in royal fashion.

Alberic decided to ask the obvious question. "Do you truly believe the king will neglect his war with Maud to invade Wales?"

"He would be a fool not to." Chester pointed to several spots on the map. "If we captured these castles, he would have bases from which to launch attacks on Bristol without stretching his supply lines. By controlling this area"—his hand covered a large area of Wales—"we would so worry Maud, she would be forced to negotiate or flee."

"They have negotiated before and come to no resolution."

"Precisely. If Maud finds herself trapped in Bristol, she is likely to flee, as she has done many times before. Except this time she has fewer choices of secure shelter. With the exception of Bristol, most of her strongholds are now under the king's control. So she gets on a ship and flees back to the continent. With Maud out of the country, her support dwindles. Eventually her supporters will treat with King Stephen to keep their lands, and we hear from the empress no more."

Making a grand hero of Chester for doing nothing more than convincing the king to help him get what he really wanted.

"Would it not be better to capture Maud?"

"Robert is an intelligent man. He will put his sister on a ship bound for Normandy before we get close enough to Bristol to prevent her leaving. Besides, if she was captured and imprisoned, then her supporters would do their best to free her. Better if she is out of sight and mind."

The reasoning made sense. Deprive the enemy of its head and wait for the body to fall.

"What happens if the king does not agree?"

"Then William and I are of a mind to go on our own, and so my reason for summoning you. As baron of Camelen you now have resources of both men and provisions. You are the first to whom I offer the opportunity to join us, as a commander under your own banner."

Alberic strove to hide the thrill that ran through him, doubting he succeeded entirely. For so many years he'd ridden in his father's wake, engaged in battle as part of his troops. For all of those years he'd longed to ride at his father's side, as a son. The offer of joining his father's campaign as a valued peer, under his own banner, came just short of fulfilling a lifelong dream.

And damnit, the earl knew it.

But the earl courted the baron of Camelen, not Alberic the son, and as a baron Alberic must make the decision.

The campaign wasn't without risks, both militarily and personally. If he committed Camelen to such a venture, and it failed, he placed his barony in danger. With the sweep of quill on parchment the king could take it away. Dare he even consider it?

He'd been quiet too long. The earl's eyes had narrowed.

"You ask much of me," Alberic stated. "What am I offered in return?"

Alberic sensed he'd asked exactly the right question.

"You get ap Idwal's holding."

He nearly leaped at the bait, and crossed his arms over his chest to hold himself back. That the earl knew of Alberic's dealings with ap Idwal didn't surprise him. News of events of any consequence flew on the winged feet of traveling merchants, pilgrims, and those informants men in high places paid to keep them apprised of happenings throughout the kingdom.

Alberic could damn near taste sweet revenge on the Welshman. But the earl did nothing without reason, his own self-serving reason.

"Do I get it free and clear, or in fealty to you?"

Chester raised an eyebrow. "We speak of Wales. Only an earl could hope to hold it within his grasp as attached to an earldom. You could not possibly hold it long on your own."

Unfortunately, Chester was probably right. 'Twould take the power of at least an earldom to hold Welsh lands securely. To hold it of royal writ would be even better.

If the king approved of and partnered this venture, Alberic knew he would accept in a gnat's breath. But Chester meant to carry through without royal approval, which meant he needed all the help he could get to avoid royal displeasure, the only penalty Chester faced. The king didn't have the right to take the earldom from Chester as he did to deprive a barony from Alberic.

And knowing this, the temptation to risk all fair screamed at him to accept.

"How large a force must I commit?"

"Twenty knights, one hundred footmen. Not an unreasonable force for a barony."

Not unreasonable at all. Chester could have required double the force, which Alberic would be expected to not only command but provision. And knowing the way armies worked, likely his men would be among the first to engage in any battle. The thought both terrified and excited him. This would be his chance, at last, to prove his mettle to his father.

The son should accept now, before the father changed his mind. But the baron knew that he didn't dare be lured so easily. Among nobility, negotiations of this type sometimes took days, even months of haggling back and forth before agreements were reached. And even then, when the battle was engaged, one was never sure if the commanders would stand their ground or pull their troops from the fray without warning. In such a manner had the king once been captured, when his earls had disengaged, leaving King Stephen standing in the middle of the field with only a few men and his own sword to defend himself.

A fleeting, fragile thing, loyalty. One could never trust in it, no matter the vows given or oaths spoken. One could only rely on oneself, a lesson he'd learned at the age of twelve and took to heart now. The earl might offer ap Idwal's holding, but if the time came to deliver, would he?

Alberic knew he had time to contemplate his answer. In fact, if he didn't take more time and ask for more than merely ap Idwal's holding, his father would think him too easily made a puppet. And that wouldn't do at all.

"You have given me much to consider." Alberic scooped his cloak from the back of the chair and draped it over his arm. "Perhaps we can talk more on the matter on the morrow."

From behind his imposing desk, the earl nodded, giving nothing of his thoughts away.

Without waiting for a dismissal, Alberic bowed out of the earl's solar, torn between the chance of achieving several goals on the one hand, and losing all he'd already gained on the other. Hellfire, the price of power was a double-edged sword he was still learning how to wield.

The hell of it was, in the learning he could easily slice off his own head, as had Sir Hugh de Leon when he'd allowed a personal grudge against Chester to cloud his judgment, getting himself and his son killed and leaving his daughters to suffer the consequences.

And something in Chester's reasoning seemed flawed. The whole plan for forcing Maud to give up her battle for the crown seemed too easy. What that flaw was, Alberic couldn't quite reach out and grab hold of.

Over the years he'd watched Chester become involved in risky schemes, putting the entire force of his earldom behind attempts to gain land and wealth. Thus far, for the most part, he'd succeeded. But Alberic sensed a day of reckoning on the horizon, and wasn't sure he wanted to be there when the day arrived.

Still, the vision of descending upon ap Idwal's holding, with a large force of Normans at his back and Camelen's banner flying high, appealed greatly. To crush Madog ap Idwal for his audacity to covet Gwendolyn, the death of two soldiers, and the burning of the village might be worth the risk.

Chapter Seventeen

GWENDOLYN RESOLVED not to gape at the wealth evident in yet another chamber, as she'd caught herself doing several times during the tour of Chester's castle.

Having finally reached the library, she took the chair Lady Mathilda indicated—a heavy piece of highly polished dark wood, the seat cushioned by a pillow fashioned of emerald velvet and gold cord. Her feet rested on a rug of what appeared to be braided wool. A huge tapestry of knights at the hunt took up the whole of one wall. Along another wall shelves of oak held both parchment scrolls and books of vellum sheets pressed between leather covers.

By the light of expensive beeswax candles in the various sconces and candle stands, Mathilda poured wine into bejeweled goblets. After handing one to Gwendolyn, the lady eased into a similar chair, stretched out her legs, and flexed her silk-slippered feet.

"I always forget how many stairs are in the castle until I show someone the lay of it. Pray, taste the wine. I hope you find it pleasing."

Gwendolyn did as bid, hoping she didn't knock one of

the jewels from its setting or spill on the rug. She was used to fine things, but not this fine, and she struggled against feeling the veriest peasant among her betters. Not that Mathilda flouted her royal status. 'Struth, she'd been most gracious and generous with her time.

The wine went down so smoothly Gwendolyn couldn't help an appreciative low moan.

Mathilda laughed lightly. "'Tis one of Alberic's favorites. I shall provide you with the name of the merchant who supplies Chester. I have also instructed the cook to give you directions for a few dishes your husband is fond of."

"You are most kind."

"Kindness has naught to do with my offer. Now that Alberic has the wherewithal to provide for himself, he should do so to his tastes." She tilted her head, her expression softening. "I admit I am most pleased at Alberic's good fortune. Unfortunately, his rise in status came at a high price for you and your sisters, and for that I am truly sorry and saddened. I have fond memories of your parents, may God grant them eternal peace."

The last caught Gwendolyn by surprise. "You knew my parents?"

Mathilda's smile returned. "My family often journeyed from Bristol to Shrewsbury, and one time my father stopped at Camelen to see Sir Hugh and Lady Lydia. A storm hit during supper, and we were forced to spend the night. That was . . . oh, dear, too many years ago. I was young, so you would have been younger still, so would not likely remember."

Mathilda couldn't be more than a few years Gwendolyn's elder, and she was married to a much older man.

Though by all accounts age hadn't diminished the earl's vibrant personality and virile good looks. If nature followed course, Alberic would live well into his fortieth year in the same good health and vigor, if he didn't get himself killed in some silly fashion, like in a war—a possibility she didn't wish to contemplate overlong.

"I fear I must have still been in the nursery, for I do not remember your visit. My sister Emma might, however. I shall have to write to ask her."

The lady tilted her head in thought. "Emma. Is she not the sister who is now at Stephen's court?"

The question reminded Gwendolyn of how closely the upper nobility kept track of the comings and goings of anyone of rank, and the familiar use of the king's name reminded her that she spoke to the king's cousin.

Here was a friendship to court—a mercenary thought, but as a baron's wife it was her duty to both her husband and Camelen to develop relationships that could prove useful later. An earl's wife, and a royal personage in her own right, Lady Mathilda could prove a valuable ally.

Influence begat power. Such was the way of the nobles.

"Emma has become a queen's handmaiden. From her one letter to me I gather she is content, for the most part."

"I should imagine any discontent would come from being surrounded by those who do not share her view of who should wear the crown. You must tell her not to overly cling to her position." Mathilda smiled in conspiring fashion. "We women must have a care. One never knows when the ability to balance family, duty, and personal feelings will be most needed."

"I shall certainly pass along your advice." Gwendolyn

put her goblet down on the table, choosing her next words carefully. Though she'd thought to seek Mathilda's advice on getting Nicole released from the convent, the conversation had taken a path Gwendolyn felt compelled to follow. "You seem to have found the point of balance. You are closely related to both the king and the empress, whom your father supports. Your husband has recently given his support to the king. It must be awkward for you to face your father."

Mathilda's sudden defensive expression sent Gwendolyn skittering to explain.

"I mean no offense, nor to pry into your private affairs. I merely hoped you might give me insights on how to cope with split loyalties to those you love. My father supported Maud, and Alberic holds Camelen for the king. No matter in which direction my feelings sway, I always feel disloyal to one or the other."

Her confession softened Mathilda's expression. "One learns to cope, though I dare say there are days when I wish I could shut Maud and Stephen in a room and not let them out until they come to terms. But both are too proud and stubborn to grant concessions, and just might kill each other if left alone too long. Then we would have a nastier mess than we have now. Maud's son Henry and Stephen's son Eustace would pick up their parents' banners and the war would continue. More lives lost. More property destroyed. More women become widows and children become orphans. A sad state of affairs all around."

"See you no end to this war, then?"

"One side must have complete victory over the other. Only then will we have peace, and an uneasy peace at that. Not only must either Maud or Stephen give up claim to the crown, but so must either Henry or Eustace. I cannot imagine either son giving up what he feels is rightfully his, can you?" She waved a dismissive hand in the air. "I digress. The truth is that neither you nor I have any say in how events will fall out. All we can do is support those who deserve our support and allow fate to have its way."

Gwendolyn couldn't say anything about her ability to influence fate by calling King Arthur from Avalon.

"So how does one decide who is the most deserving? How did you decide between your father and husband?"

"I never did, nor will I ever." Mathilda smiled. "My dear, you must not allow politics to come between you and those who deserve your support."

Gwendolyn didn't understand, and her confusion must have shown because Mathilda continued.

"When my father gave me to Ranulf, he understood that my duty would be to my husband. True, he had hoped the marriage would bring Ranulf into Maud's camp. That came to be, for a time. Ranulf aided my father in the capture of Lincoln. The alliance did not last, however, and I blame Maud for its demise." She waved a dismissive hand. "Be that as it may, my father is worldly enough to accept the loss. He also knows that I love him dearly, would do anything that I can for him, except be disloyal to my husband. Ranulf also understands that I would do anything a wife is expected to do for her husband, except hurt my father. I am both daughter and wife, and it sometimes pains me that they are on opposite sides in this war, but I find it much easier to maintain a good relationship with both if we never discuss politics."

All well and good. Mathilda simply ignored the divisive element, which wasn't an option for Gwendolyn.

"So you feel no disloyalty to your father because your husband supports the king."

"None whatsoever. Ranulf will do whatever he is driven to do. All he wants out of this war is Carlisle, which is currently in the hands of Prince Henry of Scotland. Since King David has heartily supported Maud from the beginning, Ranulf feels she would be reluctant to take Carlisle from the control of the Scots. So he now supports King Stephen, who might be convinced to hand over Carlisle if he overcomes Maud's challenge." Mathilda laughed lightly. "Of course, if Ranulf ever feels he stands a better chance of obtaining Carlisle from Maud, he will not hesitate to abandon Stephen."

How selfish! Should not an earl support either Maud or Stephen out of loyalty? A sense of duty? For what they considered the good of the kingdom?

Mathilda set her goblet on a table. "I know what you are thinking, and you must not judge Chester too harshly. When Maud presented her challenge to Stephen, each earl had to decide which claimant to the crown to support. Some joined Stephen because they could not stomach the thought of a woman on the throne. Some joined Maud because they saw a chance to gain more from her than they could from Stephen, including my father. He may actually believe in Maud's right to the throne, and love his half sister, but he also knows that if she wins he will be rewarded more handsomely than if he had sided with Stephen. Believe me, not a one of the earls made his choice out of a sense of loyalty, or for the good of the kingdom, but from whom they stood to gain the most."

And Mathilda would be in a position to know. How disheartening to realize that no one of high rank contemplated the good of the kingdom, only their own portions of it. Perhaps the time had truly come for King Arthur to sweep through and make them all see sense. Again, Gwendolyn chose her words carefully.

"I have heard the wish expressed that neither Maud nor Stephen be allowed the throne, that a third claimant, with an indisputable right to the throne, might be found to seize power and set all to rights."

Mathilda sighed. "I have heard the same. Unfortunately, other men with royal bloodlines have already been considered and discarded. Stephen will not relinquish his crown to *anyone* without a fight. 'Tis a shame my father's illegitimacy prevented him from making a claim. Were it not for the manner of his birth, as King Henry's eldest son he would have been the undisputed heir to the crown."

At least King Henry had acknowledged his son, granted him rights and honors, even granted him an earldom. 'Twas far more than Chester had done for Alberic. Gwendolyn fervently wished to ask Mathilda if she thought the earl might someday acknowledge his son, but doubted the question would be welcome. She saw no sense in offending Mathilda over a matter that rightfully belonged between Alberic and his father.

How odd that if not for the taint of illegitimacy, Robert of Gloucester might now be King Robert, and Mathilda a princess. Surely, the lady wouldn't now be wed to an earl, but to a king or an emperor.

"You have been most generous with your time and observations this morning, my lady. I thank you for your courtesy."

"Truly, our visit has been a pleasure. I suppose I should fetch the book you wished to read."

Mathilda rose and strode over to the shelves, from which she pulled a leather-covered book. "You have an interest in the history of the kings of England?"

Only one king, Arthur. And she dare not tell Mathilda of the depth of her interest.

"I have heard many tales of the ancient kings in the songs of the bards. Alberic mentioned you have a large collection of books here at Chester and was certain a copy of the *Historia Regum Britanniae* was among them. I thought it might be entertaining to compare what I have heard with what Geoffrey of Monmouth has written."

Mathilda smiled as she handed over the heavy book. "Some have dismissed his writings as no more than a collection of fables, but whether the stories are true or not, you will surely be entertained."

Gwendolyn rose, eager to begin reading the thick, heavy tome. "My thanks, my lady. I am sure I will enjoy it. If I might beg your pardon, I shall tuck myself away in my chamber until supper."

"You have my leave, but before you go, would you indulge me a moment longer?"

Something in Mathilda's tone raised Gwendolyn's guard, but she had no reason to say aught except, "Certes."

"I, too, do not wish to pry into your personal affairs, but I admit that when I learned of the earl's intention to invite Alberic to Chester, I asked him to invite you also. I do not know how much Alberic has told you of his life, but it has not been an easy one. I have always wished the best for him, and wanted to assure myself that he has found some measure of contentment."

Mathilda paused, and Gwendolyn remembered the woman's warm greeting for Alberic. Though she hadn't said it outright, the earl's wife held no ill will against her husband's bastard son. She was even fond of him.

"I know you and Alberic were married under trying circumstances," Mathilda continued. "After spending time with you, I have come to believe he made a good choice in his wife, and with you he can find the happiness that has alluded him, and he deserves. For what little it may mean to you, I wanted you to know that I approve."

The approval meant much, the compliment swelling her heart.

"I thank you, my lady."

With that, Gwendolyn took her leave of Lady Mathilda. Clutching the book to her chest, she made her way along winding passageways and sets of stairways to the chambers Mathilda had shown her as readied for her and Alberic's use.

Furnished as opulently as the rest of the castle, the small solar proved too chilly to comfortably sit and read.

Gwendolyn glanced at the door to the left, beyond which was the bedchamber Lady Mathilda indicated should be Alberic's. Was he back yet? How had gone his visit with his father?

While she wanted to know how he'd fared, the book in her hands begged reading. This was why Alberic had brought her to Chester. Not to meet the earl and his wife. Not to offer support or advice in his dealings with his father. Only to read this book.

So she turned right and entered the bedchamber she was expected to occupy. She kicked off her shoes, curled up on the velvet coverlet on the bed's luxurious mattress, opened the *Historia* and began to read.

∽

Gwendolyn heard the creak of leather hinges. She glanced up from her reading to notice the light in the chamber had dimmed considerably. 'Twas surprising to note she'd been reading for several hours, engrossed in the tales of King Arthur and Merlin's prophecies.

Alberic appeared in the doorway. He leaned against the doorjamb and crossed his arms. From his expression, she couldn't determine his mood.

"Have you been with the earl all of this time?"

"Nay, I looked in on you earlier. You were so intent I left you to your book. I checked on our horses and people, renewed an acquaintance or two. Naught of importance. I would not disturb you now if 'twas not nearly time for supper. How goes the reading?"

She was of two minds on the matter and sought to explain.

"I have learned much of King Arthur I did not know before. Have you heard tales of his attempt to invade Italy? It seems he fought his way across the continent and made it all the way to the Alps before he was forced to abandon the enterprise."

"Truly?"

"And he dispatched not one giant, but two. The second had snatched the niece of a duke and taken her to what is now Mont-Saint-Michel. Arthur was not able to rescue the woman, but managed to cut off the giant's head, so bringing him to justice."

With a disparaging smile, Alberic crossed the room and sprawled across the end of the bed, propping his warrior's body up on an elbow. "I always had a hard time believing tales of slaying giants. I have never seen one. Have you?"

Alberic didn't believe in much he could not see or touch. She was fairly sure he believed in God on faith, but everything else he questioned. Magic in particular, now giants.

"Lady Mathilda did warn me that parts of this history are considered fables by some. But while I have never seen a giant, neither have I seen the Alps yet I believe they exist."

His smile widened. "True. So which parts do you account as history and which fable?"

"I wish I knew. All is so entertaining. Did you know that Monmouth dedicated his book to Mathilda's father?"

"As he should. Robert of Gloucester contributed funds toward Monmouth's maintenance while he wrote the book. Did you also read Merlin's prophecies?"

"Aye." She'd found them very disturbing. "Apparently sorcerers prefer to utter prophecies in obscure terms."

"What do they say of Arthur's death?"

"The prophecies do not mention Arthur's name, but the story is in the history." Gwendolyn flipped through the pages until she found what she sought. "The tale of the battle between Arthur and his son Mordred is not very long. One would think so important a battle as Camblam, where so many thousands of men died, would deserve more attention. Here it says, 'Arthur himself, our renowned king, was mortally wounded and carried off to the Isle of Avalon, so that his wounds might be attended to. He handed the crown of Britain over to his cousin, Constantine, son of Cador Duke of Cornwall. This in the year 542 after our Lord's Incarnation.' Then Monmouth goes on to describe Constantine's struggles against Mordred's sons.

"'Mortally wounded.' Arthur died over . . . six hundred years ago. No one lives over six hundred years."

Gwendolyn couldn't think of a mortal soul who'd lived more than sixty years, but that didn't mean King Arthur couldn't.

"You do not take into account that Avalon is a magical isle. If his wounds were not healed, why would Merlin proclaim Arthur's return?"

"Did you find the prophecy?"

Irritated, Gwendolyn flipped through several more pages. "I find it bothersome that Monmouth chose not to include that prophecy. 'Tis recorded in other histories and legends, particularly those of the Welsh. 'Twas unconscionable for him to leave it out."

He grasped her ankle, sending delightful little shivers up her legs. "Is Arthur's return mentioned in the prophecies?"

"Not in so many words, but sweet mercy, how can one tell? As I said, most are maddeningly obscure! The prophecies begin clearly enough. Much is written about the Red Dragon, which is the Saxons, and the White Dragon, the Britains, and the various struggles between them. But after that there is mentioned a Man of Bronze, a Boar of Cornwall, a German Worm, and

German Dragon. As you might imagine, one or the other is cutting someone to pieces. There are tears, and bloodshed, and famine. Then it says here . . . 'Cadwallader shall summon Conanus and shall make an alliance with Albany. Then the foreigners shall be slaughtered and the rivers will run with blood.' A pretty picture, is it not? Have you heard of this Cadwallader?"

"Nay."

"Neither have I, so I know not if he has lived or has yet to live. And then later Merlin says a Hedgehog will hide apples in Winchester and stones will speak. What the devil is that supposed to mean?"

"I fear I am as confused as you are."

Gwendolyn pulled her knees up, removing her ankle from his grasp. How was she supposed to think when his thumb worried her ankle, especially when he sprawled on the bed, making it hard enough to follow a conversation?

"One would think if Merlin intended to tell us of future events, he would do so in an understandable manner. How am I supposed to know which prophecy deals with our time in history?"

"Is there no mention of a civil war?"

"Not in such terms, and not unless Stephen and Maud are dragons. I swear, every other prophecy deals with death and destruction. 'Twould seem England is doomed to suffer much bloodshed and slaughter, one war following the other."

Not a future she wanted to contemplate.

"Gwen, would it not make sense that one of those times of bloodshed and slaughter would be so horrific that Merlin would have assured us that in that time Arthur would return?"

So she'd hoped.

"One prophecy mentions a Lion of Justice. I thought, at first, that might be King Arthur. But he would not use the symbol of the lion, I should think, but the banner of the Welsh dragon, as he did in his lifetime. Still, it seems to me that by creating the legacy and giving it to my ancestors, Merlin left the decision of when to recall King Arthur to the people living during times of strife."

He shrugged a shoulder. "Perhaps, but an event so momentous as King Arthur's return to England would surely merit a mention in Merlin's prophecies."

Frustrated, Gwendolyn shoved the book aside. "I need to read this again. I must have missed something important. Perhaps my understanding of Latin is not as complete as I thought and I am misreading the book. What did your father want of you?"

Alberic glanced away, his mouth tightening. "Chester is putting together a plan for the invasion of Wales."

Gwendolyn hugged her upraised knees to still the lurch of her stomach. "Sweet mercy!"

"Do not concern yourself over it yet. Chester hopes to convince the king to join him in the venture. That may not happen for months. King Stephen has more urgent matters to attend to at the moment."

Ye gods. More bloodshed and slaughter. And too close to home for comfort. She thought of her Welsh relatives, who would be in harm's way.

"Why invade Wales?"

"The earl wants Carlisle. To get it, Stephen must win this war. Chester believes invading Wales is a good strategy in defeating Maud."

Chester, damn him, wanted Alberic to participate.

"What would be your part?"

Alberic's smile reflected no humor. "He offered me a position as one of his commanders. All I need do is provide twenty knights and one hundred footmen, and their provisions, of course."

'Twas a larger force than her father had taken to Wallingford, but not unreasonable numbers for a barony.

"What does he offer in return?"

"Ap Idwal."

Hellfire. A most appropriate reward. The prospect of revenge against Madog ap Idwal would tempt Alberic sorely.

"Is revenge against ap Idwal worth the risk of your own life, losing all you have gained?"

"Maybe. Either you shape your own destiny or allow others to shape it for you. Sometimes the risk might be worth the prize."

Nothing was worth Alberic's life. Nothing.

"How do you decide enough is enough, that you have all you need and do not need any more?"

"I am not sure."

"So you intend to accept his offer?"

"I have not yet decided." He slid off the bed. "You might want to put your shoes on. The bell for supper will ring soon."

He walked out of the chamber and Gwendolyn put her head on her knees, wishing they'd stayed home. Then she wouldn't be so confused about the legacy, and Alberic wouldn't now be considering making war on the Welsh.

Mathilda had been right about one thing, at the least. Men ventured onto the battlefield more for personal gain than for honor or glory or in support of a just cause. The earl of Chester would invade Wales as a means to further his own ambitions, and he hoped to drag Alberic into the fray with him.

Did not one man in the entire kingdom consider what was best for the kingdom? Apparently not!

King Arthur would, and if Arthur Pendragon seized the reins of power, no one would question his right to the crown. The war would end. The kingdom would be at peace. Alberic would no longer have to decide whether or not to participate in the invasion of Wales.

She'd come to love him, and after all she'd lost to this war, wasn't sure if she could bear to lose him, too.

Chapter Eighteen

ALBERIC WASN'T INVITED to sit at the dais with the earl and his wife, but Mathilda did him and Gwendolyn the honor of seating them at the first table below the dais, with the highest-ranking members of Chester's court.

He'd known the names and positions of most of these men for years, and with an inner smile, wondered how they felt about having a man they'd dismissed as too far below them, too unimportant to consider worth a moment of their time, taking a seat among them.

'Twas almost as satisfying as being accorded a seat at the dais. *Almost.*

Alberic assisted Gwendolyn onto the bench, her gracious smile sweeping the table. To their credit, several of the men raised wine-filled goblets to her in salute, uttering welcomes.

The man across from her, Sir David, held several manors in fealty to the earl, and his wife served as one of Mathilda's handmaidens. He raised his goblet high. "'Tis rare a lady of your beauty and wit graces us with her presence, Lady Gwendolyn. We are most pleased to have you with us. You also, Sir Alberic. I congratulate you on your rise in rank."

Alberic wondered how David knew aught of Gwendolyn's wit, but let the comment pass, having recognized the insincerity in the man's entire speech.

"Our thanks, Sir David." Alberic glanced at the empty seat across from him. "Your wife does not join us?"

"The Lady Elizabeth is indisposed this eve and begs your pardon for her absence."

"Nothing serious, I hope," Gwendolyn commented in all sincerity.

"A mild malady, I am sure."

A malady quickly cured as soon as the lady wasn't forced to dine across the mere span of a trestle table from the earl's bastard son, Alberic was sure.

Perhaps he was being too harsh and quick to judge, but his experience with the members of Chester's court hadn't been cordial, just as his relationship with the earl hadn't been close. He'd often wondered which of Chester's advisers had cautioned the earl against acknowledging a half-English, peasant-raised son all those years ago. Probably all.

Alberic doubted his rise in rank sat well with any of them. Too bad.

He raised his goblet. "To your lady's improved health, Sir David. May she not suffer unduly long."

David acknowledged the sentiment with a nod. "I will pass along your kind concern. Are you enjoying your visit to Chester, my lady?"

"Lady Mathilda has been most gracious."

Alberic almost smiled at the tightness of Gwendolyn's

tone. She'd obviously figured out that David didn't care one whit whether she enjoyed her visit or not.

As the two exchanged false pleasantries, Alberic wondered how much David knew of the earl's plans to invade Wales, of how many others at the table Chester had taken into his confidence. He hoped the topic wouldn't come up as dinner conversation, and wasn't at all upset when, at the presentation of the first course, David excused himself from the table as well, citing some vague duty, leaving both places across from him and Gwendolyn empty.

Alberic made his selections from the platter presented to him with genuine delight. "Now this is spectacular."

Gwendolyn stared down at the large wedge he placed on their trencher beside sugared dates and bits of capon. "It looks . . . interesting."

"'Tis made of eggs, cheese, almonds, fennel and . . . I know not what else."

"A favorite of yours?"

He sliced off a chunk and popped it into his mouth, allowing a low moan to answer for him.

She laughed lightly. "Lady Mathilda offered to give me directions for some dishes she claims are your favorites. Shall I request this one?"

"Oh, pray do!"

"She also offered to give me the name of the wine merchant who supplies Chester."

"Lovely. That makes this trip worthwhile."

And in a way it did. 'Twas surprising that Mathilda knew anything of his preferences. But then, the lady of the castle was trained to notice such things about those who ate in her hall. Still, before today, he'd eaten at a table at the far end, within a draft's distance of the hall's doors—too far away for Mathilda to easily notice.

"She likes you, you know."

Gwendolyn's voice was hushed, too quiet to be heard by any but him. He followed suit.

"Lady Mathilda has always been kind to me."

"Perhaps you should take advantage of her goodwill. She would be in a good position to help you gain acknowledgment from Chester."

He'd considered that a few years ago, then abandoned the idea. "I am sure Mathilda plans to have children. I doubt she would do anything to place me above them."

"She bemoans that her father's bastardy proved an obstacle to the crown. If Robert were king, she feels, there would have been no war. Given her enlightened sentiments, she may not begrudge you the earldom."

"At the expense of a son of her own? 'Tis hardly likely."

Gwendolyn picked up a chunk of capon and took a dainty bite before asking, "How long have she and Chester been married?"

Alberic had to remember how old he'd been when the earl brought his royal bride to Chester. "Nigh on five years."

"A long time. Perhaps they will have no children."

He glanced up at the dais where Mathilda sat beside Chester. She stared intently at the far end of the hall, likely at the door from which the servants who carried the food in from the kitchen emerged.

If Mathilda didn't bear the earl's children, would she begrudge him a seat at the dais, a share in the earldom? Possibly not, but he couldn't bring himself to wish barrenness on a woman he liked and respected. Should she not bear an heir, Chester would have reason to petition for an annulment in order to marry another. The degradation would be horrific.

"In order for her to have children, the earl must remain home for more than a few days at a time, not be gone for months on end." He sliced the rest of the egg wedge in two, feeding a piece to Gwendolyn before she could say any more on the subject. "Watch the end of the hall. If this meal follows suit, the next course should be a treat for the eyes."

To the blare of trumpets, Gwendolyn turned slightly, just as the platter bearers marched into the hall. "Oh, gracious me, will you look at that!"

Each platter held a swan on which the feathers had been carefully reattached after roasting. Alberic thought it silly to try to make a dead bird look alive, a waste of time to put the feathers back on again when the servers must just take them off to slice the meat.

He glanced up at Chester, who smiled broadly, enjoying the showy parade.

The two of them might look alike, but there the similarities between father and son ended. Chester loved the grandiose; Alberic preferred simplicity. Perhaps a legitimate son, born to full nobility and trained to assume the earldom, might share more of Chester's traits.

That's when the flaw in Chester's plan hit him: Chester hadn't allowed for the traits of the sons of King Stephen and Empress Maud.

Stephen fought not only to keep his throne, but for his son's right to inherit after him. Prince Eustace was a tall, solid lad, only three years from coming into his majority.

Many current royal supporters would stand behind Eustace if Stephen fell and the crown settled on a young head.

If Chester was right, if Bristol was threatened, Maud just might flee all the way to the continent, where awaited her son Henry, only a couple of years younger than Eustace. All agreed Henry was a personable lad already skilled in statesmanship. If the lad convinced his father, the count of Anjou and duke of Normandy, to back him, England would be subjected to a war of proportions not seen since the last Norman invasion of the kingdom.

This war had to end by a negotiated treaty, where one side gave up all pretensions, not by driving one particular woman out of the country.

Alberic knew then he would turn down his father's offer. If the king decided to invade Wales and called Camelen's troops into service, then he'd have no choice but to comply. But until that unlikely event happened, he preferred not to become involved in one of his father's impulsive schemes.

Chester wasn't going to be happy.

Again, too bad.

Amazingly, Alberic suddenly didn't care overmuch if he displeased the earl of Chester. As he searched for a reason why, he realized how much he'd changed over the past weeks. He had Camelen, more than he'd dreamed to ever possess. He no longer needed his father's approval, or even acceptance. Neither was necessary to his happiness because he had Gwendolyn.

Only her acceptance mattered. Only her approval and respect were important to him.

Because he loved her.

He almost choked on a piece of roasted swan, had to wash it down with a swig of wine to keep from coughing it up. And as the swan went down, he acknowledged that at some point he'd stopped trying to please Chester, and even himself, for want of proving himself worthy of Gwendolyn.

Could he ever? Perhaps not. God's truth, she had so many reasons not to consider him worthy.

But he knew she cared about him. She'd nursed him when he was injured, done many things to bolster his spirits when he'd held himself in contempt. Her advice and suggestions were usually sound. And at night, when he reached for her, she responded willingly, taking a man she'd once denounced as an enemy into her body with an eagerness that brought him such joy.

Did she still, at times, see him as the enemy? Had she put aside her enmity over her brother's death, the worst of the crimes he'd committed against her? And what of their forced marriage and her sisters' banishment from Camelen?

And his resistance to the legacy? No. She couldn't hold that against him. In time, he would prove to her that magic didn't exist. Perhaps even tonight.

How would he know he'd accomplished the impossible feat of being worthy of her?

When Gwendolyn loved him in return.

Gwendolyn's love. Now there was a goal worth pursuing, a campaign worth waging.

First he had to get her home, but before that there was the earl of Chester to deal with.

Over a confection of sugared dates and almonds,

Alberic planned his strategy. At the end of the meal, while he assisted Gwendolyn from the bench, he set it in motion.

"Are you averse to leaving on the morn?"

She raised a surprised eyebrow. "So soon?"

"I need to speak with the earl. After I tell him of my decision, I fear our welcome will end."

A smile touched her mouth, and the approval he craved lit her eyes. "You have decided to refuse his offer."

"He will not be happy."

Her smile faded. "You might forever ruin your chance for acknowledgment."

Alberic wrestled with the last bit of hope and, to his relief, it relented without much of a struggle.

"Quite likely."

She bit her bottom lip, a gesture he found endearing, but then there wasn't much about Gwendolyn he didn't find endearing. "I fear you will have regrets."

"Perhaps, but I must do what I feel is right for Camelen."

She nodded, finally accepting his decision. "You do not give me much time to finish reading the *Historia*."

He loved Gwendolyn, but her fascination with summoning King Arthur from Avalon, he could do without.

"Then you had best do so with the few hours you have left. Go. I will join you anon."

She fled the hall, and Alberic looked around for Chester.

The earl stood at the base of the dais with a group of his retainers, their expressions none too serious. Deciding he wouldn't be interrupting a discussion of import, Alberic waited until one of the men finished expounding on the qualities of his falcon before edging his way through the group to stand directly in front of the earl.

Chester's brow furrowed in surprise and disapproval that Alberic would be so bold.

Summoning all of his resolve, he forged ahead. "A word if you would, my lord. 'Twill take only a moment."

At a slight hand motion from the earl, the group faded away.

"What word?" Chester asked.

"I have given your offer much thought—"

Chester rolled his eyes. "That has always been part of your problem, Alberic. You think overmuch. You gnaw on a bone long after the meat is gone. Better to grab another bone."

Alberic refrained from countering that the earl left too much meat on the bone before tossing it aside.

"Your plan is flawed, I fear. I fail to see how an invasion of Wales will hasten an end to the war. Let us say you are right, that if Bristol is threatened, Maud will flee the country. I cannot see Henry accepting his mother's retreat with grace."

Chester waved a dismissive hand. "The lad is not old enough to lead an army."

"Not yet, but consider. If Henry craves the crown of England, and Geoffrey of Anjou feels the time is ripe to back his son, we will be dealing with an invasion."

"Perhaps, but we are talking years, and that has naught to do with my possession of Carlisle."

Which was utmost in Chester's scheme.

"You have no assurance the king will grant you Carlisle."

"If I rid the rebellion of its head, Stephen will give me whatever I request."

"Which might cast us into a war with Scotland."

Again the dismissive wave. "I have been at odds with the Scots since inheriting the earldom from my uncle, who was at odds with the Scots since inheriting from my father. Pray tell, what difference now?"

In his arrogance and ambition, Chester was willing to lay waste to Wales, and whatever portions of Scotland and England he must to obtain the honor of Carlisle. Once he had it, the rest of the country could go to seed and he'd not give a damn.

Presenting further argument against a Welsh campaign would prove a waste of breath. Chester's mind was set, and nothing would budge him from his stance.

"I have decided to decline your offer. If the king decides to embrace your cause, and demands my participation, I will join his forces. Until then, I see no sound reason to become involved."

Chester's eyes narrowed. "What of ap Idwal?"

The dangled bait tempted. He refused to bite. There were ways to deal with Madog ap Idwal other than invading Wales.

"I have no doubt he and I shall cross paths again. I will resolve my argument with him in my own way, in my own time."

Chester snorted. "So you will settle for waging petty raids on your enemy instead of grabbing at the bigger prize. No son of mine would pass up this opportunity to have all."

Alberic's stomach lurched. He stared into the earl's hard eyes, at the unforgiving mouth. Chester's words hurt, but they didn't knock him down.

He would survive. He'd found a measure of contentment and happiness that no one could rob him of. Not even Ranulf de Gernons, the powerful earl of Chester.

Quietly, he told the Norman noble who would never admit to being his father, "Then perchance you have been right all along, my lord. Perhaps I am not your son."

After a brief, parting bow, Alberic made his way across the hall and up the stairs, not stopping until reaching the door of the chamber. He pulled open the door and found sanctuary.

A warming fire glowed in the sitting room's hearth, the low crackle of burning wood a soothing sound. Candles glowed within their iron sconces, the flickering flames reflected in the furniture's highly polished wood.

In one of the chairs sat Gwendolyn, her veil dispensed with, her hair loose and pulled forward over a shoulder, strands separating to flow around her bosom, the tips flirting with her waist.

She looked up from the book on the table, the *Historia,* the question in her expression unmistakable.

"'Tis over and done," he answered.

"I am sorry, Alberic."

"I am at peace with it. Have you finished reading?"

She sighed. "Remember my asking you about Cadwallader? His tale is the last in the book. He was a king of the Britons who died in 689."

Grateful she didn't wish to pursue details of the discussions with the earl, Alberic turned his attention to the other reason he'd come to Chester.

"So now you know the prophecy concerning him is in the past."

She nodded. "In his tale I found a reference to King

Arthur. Apparently Cadwallader intended to reclaim the crown of Britain, but before he could set sail, an angelic voice told him God wished no Briton to rule Britain until the moment Merlin had prophesied to Arthur. So Cadwallader gave up the enterprise." She tilted her head. "Does that allude to Merlin's prophecy that Arthur would return?"

Wonderful. Now angelic voices ruled men's actions. Better that, Alberic supposed, than prophecies and magic. He plopped down in a chair at an angle with Gwendolyn's.

"Do any of Merlin's latter prophecies mention a Briton ruling Britain?"

"Nay." Then she smiled. "Not, that is, unless the Ass of Wickedness or the Dragon of Worcester or the Charioteer of York are Britons who manage to become kings. Sweet mercy, Merlin would have made the future much easier to discern by using names instead of these high-flown titles!"

"So is the Ass of Wickedness in our past or someone to be wary of in the future?"

Gwendolyn closed the book with a decisive thump. "In our past, I pray, but I cannot be confident of the conjecture. I am no closer to determining our place in history among the prophecies than I was before."

He heard her frustration, but it was tinged with humor. If he couldn't get her to disavow the legacy completely, perhaps she would, in the interest of peaceful marital relations, come to view it less seriously.

But that wouldn't do him much good if she ever came to the conclusion that England truly needed the services of King Arthur.

"Tell me this, then. From among the prophecies, can you determine England's time of *most* dire need?"

Gwendolyn ran her hand over the book's cover, as if seeking an answer from within its pages. "The early prophecies tell of death, famine, and calamity. The last prophecies are just as disturbing. In the last, even the stars in the heavens weep. 'Twould seem that England flows from one tumult to another with few periods of peace between."

"Of the early prophecies of death, famine, and calamity, would not the guardian of the legacy consider that time most dire?"

She looked away and pursed her lips, so he pressed on.

"Gwendolyn, you must realize that over the past several hundred years one of the guardians has considered her time in history the most dire. Would she not have tried to summon King Arthur?"

"No one has tried as yet. The legacy can be invoked only once."

"Or she tried and the spell failed because there is no such thing as magic."

She turned those wide brown eyes on him. "If it failed, then the conditions of the legacy were not met."

"Or the legacy is false. Mortal men cannot be summoned from the grave."

She stared at him a long while before getting up, looking so sad he wanted to take her in his arms and comfort her. He was about to when she raised her chin.

"You and I might never agree on this, I fear."

Damn. He thought she'd seen reason.

"Apparently not."

"Can you remove the ring?"

Back to that again, were they? "I have not tried of late."

Gwendolyn crossed her arms, her expression daring him to give the ring a tug.

He looked down at the seal of the dragon, the gold claws gripping the onyx and garnet, wishing he'd never put the thing on his finger. He tugged, and turned, and twisted, until his knuckle turned red from the chafing of bunched skin against gold.

Ruefully, he admitted, "Not as yet."

Smugly, she smiled. "When you can prove to me that anything *but* magic keeps that ring on your finger, we will speak of this again."

She flounced off into her bedchamber.

Alberic slumped in the chair.

Why, on this night of all nights, when all he wished to do was glory in his love for Gwendolyn, had they butted heads?

He shouldn't have asked her about the *Historia*. He shouldn't have attempted to sway her from her beliefs. He *should* have taken her off to bed and made love to her until dawn.

He still could, not doubting he would have no trouble coaxing Gwendolyn into a lusty mood.

Except this damn ring had to come off, and right outside the castle wall dwelled a blacksmith, and a bit farther down lived a goldsmith. Surely one of them would solve the problem, and if he hurried, there would yet be several hours before dawn to spend in her bed.

Confident, Alberic sped off into the village.

Two hours later, shaken to his core, he slumped in the

same chair, his hand aching and useless at the end of his arm.

Thank God, Gwendolyn slept so he need answer no questions, for indeed, he found the answers revolting.

He'd gone to the goldsmith first. They'd lathered his hand with soap, then coated it with grease, then applied a truly nauseating liquid Alberic couldn't name. The ring hadn't budged.

So he'd hastened to the blacksmith, who pried and poked with both pincers and file, then gently and carefully wielded a saw. When the blacksmith scratched his head and suggested smashing the ring with his sledgehammer, Alberic declined.

He stared at the ring that had been subjected to brutal punishment and refused to come off. The stones shone brightly, the gold remained unmarred. Only his hand suffered the penalty of the evening's folly.

He didn't believe in magic, still wasn't prepared to embrace the notion it existed. But neither could he explain the ring's stubborn grip on his hand.

What he'd heard of magic wasn't heartening. The use of it was always associated with dark, unholy forces, inflicting suffering on the object of the spell and sometimes resulting in injurious, even deadly consequences to the wielder.

Its use involved great risk, far more than he wished to undertake. Infinitely more risk than he would allow Gwendolyn to take.

Several hours remained until dawn. He should go to bed, get some sleep, put the evening's incredible events out of his head. Surely, with a few hours' rest things wouldn't seem so bleak. So impossible.

Except if he didn't do something to assure himself that neither he nor Gwendolyn was endangered, he wouldn't sleep.

He knew of no witch or conjuror or sorcerer to consult on the ways of magic . . . save one: Merlin.

From the table, the *Historia Regum Britanniae* beckoned.

Reluctant, but knowing of naught else to do, Alberic opened the book, found the prophecies that had so frustrated and angered Gwendolyn, and began to read.

Chapter Nineteen

A T MIDAFTERNOON, Gwendolyn sat atop her horse, waiting for Alberic to come out of the inn and tell her whether or not he'd procured a room for the night.

She'd thought they would go straight back to Camelen. To her amazement, Alberic decided to stop in Shrewsbury. Not that she minded spending the night at an inn instead of in a tent, and this one, within the shadow of the Benedictine Abbey of St. Peter and St. Paul, seemed neatly kept.

A baron, Alberic could have availed himself of Shrewsbury Castle's hospitality. So why didn't he?

While her curiosity nagged at her, she forswore questioning Alberic. Neither of them was in a good mood, and she didn't want to risk arguing with him again. Their disagreement last eve over the legacy yet smarted, the wounds still fresh after all these hours.

As far as she knew, Alberic was more convinced than ever that Merlin's prophecies proved him right and her wrong. But sweet mercy, if Merlin hadn't intended for King Arthur to rule England a second time, then why the devil bother to devise the legacy?

She knew Alberic had left their rooms shortly after she'd childishly escaped into her bedchamber. Where he'd gone she didn't know, but he didn't appear to have gotten much sleep.

He strode out of the inn, pointed the cart's driver toward the stables, and then came to her. No matter Alberic's mood, he was ever gallant. As he assisted her from atop her horse, she wished he would hold her for a moment, tell her everything would be all right again soon, but he let go of her the moment she was steady on her feet.

"I have arranged for a private room for you and me. The others shall have pallets in the common room or in the stables. Do you wish to go up to the rooms now or walk around a bit to stretch your legs?"

She heard no anger, only weariness. "I shall defer to your preference, my lord."

He raised an eyebrow, likely surprised at her acquiescence, and likely wishing she would defer to him as easily in other matters. As much as she loved Alberic, wanted peace with him, in some things she had no choice but to stand her ground.

"I planned to visit the marketplace. You are welcome to accompany me."

If he thought she would pass on the chance to visit the merchants' shops, he had best think again.

"Might we visit the apothecary?"

His brow scrunched. "Are you ill?"

His concern made her wonder if he was as wroth with her as she believed. "Nay. We are low on some healing herbs, is all. As long as we are here, I should replenish them. Is there a shop in particular you wish to visit?"

"A goldsmith."

She waited for him to tell her why. He didn't; merely turned to Garrett and told him to ensure everyone in the retinue was settled, then asked her if she was ready.

As at Chester, one was hard-pressed to see signs of the war in Shrewsbury. Children dashed through the narrow dirt streets, playing games with no apparent concern for their safety. Monks from the abbey strolled by on their errands. Merchants conducted business, the items they hawked no different from the last time she'd inspected their wares. The tanner's shop still stank, and the abbey's bells sang the canonical hours.

Hard to tell, now, that near the beginning of the war, the castellan of Shrewsbury Castle had declared allegiance to Maud. Incensed, Stephen had laid siege to the castle and, in the end, hanged all ninety-three members of the garrison.

Alberic guided her into the apothecary where bunches of drying herbs and flowers hung from the rafters. The aroma of rosemary and sage mingled with the scents of lavender and roses, nearly overpowering the small shop. His nose scrunched. He reached into the leather purse tied to his belt and handed her a few coins.

"I will be across the street," he announced. "Do not go farther without me."

Gwendolyn watched him head toward the goldsmith, wondering what he wished to purchase. Knowing she'd likely find out later, she attended to her own task.

She bought willow bark and feverfew for aching heads, though with Emma at court they no longer needed to stock as much. Chamomile to soothe the spirit after a trying day. Woad to stanch blood flowing from wounds, which she hoped never to use.

Finished, she stood in the apothecary's doorway to await Alberic. The aroma of meat pies wafted on the light spring breeze from a vendor's cart not far down the street. Her stomach grumbled, but though she might have enough coin for the purchase, she dare not move.

Alberic hadn't needed to warn her about wandering the town's streets on her own. No matter how safe it seemed, rabble always lurked about, mostly beggars and footpads who preyed on the unwary.

She deemed as harmless a bent-over old woman, a basket hanging from her arm, who shuffled toward the apothecary shop. But instead of going inside, the woman stopped and displayed a toothless grin.

"'Ere, milady. Be ye needin' a charm or two? Fer good luck, mayhap, or to ward off curses or evil spirits?"

Gwendolyn sighed. The last thing she needed was another object that purported to possess magical qualities. The pendant and ring were enough to deal with.

"Nay, I—"

"Ach, do not be hasty, now." With gnarled fingers she pulled what looked like a rotted nut from her basket. "This charm 'ere is one o' me better sellin'. Hang this around yer neck and ye'll ne'r be pestered by lice."

Nor pestered by any other living creature, given the smell of the ugly charm.

"I thank you, but—"

"Or grind it up and put it in yer wine. Cures whatever ails yer belly or bowel."

Just the thought of it churned her stomach.

"Old woman, I need no charms. Be gone with—"

"Ah! I 'ave just the potion all young women cannot do without." From the basket she plucked a small vial containing a blue liquid. "Love potion. Ne'r failed to work. I can name ye a flock full of satisfied ladies, some most noble. Ye put this in the man's drink, and next thin' ye know"—she snapped her fingers—"he be fallen at yer feet, heart in hand. 'Tain't that worth a pence to ye?"

'Twould be worth several pounds if it stood a chance of working. Gwendolyn glanced toward the goldsmith's shop, wishing Alberic would come out and rescue her. When he did leave the shop, he shook his left hand as if it hurt.

"I am already married," she said absently, guessing at why he'd gone to a goldsmith.

Alberic hadn't wished to make a purchase, but to enlist the goldsmith's aid in removing the ring. Apparently, whatever they'd tried hadn't worked. The ring yet sat on his hand, his *reddened* hand.

"That yer 'usband?"

"Aye."

The woman sighed. "Can see ye need no love potion, but I am willin' to give ye a more than fair price on— Hey, where ye goin'?"

Gwendolyn was halfway across the street before Alberic spotted her and quickly slipped on his riding glove. His expression dared her to comment. She bit her bottom lip and refrained. The middle of a Shrewsbury street was no place to question him about the ring.

"Shall we return to the inn?" she asked instead.

"Not just yet."

She tossed her head toward the pie vendor. "Hungry?"

"I could be."

They shared hot pastry-wrapped pork and gravy as they ambled through the streets. Gwendolyn stopped to look at a length of blue linen, but passed it by. Neither of them slowed at the potter's shop. Alberic found a shoemaker's wares interesting, and ordered a pair of boots to be delivered to Camelen a week hence.

The silence lengthened, but the tension eased.

They rounded a corner, and at the edge of her vision she caught sight of a man who struck her as familiar, but when she turned to look fully, he was gone. Still, the back of her neck tingled, and she struggled to put a name to the fleetingly glimpsed face.

Except she knew no one in Shrewsbury, and doubted anyone she knew would also be wandering its streets. Surely, she was mistaken. Still, her unease continued until they found the cooper's shop, where a sighting of a different sort banished all else from her thoughts.

Alberic grinned from ear to ear. "There it is, Gwendolyn. Our tub."

The tub was huge, oval in shape, and long enough for Alberic to stretch out his legs. Room enough for two.

She knew she blushed, picturing him in the tub, naked, guessing at where he would invite her to sit.

"Do you have any notion of how much water we shall need to fill it?" she protested.

"Nigh on twice the buckets, I imagine."

"You will have to hire a carter to haul it to Camelen."

He ran a hand along the length of smoothed wood banded with iron, utterly enraptured. "All we need do is unpack the cart we have, pick up the tub, then put all our belongings inside of it." He turned to the cooper. "Master Cooper, how much?"

While Alberic haggled with the cooper over the price, Gwendolyn stepped away to allow her cheeks to cool, convinced the cooper knew precisely why Alberic wanted the big tub. 'Twas an extravagance, all for one purpose, and to her chagrin she could hardly wait to get it home to test it.

She sighed. For all that was wrong between them, her love for Alberic hadn't diminished, nor her desire. He hadn't shared her bed last night and she'd missed him. Tonight they would share a room at the inn and most likely end up with limbs entwined and bodies joined.

Thank the Lord he hadn't taken the earl's offer. Alberic wouldn't be going off to invade Wales instead of spending his days overseeing Camelen and his nights making love to her. 'Twas selfish of her to want to keep him home, but she also knew the day was coming when he'd be called upon to involve himself in the war once more.

All knights owed military service to their liege lords, and unless this war ended quickly, eventually the king would call on the baron of Camelen to serve his forty days.

'Twas probably also selfish of her to wish to summon King Arthur so he could put the whole mess to rout.

Poor Alberic. He'd made an attempt today to remove the seal of the dragon. Soon, he would be forced to admit that no physical reason explained the ring's stubborn grip on his hand. She would give him time to come to terms with his involvement in the legacy . . . and then?

Whether or not the two of them decided to summon King Arthur, for the sake of the legacy's continuance, she had to prove to him that they could. Elsewise, he wouldn't allow her to pass the legacy to their as yet unborn daughter.

This meant another test, and as sure as Alberic would adore testing the tub, he would hate testing the ring.

The following sunny morning, an hour out of Shrewsbury, riding beside Gwendolyn, Alberic surrendered.

"I cannot remove the ring."

To her credit, when she looked over at him, he saw no smugness, only sympathy.

"How is your hand?"

So he hadn't put on his glove quickly enough, and she'd guessed why he'd gone to the goldsmith. Or she might have noticed the redness and swelling last eve while they'd dined, or later, though he was sure he'd pleasurably distracted her from his hand. Either way, she knew only part of what he'd done at the goldsmith. His gift for her remained secret.

"Sore."

She looked forward again, down the road that led toward Camelen. "I would tell you I was sorry if I were, but I cannot be sorry that the ring is content with you as my partner in the legacy."

He remembered putting it on all those weeks ago at Wallingford, of the odd feeling the ring had somehow been made for him. This coming to terms with the possibility of magic, that the ring had somehow deemed him worthy to wear it, still tightened his gullet. He also remembered Gwendolyn's first reaction to his wearing it: utter horror.

Not sure he wanted to hear the answer, he asked, "What changed your mind?"

"Not one thing in particular, and make no mistake, 'twas not easy to accept that you were not at fault for tilting my world upside down."

She no longer held him solely responsible for her brother's death, then, or for accepting the gift of Camelen from the king.

"I would tell you I was sorry if I felt the least bit regretful that events led me to Camelen and to choosing you as my wife."

She smiled. "I do not think you had a choice, but I wonder what would have happened had you chosen Emma. The ring might have slipped from your finger and refused to return. Would not that have raised an eyebrow or two?"

He smiled back, refusing to tell her that his own musings had been darker. Would the ring have remained on his finger and something untoward happened to Emma? While he was forced to accept the possibility of magic, he yet distrusted it, and doubted he would ever feel comfortable with it.

"Magic or no, legacy or no, I would have chosen you, Gwendolyn."

Her smile faded. Her sharp glance his way asked "Why?"

"I think I knew from the moment I saw you on the battlements in chain mail and helm. You took me by surprise, at first. Then I had to admire your good sense, and your courage and inner strength. And, truth to tell, whenever I looked at you I felt a rush of desire. Still do. Likely always will."

She nodded. "And I for you. The legacy states the partners must be of faithful hearts. I imagine the magic ensures we remain attracted so—"

She reined in, alarmed.

He followed suit, spotting the threat.

Madog ap Idwal sat atop a pony in the middle of the road. Many of the same men who'd accompanied the Welshman on his first visit to Camelen arrayed themselves behind him, including Edgar the archer.

Alberic gave brief thought to the well-being of the two soldiers who today served as point guards, and had obviously been overtaken.

And now he truly wished he'd listened to Gwendolyn when she'd advised him that a baron should travel with a larger retinue. He also wished he'd put on his chain mail this morn. Too late for wishes.

"Gwendolyn, you know what he wants."

"Aye."

Her distaste almost made him smile. "Your horse can easily outrun their ponies. Should things go sour, you are to take the road back to Shrewsbury and seek refuge at the castle."

"As you say, my lord," she said with equal distaste, making him wonder if she would obey.

Most times she followed orders, but at others defied him, most notably on the night she'd refused to hand over the artifacts. The woman could be stubborn.

She sighed. "I know now who I caught a glimpse of yesterday in the marketplace. My apologies for not recognizing him immediately, Alberic. With warning, we might have avoided this."

"I have my doubts. Stay here."

Alberic nudged his horse forward, putting himself between ap Idwal and Gwendolyn. His warrior's instincts rose to the fore. Hatred for ap Idwal and the desire for revenge burned in his heart, tempered only by the need to protect Gwendolyn.

"Last I heard the road was open to all, ap Idwal. Stand aside."

The man didn't move. "So the tale is true. You recovered. How unfortunate."

"Now that you have satisfied your curiosity over my health, there is no reason for you to linger."

"Oh, I have reason, Norman. I have a bargain to keep, and you stand in my way."

"You seek to keep a questionable bargain with a dead man. Give it up, ap Idwal."

"Give it up?" he asked quietly, his face contorting with anger. "Norman arrogance knows no bounds. You are forever ordering both the English and the Welsh to give up something to you. No more. Gwendolyn should be mine. Camelen should be mine. The ring should be mine. And I shall have them."

The ring? Did ap Idwal know about the legacy? Had Sir Hugh told him? Perhaps. Or did ap Idwal see the ring as Alberic once had, as proof of lordship?

He heard the soft footfalls of Gwendolyn's mare coming up beside him, dread coiling in his stomach. Though she went no farther than his side, he didn't like having her exposed.

"Your bargain with my father no longer stands," she declared. "Another man has been chosen, and I am content with the choice."

"Who the hell cares what you want? *I* was chosen, and

I will have what I was promised!" Ap Idwal dismounted and pulled his sword. Alberic tensed. "I challenge you, Alberic of Chester, for the rights to Lady Gwendolyn and Camelen."

And hadn't he known all along it would come to this? He and ap Idwal, sword to sword. For the possession of Camelen, of Gwendolyn, and now the seal of the dragon and a legacy he barely believed in.

Resigned, he prepared to dismount.

Gwendolyn's voice stopped him.

"Your hand," she said softly. "Will it hamper you?"

"Nay," he answered, hoping he told the truth.

She smiled at him, a blessing from a goddess. "Then I leave him to you."

"Remember what I said about seeking shelter at the castle."

"I heard you, but it will not be necessary."

A smile and a profession of confidence. She didn't even tell him to have a care before she backed up her palfrey several steps.

Dismounted, Alberic pulled his sword from its scabbard and perused the battlefield. He saw no advantage or disadvantage. He wore no helm or mail, but neither did ap Idwal. The road was rutted, but not deeply, favoring neither man. His only concern was ap Idwal's supporters, Edgar in particular, the man's bow a nasty reminder of an arrow whizzing past his head to pierce the village church's door.

"What assurance have I that your men will not interfere?"

"You have my word of honor."

"An honorable man would not have set fire to the village before his stated deadline had passed."

Mouth pursed in a hard line, ap Idwal called over his shoulder. "Toss down your weapons, all of them."

Soon swords, daggers, a bow, and a quiver of arrows all lay on the road.

Ap Idwal waved his sword. "And your assurance?"

Alberic looked over his shoulder to Garrett. "Ride back and see that our men do the same."

The old knight frowned. "This is madness, my lord. Allow Roger or I to take your place."

He shook his head. "Do as I say. No one is to interfere."

Garrett jerked his horse around to obey, riding to the back to relay the order to the soldiers who guarded the rear. Roger looked none too happy about the disarming, but soon the soldiers of Camelen piled their weapons on the side of the road, within ap Idwal's sight.

As the last dagger clanged onto the pile, ap Idwal rushed forward with a cry devised to curdle a man's blood, his sword in position for a punishing blow. Alberic waited until the sword reached its peak, then deprived the cold steel of its target. He ducked fast and low, the maneuver perfectly timed. The edge whistled over him, the weight of the sword spinning ap Idwal clean around.

"A new dance, ap Idwal? Prettily done."

"Put up your sword, whoreson, or do you plan another retreat?"

"I yet wait for an attack worth countering."

"Bastard!"

Ap Idwal's anger drove him to yet another forceful but ill-planned attempt to skewer his enemy, and Alberic knew he had his opponent's measure. Too often men fought with their brawn and not their brains. All he had to do was block a few thrusts, let the Welshman wear himself out with his wildness, and then he'd have him.

'Twas almost a shame.

So Alberic began to circle, mostly staying on the defensive to draw ap Idwal into a false sense of having the upper hand, the tactic learned on the earl's practice yard. How odd that he had Chester to thank for being hard on him, driving him to spend hours sparring against skilled knights, believing he trained to please his sire. He knew differently now. All of those hours had prepared him for this one battle alone, the most important of his life.

Blow after blow rained down, each blocked and thrown off, though not with ease. Ap Idwal was strong, his blade heavy and finely honed, and he fought for a prize he believed rightfully his. Such men often won with a lucky stroke.

But not this time.

His attention divided between ap Idwal's sword and eyes, Alberic saw the flash of doubt and moment of hesitation. On the next stroke he countered differently, letting ap Idwal know that he, too, fought for what was rightfully his: Gwendolyn, Camelen, and aye, the damn legacy if it proved true. All were tightly bound together. To lose one was to lose all.

Nay, not quite true. He could lose Camelen and go on with his life, and the legacy could go hang. But to lose Gwendolyn would tear the heart and soul from him, leave him a shell of a man. His love for her overshadowed all. She was his reason to live, to fight.

Alberic pressed his offense. With stroke after stroke

he hammered at ap Idwal, punishing him for daring to covet the woman he loved. For the deaths of two soldiers and the burns on Mistress Biggs's legs. For the dishonorable firing of the village and the knock on the head in the graveyard that had put him in bed for several days, and worse, had led him to doubt himself.

Sword slid against sword, emitting a lethal metallic hiss. In those few moments when he stood chest to chest with ap Idwal before pushing away, he heard the man's labored breathing, saw clearly the man's hatred and determination.

Alberic's own breath was as labored. His hand hurt, his arm grew weary. Dust swirled around them, rising from the churned-up road. Yet he patiently waited for that moment when ap Idwal left his guard open too long. When it came, his sword flashed, drawing first blood with a slash to ap Idwal's left upper arm. The man howled and spun away, but with the tenacity and fury of an injured beast, he viciously flung himself back into the fray, exactly as Alberic had hoped.

Ap Idwal barreled at him with the intent to deliver a finishing blow. Alberic changed his grip on his sword. He took his stance, his foot landing at the edge of a rut. Pain pierced his ankle and shifted his balance. He remained upright, but not steady. Sharp steel flew toward him. Alberic countered at the angle he'd planned and, to his relief, the maneuver worked despite the flawed arc of his sword.

Ap Idwal's weapon flew out of his hands. Alberic hit the dirt road and rolled, barely catching sight of his opponent pulling a dagger from his boot. He rolled once more, bracing for the lunge that was sure to come.

That never came. Ap Idwal spun on his heel and ran toward Gwendolyn.

Nooooo!

Heart in his throat, he shouted, "Gwendolyn, flee!"

But even he could see she had no time.

He gained his feet and began to run, hearing shouts of outrage from his soldiers. Garrett had dismounted, and though Alberic gave valiant effort, his limp wouldn't allow him to reach Gwendolyn ahead of ap Idwal. Roger gave heel to his horse, but he was too far away to give aid.

Then Gwendolyn shifted in the saddle, her expression a mix of outrage and resolve.

Yes! Wait. Wait. Gwendolyn's legs tightened around her mare. Ap Idwal lunged for the horse's halter. *Now!*

She reared the horse. The front hooves rose high off the ground, one iron-shod hoof catching ap Idwal in the chest, knocking him over. The steep angle was too much for Gwendolyn to maintain her balance on the mare's back. She slid off, arms flailing, and hit the dirt with a sickening thud.

Ap Idwal got up.

"My lord, behind you!" came Roger's warning.

Alberic didn't turn around, his entire being torn between wanting to tear ap Idwal limb from limb and reaching Gwendolyn. He heard the arrow's angry buzz, knew it was aimed at him, and braced for the impact. He heard the arrow bite into human flesh, but felt no pain.

Ap Idwal jerked and flung his arms wide, the dagger dropping from his hand, an arrow protruding from his back. He fell first to his knees, pausing there for an eternal moment before his body toppled forward.

Within the space of two heartbeats, Alberic reached

Gwendolyn, who'd risen up to lean on her arm. Relief flooded him as he looked her over. No blood.

He dropped to his knees and gathered her in his arms, his fears easing, though his heart still pounded against his ribs. Pressing his face into her neck, he breathed in her sweet scent, kissed the steady pulse at her temple, and allowed himself to believe everything might be all right.

"Good God, Gwendolyn, you scared me."

She laughed lightly. "Not nearly as much as you frightened me, I warrant. When you fell . . . and then the arrow . . ." She gulped in air. "Are you all right?"

"I will be. You?"

"I shall have a large bruise on my hip, but am otherwise unhurt."

He would tenderly rub salve on that bruise as soon as he got her home. "Are you sure?"

"Aye, my love, I am sure."

My love.

The words flung his thoughts in another direction, a path he refused to follow while kneeling in the middle of a dirt road. His heart soared even as he fought the elation, unsure if Gwendolyn truly meant the words as he wanted her to mean them.

So now he had further reason to get her home, get her alone, and find out if the woman he'd forced into marriage, whom he didn't deserve, had come to love him as much as he loved her. 'Twould make his life complete and full. And as much as he preferred to remain here a few moments longer and cling to Gwendolyn, now assured no undue harm had befallen her, 'twas time to get up.

He allowed himself only a kiss to her cheek before he helped her to stand. His arm around her shoulders, and hers around his waist, they walked over to where Garrett and Roger stood guard while Edgar pulled his arrow from ap Idwal's back. Only then did Alberic wonder why the archer had disobeyed the order not to interfere, and why the arrow wasn't planted in *his* back.

"Why?" was all he asked.

Edgar bowed, then squared his shoulders. "I would have allowed him to slice you in two, Lord Alberic, but had Lady Gwendolyn suffered injury I would never have forgiven myself." He bowed to Gwendolyn. "My lady, please know I never meant you harm. Always I believed the man chosen by Sir Hugh as your betrothed to be the better man, deserving of the lordship of Camelen, even when I deplored his methods.

"Madog ap Idwal's dishonorable and cowardly attack on your person proved me wrong. I found it unforgivable that he broke his own bargain, and unpardonable that he meant to somehow use you against Lord Alberic. I most humbly beg your pardon, my lady. If you can find it in your heart to forgive me, I offer my bow and my life to your service."

Alberic raised a surprised eyebrow. Gwendolyn's arm tightened on his waist. She looked up at him, seeking guidance. He couldn't give it to her, his feelings too mixed about the man who'd once tried to take his life, but today had possibly saved Gwendolyn's.

"I am grateful for your accurate arrow," she said. "As to your service, I am in a quandary. You were in company of those who robbed Camelen's horses, killing two soldiers. How do you propose to face the garrison, to say naught of Mistress Biggs?"

"I had charge of the horses, and had naught to do with the deaths. Roger can testify to my innocence on that score."

All looked to Roger, who scowled. "I fear I must say he is right. Edgar left the camp before the attack occurred."

Edgar continued, "Nor was I aware of ap Idwal's plan to fire the village until I saw the flames. I swear to you, neither was done with my knowledge or approval."

"Our point guards?" Garrett asked.

"Up the road, bound and gagged but otherwise unharmed."

Silence reigned until once more Gwendolyn spoke. "Have we your pledge to nevermore aim an arrow at Lord Alberic?"

"Henceforth my arrows shall be aimed in his defense, my lady, this I so thee pledge."

"Then I give my blessing, but the decision must rest with his lordship."

It really wasn't a decision. The man had protected Gwendolyn when most needed. Such a man was welcome, though Alberic wasn't ready to have the man too close at hand yet.

"Garrett, take Edgar and two others and lay claim to ap Idwal's holding in my name." He glanced at the Welshmen who stood by their ponies, their weapons still in a pile in the dirt. "Will there be trouble on that score?"

Edgar shook his head. "Not likely. You will note that none of ap Idwal's men moved to stop me from picking up my bow and an arrow, and I believe all knew whom I intended to aim for. When the extent of ap Idwal's shame becomes known, I doubt anyone will raise a blade to defend his right to the holding."

With a last look at Madog ap Idwal, Alberic realized he'd obtained his revenge and would lay claim to the Welsh holding without the earl's help. Although he hadn't done it in his own time and certainly not by himself. But then, he no longer had to prove himself worthy. Not to the earl, not even to himself.

He had several loyal men, and one incredible woman, upon whom he could rely.

Never again must he be alone.

A humbling and heartening thought.

Alberic turned Gwendolyn around and whispered, "I need a bath. Let us go home."

Chapter Twenty

'TWAS NIGH ON MIDNIGHT, THE DARK, silent *between* time.
Gwendolyn lit every candle in the bedchamber, now five in all, then swished a hand through the steamy water in the new tub, not caring what the servants thought of their lord and lady bathing at such an odd hour. A soak in lavender-scented water would do them both good.

She ached all over and imagined Alberic did, too. The bruise on her hip wasn't as bad as she'd thought it might be, and he'd uttered no complaints of physical discomfort. But damn, she'd come close to losing Alberic today, and the need for closeness, to make love to him, was almost unbearable. So she'd ordered the tub filled while he made a final round of the battlements to ensure the guards were in place and assure the garrison once again that he'd come through today's ordeal whole and hardy.

She knew he'd suffered no wound, but she would never forget the moment he'd slipped on the road, forever remember the sight of that arrow flying through the air. With a hard shake of her head she banished the memories, not wanting to greet Alberic trembling with terror.

Soon, he would come up the stairs. Shortly, she would have him right where she wanted him. Safe in her arms.

My love.

Had Alberic noticed the unintended endearment? Had he heard she truly loved him? He'd not reacted in any way. Not happy, or surprised, or revolted. No matter. Her love for him didn't depend upon whether he knew of her love or if he returned it.

Gwendolyn rose from beside the tub and undressed, leaving on only her chemise to ward off the chamber's chill. No need to light a fire in the hearth. She'd be warm soon enough, and the way she would be warmed sent tingles of anticipation flickering over her skin.

She undid her braid, raking her fingers through the kinks and tangles until her hair flowed free before subjecting the tresses to a comb. When nearly done, she heard his footfalls in the passageway.

He came through the door and stopped abruptly when he spotted the tub. He closed his eyes and took a long sniff of steamy lavender.

"Oh, joy. Oh, rapture!"

She chuckled at his approval, but said not a word as he threw the bolt on the door and tore off his garments. Gloriously naked, his warrior's hide thankfully intact and unmarked, he padded over to the tub and dipped in a hand.

He sighed. "You like your bathwater hotter than I do."

She twisted her hair and pinned it to the top of her head before she approached him. He held out an arm in invitation, and she slid easily and firmly into his embrace. Pressed breast to chest, her arms around his neck, his hands at her waist, she placed light kisses along his rugged jawline.

"The water must be hot so it does not cool too soon."

His hands slid down to cup her bottom, pulling her lower body up and more firmly against his hardening phallus. "How long do you plan to linger in the water?"

"As long as it takes."

She felt his fingers gathering up her chemise, the fabric rising and teasing her sensitive skin.

"For what?" he asked, his voice low and gruff.

"For you to pleasure me so throughly I do not notice when the water cools."

The chemise bunched at her waist, his long fingers splayed against her bared bottom, he again pulled her in tight against his now fully engorged arousal.

"You ask much of your husband so late at night."

She wiggled against the hard rod she wanted to ease her deepest ache. "I have never known my husband to fail to please me, no matter the time of day or night. The water cools. Get in."

He pushed her chemise upward, over her head. "We have time to rub salve on your bruise. How feels your hip? Still sore?"

"Other parts of me hurt more. The salve can wait until after."

Finally, he surrendered to her urging, easing slowly into the water, stretching his legs the length of the tub. She followed, sinking into the soothing heat to sit between his legs and melt back against his chest.

She couldn't help a sigh. "So this is heaven."

His arms came around her. "Our own piece of it anyway. Lord, what a day this has been."

"I prefer not to think about today, or even tomorrow. 'Struth, I just want to be with you and not think at all."

He scooped up a handful of water and dribbled it over her shoulder. The rivulets trickled down her arm and over a breast. With a finger he traced the path of one drop to slide over her nipple, then paused to circle the nub. Her body responded as it always did to his fondling, greedily begging for more.

"Do you know how beautiful you are, Gwen? I could sit here and look at you all night long and never tire of the sight." He kissed the side of her neck. "And touch. Your skin is so soft beneath my fingers and mouth. Delectable."

She shivered beneath his warm kiss and tried to turn around to kiss him, too.

"Not yet. Let me look, and taste, and touch a while longer. Do nothing but enjoy."

"You will let me have my turn at you, then."

He chuckled. "Without a doubt."

Then Alberic reached for the bar of soap atop the stack of towels next to the tub, and Gwendolyn reveled in the most erotic of baths. His hands slick and skilled, he kneaded her shoulders, stroked her arms, then thoroughly washed her breasts until she nearly screamed for mercy. Her respite came when he washed her hands, his fingers gliding over and around hers, giving her a chance to inspect his beleaguered hand.

The seal of the dragon glittered, remaining firmly fixed in place. No amount of tugging would remove the ring, and 'twas obvious he'd tried all manner of ways to get it off. She interrupted his ministrations to take his left hand in both of hers to massage away the soreness. After dunking it in the water, she brought his hand to her mouth and kissed the knuckles.

"You said this morn you had no regrets. Can you say that still?"

His hand tightened on hers. "I would be the veriest fool to regret whatever brought me to Camelen and to you. I swear, I would not rather be anywhere else but here, and with no other woman but you. What of you? Are you truly content?"

"I would not have said so if I were not. I hated the reason why you came, and all the heartache. But now I cannot imagine my life without you here with me."

From far off she heard the sound of church bells pealing the hour of matins. Midnight. The time between, the time of magic.

Alberic wrapped her in his arms again and bent his head, his mouth hovering next to her ear, his breath warm and soft. "I love you, Gwen. With all my heart and soul, I love you. With each breath I love you more, and vow that at my dying breath I shall love you most of all."

Joyous tears welled in her eyes and spilled onto her cheeks. This time when she turned he didn't stop her. On her knees, fingers threaded into his hair, she tried to swallow the lump in her throat so she could tell him she loved him, too. But couldn't. So she ravaged his mouth, willing him to *know* what she couldn't say yet.

Then speaking proved impossible. Coherent thought became hopeless. Alberic's roving hands demanded more than kisses, more than vows. She surrendered up body and soul to the searing heat he ignited between her legs, the slow stroke of his fingers driving her wild. She arched back when he hungrily sought a nipple on which to suckle, feeling more alive, and beautiful, and loved than she'd ever felt before.

Ravenous for the joining, one at a time she spread her legs farther apart, placing them outside Alberic's. He knew what she craved, and with hands on her hips guided her to that which she sought. With the brief thought that she'd never taken her turn to look and taste and touch, she lowered onto him with the intent of just sitting there, joined to the hilt, then caress whatever other parts of him she could reach.

Except he scooted forward, sloshing water, moving her legs so they circled around him.

She hadn't known a man's penis could pierce so deeply, or with the slickness of soapy water to aid him, all Alberic need do was contract a few muscles to set her to squirming. Gwendolyn tightened a few muscles of her own, encouraging him to continue. He pumped faster. She spurred him onward.

His lips pursed, his green eyes closed.

Gwendolyn tilted her pelvis, changing the angle of his thrusts and increasing the depth and breadth of each stroke. She bloomed in a sharp burst, the petals of her spirit opening to greet the new day in a riot of vivid color and heady triumph. Alberic shuddered beneath her, his release accompanied by a low, satisfied groan.

She collapsed against him, her heart thudding against his, vowing there would be more midnight baths in their future.

Between heavy breaths she managed to utter, "I love you, Alberic. I love you. I love you."

He almost crushed her with an embrace. "Who would have thought we would come to this? When I chose you as my wife the most I dared hope for was an accord, that we could find a way to get along."

"I dare say we did!"

He laughed lightly. "I dare say you are right."

The next kiss was the sweetest they'd ever shared. A vow to each other that nothing could ruin the love they'd found.

"You kept your word," she told him when coming up for air. "I did not notice the water had cooled until we were done."

"'Tis finally comfortable."

"Then enjoy."

After a long parting kiss, Gwendolyn climbed out of the tub to find water all over the floor and the towels soaked through. She used her chemise to dry off, took the pins from her hair, and climbed into bed.

Alberic didn't remain in the water. He, too, used her chemise, then blew out all but one candle. He grabbed the jar of balm before he sank onto the mattress, and soon his hand was circling on the bruised hip she'd forgotten he'd promised to tend.

She closed her eyes, enjoying the tending.

"Feels good," she whispered.

His failure to answer prodded her eyes open again. Alberic stared at her hip, frowning deeply.

"Truly, Alberic, it does not hurt much."

He acknowledged with a nod of his head. "I was considering what you said this morn, before ap Idwal made his *last* appearance in our lives. I gather you believe the magic will ensure we remain attracted. Is that what our love is, an obligation for the convenience of an ancient legacy?"

Would she have fallen in love with Alberic if he didn't wear the ring? Had Alberic given her his heart because the magic compelled him to love the guardian of the legacy?

She hated to think that might be so.

"I know not," she confessed.

He smiled wryly. "Perhaps 'twas not such a foolish notion to rid myself of the ring by chopping off the finger."

"You had best not!"

"Then how will we ever know for certain if we love of our own free will or are compelled by a magical spell?"

How, indeed? Gwendolyn thought back on all she knew of the legacy, which Alberic no longer denied as nonsense. She should be glad he acknowledged the existence of magic, but he now had questions she'd never thought to ask and wasn't sure she wanted answered.

"We may never know for certain, but I believe the legacy requires the partners to love each other before the spell can be cast, not that it can compel the partners to love."

"Perhaps," he said before he put the jar on the night table then lay down so she could cuddle up against him.

Gwendolyn lay awake a long time, listening to the beat of his heart that now belonged to her, hoping it was given freely.

∽

The following morning, shortly after they broke fast, Alberic shocked her with a startling, unreasonable, impossible request.

"No one is to know of the legacy except the partners," she argued against his plan.

"Except neither of us knows what is expected of us. You once told me you believed Rhys had come to Camelen with your mother against the possibility she may need his help. We both know the bard is trustworthy. I say we show him the scroll and let him tell us what it says if he can."

She understood his reasons, truly she did, but her parents' warnings to maintain secrecy yet whispered in her ear.

"What if I am wrong and telling Rhys voids the spell?"

"I am quite willing to take the risk. Tell me true, Gwen. Let us say we never decide that England has come to its most dire moment, and the time comes to pass the artifacts on to our daughter. You have lived with questions and doubts since your mother gave the artifacts to you without explaining their use fully. Do you wish the next guardian to endure the same?"

She opened her mouth, then closed it again. Nay, she didn't wish those fears and uncertainties on anyone, much less her own daughter. And without having her uncertainties answered, she couldn't help the next guardian.

Alberic continued, "After reading Merlin's prophecies I am convinced that if we try to invoke the spell without knowing the consequences, we could summon one of the dragons, or giants, or even the Ass of Wickedness instead of King Arthur."

That surprised her. "You read the prophecies?"

He nodded. "The night before we left Chester."

The night they'd argued and she challenged him to take off the ring. Obviously Alberic had given the matter a great deal of thought since. And perhaps he was right to delve further into the mystery, which she'd never had the courage to do. Perhaps that time was now.

Still she heard her parents' warnings.

"On one condition. We do not tell Rhys beforehand what we wish to know. If he can read the scroll, then fine. But if not, we come away no worse than before."

"Agreed."

Not long after, Gwendolyn's stomach in knots, the scroll secreted away in her cloak, she and Alberic approached the bard's cottage. Harp music wafted through the air, a sound she usually found soothing. Not today.

Rhys opened the door to Alberic's knock.

The bard raised a quizzical eyebrow. "I am honored, my lord, my lady. What brings you to my humble hut?"

"We ask a boon," Alberic answered. "We are in possession of a scroll neither of us can read. We should like you to try."

Rhys smiled. "I should be pleased to be of service. Pray enter."

Gwendolyn pulled out the scroll, and with shaking hands offered it to the bard.

For tortuous moments he stared at the unrolled parchment, saying nothing. When he looked up, he seemed confused.

"May I ask how this came into your possession, my lady?"

Gwendolyn almost refused to give him any information, but not yet knowing if he could read it and out of courtesy to a revered Welsh bard, she answered, "'Twas among my mother's belongings."

"How odd. This is written in no language I can name. Were I to guess, I would say it was that of the Moors. I wonder how your mother came by it?"

The Moors?

Stunned, she looked to Alberic, who circled behind Rhys to look at the scroll. His brow furrowed, likely as puzzled by Rhys's statement as she. 'Twasn't possible for her and Alberic to recognize the writing as some form of Welsh and for Rhys to see another language altogether. She could think of no explanation for his error other than failing eyesight.

"'Tis no wonder why we cannot read it then." Alberic held out his hand for the scroll, which Rhys promptly handed over. "We thank you for looking."

"If you wish, I could inquire of other bards—"

"Not necessary," Alberic answered abruptly. "When I am called to the king's court, I may make inquiries."

Rhys bowed his head in acquiescence. "As you say, my lord."

With his hand in the middle of her back, Alberic urged her toward the door. She knew she should obey without hesitation, but for most of her life she'd believed Rhys had come to Camelen with her mother as an aid to the legacy. With that notion now shattered, another question nagged.

"I have always wondered why a Welsh bard settled on England's soil. What brought you to Camelen?"

His smile was soft. "Your mother. She worried her children might grow up too Norman. She asked that I come to keep the Welsh traditions alive for you and your siblings. When a Welsh princess asks, one relents."

So simple an answer.

"And will you stay for my children?"

The bard's smile widened. "If my lady wishes."

"She does. Good day to you, Master Bard."

Finally outside, her attention again turned to the scroll, and her frustration increased.

"Moorish. That makes no sense at all. I fear Rhys's vison fails him."

Alberic slowed, and Gwendolyn realized he'd led her to the middle of a field, not in a straight path to the keep.

"Have you looked at this of late?"

The tone of his question stopped her, and a quiver tingled along her spine.

"I had no reason to since showing it to you."

His hand shook as he handed her the scroll. "Tell me what you see."

She still saw ancient Welsh, but could read *more*. And what she read nearly buckled her knees.

Faithful hearts, honorably bound.

Then she understood why Alberic's hand shook.

"You can read it, too."

"Though the whole of it still appears to be in Welsh, I can now see whatever you see in Norman-French."

Welsh. Moorish. Norman-French. All on the same parchment? Three people seeing three different languages?

"Not possible."

"I swear to you, I see two phrases in Norman-French. Perhaps Rhys truly sees Moorish. Consider. The legacy was devised by Merlin, a mighty sorcerer. He gave the artifacts into the guardianship of the women descended from the line of Pendragon, whom he trusted to keep the legacy secret. But knowing the failing of humans, he must also have known that the artifacts could fall into untrustworthy hands. 'Twould be meet to place a spell on the scroll so those who are not supposed to read it cannot."

How very sensible and safe. Except for one thing.

Gwendolyn flung a hand in the air. "But until now you were not able to read a word of it despite being chosen by the ring."

"By the ring, perhaps, but until of late I did not believe in magic, nor was I accepted as partner by the guardian. It needed for you to love me first, Gwen. And that, I vow, is a magic unto itself."

Gwendolyn melted into the arms of the man with whom she shared a magical love. And if his conjecture was right, then she also had to admire Merlin's genius.

"So as time passes, the scroll will tell us what we need to know. And when the time is right to issue the summons, whoever is meant to invoke the spell will be able to read all."

"I believe so, and I would be most pleased to pass through this life never being able to read the whole. What say we put this away and not take it out for, say . . . fifty years."

∾

Gwendolyn sat on their bed, watching Alberic inspect the lid of her mother's trunk, looking for evidence of a hiding place for the scroll and pendant.

Faithful hearts, honorably bound.

Comforting words, for surely that meant the magic hadn't forced her and Alberic to love each other. She silently thanked Merlin for putting the doubt to rest, even though she was irked he hadn't done so sooner.

But she shouldn't be surprised by the unusual way of revelation. One had only to look at Merlin's prophecies; every one of them written in an unclear manner. Such, she supposed, was the way of sorcerers.

At least now she could put the artifacts away and not worry over them.

"Any luck as yet?" she asked.

He grunted, then asked, "Do you still wish to visit Nicole?"

Letters from both Nicole and Emma had arrived while she and Alberic were at Chester. Both disturbed her, especially Nicole's. She'd been ready to leave for Bledloe Abbey right then, but after having time to reread the letter, had changed her mind.

"Nay. I suppose I should accept that Nicole has truly made peace with her fate and not interfere. My going to visit her may disrupt her contentment."

"Nicole does seem to enjoy her time in the infirmary. She showed no interest in herb lore before, did she?"

"She showed little interest in learning of any kind. Perhaps that is why I am surprised she has delved into a subject so deeply and, if she persists, perhaps she will find the cure for Emma's headaches she seeks. I should be thankful she is content, especially since Emma cannot yet petition the king for Nicole's release."

Where Nicole was most content, Emma wasn't. She'd suffered two headaches since arriving in London, bemoaned her lack of progress where Nicole was concerned, and sounded lonely. Apparently, she'd made only one friend, another of the queen's handmaidens. Gwendolyn's heart bled for her sister, but there was little she could do for Emma, either.

"Found it!"

Alberic pushed a panel aside to reveal an empty space behind it. He stood up and dusted off his hands, looking very proud of himself.

"Well done, Alberic."

He shrugged a shoulder. "One would never find the secret space if one did not suspect it existed. Shall we?"

Gwendolyn slid off the bed and fetched the black velvet sack containing the pendant and scroll from the table. Alberic tucked the sack into the hiding place and pushed the panel back in place. Almost, she could hear him sigh with relief. He now believed in the legacy, but it still bothered him. Understandable. While she could put the reminders of her guardianship out of sight, he could not. The seal of the dragon sat on his hand, reminding him daily of his partnership in the legacy and the responsibility it entailed.

Gwendolyn smiled. The ring couldn't have found a better man on whom to cling, for Alberic took all of his responsibilities most seriously. Nor could she have found a better man to love. Truly, she could ask for no more.

"We should go down to the hall," she said. "'Tis nearly time for nooning."

"A moment more. I have a gift for you."

He crossed the room to where his cloak hung on a peg next to hers. Whatever it was he fetched, he could hold it in his closed fist. No gloves, then. Or hair ribbons. Her curiosity nigh on bursting, she held out her hand, and gasped at what he gave her.

A clasp for her cloak. Twin trefoils fashioned of delicate strands of intricately woven gold. In the center of each trefoil winked a jewel, one of garnet, the other of amethyst. She had no trouble determining its meaning. The garnet for Alberic, the amethyst for her, their future linked together.

"'Tis beautiful," she managed to say before tossing her arms around his neck, squeezing tightly. "Where did you find such a piece?"

"Day before yesterday, at the goldsmith in Shrewsbury. When I saw it, I could not pass it by. I gather you approve?"

"Heartily! I am tempted to wear my cloak to meal so everyone can see it." Then she backed away a bit. "Alberic, you do realize *any* trefoil is considered magical."

He shuddered and sighed. "Aye, but I reasoned that this was fashioned by a man, not a sorcerer, so whatever magic it might contain cannot be as forceful as your pendant."

"True."

She kissed him long and tenderly, an inadequate thanks for so special a gift, vowing to show greater appreciation later. Before they left the chamber, she attached the clasp to her cloak, noting how grand it looked. She would wear it always, and proudly.

Hands clasped, they headed down the passageway to the stairs.

"Now that we have put urgent matters aside," he said, "I can pursue other endeavors."

"I suppose you must hie off to Wales to inspect your new holding."

"Aye, that, too, but first I want to learn some of the

language. I thought to ask Rhys. A Welsh bard should be a good teacher, I would think."

A wise choice.

"I can help you with your studies, teach you a few phrases." And Gwendolyn knew just the phrase she wanted Alberic to learn first. *"Yr wyf i yn dy garu di."*

"Yr wyf i yn dy garu di."

He said it clumsily, so she repeated it.

He echoed her more fluently this time, then asked, "What does it mean?"

She squeezed his hand. "'I love you.' You shall have to say the phrase often so you remember it."

Alberic stopped at the top of the stairway, and just before he kissed her, with heartfelt sincerity he said again, *"Yr wyf i yn dy garu di."*

He didn't say the words perfectly, but Gwendolyn didn't care. She would forever love hearing those words from Alberic, in whatever language.

ABOUT THE AUTHOR

SHARI ANTON's secretarial career ended when she took a creative writing class and found she possessed some talent for writing fiction. The author of several highly acclaimed historical novels, she now works in her home office where she can take unlimited coffee breaks. Shari and her husband live in southeastern Wisconsin, where they have two grown children and do their best to spoil their two adorable little grandsons. You can write to her at P.O. Box 510611, New Berlin, WI 53151-0611, or visit her Web site at www.sharianton.com.

More
Shari Anton!

Please turn this page

for a preview of

Twilight Magic

Available in mass market

Fall 2006.

Chapter One

England 1145

Not this morn, Lady Emma. The king has matters of great import to discuss with his counselors, so he will be occupied for the greater part of the day."

Another of the chamberlain's clerks had told her the same thing yesterday, and she'd heard similar excuses on other occasions throughout the past summer. With the king so rarely in residence at Westminster Palace, Lady Emma de Leon's opportunities to speak to the king had been few, and she was determined to gain an audience before he left again.

"On the morrow, perhaps?" Emma asked of the pale little man with the graceful hands and up-tilted nose.

He sniffed. "There is a war being fought, my lady. Events will dictate who will be allowed into the royal presence based on urgent need."

Emma understood all about the damn war. If not for the war's horrible effect on her family, she wouldn't be forced to plea for royal intervention on her youngest sister's behalf.

"A child's fate depends upon a royal decision, and I require only a few moments to make my request. Surely the king can spare a moment for an act of mercy."

The clerk's tight smile didn't bode well. "If I granted time to everyone who requested a few moments, his majesty would be an old man by the time all were done."

Emma tamped down her ire, striving mightily to be pleasant to the guardian of the royal chamber's door. "I realize the king's time is precious, and if any other person could act on my request, I would not bother his majesty. But King Stephen is the only one who can make decisions over his ward's fate."

"Is the child in grave danger?"

"Nay, but . . ."

He waved an irritatingly dismissive hand. "Then the matter is not urgent and does not require the king's immediate attention. Indeed, I suggest you put your request to parchment for the king to consider at his leisure."

"I did, several months ago, but have been given no answer. I can only assume my request has been . . . misplaced."

Lost on purpose, no doubt. Shoved aside by the chamberlain's clerks as unimportant. Her deceased father, Sir Hugh de Leon, was considered a traitor, and no one at court felt any obligation to show kindness or mercy to the traitor's daughter.

The clerk's eyes narrowed. "Naught which is overseen by the chamberlain becomes misplaced. You must have patience, my lady. The king will consider your petition in due time."

With that he strode off down the marble-floored hallway to the royal residence leaving her standing alone and with no recourse. Naturally, the guards opened one of the huge oak doors and the clerk swept through without a challenge.

The clerk belonged; she did not.

She was tempted to rush the door and force her way in, but she knew she might hurt her cause if she were to be so bold. So Emma fled in the opposite direction.

All the way back to the queen's solar, where Emma spent most of her days and nights, she fought the urge to scream and make *someone* listen to her. No one would, however. Not even if she screamed.

Since her arrival in London, she'd been shunned, considered the undesirable outcast. Emma had known from the moment she'd been informed she was being sent to court that she wouldn't be popular. But she hadn't expected to be treated with contempt.

As now, upon entering Queen Matilda's sumptuously furnished solar. Several elegantly garbed women who served as the queen's handmaidens looked up from their embroidery, or loom, or book to see who had entered. Each immediately turned away when they saw who came through the door.

No one of importance, their looks said. *Only the traitor's daughter,* their malevolence shouted.

Having expected no less and intent on ignoring the hurtful dismissal, Emma took a seat on a bench at the far end of the room, near the open window slit. As the rain splattered against the palace's thick stone walls, she took a deep breath to help calm her upset and ease the urge to blame her father or her new brother-by-marriage for placing her in an untenable situation.

On the day of her father's death, King Stephen had

made Alberic of Chester a knight and gifted him with her father's barony. Then the king had ordered Alberic to marry one of the three surviving de Leon daughters, send another to court and give the last to the Church.

Alberic's decision on which daughter to marry hadn't surprised Emma. Gwendolyn was by far prettier and more likeable than her older sister. Besides being too young for Alberic's taste, Nicole had also tried to stab him with a dagger. Still, Alberic would allow the girl to return to Camelen, which only proved her brother-by-marriage possessed a generous heart.

Emma had promised Nicole she would petition the king to allow the girl to leave the nunnery at Bledloe Abbey and return home. Of late, Emma had considered adding a similar plea of her own, but admitted she didn't particularly want to go home. Being dependent upon her slightly younger sister and her new brother-by-marriage didn't appeal. Sweet mercy, she'd come to court with hopes of finding a place for herself but found only misery. 'Truth, she didn't particularly want to remain here either.

For now, however, she had to put her own problems aside to solve Nicole's. Once assured the girl was suitably taken care of, she would worry about her own future.

Not that she had any control over her own fate, for that, too, rested in the king's hands. A king whose time was limited and guarded by wretched, unmerciful clerks.

A stirring at the doorway signaled the return of Queen Matilda from her daily walk in the garden, accompanied by the flock of men and women who comprised the cream of the queen's court. Everyone in the solar stood, giving the queen the honor due her royal rank. Not until she crossed the room to her ornately carved, armed chair, and gave a small hand signal, did everyone return to their occupations.

Emma wondered if she should again ask the queen to intervene on her behalf. Matilda, however, showed no more inclination to assist the traitor's daughter than the chamberlain's clerks. Nor were any of the people closest to the royal couple interested in Emma's problems, save one brave, caring soul who now came toward her.

Lady Julia de Vere, the lovely niece of the earl of Oxford, had come to court years ago as a hostage to her uncle's continued support of the king's efforts to hold onto his crown. Though held in the sumptuous cell of Westminster Palace and not the dreary White Tower, both Emma and Julia were prisoners of the crown. But the fundamental difference between them was that Julia de Vere was treated with the utmost courtesy and respect by all and sundry. Emma didn't know why Julia didn't consider her a social leper, but she was grateful the woman deigned to be friendly.

She tried hard not to notice how favorably Julia's blond hair compared to her own drab brown, or how much better was Julia's surcoat of sapphire silk, shot through with gold thread, which fit into the elegant surroundings better than Emma's well-made but now faded green wool.

Emma accepted the difference in their position at court even though she actually outranked the niece of an earl. Being the daughter of a Norman baron placed Emma within the ranks of the nobility, and being the daughter of a Welsh princess should boost her far over Julia. Her high birth was, perhaps, the reason she resided in the palace and not the Tower. However, no one at court felt inclined to acknowledge her station further.

Julia's smile went far to lighten Emma's mood. She took a seat on the bench, careful to spread the sapphire silk skirt to show it to the best advantage. "How is your head today? You seem less pale."

"Better. I appreciate your concern."

"Four days is a long time to spend on pallet in a dark corner with a pounding head. I still believe you should allow a surgeon to examine you."

Julia meant well, and Emma would heed the advice if she didn't already know why the headaches occurred and what she could do to make them cease. However, she considered the cure worse than the agony. She would willingly suffer the pain rather than allow the cursed, devil-sent visions to overtake her as they had in her childhood. Since discovering how to both evade and fight off the visions, she'd done so—though not with complete success.

"The surgeon's time would be wasted. The pain must run its course. How went your walk in the garden?"

"The flowers are fading. Michaelmas is but a fortnight away and with it will come harvest time's chill. You should come with us next time. It may be our last opportunity to take the boats into the pond and feed the swans. Were you able to make your request of the king's clerk?"

Unwilling to tell Julia why the thought of going near the pond, swans or no, made her shiver, Emma merely answered Julia's question.

"Apparently the king is too busy today to attend to anything not concerning the war. Tomorrow as well. Perhaps I will have better luck the day after."

Julia leaned closer. "I gather you did not offer to bed the clerk."

They'd had this discussion before. Emma smiled,

remembering her horror the first time Julia had declared that officious, pompous clerks must be bribed into granting favor, either with body or with coin. Julia accepted the practice as a means of getting her way. Her uncle kept her well supplied with coin, but depending upon what she wanted and from whom she wanted it, Julia wasn't above spending a night or two in a man's bed, though she was selective in her bed mates and most discreet.

Indeed, taking a lover was common practice. At night, after the queen retired to her private bedchamber, a veritable parade ensued of men coming in and women going out of the solar. Emma had moved her pallet to a dark corner of the large chamber to avoid being stepped on or mistaken for another woman, as much as for a quiet place to endure her headaches.

"Nay. I refuse to offer up my virtue to so mean a little man. Nor do I have the coin to offer him. And nay, I shall not take your coin because I have no way to repay you. Allow me my pride."

"Pride will not open the king's door."

Perhaps not, but she wouldn't take Julia's coin for such a purpose. As for bedding the clerk—well, not only did the pale little man not appeal to her, but even if she offered herself to him she doubted he would accept. She wasn't slender and pretty as were the majority of the ladies who lived in the palace, and she would be utterly mortified if she offered the clerk a tumble and he backed away in horror.

Besides, she already *knew* the man to whom she would give her virginity, and he certainly wasn't one of the clerks, thank heaven above.

"Then I must find another way into the royal chambers. Perhaps I should make my request of the chamberlain instead."

"Tsk. The chamberlain is as hard to gain an audience with as the king. The clerks guard both zealously. 'Struth, Emma, you must somehow bribe one of the clerks or you will never get through the doors!"

Emma sighed inwardly. Julia was probably right. But she had nothing a clerk might want.

"There must be another way."

"Then you must find a means of entry quickly. I understand the king will be in residence for four more days before he returns to the field."

Four days. Damn.

Well, if she couldn't go through the clerks, or appeal to the chamberlain above them, then she would have to go around them. Make a direct assault on the royal chambers. Somehow get past the doorway's guards.

Fortunately, she had one effective weapon in her. Bravado.

She would give the king today and tomorrow to meet with his counselors. Early on the morning after she would be among the throng of courtiers, advisors, and attendants milling outside his chamber door, prepared to sneak, bluff, or push her way inside.

No matter if she lowered her standing at court. After all, she was already so low she didn't see how she could sink any further. But she would keep her promise to Nicole.

❧

Darian of Bruges strode through the passageways of the royal residence beside William of Ypres, commander of the Flemish mercenaries, matching his stride to that of his shorter and rounder mentor.

He'd made this trek several times over the past years. Each time Darian was amazed that he was allowed onto Westminster Palace's grounds, much less into the royal chambers. Of course, there were people who would prefer that a man of his ilk not be allowed in the city of London much less inside the palace.

Too bad.

King Stephen needed men such as Darian if he hoped to win his war against the Empress Maud. Men willing to take risks. Men capable of accomplishing those tasks men of refinement hesitated to undertake.

His boot heels clicked against the marble floors, an unusually loud noise for a man so devoted to silent approaches. But then, he wasn't in the field. His only task this morn was to act as an added set of ears and eyes for William.

A task few others could perform. Not only did his commander trust Darian's keenly honed ability to assess his surroundings, catching details others missed. But he was one of a handful of men who knew William's eyesight had begun to fail. Not even the king knew yet, and William didn't plan to tell him until the problem interfered with his ability to command his troops in battle. Thankfully, the surgeon felt that time might not come for many years yet.

"Do you know why we have been summoned, or who else will be present?"

William shook his head. "The clerk did not say, though I would not be surprised to see Henry. He did not approve of the plan we decided upon yester noon. I fear he may have convinced the king to change his mind."

Damnation. If the king changed his mind, then Darian wouldn't be leaving London anytime soon and Edward de Salis, a vile, evil man, would continue to ravage villages and maim and murder innocents. The bastard must be stopped soon, and Darian itched to bring the bastard to his knees, then send him to hell.

Unfortunately, Henry, bishop of Winchester, the king's brother, was quite adept at convincing Stephen to change his mind. But then, one of the complaints often heard about Stephen was his inability to withstand a convincing argument.

One would think a king would have more confidence in his judgment and stand firm on his decisions. Apparently not. Especially when arguments came from the brother whose support and machinations helped put the crown of England on Stephen's head.

But politics were for others to contemplate and argue over. A native of Flanders, Darian didn't care who sat on the throne of England. He had his own reasons for becoming involved in this war, his loyalty belonging only to William of Ypres.

"Henry might feel differently if his villages were being burned and his people harmed."

"Too true. Do you see him?"

They were nearing their destination. Darian's height proved useful as he glanced around at the men and women milling in front of the doors to the antechamber.

"Nay. Nor do I see any of the earls or other advisors present yester noon."

A good sign. If Henry had indeed won Stephen over, the bishop would surely be here to gloat.

"Perhaps they are already in the king's chambers. Ah, the doors open."

The huge oak doors swung wide. The crowd rushed forward to enter the antechamber. Pushing and shoving ensued, each person trying to gain advantage over their fellows. Their efforts would do them no good. The clerk would decide on the order people were allowed into the royal presence. Unless they'd been summoned by the king or had paid the clerk a goodly sum ahead of time, they would be forced to wait until the clerk deemed them worthy.

One woman had apparently come to that conclusion. Garbed in a white chemise covered by a topaz-hued surcoat, the softly rounded, dark haired woman actually seemed hesitant to pass through the doorway. Darian saw her nervousness in the way her hand smoothed over a gauzy veil that was anything but ruffled. He couldn't see her face, but could well imagine the doubt he might glimpse in her eyes.

When he found himself wondering what color those eyes might be, he pulled his attention back to where it belonged.

He and William edged forward at the back of the crowd, the king's summons guaranteeing they would be among the first admitted to the king's inner chamber. It suited Darian immensely. He didn't like crowds, and found the air in the palace stifling. Better this audience was over quickly so he could get out into the field and not have to deal with personages of noble birth, most of whom couldn't be bothered with anything other than their own petty concerns.

The woman in topaz bowed her head and positioned

herself close behind two large men who shouldered their way through the middle of the crowd, doing her best to avoid notice by the guards on either side of the door. She slipped into the antechamber without challenge and he could almost feel her relief.

She's not supposed to be here.

He admired the woman's boldness, but knew her efforts were for naught. She may have sneaked past the first set of guards, but would never get past the clerk if she wasn't on his list of those who would be allowed to speak with the king. And he highly doubted she was on the clerk's list.

But her problem wasn't his problem. There was nothing he could do to help her even if he'd wanted to, which he didn't.

Still, his curiosity prodded him to nudge William and ask softly, "The woman in topaz. Do you know who she is?"

William squinted. "Lady Emma de Leon. Have you heard her tale?"

He'd heard of her and her plight.

"Daughter of Sir Hugh de Leon, who had the misfortune of dying while fighting for Maud. King Stephen's ward. Barely tolerated at court." As he was grudgingly tolerated. He brushed aside an unwanted pang of kinship. "Must a royal ward be on the clerk's list for her to speak with the king?"

William huffed. "Probably. Why?"

"Merely wondering."

Thankfully, William accepted the explanation without comment because Darian truly couldn't explain his curiosity with the king's ward.

Lady Emma glanced furtively from side to side, likely looking for a place to hide, giving him brief glimpses of her profile. Young. Smooth skin. Straight nose. Strong jaw. Wide set eyes. Not pretty, but handsome enough for a man to give a second look.

He still wanted to know the color of Emma's eyes, but he didn't have the chance to look more closely. Duty called. He followed William to the next doorway, this one guarded by an imperious clerk as well as two burly soldiers.

The clerk bowed. "Lord William, you are expected."

Darian almost smiled at the clerk's obeisance to the mercenary captain. Indeed, the king had granted William enough land and rights and fees that, were he not a Flemish mercenary, he would hold the title of earl of Kent. Accustomed to becoming lost in William's shorter shadow, Darian wasn't surprised when the clerk didn't acknowledge him, but merely gave a hand signal to the guard to open the door.

Then the clerk glanced up, and a sly gleam within his eyes sent a shiver down Darian's spine. Something was amiss.

He entered the inner chamber behind William, his senses alert. All seemed calm and normal enough. King Stephen sat in his ornate armed chair, the chamberlain standing beside him. Waiting. Their expressions gave nothing away.

No one else was in the room. Not even a servant.

Still, Darian sensed a threat and, for the life of him, couldn't figure out why the back of his neck tingled—until he heard shouts through the still open doors to the antechamber.

"Make way for the bishop! Stand aside! Make way!"

The bishop had to be Henry, Darian realized, when he heard the man's voice.

"Let them in! Let them all in to witness the king's justice!"

"What the devil is Henry about?" William muttered.

Darian didn't know, but sensed whatever the bishop was up to couldn't be good.

Henry, bishop of Winchester, burst into the chamber, garbed in the full regalia of his office. He hustled toward King Stephen followed by four soldiers bearing a litter.

The room filled up with people. The air grew close and overly warm.

Henry pointed to a spot on the floor in front of the king. The men lowered the litter.

Darian heard the buzz of voices and could feel William uncomfortably shifting his stance, but nothing could tear his gaze from the face of the obviously dead man on the litter.

The face of Edward de Salis, the vile, evil man who yester noon the king had given Darian the order to assassinate. But someone had gotten to de Salis first.

"Darian of Bruges!" Henry, bishop of Winchester shouted. "I accuse you of murder!"

THE EDITOR'S DIARY

Dear Reader,

All's fair in love and war . . . even a few white lies, a little bloodshed, and a dash of attempted burglary. And that's just in love. Check out our two Warner Forever titles this December to see why.

Romantic Times BOOKclub Magazine raves **Shari Anton's** previous book is a "charming delightful romance" that "sparkles with originality." Well, prepare to be enchanted by her latest, **MIDNIGHT MAGIC**. Though she is betrothed to another, Gwendolyn of Leon finds the King has given her hand in marriage and her land to a knight with her family's blood on his hands. His arrogance astounds her, his steady gaze and teasing smile intrigue her. But on this knight's hand rests the ring Gwendolyn needs to activate an ancient magical legacy . . . and she will do anything necessary to wrest it away—even seduce him. With the seal of the dragon slipped on his finger, Alberic of Chester has gone from landless knight to titled baron. Marrying Gwendolyn would secure his position and Alberic is intent on taking what is rightfully his by king's decree. But winning the heart of his sensuous and fiery wife-to-be may prove his most daunting fight yet.

Good girls never lie . . . unless it's their job. Lettie Campbell from **Kelley St. John's GOOD GIRLS DON'T** knows that all too well. As a well-paid cheating consultant for *My Alibi*, the cover stories come easily to Lettie . . . until she discovers the man on the receiving end of one of her whoppers is none other than Bill Bannon—her best friend in high school. How can she lie to him now? But even more shockingly, when did the boy next door have the power to make her heart flutter and her toes curl? As the lies pile up and Lettie and Bill start to burn up the sheets, Lettie knows she has to come clean. Will she 'fess up before Bill discovers he's been conned? Grab a copy of this sassy and sensual debut from brand new Warner Forever author Kelley St. John today.

To find out more about Warner Forever, these titles, and the authors, visit us at www.warnerforever.com.

With warmest wishes,

Karen Kosztolnyik, Senior Editor

P.S. Believe in love and the afterlife vampire-style in these two irresistible novels: **Susan Crandall** delivers the poignant story of a woman who lost her husband and unborn child in a fire and the man who gives her a reason to believe in love again in **ON BLUE FALLS POND**; **Michelle Rowen** tells a death-defyingly funny debut about a girl who goes on a blind date and comes home a vampire in **BITTEN & SMITTEN**.